For a whole year Maria had lived in exile; and all that time he had never wavered. Surely that was proof enough of his devotion?

And if marriage could be arranged that would not offend the laws of the Holy Church . . .

But it would, of course it would.

Two voices argued within her. She knew that one was prompted by her head, one by her heart; and it was the first to which she should listen.

But she was lonely; she was homesick; and this year away from him had taught her one thing: she loved the Prince of Wales.

SWEET LASS OF RICHMOND HILL

Jean Plaidy

FAWCETT CREST • NEW YORK

A Fawcett Crest Book
Published by Ballantine Books
Copyright © 1970 by Jean Plaidy

Library of Congress Catalog Card Number: 87-34312

ISBN 0-449-21740-X

This edition published by arrangement with G. P. Putnam's Sons, a Division of the Putnam Berkley Group, Inc.

Manufactured in the United States of America

First Ballantine Books Edition: July 1990

CONTENTS

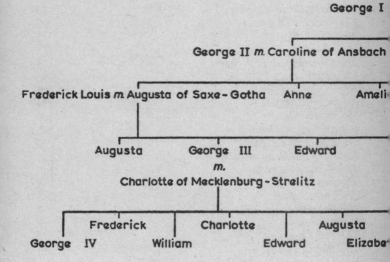

George I

George II *m.* Caroline of Ansbach

Frederick Louis *m.* Augusta of Saxe-Gotha   Anne   Ameli

Augusta   George III   Edward
                 m.
        Charlotte of Mecklenburg-Strelitz

                Frederick   Charlotte   Augusta
George IV   William   Edward   Elizabe

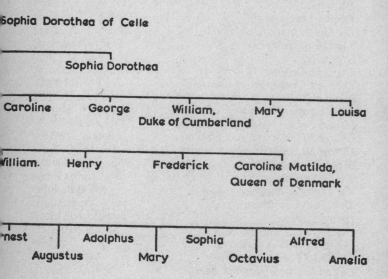

Sophia Dorothea of Celle

Sophia Dorothea

Caroline   George   William,   Mary   Louisa
Duke of Cumberland

William.   Henry   Frederick   Caroline Matilda,
Queen of Denmark

Ernest   Adolphus   Sophia   Alfred
Augustus   Mary   Octavius   Amelia

BIBLIOGRAPHY

Mrs. Fitzherbert and George IV	W. H. Wilkins, M.A., F.S.A.
The Life and Times of George IV	The Rev. George Croly
George The Fourth	Shane Leslie
Memoirs of George IV	Robert Huish
George the Fourth	Roger Fulford
The First Gentleman	Grace E. Thompson
The Good Queen Charlotte	Percy Fitzgerland
The Life of George IV	Percy Fitzgerland
George III	J. C. Long
The Four Georges	Wm. M. Thackeray
The First Gentleman of Europe	Lewis Melville
Loves of Florizel	Philip Lindsay
Memoirs and Portraits	Horace Walpole
Memoirs of the Reign of George III	Horace Walpole
George III, Monarch and Statesman	Beckles Wilson
George III, His Court and Family	Henry Colburn
In the Days of the Georges	William B. Boulton
The Four Georges	Sir Charles Petrie
The House of Hanover	Alvin Redman
The Great Corinthian	Doris Leslie
Fanny Burney	Christopher Lloyd
The Story of Fanny Burney	Muriel Masefield
George, Prince and Regent	Philip W. Sergeant
The Years of Endurance	Arthur Bryant
England in the Eighteenth Century	R. W. Harris
The Reign of George III	J. Steven Watson
The Dictionary of National Biography	Edited by Sir Leslie Stephen and Sir Sidney Lee
British History	John Wade
National and Domestic History of England	William Hickman Smith Aubrey

A Birth in Tong Castle

Dusk was beginning to throw long shadows across the Red Room in Tong Castle as Mary Smythe pushed aside the red hangings about the bed and sat down uneasily. It was too early as yet for the child to make its appearance—but how could one be sure? Children had a habit of coming before their time.

She wished that the child could have been born in their own home. Walter had said that as soon as they had a child they must certainly look for a house, and she anticipated with great pleasure the prospect of choosing her own furniture and making her own home; it would be quite different from living in her brother-in-law's mansion at Acton Burnell or here in Tong Castle.

It was of course very kind of the Duke of Kingston to lend them his castle until after the birth of the child; he preferred to have someone living there during his absence, to keep the servants in order and see to the running of the place, so why not his good friend Walter Smythe whom he knew was longing to leave the parental roof now that he had acquired a wife?

She had been delighted to come to Tong Castle, as grand and impressive an edifice to be found not only in the county of Shropshire but in the whole of England. But it was not one's own home. She had tried to make it so by installing the prie-dieu in a corner of the room, the crucifix over the bed and the flask of holy water on the carved mantelpiece. But whenever she was conscious of the manner in which the servants eyed these things, an irrepressible indignation swept over her. She would never be reconciled to the laws of England which, while they did not go so far as to forbid Catholics to worship as they pleased, excluded them from their civil rights and penalized them in a hundred ways.

Mary clenched her hands together and reminded herself that she would be ready to die for her faith in the same way in which those of her own faith were murdering those not of theirs throughout the world.

Walter came into the room. He was the best of husbands, good looking, financially secure and, most important of all, a Catholic. The marriage would never have taken place if he had not been. She had brought him a good dowry; they were even remotely related to each other, which was often the case with Catholic families in England, for few married outside their own religion.

He looked startled when he saw her. 'Mary?' he cried questioningly. She nodded. 'I am not sure. But it may be.'

'It's a little soon.'

'It often happens so, I believe.'

'Should I call the midwife?'

'Not yet. Wait a little. She will laugh at me for being over-anxious.'

He sat down beside her and took her hand.

'It's strange,' he said, 'that the child should be born in a castle.'

'I'd rather he were born in our own home.'

'We'll find a house as soon as you are ready.'

'I should like to settle near my brother in Hampshire.'

'In Red Rice?' mused Walter. 'An excellent spot, as it is not far from Winchester.'

'Walter, after your adventures in the Austrian Army do you think you can settle down?'

'With you . . . to raise a family, yes.'

To raise a family. She saw the gracious house, the garden with its peaceful lawns and the children they would have clustered about them. It was a pleasant picture; and the subsequent births would be less tiresome than this one. The midwife had told her that the first was always the most difficult.

'A house,' she mused, to take her mind off the pains which she fancied were becoming a little more frequent, 'with a chapel.'

'Perhaps it would be a little unwise to have a chapel in the house, my love.'

'Oh, Walter, why should we be persecuted?'

Walter admitted that the intolerant laws were a burden to all

Catholics, but being a fair man he pointed out that they were less severe in England than in any other country in the world.

'Yet . . . we are penalized,' cried Mary, her eyes flashing. 'If this were not so we should have our own house now. You would not have had to leave England to follow a career.'

'Well, I have at least travelled and seen service in the Austrian Army.'

'And that was England's loss,' cried Mary vehemently. 'Oh, Walter, if only it had gone differently at the '45.'

'But it did not, Mary, and we know full well that the Stuarts lost all hope after Culloden. Charles Edward will never come back now. He is drinking himself to death across the water and the Hanoverians are firmly on the throne. They say young Prince George is a good young man, and popular with the people. No, Mary, the Hanoverians are here to stay so we had better make the best of it.'

'But to live as we do . . . hearing Mass almost by stealth, being debarred from privileges. What of our children? Are they going to grow up in a society which will deprive them of their rights because they worship God in the only true way?'

'You must not excite yourself, my dear. One thing is certain. Our children will worship God in accordance with the laws of the Roman Catholic Church no matter what the laws of the country.'

Mary sighed. Anything else was unthinkable, of course.

'You should not concern yourself. As long as the laws are not made more harsh we shall be able to look after ourselves.'

Dear Walter! He was so resigned. Perhaps she was apt to become excited over this matter simply because she was about to bear a child. The future looked bright enough. Soon the uncomfortable business of childbearing would be over; they would have their house and she would be a happy matron. How different that would be from sharing her brother-in-law's house at Acton Burnell—large and comfortable though it was. Perhaps the Duke of Kingston hoped they would buy Tong Castle, for he wanted to sell it. But no, Tong Castle was too grand for them; they would not be able to keep it up, for in spite of her dowry they were not rich according to the Duke's standards as Walter was the second son of the late Sir John Smythe and naturally his inheritance could not equal that of Sir Edward, his brother, who had inherited the title and the bulk of the family estates.

She caught her breath suddenly. 'Walter, I think . . . I am almost certain . . . that my time has come.'

Walter lost no time in summoning the midwife.

Mary was right. Within a few hours she had become the mother of a daughter.

She was a little disappointed, having hoped that the first-born would be a son; but the child was healthy and perfect in every way. She was named Mary Anne; but as her mother was Mary the baby soon became known as Maria. Little Maria grew prettier every day; and very soon her mother was once more pregnant.

Mary Smythe was determined that her second child should be born in a home of her own; so when Maria was only a few months old her parents gave up their custodianship of Tong Castle and came to Red Rice to stay with Mary's brother, Mr. Henry Errington, while they searched for a suitable residence. This did not take long to find; and before the birth of little Walter they had settled into a large country house in Brambridge which was not very far from Red Rice and had the additional advantage of being close to the town of Winchester.

Here Mary settled happily and during the next few years increased her family. John followed Walter; and after him came Charles, Henry and Frances—a pleasant little family, living comfortably in the country, undisturbed by great events in the capital. The old King died and young George came to the throne; they heard of his marriage to Princess Charlotte of Mecklenburg-Strelitz, of his coronation and the birth of the Prince of Wales, which was followed in due course by the birth of a second son.

'Oh yes,' repeated Walter Smythe, 'the Hanoverians are here to stay.'

Life in Lulworth Castle

Maria Smythe lay on the hard pallet in her sparsely furnished room—which was more like a cell—and wept silently, asking herself how she could bear to be torn away from this place which had been her home for so many years.

Tomorrow Papa would come to take her away and she would leave her school-fellows, the dear nuns, the Mother Superior, the routine of the convent and Paris, and go back to England. How strange it seemed that when she had known she was to come here she had wept as bitterly at the thought of leaving her home in Brambridge as she was now weeping at the prospect of leaving the convent.

Maria sat up. Perhaps there was comfort in that. Perhaps she would become reconciled to life in Brambridge just as she had to life in the convent before she had grown to love it. But it would be different, of course. At home she would have to think about marrying for she knew well enough that this was the reason why she was being brought back to England. It happened with regularity to all the girls. They came here to be educated as good Catholics in the Convent of the Blew Nuns: then they returned home where suitable husbands were found for them; they produced children and, if they were girls, they in their turn came to the Convent. That was the pattern of Catholic girlhood.

The door opened slightly and her sister Frances appeared. Frances's eyes were red with weeping and she sniffed pathetically as she ran to the pallet and threw herself into Maria's arms.

'It's all right,' soothed Maria. 'You'll be all right when I'm gone. And in a very short time it will be your turn.'

Frances looked up at her sister with adoration. Maria was not only the most beautiful person she knew; she was the kindest. What was little Frances going to do—newly arrived at the convent—with no Maria to protect her?

Maria immediately dismissed her own misgivings in order to comfort her sister. She pushed the heavy corn-coloured hair out of her eyes and said: 'Mamma and Papa will come and visit you perhaps. Perhaps I shall come myself. And in a very short time— far shorter than seems possible now—*you* will be feeling sad because it is your turn to leave all this.'

'But *you* will not be here, Maria.'

'I shall write to you.'

'But they will find a husband for you and even when I come home you won't be there.'

'I shall invite you to my house and find a husband for *you*. You will live close by and we shall see each other every day.'

'Oh, Maria, is that possible?'

'With Maria Smythe all things are possible.'

Frances began to giggle. 'Oh, Maria, Reverend Mother would say that you blaspheme.'

'Then I pray you do not tell her or I shall be summoned to her presence.' Maria folded her arms in an imitation of Reverend Mother. ' "Maria Smythe, I hear that you believe yourself omniscient." "Yes, Holy Mother." "Then I pray you go to Versailles and tell the King that he must give up his evil ways." "Yes, Holy Mother." ' She began to laugh. 'Oh, I am ridiculous, am I not, Frances? Still, you are laughing.'

'But you did go to Versailles, Maria, once.'

Frances was asking for the story which she had heard before, so Maria obligingly told it.

'It was when Mamma and Papa came to visit me here . . . as they will come to visit you. And naturally they took me to see the sights. One of the most exciting of these was a visit to Versailles. Oh, Frances, you will love to visit Versailles. There is not another palace in the world like it. The gardens, the fountains, the statues . . . they are like something you have dreamed of. And the great palace with all its windows that sparkle like diamonds when the sun is on them.'

'I wish we could go together, Maria.'

'Well, we will talk about it when you come back to England. And we shall laugh together. Oh, you will love it here. Everyone seems so gay.' Maria's face clouded for a moment. 'Except some of the poor people. But you will love Versailles and you can go into the Palace and see the King having his dinner. It is so funny. There he sits in state behaving as though he is quite alone and only the barrier separates him from all the people who have come to watch him eat. I have heard that the funniest thing is the way in which he can knock the top off his egg at one stroke. But, alas, he was not eating an egg on the day Mamma and Papa took me to see him dine.'

Frances was already beginning to laugh at what was to come, but Maria had no intention of arriving at a hasty conclusion.

'It is necessary to have a ticket to get into the Palace and this Papa had. Anyone can go in provided they have a ticket, except begging friars and people marked with the small pox, but before you go in you must have a sword and a hat and there are people at the gates selling these. You will laugh at the people, Frances. They put on their hats and flourish their swords and some of them have never carried a sword before. And then into the Palace. You will never forget it. It is quite magnificent. The hall of mirrors! You can see yourself reflected again and again and again.'

'Yes, Maria, and when you came to the apartment where the King was dining . . .'

'Oh, Frances, what a disgrace! There we were close to the rope which held us back. Papa had brought me to stand in front of him so that I could see everything.'

'And the King of France . . .'

'Is a very old man, Frances. The Dauphin is his grandson. He is not nearly so handsome as his grandfather, for although the King is so old you know just by looking at him that he is a king. But the Dauphin's wife is lovely. She is like a fairy. I saw them together. She is Austrian.'

'Where Papa served in the Army,' said Frances. 'I wonder if he saw her there.'

'I doubt it. But I was telling you about the King at dinner. Well, Frances, his servants brought in a chicken. They kneel before him when they serve him; and he is so fastidious, with the most beautiful white hands sparkling with diamonds, and suddenly he picked up a chicken and tore it apart with his hands. Oh, Frances, it seemed to me so *funny*.'

'Go on, Maria. Go on.'

'There was silence. Everyone was watching the King and suddenly . . . I laughed. I laughed out loud and I could not stop laughing, Frances, because for some silly reason it seemed so funny.'

'Yes, yes?'

'And the King said to the man who was serving him, "Who is that laughing?" And Papa held my hand very tightly and I stopped laughing for the man came right over to where I was standing. He said: "Who are you and what is your name?" Papa was about to speak and I thought: No. I will not let Papa take the blame. So I said very loudly and very quickly, "I am Maria Smythe, an English girl from the Conception Convent in the Faubourg St. Antoine. It was I who laughed at the King." '

Maria became convulsed with laughter in which joined Frances, temporarily forgetting the imminent parting. 'Oh, Frances, the ceremony! It has to be seen to be believed. The King went on eating his chicken as though nothing had happened, and I stood there shivering, thinking that I should be carried off to prison and wondering what it was like living in a cell in the Bastille or the Conciergerie. I watched the man bowing and speaking to the King; then he took something from the table and came over to where I stood. I realized how grand *he* was when he spoke. "Mademoiselle, I, the Duc de Soubise, have the honour to present to you His Majesty's compliments. His Majesty wishes you to do him the honour of accepting this gift which he hopes will *amuse* you." He then presented me with a silver dish.'

'Which you still have,' said Frances.

Maria nodded. 'And which,' she went on, 'was full of sugar plums.'

'Show me the dish, Maria.'

Maria went to the bag which was already packed and took out a beautiful dish of silver on which a delicate pattern was traced.

'It's lovely,' cried Frances. 'And you had it just for laughing. It's a royal gift, Maria. The first royal gift you have ever had.'

'And the last, I dareswear,' said Maria lightly. 'But it is a lovely dish and I still laugh when I see it. And I envy you, Frances, to stay in Paris, for how I love Paris! I love it in the mornings when it is just beginning to wake up and there is an air of excitement everywhere and the streets are filled with the smells of cooking and the shops open and people are all scuttling about in the excited way they have. You can't help catching the excitement. Brambridge seems very dull in comparison.'

'Brambridge *is* dull,' admitted Frances. 'The only excitement is going to Mass.'

'So that is the same, is it. Do they still lock the door of the chapel when Mass is celebrated?'

'Yes. And apart from that it is all so quiet. Lessons every day and a little riding in the park and we don't know many people because most of our neighbours are Protestants and Mamma and Papa won't allow us to know them.'

It was Maria's turn to be mournful. 'Oh, lucky Frances!' she sighed.

A happy phase of her life was over; a new one was about to begin. She would have to learn to adjust herself to life at home as she had in Paris—and at least she had succeeded in comforting Frances.

The house in Brambridge seemed smaller than she had been imagining it. Perhaps, she thought wryly, she had compared it with Versailles. On the journey back they had passed through London and an excitement had touched her then, for the capital city reminded her of Paris. Perhaps this was because in Paris there had been a craze for all things English and the Parisians had been copying the English style of dress . . . masculine of course. The men wore severely cut coats and white cravats and riding boots; and shops were advertising *le thé* as drunk in England. Maria had felt excited by the big city, but of course they could not linger there. And when they had at length arrived in the beautiful county of Hampshire and passed through Winchester on the way to Brambridge and the carriage took them up the avenue of limes she felt a certain emotion, for this after all was home. Yet she did remember that the Mother Superior had embraced her with affection when she had left and had told her that if ever she wished to return to the Blew Nuns there would always be a welcome for her, implying that Maria Smythe would always remain one of the favourite pupils.

There was the house—a country mansion, the home of a squire and his family. Mamma was waiting to welcome her and embraced her, then held her at arms' length. 'Let me look at you, Maria. Why, how you have grown! Who would have thought that this was my little Maria?'

'Oh, Mamma, it is so good to see you.'

'And you have been happy with the nuns?'

'They were very kind to me.'

Mary Smythe smiled. Who would not be good to this charming young creature? How wise they had been to send her away. She had poise and charm and of course she spoke French like a native. Consequently they had a beautiful, intelligent and educated girl to launch on society.

'Come into the house, daughter. You will have forgotten what it looks like after all this time.'

Arm in arm, mother and daughter entered the house and there were the boys waiting to give her a boisterous greeting.

'Be careful, boys,' cried their father, 'you will harm Maria's Paris coiffure.'

John reached up and tried to pull down the golden hair which was piled high on Maria's head.

She jerked away from him, laughing. 'We all have to wear it high because Madame la Dauphine has a high forehead and wears hers so. It's the fashion.'

'And a most becoming one,' said Mary.

'I'm so pleased you approve, Mamma.'

'Come, my dearest, to your room. I have had a larger one prepared for you. It overlooks the lime avenue. I trust you will like it.'

'Oh, Mamma, I *am* happy to be home.'

'I feared that you would not wish to leave the nuns.'

'Nor did I. But I wanted to be home, too.'

'You are fortunate, my dear, to have so much that you enjoy. I hope Frances will feel the same.'

'But of course she must, Mamma.'

Mary smiled, well pleased with her daughter. The boys were merry but inclined to be too boisterous and a little selfish. And Frances? Well, they would see. But perhaps there was only one Maria.

Later Walter and Mary discussed their daughter.

'She is charming,' said Mary. 'And a beauty. Her hair is quite lovely and her eyes . . . that lovely hazel colour! Her complexion is quite perfect. It is like rose petals.'

'You are a fond mother.'

'Can you deny what I have said?'

'She has my nose. It would have been better if she had yours.'

'What nonsense! It adds *character* to her face. I think an aquiline nose is so attractive. Without it she would be insipid.'

'You are determined to eulogize your daughter, Madam.'

'Well, sir, tell me if you can see one fault in her.'

Walter looked dubious and Mary cried triumphantly, 'There, you cannot. You are as proud of her as I am.'

'I admit to falling under the spell of our Maria. She has returned from France even more delightful than when she went.'

'Even the King of France was delighted by her.'

'Oh, those sugar plums. He would have behaved so to any child.'

'I don't agree. He saw her, was enchanted by her, and wished to make her a present.'

'I do not like to think of that man's making gifts to our daughter . . . even though he thought of her as a child.'

Mary nodded. 'A sad state of affairs. No wonder the French are displeased with their king. Maria was telling me that he never goes to Paris at all because the people dislike him so much. They feel differently towards the Dauphin and his young Austrian wife. At least our King leads a good life, although there have been rumours about his early indiscretions. Did you know, I heard the other day that he had kept a Quakeress before his marriage and had even gone through a ceremony of marriage with her.'

'Rumours, Mary, to which it is unwise to listen and more unwise still to repeat.'

'Well, here's a more pleasant rumour. I have heard that he is inclined to be tolerant to religious minorities. The Quakers for one.'

'So here we are back to the Quaker rumour.'

'Well, is it not important to us? If he is lenient towards Quakers why not to Catholics? I think we are lucky to have such a king and he will do something for us. Oh, Walter, it infuriates me to think we have to go almost stealthily to Mass and lock the door of the chapel.'

Walter checked this flow by bringing the subject back to Maria.

'Our beautiful daughter is seventeen. Is it not time that we looked for a husband for her?'

Mary sighed. 'It's true, of course, but I wish it were not so. I should love to keep her with me for a little longer.'

'Well, there is no hurry, but we have our duty to her, you know. She will not have a big dowry.'

'Her dowry will be her beauty and her charm, and have you noticed Mr. Smythe that she has in addition to these the sweetest of natures?'

'Your daughter is a paragon, I doubt not, Madam. Therefore, in spite of her small dowry I am sure she will make a most satisfactory marriage.'

'But who is there here in Brambridge?'

'No one worthy of her, I agree. That is why I have come to discuss with you the possibility of sending her to your rich brother at Red Rice for a visit. I am sure he will be eager to do all that is possible for his charming niece.'

Maria's parents were right when they said that Henry Errington would be delighted to welcome his charming niece to his mansion in Red Rice. He had heard accounts of her beauty and when he saw her he was impressed.

He would invite some wealthy and eligible young men to the house if he could find them. That was the problem. He had wealthy neighbours with eligible young sons, but they were Protestants and the most important quality the bridegroom must have was that he must be of the approved religion.

Still, he would do the best he could and he would invite his old friend Edward Weld to come and stay that he might ask his advice. Edward's first wife had been a daughter of Lord Petre, and although unfortunately she was dead, Edward did entertain now and then at Lulworth Castle. Henry knew he would be pleased to help.

In due course Edward Weld arrived at Red Rice and Henry took him to his study to discuss the problem.

'My niece is a delightful creature, educated as few girls are today and in addition lovely to look at and of an engaging disposition. I don't feel it will be difficult to find a husband for her in spite of her lack of dowry.'

'How old is she?' Edward Weld wanted to know.

'Seventeen.'

'Very young.'

'Yes, but my sister has another daughter and she would like to see Maria suitably placed. I wondered, my dear friend, whether you could help me in this matter.'

'I'll do everything I can, of course. What do you suggest?'

'Perhaps you could invite me to Lulworth and include my niece in the invitation?'

'Easily done. You and your niece are invited.'

'We have great pleasure in accepting.'

'Without consulting the young lady?'

'Maria is the most obliging of young women. I only have to say that I wish to go and her to accompany me and she will wish to please me.'

'I must say you make me eager to see this charming creature.'

'I love the girl although I have only just made her acquaintance so to speak; she's been in Paris so long and was only a child when I knew her before she went to France. I am not so sure that I'm all that eager for her to marry. I'd like to adopt her and keep her with me.'

'Her parents would never agree to that, I'm sure.'

'And I'm equally sure of it. But come into the gardens. I think we shall find Maria there.'

Maria was picking roses and her uncle was delighted with the impression she made on his friend, for he had seen that Edward had dismissed his praise of his niece as avuncular pride.

'Maria, my dear, come and meet Mr. Edward Weld.'

She looked up from the rose bush and the flowers, thought her uncle fondly, were not more lovely than she was, as setting down her basket she dropped an enchanting curtsey.

'Mr. Weld has invited me to Lulworth Castle, Maria, and has suggested that you accompany me. How would you like that?'

'It sounds delightful and I shall be most happy to go with you, Uncle.'

'There, Edward,' said Henry Errington, 'your invitation is accepted.'

Edward Weld smiled, well pleased, and Henry noticed with pleasure that his friend found it difficult to take his eyes from Maria.

Before Edward Weld left the house he told Henry Errington that he wished to speak to him confidentially and Henry asked him to come with him into the library for this purpose.

As soon as they were alone Edward burst out: 'You may have noticed how I feel about Maria. Henry, what chance do you think I should have if I asked her to marry me?'

'*You* . . . Edward!'

'Oh come, Henry, I'm not as old as all that, I am forty-four years of age. Maria is almost eighteen. A disparity I admit, but I cannot help but love her and I—and you too—can assure her parents that I will cherish her and give her everything that—and more than perhaps—she has been accustomed to.'

'I am sure you would, Edward. Have you spoken to Maria?'

'Certainly not. I have spoken to you first. I should want Maria's family's permission before I spoke to her. Well, Henry?'

Henry was thinking: Edward Weld, a Catholic, a good living man, a rich man, the owner of Lulworth Castle, a widower who had enjoyed one happy marriage with a wife who had been the daughter of a lord. He was sure that Maria's parents could find no fault with such a match.

'There is one thing,' said Henry, 'my sister and brother-in-

law dote on the girl. I doubt they would force her into marriage.
The answer would depend on her.'

'Perhaps she would be so delighted with the Castle . . .'

'I doubt it. Maria would never be tempted by material gain.'

Edward looked a little uneasy. His health was not good; he
was not of an age to shine in courting a young girl; he had hoped
to dazzle her family with his wealth, but if that was of no account
his chances would be small.

His friend laid a hand on his arm. 'Maria is fond of you, I
am sure, but I think though that she regards you in the light of
an . . . uncle, which is natural considering you are my friend.
Perhaps that will change. I should not declare your intentions
immediately, but I will write to her parents and let them know
what they are. In the meantime we will go to Lulworth as arranged.'

Lulworth! What a delightful spot. And Mr. Weld seemed a different man in his own home. She wanted to hear all about the
castle; she wanted to explore it. Would she allow Mr. Weld to
take her on a tour of inspection? She did not wish to encroach
on his time because she was sure he had serious business which
did not include wasting his time on a girl like herself. But no,
Mr. Weld would be delighted; he was gratified that she should
be so interested in his home and he would allow no one to show
it to her but himself.

'It is not old . . . as castles go,' he told her. 'My family
bought it little more than a hundred years ago, in 1641, for
although the foundations were laid about the time the Armada
was defeated, the castle wasn't completed until some forty years
later.'

'It must be most exciting to *live* in a castle.'

'I find it so. Do you think you would?'

'I'm sure I should.'

'Well, who knows, perhaps you will.'

She laughed lightheartedly. 'I hardly think so. I shall have to
be content with our house which is very pleasant but by no
means a castle.'

'But perhaps you won't live there always. Perhaps you will
marry and er . . .'

'Who can say? Have you a chapel in the castle?'

'Yes. Would you like to see it?'

'Very much. At home we have to worship in the priest's house.

Papa has made a chapel there. It must be wonderful to have your own chapel.'

He laid his hand on her arm and she showed no objection. She thinks of me as an uncle, he thought despairingly. And how lovely she was! How young! How full of health and vigour.

On the way to the chapel he pointed out the round towers at each corner of the building, battlemented and made of Chelmark Stone. She was deeply interested in everything and delighted when he pointed out how the chapel had been built in four sections to make a cross.

She thought the views from the park were delightful, looking across the Dorset coast as they did, and she suggested climbing to the top of one of the towers for a better view.

She led the way up the narrow stone spiral staircase. The way was steep; it was years since he had been up there; he followed her, trying to keep up, trying to hide his breathlessness, and when he finally stood beside her at the top of the tower she turned to him in alarm and cried: 'Mr. Weld, are you feeling ill?'

'No, no . . .' he gasped.

'But you are. Oh dear, how careless of me! I *ran* up those stairs. Pray sit down. Yes, you must, Mr. Weld.' She insisted he be seated on a stone ledge and she knelt beside him, looking up at him anxiously. He thought how beautiful she was in her concern and he loved her more than ever, but hopelessly, he thought. He had meant to impress her by his castle and all he had succeeded in doing was showing her that he was an old man.

'I am all right.' He made to stand up.

But she would not hear it. She was charmingly authoritative. 'Oh no, Mr. Weld. I insist.'

'*You* insist.'

She blushed. 'I am sorry. But I really am a little anxious.'

'I find it delightful that you should care for a poor old man.'

'But of course I care. And you are *not* an old man. *I* have been stupid. I ran up those stairs. Mamma says I am sometimes thoughtless and I'm afraid I am.'

'I . . . I find you charming. I would not change you.'

'Careless or not?' Her laughter rang out.

'And what are you thinking of me?'

'That is was very kind of you to allow me to come here with Uncle Henry and to show me your beautiful castle and . . .' She had paused to look at him. Then she added severely: 'But I can see I shall have to make you more careful in future. There! I've been impertinent again.'

'Please go on . . . being impertinent.'

'Do you know, Mr. Weld, you are not in the least like an uncle. Do you feel rested now? Shall we go down?'

He rose and said: 'One moment. Let us look over the parapet so that you can see the countryside.'

She stood with him so close that a strand of her long hair blew across his face.

Ask her now? Say: 'All this is mine. Share it with me.' If she were mercenary . . . but she was not. She was just sweet, innocent and infinitely desirable.

'Maria,' he began.

She turned to him, her eyes shining with pleasure in the beautiful landscape.

'Yes, Mr. Weld?' she prompted.

'You like . . . all this?'

'Certainly. Who could help it?'

'You would like to live here?'

'I think it's the most delightful spot.'

'Then . . .'

She looked at him expectantly.

'No,' he said. 'I am too old . . . and you are too young.'

Then she understood.

She was bewildered. She wanted to get to her room and think.

There was a letter from Mamma. Mr. Weld had offered marriage. Mamma and Papa had thought a great deal about this offer. Uncle Henry could vouch for Mr. Weld who was a good man and belonged to one of the foremost Catholic families in England. He was devoted to Maria; he did not ask for a dowry which, Maria would realize, was a great consideration, poor Papa's affairs being what they were. Mr. Weld had already proved himself a good husband to a lady of high rank. It was flattering that he should wish their dearest Maria to take her place, so Maria should think very seriously about this. It was not that they would *force* her to marry where she did not wish; they would not even *urge* her to do so; but what they would do was ask her to think very carefully of her position. She was not rich; she had little to offer but her beauty; there were the boys and Frances to consider. And while Mamma and Papa would not for one moment suggest that she *accept* Mr. Weld's offer if she did not wish to, they would be very *happy* if she decided to be wise and do so.

Maria read that letter over and over again.

Mr. Weld was so kind, so good, so very anxious to show her that he would understand perfectly if she refused his offer. Uncle Henry obviously wanted her to make his old friend happy; and she wanted to please everyone.

She took a delight in seeing that Mr. Weld did not exert himself. This pleased and yet disturbed him. He enjoyed her attentions, but at the same time was aware that they stressed his age.

And one summer's day when Mr. Weld seemed to find the heat too much for him and she exerted her charming tyranny and insisted that he sit in the shade with her instead of going to ride, she thought he seemed a little sad and she mentioned this.

He said: 'There is only one thing that makes me sad, Maria. It is because I am not twenty years younger.'

'Why should that make you sad? The young are often very foolish.'

'It makes me sad because I am not your age. Then I could ask you to marry me and if you said yes I should no longer have any reason to be sad.'

'You might ask me to marry you,' she told him severely, 'which is something you have not done yet, although you have spoken to my uncle and my parents on this matter. Perhaps if you were to ask *me* . . .'

A look of great joy came into his face.

'Maria,' he said, 'will you marry me?'

'But certainly I will,' answered Maria; and she laughed with pleasure to see his joy.

Edward Weld was delighted with his marriage; as soon as Maria had agreed he had hurried on the ceremony and Walter and Mary Smythe congratulated themselves that their eldest child had done very well. With little effort and no expense they had arranged for her an advantageous union, for at eighteen years old she was comfortably settled; her home was a castle; her husband was rich and indulgent and most important of all a Catholic.

As for Maria, she was very happy. It was gratifying to know that she could make her husband so happy; he delighted in showing her off to his friends and there were frequent house-parties at Lulworth Castle. Maria quickly learned to become a good hostess; the poise she had acquired in France was an additional asset and she could converse with the grace and ease of a much older person; and as she matured a little she grew even more beautiful.

Edward Weld could not do enough for her. Her portrait must be painted. He must always be able to see Maria as she was during this first year of marriage. He would have her painted beside him. There was a picture of him in the castle hall in which he was portrayed with his first wife, and as there was room to paint in Maria on the other side of him this was done. He was delighted with the result and whenever he came into the hall he would stand for a few moments looking at himself with the two women on either side of him, but his eyes would linger on Maria.

Then he decided that Maria should have a portrait to herself and he summoned Gainsborough to Lulworth.

When the artist arrived he was delighted by the beauty of the sitter but a little surprised that she wore her hair in its natural state. He commented on this.

'Madam, the ladies of the Court wear wigs or powder their hair.'

'Do they indeed, Mr. Gainsborough?' reported Maria. 'I do not.'

Mr. Gainsborough could not hide his dismay, for this portrait would not look like those which he was accustomed to painting. It was clear that he wished his sitter would make some concession to fashion.

Maria had spirit, her husband was not displeased to note. He liked to see a little fire in his goddess; she quite clearly had not taken to Mr. Gainsborough; but he was surprised when after the first sitting she came to him, her eyes flashing with an indignation he had never seen before.

'Would you believe it, Edward, that man has given me a grey wig!'

Edward went to see the portrait and it was true that Gainsborough had sketched in her curly hair with grey impaste.

The next day, however, Maria told Mr. Gainsborough that she had no intention of giving him another sitting. The painter shrugged his shoulders; he would be paid for what he had done and there were many people more important that Mrs. Weld of Lulworth who were asking for his services.

'Why,' said Mr. Weld, as the artist drove away from the castle, 'what a determined young person you are to be sure!'

Maria laughed. 'Was I right, Edward, in thinking that you wished for a portrait of your devoted wife?'

'You were indeed.'

'Well, I was determined that you should have that or nothing. Do you imagine I wished Mr. Gainsborough to present you with some Court beauty who bore no resemblance to her whom you have honoured with your name?'

Edward smiled fondly.

'We'll find an artist who will give me exactly what I want—which is my own Maria.'

Edward Weld was forty-five—not a great age certainly, but since he did not enjoy good health it occurred to him that the time had come for him to make sure that in the event of his death Maria would inherit all he had, for if he did not make a new will the castle and everything he possessed would go to his brother Thomas.

He therefore took the first opportunity of going to see his lawyers and instructing them to draft a new will which was to be brought to the castle at the earliest opportunity.

This was done and delivered at the castle for his signature. He could not resist telling Maria what he had done, so he sent one of the servants to her room and asked her to come to him in the library.

She came in a riding habit of a most elegant cut, for another thing Maria had learned in France was how to dress to advantage, and as ever Edward was deeply conscious of her beauty.

'Ah, my love, how delightful you look.'

'Such a lovely morning, Edward. I have come to insist that you come riding with me.'

'It will give me great pleasure. But first I have something to show you. I have made a new will.'

She looked alarmed and he laughed at her. 'I am not going to die, dearest Maria, simply because I make a will.'

'I hate talk of wills.'

'Bless you. But these things have to be. This will be signed and put away and then we will talk of it no more and I shall have the satisfaction of knowing that should anything happen to me, my Maria is comfortably settled.'

'You are so good to me, dear Edward.'

He smiled at her fondly and she sat down while he read the contents of the will to her. Apart from a few legacies everything was for her.

'Now,' he said. 'The witnesses have to sign. We will get this settled immediately.'

'But then it will be too late to ride. Have you forgotten that the Framptons are coming over from Moreton. There is just time to ride if you have to change. The will can be signed after the Framptons' visit.'

Ever ready to please her he put the will into his bureau, locked it and went to change into his riding clothes.

It was a lovely morning. Galloping across the fields, walking their horses close to the sea, they talked of the Framptons and other friends and new furnishings Maria had decided on for certain rooms in the castle.

The time passed quickly and soon Maria was reminding him that they must return to the castle if they were to change in time to greet the Framptons.

As they cantered across the park surrounding the castle Edward's horse stumbled over a molehill and he was thrown right out of the saddle. He lay still on the grass while the horse cantered back to the stables.

Maria hastily dismounted.

'Edward,' she cried. 'Oh . . . my dearest . . .'

Edward opened his eyes.

'Thank God,' she cried. 'Edward, I am going to get help . . . Just lie still . . . and wait.'

Edward was apparently uninjured by the fall but his doctors advised him to remain in bed for a week or so. The incident had been a great shock to him, they said.

Maria proved herself to have another excellent quality: she was a good nurse. A week passed and Edward did not recover. No bones were broken, but it was certain that the fall had had an adverse effect. He seemed to have aged considerably and although he was at peace while Maria was at his bedside his memory seemed to be failing.

Two weeks passed. The doctors shook their heads. They did not understand his condition. The fall had not appeared to be serious and yet after it he changed considerably.

'Good nursing is what he needs,' they told Maria. 'But keep him quiet for a little longer.'

Maria rarely left the sick room; but she noticed that each day her husband was growing more feeble.

And one morning when she went into his room and spoke to him he did not answer.

She went close to the bed and stared at him. One glance was enough to show her that she was a widow.

Mrs. Fitzherbert

It was not until the will was read that Maria realized what had happened and that she alone was responsible for her position. The new will had lain unsigned and forgotten in the bureau during Edward's illness and in the old one there was no mention of Maria. How could there have been? Edward had been unaware of her existence when he had written it. The Castle and Edward's fortune therefore had all gone to his brother Thomas and there was not a penny for Maria.

Thomas—Edward's brother—arrived at the castle. He was sorry for Maria and assured her that she would not be left without means of support.

'You should not concern yourself with me,' she told him. 'I shall return to my parents.'

Thomas thought that would be the wisest plan; he would however insist on making her a small allowance which he was sure was what his brother would have wished.

Maria knew that what her husband had wished was to leave her the castle and the bulk of his fortune, but she did not remind Thomas of this. She herself was to blame. Who would have thought on that sunny morning when she had persuaded Edward to postpone the signing of his will that such an act could have the effect of making her a poor widow instead of a rich one?

But she was young and she could not regret the loss of a fortune. She was still mourning for Edward whom she had loved, if not passionately, with devotion and gratitude.

She was delighted when Papa arrived to take her back to Brambridge.

* * *

Mary Smythe was glad to have her daughter at home, but she did deplore what she called her lack of worldliness. Edward had been ready to sign his will and what had stopped him was Maria . . . the chief beneficiary!

'My goodness!' cried Mary. 'What irony! A fortune handed to you and you calmly say, "Later, please. Let us ride first." Really, Maria!'

'Oh, Mamma, how was I to know . . . ?'

'No, no, my dearest, of course you did not. But I think you should try and take a slightly more practical view in future.'

'Mamma, it is over. Dear Edward is dead and I am not rich, though I have enough. I must be content with that.'

Mary Smythe sighed. Her daughter grew more beautiful every day. Would a young widow have as much chance of finding a husband as an unmarried girl? She was not sure, for the widow was very little better off than the young girl had been.

Maria stayed at her parents' house for some months and then decided to take a cottage nearby on Colden Common, which was not a bad idea. 'It makes her status clear,' said Mary to Walter, 'and after a year of mourning there is no reason why Maria should not go into society again. She will then be under twenty which, Walter, you must admit is very young. And I begin to think that our Maria is beautiful enough to do without a dowry.'

'No one is beautiful enough for that, Mary.'

'You are a cynic, Walter. Maria married Edward did she not? She would have been rich but for her own folly . . . well, hardly that—heedlessness. But I doubt not that she has now learned that financial affairs should be settled at the earliest possible moment—and that is a very valuable lesson learned.'

'At the price of a fortune, yes.'

'Perhaps my brother will help again. He was very useful before. But Maria must have her year to mourn poor Edward. Then we shall see.'

So Maria settled quietly in her cottage.

Henry Errington was very interested in his sister's family, having none of his own, and he made up his mind that having succeeded in finding Maria a husband once he would do so again; but like his sister and her husband he agreed that the year of mourning must first be lived through.

Maria found life in her little cottage with the one servant she could afford, suited to her mood. She thought a great deal of that short period when she had been mistress of Lulworth Castle and was sad mourning poor Edward who had loved her so devotedly and had doubtless shortened his life in trying to keep up with her youth. There had been no need. She had not wished him to.

But she was sensible enough to know that her feeling for him had been no deep-rooted emotion. She had tried to please him because she enjoyed pleasing people; and after a few months she began to find the quiet life at the cottage very much to her taste. She read a great deal; she studied politics, for she quickly realized that she was living in momentous times. The conflict with the American colonies was certainly one of vital importance; she followed the activities of Pitt—now Lord Chatham; and she thought often of affairs in France and was a little sad because the King who had presented her with a dish of sugar plums had died and on the throne was now that gauche young Dauphin and his dainty Austrian-born wife.

Well, nothing remained the same and she wondered how long she would stay in her little cottage on Colden Common. She knew that Uncle Henry had his eye on her. They would soon start matchmaking again. But at the moment there was respite, and she could enjoy it.

As her brother Walter came breathlessly into the cottage, one glance was enough to show her that something was very wrong.

'Maria,' he said, 'come home at once. Papa has been taken very ill.'

She snatched up her cloak and climbed into the trap. She had never seen Walter so serious.

'Tell me what happened,' she demanded.

'Mamma went to see what had happened to him and found him in his chair unable to move.'

Through the avenue of limes they went as fast as the pony would take them and as soon as they stopped by the door Maria leaped down and ran indoors.

Her mother, white faced and silent, embraced her. The doctors were with Walter Smythe; and it did not take them long to give their verdict. He had had a stroke which had paralysed him.

Life had indeed changed in the house in Brambridge. Maria gave up the cottage and went home to console her mother, but with poor Papa an invalid who would never walk again, nothing was the same.

Uncle Henry came over and was a great consolation; he would be a father to the family, he said. Frances should remain with the Blew Nuns to complete her education, for no good could come in bringing her home; and the boys would have to be found careers, which was not easy, as being Catholics they would be debarred from the professions most suited to their position in life, such as government posts, the Bar or the Army or Navy.

Uncle Henry stayed with them for a while but Maria discovered that her uncle, although a delightful host, a man who loved to entertain and who enjoyed good food and wine, was not really suited to be the guardian of boys who were fast becoming men. The discipline imposed by their father was completely lacking and Maria had some uneasy moments contemplating their future.

It was now that she regretted her ill luck or lack of prescience which had prevented her from seeing that the will was signed before that fatal ride. What a lot she could have done for her family if she had been the rich widow of Lulworth Castle instead of the poor one of a cottage on Colden Common!

Uncle Henry was, however, very interested in his beautiful niece and he was constantly endeavouring to see that she was not hidden from sight. One of his friends was Thomas Fitzherbert, a rich Catholic squire who had estates in Swynnerton in Staffordshire and Norbury in Derbyshire; but was some thirty years old—older than Maria, it was true, but Maria was now no inexperienced girl. Uncle Henry was right when he guessed that Tom Fitzherbert would be impressed by his niece.

'She is delightful,' he cried. 'I am sure, Henry, that I never saw a more lovely girl.'

Uncle Henry chuckled. If Maria married Tom Fitzherbert she would have a life more suited to her than that she had had through her first marriage. Edward Weld had been very worthy, a good rich Catholic husband, but he had been somewhat old for Maria and he had really lived too quietly at Lulworth. Tom Fitzherbert knew how to live well—which was in that manner so enjoyed by Henry Errington. Maria would really have been wasted at Lulworth where comparatively little entertaining had been done.

As Henry predicted it was not long before Tom Fitzherbert was making his intentions clear; and Maria, like the good sensible girl she was, accepted him.

Maria was just turned twenty-one when she became Mrs. Fitzherbert.

* * *

Maria was quickly to discover that life with Thomas Fitzherbert had a great deal more to offer than that which she had enjoyed with Edward Weld. Now she had an energetic husband, who was as devoted to her in his way as Edward Weld had been in his. Maria was beautiful, goodnatured, poised and intelligent and Thomas Fitzherbert was certainly not disappointed in the marriage—nor was Maria.

They had plenty of money; they entertained lavishly, not only in the country but in London where they had a house in Park Street, off Park Lane. Here politicians and members of the aristocracy came often and the conversation was witty and amusing. Maria Fitzherbert began to be known as one of the most successful hostesses in London; and how much more to Maria's taste was London life than that of the country!

Mr. Fitzherbert, though an ardent Catholic, was liberal in outlook and fully supported the monarchy. He had great faith in the King whom he knew was anxious to abolish intolerance and he had hopes of seeing a reform in the laws against Catholics.

In her new affluent circumstances Maria did not forget her family, and when it was time for Frances to leave the convent she suggested that her sister come and stay with her.

It was a great joy to see Frances again—grown into a tall and pretty young woman. The sisters embraced warmly and Maria was interested to discover that her sister had been as regretful to leave the Blew Nuns as she had been. She had tales to tell of Paris, the scandals of the Court, the inability of the King and Queen to get children until the recent birth of a Princess to them—Madame Royale.

Maria listened eagerly and with pleasure to her sister's accounts of life in France and told her what had been happening at home.

'You will not find it difficult to settle down,' she assured her.

'I should have hated to be shut away at Brambridge, Maria. Oh, it is so changed! Poor Papa! He is just *there* . . . not like his old self at all; and Mamma seems to have lost her spirit and the boys are so wild. How glad I am that you married Mr. Fitzherbert and have invited me to stay with you.'

'I am glad about both of those things also,' Maria told her.

Maria enjoyed launching her sister on London society and when she took her to Swynnerton, Frances was a success. She was exceptionally pretty, charming, gay and goodnatured; but a pale shadow of Maria, most people agreed.

There was one young man who was entertained frequently at Swynnerton who did not however agree with this verdict.

Frances came into her sister's bedroom while Maria was at her dressing table. Maria, who liked to dress her own hair, had dismissed her maid. She still wore it naturally. She was secretly proud of those thick corn-coloured curls and was not going to have them disfigured by powder; and as her own hair was abundant she had no need to pad it. Besides, she preferred to follow an original style.

Frances sat on the bed and watched her sister.

'You should see the hairstyles in Paris. They get higher and higher. Women are wearing feathers and even country scenes in their hair. And the Queen leads the fashion, which becomes more outrageous every day. Monsieur Léonard, her hairdresser, goes rattling along in his very fine carriage every day from Paris to Versailles to dress the Queen's hair.'

'I shan't change my style . . . not even for the Queen of France,' said Maria.

'I don't blame you. Yours looks lovely. Maria, I have come to the conclusion that you are a very unusual woman.'

'Have you only just come to that conclusion?' asked Maria lightly.

'Well I've always known it. You're very happy with Tom, are you not?'

Maria agreed that this was so.

'But then you were happy with Mr. Weld.'

That was also true.

'I wonder whether, Maria, you are the sort of woman who would be happy with *any* man.'

'I'm sure I should not.'

'But *two* happy marriages. You are, of course, very goodnatured, amusing, clever and beautiful.'

'Please, you are making me blush.'

'But you are also wise, so you know these things. How much am I like you, Maria?'

'Quite a bit, I believe.'

'I wonder if I shall be happily married.'

'I am sure you will if you marry wisely.'

'Are people wise when they are in love?'

Maria was thoughtful. She had married what was considered wisely twice. Yet she hesitated to answer that question. A thought came into her head. Had she ever been in love? She was fond of Thomas, of course; she had been fond of Edward, but . . .

Frances was looking at her intently.

'I think,' said Frances steadily, 'that I could feel the same for Carnaby Haggerston as you do for Thomas Fitzherbert.'

Maria was excited. 'Frances. He has . . .'

Frances nodded.

'And you have accepted?'

'Not exactly. I wanted to talk to you first.'

'But you are fond of him, Frances? I have seen you together. I know.'

'Yes,' said Frances, 'I'm fond of him.'

'I'm delighted.' Maria rose and embraced her sister. 'Mamma will be so pleased and so will Papa . . . poor dear Papa . . . if he is able to grasp what this means. Uncle Henry and Thomas will both be so . . . gratified. It is just what we should all have wished.'

Frances nodded and kept her eyes on her face. Maria was happy; and her happiness had come through wisdom. No one could deny that Sir Carnaby Haggerston of the Northumberland *Catholic* Haggerstons was not an excellent match.

With Frances safely married and the chance of helping the boys which marriage with Thomas gave her, Maria was at peace. Occasionally she invited her mother to spend a little time with her in the country. Poor Mamma, she had changed a great deal since Papa's stroke and Maria feared she sighed nostalgically for the past. Walter had gone into the Austrian Army since his religious opinions debarred him from joining that in his own country; and Uncle Henry was often at Brambridge. But he was too indulgent and the boys, Maria feared, sadly missed a father.

She was growing closer and closer to Thomas whose activities were of the utmost interest to her; and for him it was a great pleasure to have a well-informed wife with whom he could discuss those issues which were of such importance to him.

There was only one disappointment in their marriage; there was no sign of any children. But Maria was very young and they had their whole lives before them. Thomas was certain that such a paragon as Maria could not fail to give him all he wanted.

He delighted in those occasions when they could dine alone together. These were rare because there seemed to be a continual round of entertaining, for he had always been a jovial man who liked to surround himself with friends; he was wealthy; he had fine houses in which to entertain, and as there were three of them in different parts of the country and he had so many friends in each part, naturally there was a constant round of visits.

But there were rare occasions when he and Maria could dine intimately together and this was one of them. How beautiful she looked with her golden hair falling about her shoulders, so simply dressed and so charming. He thought that in her muslin gown with the blue ribbons she was more beautiful than in a satin silk velvet or brocade evening gown.

Driving home through the Mall they had passed a young woman in a carriage—a flamboyant, overdressed young woman in pale pink satin and big straw hat decorated with pink and green feathers. An undoubted beauty but, in Maria's opinion, decidedly a little vulgar. Thomas had told her that the woman was Mrs. Robinson, the actress who was known as Perdita because she had been playing Perdita in *The Winter's Tale* when the Prince of Wales had first noticed her.

While they dined they discussed the woman and the scandal she was causing.

'I am sorry for His Majesty,' said Thomas. 'The Prince is a great trial to him.'

'He is young yet,' replied Maria. 'Doubtless he will grow wiser as he grows older.'

'But when the heir to the throne lives openly with an actress it is certain to cause distress to all good subjects of the King who, I have heard, spends many a sleepless night worrying about what the Prince is doing.'

'I am surprised that he should have become enamoured of such a woman.'

'Actresses have a great appeal for the very young and she is reckoned a beauty.'

'She is undoubtedly that,' agreed Maria.

'And clearly well aware of it. I give her another three months. They say His Highness is already wavering.'

'Poor woman! What will she do then?'

'Find another protector, I dareswear. That is usually the way of such women.'

'I am sorry for her. She is so pretty, too.'

'You waste your pity on such a woman, my love. I wonder what influence the Prince will have on political issues. I have heard that he is seen often in the company of men like Burke and Charles James Fox.'

'So it would appear,' said Maria, 'that he does not spend all his time with the actress. He must be interested in politics to have such men as his friends.'

'This could be so.'

'And do you think he will be on our side?'

Her husband smiled. 'The Prince will always take sides *against* his father. But the King gave his assent to our Bill nearly two years ago, so doubtless His Highness would not have given his if he had an opportunity of doing so, which fortunately he has not. He will have to wait until he is twenty-one before he can have an influence on politics . . . and that is three years away.'

'Is he so young then?' said Maria.

'Very young. Six years younger than you, Maria.'

'Six years.' That was about the time she had married Edward Weld! She had seemed very young then. She was silent, thinking of the Prince who caused such distress to his father and who was very wild and gay and, so it was said, extremely charming and undeniably handsome.

Poor woman, she thought again, as a vision of the woman in the Mall rose before her, overdressed, her hair heavily powdered, her face a mask of rouge and white lead.

The subject was distasteful so she changed it.

'How gratifying it is that that cruel law has been changed. I remember my parents talking about it long before I went to France. One of the most cruel aspects was that which enabled the son of a Catholic turned Protestant to take over his father's possessions. Just imagine if Walter, John or Charles had done that. What a dreadful law!'

'All laws against minorities are monstrous. But we are fortunate in our king, Maria. He has always stood for tolerance and he is a good man. I know many people laugh at him . . . call him "Farmer George" because he is fond of the land, and "The Button Maker" because he is interested in handcrafts. They call him dull because he is a faithful husband—but I think he is a good man.'

'But a good man is not necessarily a good king. What of the Colonies? I fancy King George has played an important part in that disastrous affair.'

'You have a point there, my dear,' Thomas admitted. 'But I was referring to his tolerance. He has protected Methodists and Quakers in the past—and I believe he has always been sympathetic towards us.'

A servant came in at that moment to announce that Sir Carnaby Haggerston had called.

Maria rose to greet her brother-in-law and drew back in dismay when she saw how agitated he was.

'Lord George Gordon is mustering the Protestant Association and I've heard that he is inciting them to rise up against the Catholics of London. My God, I pray we are not going to have riots here . . . as they've been having in Scotland.'

'Impossible,' said Thomas. 'The Protestant Association is a worthy body. I'm sure of this.'

'But,' said Haggerston, 'I hear that Gordon is a madman.'

Maria sat at an upper window in the house in Park Street. Terror had struck London and she knew that at any moment the mob might come running into this very street, stop at this very house, break down the doors and destroy or burn their possessions.

Thomas had urged her to leave London, but that she would not do. It was his duty, Thomas said, to stay here. The houses of his friends had been looted and some of their priests were in danger. He must do all he could to get them removed to places of safety. He would not be true to his Faith if he ran away to the country to hide himself there. Besides, who knew when these riots would spread even into the country. But he deplored the fact that Maria was in the centre of the trouble.

Maria for once was in disagreement with her husband. Her mouth set into firm lines, for Maria could be very firm when she considered it necessary to be, and she said: 'If you stay in London, Thomas, I shall stay too. You may need my help.'

And Thomas found it impossible to persuade her.

The trouble had seemed to break out suddenly. At the heart of it was mad Lord George Gordon, an insignificant younger son of a noble house, good looking, a *bon viveur*, a Member of Parliament who could not get himself taken seriously.

That, Maria had said to Thomas, was at the root of the trouble. Lord George was determined to call attention to himself no matter if he laid waste half London to do so. He was a Protestant, and when he had been elected President of the Protestant Association of England he believed he had that chance. He announced his intention of bringing about the repeal of the Catholic Act, that Act which had given the rights to Catholic subjects of England which had so long been denied them. He had spoken in Parliament where his diatribes had not been given serious attention; he had had an audience with the King which had brought no success.

To a man such as Gordon, obsessed by the need to call attention to himself, these rebuffs only strengthened his resolution. The Parliament and King rejected him; very well, there was the mob.

The nightmare days followed. Members of the Protestant Association collected in St. George's Fields; they marched round the fields singing hymns and holding banners aloft; but it was not the orderly members of the Association who would be of use to Lord George; it was the mob he collected on his march to the Houses of Parliament. Beggars, criminals, prostitutes, all looking for sport and chiefly gain, joined the throng which had grown to over twenty thousand.

'No Popery!' they shouted. They flung mud at the carriages of Members of Parliament; they waited outside the House while Gordon entered it; but they were not interested in talk; they wanted action. Many did not know what the point at issue was but they screamed the parrot cry of 'No Popery'; and the pillage began.

Maria shivered; looking out she could see the red glow in the sky. They were burning Catholic chapels and the houses of well-known Catholics. The Fitzherberts were not unknown. When would their turn come?

A carriage drew up at the door and Frances stepped out and hurried into the house. Maria ran down to greet her.

'Frances! To come through the streets!'

'But Maria, Carnaby is out . . . I know not where . . . and I could not stay in the house alone. I had to be with you. So I took a chance. Oh, Maria, it was terrible. I saw houses ablaze . . . the houses of our friends . . . What will happen next?'

'How can we know? Sit down and have a glass of wine.'

The servant brought it. Was she watching them furtively? The girl was a good Catholic—she would not have been employed in the household if she were not—but what were the servants thinking? It was the rich Catholics who were the targets for the mob.

Frances drank the wine and looked at her sister, asking for comfort.

'It cannot go on,' said Maria.

'Why not!' demanded Frances. 'They could burn the whole of London. They have attacked the house of a magistrate who attempted to warn them that they were breaking the law. On my way here I saw seven big fires. Oh, Maria, Maria what next?'

'They will have to stop it. They will have to call out the Army.'

'Then why do they not? What do they let this go on for? The mob has freed the prisoners from Newgate; they have set the prison on fire. Felons are walking the streets. What will become of us?'

'That's something we never know from day to day—Gordon riots or not. It is no use agitating yourself, Frances. It does no good. At any moment we may be called upon to play our part and we have to be ready for that.'

'Where is Thomas?'

'He is out . . . helping our friends. He is trying to get some of the priests out of London. It is their only hope.'

'They would have no compunction in murdering *them*,' said Frances. 'Listen.'

The shouts seemed to be coming nearer, the red glow in the fire more fierce.

Maria prayed silently that no harm should befall her friends, her sister and herself. If the riots spread to the country . . . she thought of the house in Brambridge and her father, that poor helpless invalid, and the boys. What of Uncle Henry who would, like Thomas, not stand idle? And men like Thomas who were taking an active part in all this were the ones who were in most danger.

Thomas must be safe. How she wished he would come in.

The shouting had become more muted.

'They are not coming this way,' said Frances.

Maria sighed with relief. But where was Thomas?

It was midnight when he returned; his clothes were singed and blackened by smoke and he was exhausted.

Maria cried: 'Thank God you are home.' She did not ask questions; it was imperative to get him to bed. She would not allow the servants to wait on him, for how did one know whom one could trust?

'I must wash this grime from me, Maria,' he said.

'I will prepare you a hot cordial while you do so.'

Bathing exhausted Thomas and before he could drink the cordial he was asleep.

In the morning Maria was alarmed by his looks; he had lost his usually healthy colour and he coughed incessantly. She wanted to call a physician, but Thomas said it was only a chill and would pass. There was work to be done. More of the priests were in acute danger and it was the duty of men such as himself to bring them out of it.

But when he tried to rise from his bed he could not do so and Maria decided that whatever he said she was going to call a doctor.

She was scarcely aware of what was going on outside because Thomas was very ill, through an inflammation of the lungs; Maria was at his bedside day and night listening to his delirium.

Meanwhile the rioters were threatening St. James's Palace and the Bank of England, and the King, realizing drastic action was necessary, called in martial law. The troops fired on the mob and after several hundred rioters had been killed, order was at last restored.

The Gordon Riots were over.

But Thomas Fitzherbert was very ill indeed: and even though the fever subsided, he did not regain his former good health.

With the coming of that winter as his health did not improve, Maria decided to take him to the South of France where a warmer climate might be beneficial. They took a villa near the sea where Maria devoted herself assiduously to his comfort. But it was no use. Thomas's lungs seemed permanently affected.

Never before had Thomas realized what a blessing his marriage had been. In Maria he had the perfect nurse. Every hour of the day she devoted to him; she would sit with him at the open window looking out over the sea and talk about events in England, for which Thomas was homesick. Not so Maria. Those early years in France had given her a love of this country and she would not have objected to settling there altogether.

But as the winter wore on it became apparent that Thomas was no better in France than in England and that far from improving he was growing steadily more feeble.

He grew anxious about Maria's future, knowing what had happened in the case of her first marriage, how the will which would have left her very comfortably off had never been signed, he was determined that nothing like that should happen again.

He told Maria that he had made a will and that if he died she would be a comparatively rich woman.

Maria said that she did not wish to talk of such an unlikely eventuality, but he insisted that she did.

'The estates at Swynnerton and Norbury will have to go to

my brother Basil. They were left to me with that provision. It is always a male heir who must inherit . . . and if we should have no son . . .'

Maria nodded. The hope of children was one which she had been obliged to subdue, for it was almost certain now that Thomas would never father a child.

'But that will not prevent my looking after you, Maria. The lease of the house in Park Street is not part of the family inheritance. That shall be yours, with all the furniture in it, also my horses and carriages, and in addition there will be an income of two thousand pounds a year—so, my dear, although you will not be as rich as I should like to make you, you will be well provided for.'

'Oh, Thomas, do not speak of these things.'

'Nor will I again. This is settled. I can now have the consolation of knowing that if I should die, you will be comfortably placed.'

'Nonsense,' she said sharply. 'You are not going to die. When the spring comes . . .'

But the spring came and there was no change in Thomas's condition. His cough grew worse and when she saw the blood on his pillow she knew.

That May he died. He was only thirty-seven; she was twenty-five years old—and once more a widow.

An Evening at the Opera

She was no longer young; she had been twice widowed; and now she was completely free to live the life of her choice. Deeply she missed Thomas; she thought affectionately now and then of Edward her first husband; but she discovered that freedom was pleasant. She was no longer beholden to anyone and she had enough money to live in the utmost comfort.

She did not return to England when Thomas died, but stayed on in Nice, and when she had a desire to be once more in Paris she decided she would stay there for a while. What joy to be back in Paris, the city of gaiety which she had once loved so much. To ride through the streets in her carriage, to mingle with the fashionable people in the Bois, to visit the dressmakers, to meet friends on the fringe of the Court, all this was interesting. But Maria wished to do something practical and since Thomas had died for his Faith (for his work during the riots, she insisted, had been the beginning of his illness) she would found a house where Roman Catholic ladies could find refuge in Paris if life was not tolerable for them in England.

She grew a little saddened during her study in Paris, for she soon discovered that it was not the same as it had been a few years back. There was an air of brooding tension in the streets which she was quick to sense. The people hated the Queen and this was made obvious by the unpleasant cartoons in which she was depicted. In spite of the fact that a little Dauphin had been born the murmurings continued and Maria began to think of returning to England. Moreover, her family were writing to her and asking her to come home where, they pointed out, she could live in the utmost comfort; and Maria, growing more and more

35

sensitive to the atmosphere in her beloved Paris, and feeling a little homesick, crossed the Channel and decided to look for a house near London.

Marble Hill was not for sale, but Maria had no wish to buy it since it could be let to her, and as soon as she saw it she was eager to begin the tenancy.

Ideally situated in Richmond, it had been built by the Countess of Suffolk, mistress of George II, and been called Marble Hill because it stood on the top of an incline and was of dazzling whiteness; on either side it looked down on lawns and chestnut trees and from the windows a very fine view of Richmond Hill could be seen.

Here, Maria thought, she could indeed settle and be content. She had no desire to entertain lavishly; she assured herself, her friends and her family that she preferred to live quietly.

She was too beautiful and accomplished to shut herself away from the world was the general opinion, and Lady Sefton, a distant relation on Maria's mother's side, was soon calling at Marble Hill. She wished, she said, to launch her charming kinsman into London society. Maria protested, but so did Lady Sefton.

'Why, my dear cousin,' she said, 'you are far too young to live the life of a recluse. I was talking to the Duchess of Devonshire about you and she is eager to make your acquaintance.'

'My dear Lady Sefton . . .'

'Oh, come, Christian names between cousins. Isabella if you please.'

'Well, Isabella, I have no great desire to go into society as yet. I am happy here in Marble Hill and my friends and family are frequently with me.'

'When Georgiana Cavendish asks to meet people they are expected to be delighted. Moreover, you will be so interested in her. She has the most exciting *salon* in Court circles. Everyone . . . simply everyone of interest is there. Fox, Sheridan . . . even the Prince of Wales.'

'But my dear Isabella, I am a simple country woman.'

'What nonsense! I never knew anyone more poised. You are not going to waste your talents on the desert air of Richmond, cousin, I do assure you. I shall not allow it. You shall come with me to the opera, I insist. Why, you have a place in Park Street. What could be more convenient. It was clearly *meant*.'

Maria wavered. She did like society. It might be that she

would soon tire of the quiet life at Marble Hill, and enjoy meeting the famous people of whom she had heard.

'So it is settled,' said Lady Sefton. 'You will come to Park Street; and I shall show you off in my box at the Opera. I think society is going to be very impressed, for, my dear Maria, you are not only a beauty, you are such an original one. No one at Court or in society looks quite like Maria Fitzherbert.'

Maria prepared for her visit to London. She would miss the fresh air of Richmond, she reminded herself. Well, she was not far away and it would be simple enough to come back whenever she wished; moreover, she would enjoy a stay in London; and it was as well to make sure that all was well in the Park Street House. She would need clothes, but would arrange that in London. Yes, she was looking forward to a little town life.

But the country was charming; she loved to stroll along by the river towards Kew on these lovely spring days when the trees were budding and the birds in full song.

One day when the sun was shining she slipped a cloak about her shoulders and not bothering to put a hat on her glorious hair, worn loose and unpowdered, she strolled out into the sunshine.

There were very few craft on the river; she supposed that it would be busier between Kew and Westminster, with so many people going back and forth between the royal palaces. That was another reason why Richmond was so restful.

She paused suddenly; she heard the sound of laughing voices; a small party of men and women came into sight. She would have turned back, but they had seen her and she did not want to have given the impression of avoiding them. She noticed at once that these people were most elegantly dressed, their hair powdered, their coats of velvet and satin. A party she guessed from the Court, strolling out from Kew Palace.

One young man of the party stopped suddenly a little ahead and made a gesture as though bidding the others not to walk beside him; the rest of the party slackened their pace and as he approached Maria she saw the diamond star on his coat and a suspicion came to her that he must be a very distinguished personage indeed.

He was young, fresh complexioned, blue-eyed, inclined to be a little plump, rather tall and undoubtedly handsome.

As she approached he gave her the most elaborate bow she had ever seen. She bowed and quickening her step, hastily walked on and took a path winding away from the river. She did not look back; her heart was beating faster; she wondered briefly whether she was being followed. But no. She could hear the voices of the party she had just passed; they were still on the towpath. By a round-about way she came back to the river. She was relieved that there was no sign of the elegant party. She had guessed of course who the young man was who had bowed so elegantly. It was none other than the Prince of Wales.

Now she was pleased that she was going to London for she had a notion that if she strolled out along the towpath at precisely the same time the next day she would encounter the same party.

She did not wish for that. The Prince of Wales had already acquired a rather dangerous reputation where women were concerned; he took a delight in romantic adventures. She was sure that he would have thought a chance meeting on a towpath a most amusing meeting place. But Maria Fitzherbert was no Mrs. Robinson. Yes, it was time she appeared in society as a reputable matron of irreproachable character.

No sooner had she settled into Park Street than Isabella Sefton descended on her. They must pay their suggested visit to the Opera, but first Isabella wished to launch her dear Maria into society through a ball she was giving the next day.

It was pleasant to be in a society which was more glittering than anything she had experienced before, though Isabella assured her that her ball was homely compared with those given at Devonshire House or Cumberland House . . . to say nothing of Carlton House.

'You are not suggesting that we shall be invited to Carlton House!' cried Maria.

'It would not surprise me in the least,' laughed Isabella.

Maria thought a little uneasily of that encounter on the river bank; but perhaps she had been mistaken, perhaps that elaborate bow was the manner in which he greeted any of his father's subjects. After all, he had to woo their popularity; and the most elegant of bows would be expected from royalty. She had heard that his father, the King, strolled about Kew and talked to people as though he were a country squire.

She was surrounded by admirers. Not only her beauty was admired, but the fact that she looked so different from everyone else. The women with their powdered hair, their elaborate styles, were not dissimilar; but Maria Fitzherbert was different. Not only was her hair unpowdered but her complexion, which was flawless, was untouched by rouge or white lead; she had a delightful combination, the youthful skin of a young girl and the fully developed bosom of an older woman. It was impossible not to notice her. Maria Fitzherbert, because she was different from all other women, was the belle of the ball.

The next day a paragraph appeared in the society columns of the *Morning Herald*. It said:

A new constellation has lately made an appearance in the fashionable hemisphere, that engages the attention of those who are susceptible to the power of beauty. The widow of the late Mr. F . . . h . . . . . t has in her train half our young nobility; as the lady has not, as yet, discovered a partiality for any of her admirers, they are all animated with hopes of success.'

When Isabella brought the paper to show her Maria was annoyed.

'It is absurd. I have only just arrived. And to talk of my partiality. It is quite ridiculous.'

'Such notoriety is something we have to endure when we become famous, Maria.'

'Famous. For appearing at a ball!'

But Isabella laughed. Maria was fascinating. She was so different.

Maria surveyed the audience from the Sefton box at Covent Garden. Many eyes were on her. Perhaps, she was thinking, I will curtail my stay in London. It would certainly be more peaceful at Richmond; or perhaps she would go to stay for a while at Brambridge or with Uncle Henry.

Then she was aware of the changed atmosphere in the theatre. She was no longer the focus of attention. Something was happening.

Isabella leaned towards her and whispered, 'This is to be a royal occasion.'

And into one of the boxes opposite stepped a glittering figure. His coat was of black velvet spattered with blue spangles and on his breast he wore a flashing diamond star.

A cheer went up as he came to the edge of the box and Maria saw a repeat performance of that most elegant bow; he was smiling at the audience which greeted him with such warm affection. So she could no longer doubt that the gallant young man she had met on the towpath was the Prince of Wales.

He sat down and leaned his arms on the edge of the box; the curtain rose; and glancing across at the Prince, Maria saw that his gaze was fixed on her.

Quickly she lowered her eyes, but not before she had caught the smile, the look of undisguised admiration.

It was impossible to pay attention to the singing; she could not but be aware of him. As for him, he made no pretence of being interested in what was happening on the stage but continued to gaze at her.

Isabella was chuckling.

'Ha, ha, cousin,' she whispered. 'I see you are making quite an impression on his susceptible Highness.'

'This is most . . . embarrassing.'

'Many would find it most flattering.'

'Isabella, I do not. I wish to hurry home after the performance. I think perhaps I should return to Richmond.'

The Prince was leaning forward. He had seen that they were talking together and seemed to want to hear what they were saying.

Did he often behave like this? wondered Maria. There was that disgraceful affair with the actress. How very embarrassing! He would have to realize that she was a respectable widow. But how convey this to a Prince who was quite clearly accustomed to having women run when he beckoned.

But not Maria Fitzherbert.

The curtain had fallen. The applause rang out. The Prince joined in it heartily. He had had a most delightful evening and he was grateful to the performers even if this was not due to them.

Maria said quietly but firmly, 'I shall leave at once, Isabella. My chair will be waiting.'

Isabella was amused. She wondered how deeply the Prince was affected. After all, Maria must be about six years older than he was. Mary Robinson it was true had been about three but she was only twenty-one at the time of that liaison and Maria must be about twenty-seven or eight—the Prince twenty-one.

'Very well, my dear,' she said. 'But you will certainly meet him at someone's house sooner or later.'

'Not if I return to Richmond,' said Maria.

Her servant was waiting with the chair and she gave instructions that she was to be carried with all speed to her house in Park Street.

* * *

As her chair was carried through the streets she was more disturbed than the occasion warranted, she told herself. Perhaps he had not been looking at her. Perhaps it had been a mistake. That paragraph in the paper had made her imagine that she really was as fatally attractive as the writer had made her out to be. He had been bored with the Opera and had merely diverted himself.

They had arrived at the house and thankfully she alighted, but as she did so she saw another chair entering the street.

She hurried into the house, her heart beating faster. The door was shut. She felt . . . safe.

But she could not resist going to the window.

She saw the chair stop; someone alighted.

Oh no, she thought. It is not possible!

But it was. He was standing there in his spangles and diamonds.

The Prince of Wales, like some lovesick country swain, had followed Maria Fitzherbert home.

Adventures of a Prince

During the summer of 1783 when the Prince of Wales was approaching his twenty-first birthday he believed that he was the most fortunate man in England, and he was surrounded by men and women who confirmed him in this belief. He was at last escaping from the restraint which his puritanical parents had put on him, and was free to be the companion of the most brilliant men in the country; he could indulge his passion for architecture in Carlton House, that old ruin which his father had flung to him and which he was fast converting into the most elegant residence in Town; he could run his own horses at Newmarket; he could take his place in the House of Lords; and he could, without any attempt at secrecy pursue the greatest diversion of all—women.

Let the King splutter his threats and warnings; let the Queen alternately scold and declare her sentimental fondness for her first-born; they could not deter him. He was the idol of the people, the quarry of every fashionable hostess—for no ball was of any significance without him—and almost every woman longed to be his mistress. There were a few exceptions; Georgiana, his dearest Duchess of Devonshire, among them, but this only made this most delightful of all occupations the more piquant, and while he could sigh for the unattainable he could always soothe himself with the eagerly accommodating.

Life was very good that summer for the Prince of Wales.

Some months before he first set eyes on Maria Fitzherbert his Uncle, the Duke of Cumberland, had suggested he come down to visit him at a house he had rented from a certain Dr. Russell and which was situated in a little fishing village called Brighthelmstone.

'What,' demanded the Prince of Wales of his equerry, the Earl of Essex, 'should I want of a little fishing village called by such a name as Brighthelmstone?'

'I have heard of the place, Your Highness,' answered Essex. 'It is also known as Bredhemsdon.'

'Which is no more pleasant to my ear than the other,' retorted the Prince.

'No, sir, but they say the sea bathing there is very beneficial to the health—and it is not so far from London to make the journey tiresome.'

Sea bathing! thought the Prince, and touched his silken neck-cloth. Recently he had been affected by a slight swelling of the throat and he and Lord Petersham had together designed a neck-cloth which would completely hide it. Hence neckcloths in exquisite designs and colourings were the height of fashion now. The Prince's physicians had suggested that sea bathing might be good for his throat; he had not taken the idea very seriously, but Essex's remark reminded him of it.

'I confess it would be amusing to see how my aunt Cumberland *amuses* herself in a fishing village.'

'I am sure, sir, that where the Duchess found herself there would she find amusement.'

The Prince laughed aloud. He was fond of the lady who had inveigled his uncle most unsuitably into marrying her, and being banished from the Court because of her. She was a fascinator—a woman of wide experience; the very manner in which she fluttered her eyelashes which had become a legend since Horace Walpole had referred to them as being a yard long, was in itself a promise. The Prince delighted to call her by what seemed to him such an incongruous title as 'Aunt', and as she was constantly urging him to honour Cumberland House with his presence he had seen her and his uncle often since he had been free to do so—much to the chagrin of His Majesty, of course, who believed it was just another trick of his son's to plague him, which in a way perhaps it was.

At least his uncle had had the courage to marry the woman of his choice, thought the Prince, whereas his father, the King, by all accounts had meekly given up Lady Sarah Lennox for the sake of that plain German Princess, Charlotte, who was the mother of that large family of whom he, the Prince, was the eldest son.

Yes, he would go to Brighthelmstone or whatever they called it. Perhaps Essex should be one of those who accompanied him.

They were good friends, he and Essex. The Earl had served him faithfully as go-between in the affair of Perdita Robinson—Lord Malden he had been at that time, having recently inherited his earldom. Malden it was who had carried those letters between them, arranged those assignations on Eel Pie Island and persuaded the lady to do what she had intended from the first— surrender.

The Prince smiled cynically. He would never again be caught in that way. But it was no fault of Essex that Perdita after promising to be the love of his life had turned out to be nothing but a sentimental bore—and a scheming one too. The Prince flushed with anger even now, remembering the humiliating scene with his father when he had had to confess that his ex-mistress was threatening to publish letters which she had in her possession and which had been written by the flowery but very indiscreet pen of the Prince of Wales.

This was yet another reason for his friendship with his uncle. Cumberland had written indiscreet letters to Lady Grosvenor and Lord Grosvenor had brought an action against him which had cost £13,000. The Prince's had cost £500 a year for as long as Perdita should live and after that £250 for her daughter's lifetime.

To the devil with Perdita! She was ancient history and she had had many successors. No . . . not quite. There had never really been another like Perdita, for he genuinely had believed in the early days of their liaison that he would be faithful until death; and he had never seriously believed that of any of the others. But then he had been so young . . . only seventeen when he had gone with the Royal party to Drury Lane and seen Mrs. Robinson as Perdita in *The Winter's Tale*.

But what had Perdita to do with this fishing village with the ridiculous name?

'I shall drive myself down,' he said. 'It will be good exercise for the horses.'

So on a September morning when the countryside was touched with golden sunshine and the weather was as warm as midsummer, the Prince of Wales rode down to Brighthelmstone. He drove his own phaeton with three horses after the manner of a wagon team; and riding with him were only an equerry and one postilion. The rest of his suite would follow.

The phaeton rattled along at a dangerous pace, for the Prince liked speed. He was a man of contrasts, for while he would spend hours with Lord Petersham discussing the shape of shoe buckles, the cut of a coat, the material most suited to a neck-cloth, the excellent idea of having one's snuff boxes to match one's ensemble and the season, he could also take a turn in the boxing ring, for he practised fisticuffs regularly under the skilled tuition of a certain Angelo, who also taught him to fence. He could sing pleasantly, dance well, was at ease in the saddle and could write fluently and with grace. He could join in an intel-lectual discussion and shortly afterwards be indulging in an in-fantile practical joke. With his gifts he should have been an ideal son; but with his indiscretions and his waywardness he gave his father many a sleepless night.

He was not thinking of this as he rode to Brighton; his mind was on a subject which was never far from his thoughts: Women. The situation at the moment was satisfactory enough; there was always comfort in numbers, he had discovered. The most agree-able time had been when Grace Elliot and Lizzie Armistead shared his attentions. Grace had been something of a romp, never attempting to be faithful and making no pretence about it. He was by nature sentimental, but just having escaped from Perdita at that time Grace with her frank unabashed attitudes had been just what he needed. There had been a daughter which might have been his—or one of two other men's—but Grace had christened the child Georgiana, which was a nice touch since she made no demands. Now she had gone to that Frenchman, the Duc d'Orléans, who was resident in London for a while. Good luck to Grace; she wouldn't need it, for she would always know how to look after herself. He had heard that Orléans made her a handsome allowance. She would deserve it, for Orléans was an ugly fellow who suffered from a horrible skin disease which made his hair fall out and his skin a hideous colour.

And Lizzie Armistead? There was a fascinating woman. Lady's maid at one time to none other than Perdita, and it was at the house in Cork Street that he had met her; but others had seen her first. Charles James Fox for one. Trust Fox to pick out a winner among the women. If only he could do as well at the races he would be a rich man. As it was, he was in constant financial trouble. Not that it worried Charles as long as he kept his grip on politics. He'd be Prime Minister one day and he wouldn't have a more faithful friend and supporter than the Prince of Wales. That—and Lizzie. What more could he want?

Lizzie had gone back to Charles and he was living with her now in her house at Chertsey, the house she had managed to acquire through her own skilful management of her affairs. It was funny. There was Charles, the son of Lord Holland, and at one time the possessor of a fortune, several times bankrupt, now living on the bounty of the lady's maid who had saved enough from her generous lovers—the Prince included—to put into a little house in Chertsey where the most brilliant politician of his day should have a refuge.

Lizzie and Charles were two of his best friends. What interesting, amusing and exciting people! How different from the household at Kew, with his sanctimonious father, his dreary mother, his poor sisters who had never had—nor would ever have if his parents had any say in their upbringing—any chance to enjoy life. How could poor Charlotte, Augusta, Elizabeth and the rest know anything about the brilliantly gay, the witty and amusing outside world and people like Charles and Lizzie, Richard Sheridan the playwright, Edmund Burke the philosopher, Georgiana the brilliant leader of fashion, beautiful and witty. Poor little Princesses wilting away at Kew when there was the world to be explored!

He thought of Lady Melbourne with whom he had liked to fancy himself desperately in love. He had always wanted to be seriously in love; and the light affair did not give him the same satisfaction as what he was pleased to believe, while it lasted, was the love of a lifetime. That was why Perdita had been so important. The long wooing, the sighing, the locks of hair, the tender messages engraved on miniatures and lockets, this was what he craved. He took great pleasure in writing of his sufferings and aspirations and even the fate of those letters which he had written to Perdita could not deter him. He recognized the difference between lust and love—and although he was as ready to indulge in the first as any of his companions, he never forgot the worth of the second. He often told himself, and others, that what he wanted was to settle down with the woman of his choice, marry her and live happily—and faithfully—ever after.

For a short time he had deluded himself with Lady Melbourne; she had even borne a child which was said to be his—a boy this time and named George of course.

Actresses had always interested him. There was the fascinating young German actress known as Mrs. Billington who had a house near the Thames at Fulham. She was a pretty and very lively young woman with the most original methods of making love. Most intriguing, and at one time he had been constantly at the theatre—not to see the play, of course, but Mrs. Billington. It had been so easy to visit her, she being so near the river; and every night when she was not playing she would have musical evenings, for Mrs. Billington was noted for her singing; it gave him great pleasure to sing duets with the ladies who attracted him. His voice could not of course compare with that of Mrs. Billington, which was of remarkable compass and one of the most melodious he had ever heard.

But although her eccentric methods had excited him in the beginning he had tired of them. Mrs. Billington might have been amusing but she was not romantic. He did not care for her coarse approach, and when he remarked to Fox: 'The only pleasure I have in that woman's company is when I shut my eyes and open my ears,' Fox knew, and so did the Prince, that the liaison was nearing its end.

What would please him would be to fall deeply in love; he longed to experience all those emotions which he had known in the early stages of his affair with Perdita. He might be the leader of fashion; he might find pleasure in horse-racing and boxing, riding and hunting; he might enjoy dabbling in politics and the friendship of brilliant men—but the overriding need in his life would always be Romance. And whenever he visited any banquet or ball, any place whatsoever, the thought always in his mind was what women would he meet on that occasion.

So it was not surprising that on his first visit to Brighthelmstone, he should be thinking of women.

The inhabitants of the little town were aware of the honour which was about to be done them and they had turned out in strength to welcome him.

How enchanting it was with the shingle beach and the ocean—today deep blue and placid as though on its best behaviour to welcome the Prince of Wales. There were gulls on the brown roofs, and on the three-cornered stretch of grass fishing nets and lobster pots; a salty tang was in the air; and as the phaeton dashed into the town a great cheer went up. His Highness the Prince of Wales had come to Brighthelmstone.

People crowded about the house on the Steyne which had been taken over by the Duke and Duchess of Cumberland. The Prince embraced the Duke to the cheers of the crowd; with even greater fervour he embraced the Duchess.

'How handsome he is!' was the universal comment; and so he was in his exquisitely cut coat of the finest green cloth with the diamond star flashing on his breast. He stood on the balcony between his aunt and uncle and acknowledged the cheers, his beaver hat in his hand. This enabled the crowd to see his abundant hair, which was frizzed and powdered most elegantly; his eyes looked very blue, his smile so friendly.

'God bless the Prince of Wales!' cried the people of Brighthelmstone.

And when they had retired into the drawing room the Duchess lifted her green eyes, so miraculously black-fringed, to his face and echoed: 'God bless you, my dearest Prince of Wales. How kind of you to take pity on us and visit us here in our little sea village.'

'Dearest Aunt, I could not resist the temptation to see how you amused yourself here.'

'This is what you shall discover, gracious nephew. Wait until you have taken a dip in the sea water. I can assure you it is most refreshing. But there is one drawback which I know will cause Your Highness some concern. The ladies and gentlemen do not bathe together. The ladies take possession of the shore west of the Steyne and the gentlemen to the east. In any case the ladies all wear long and hideous flannel gowns and the gentlemen bathe much more charmingly naked.'

'I am sure your flannel gown is most becoming.'

'But of what use, since there are no gentlemen to see it . . . only the fat old fishwife who dips me.'

'What a fantastic pastime. Does the sea really benefit you enough to make the performance worth while?'

'I believe it does; and I am certain that once you have tried it you will wish to repeat it.'

'And when shall I take my sea bathe, pray?'

'Tomorrow, of course.'

'I trust the whole town will not turn out to see me.'

'My beloved nephew, since so many people turn out to see Your Highness in his clothes, how many more would arrive to see you without them. But have no fear. It is all very discreet and the old fellow who dips you knows his job perfectly.'

The Prince was amused; and since the Duke and Duchess had naturally brought with them many of their most entertaining friends, his first evening in Brighthelmstone was most pleasantly spent.

The Prince stayed for eleven exciting and interesting days. He took to the sea bathing and found it most invigorating, and every day went into his bathing machine and undressed. It was then taken down to the edge of the sea by the bathing machine attendant and his horse, when the Prince would emerge and enjoy immersing himself. He hunted on the downs beyond Rottingdean, danced in the Assembly Rooms, strolled about the town meeting the people and accepting their loyal greetings with affable smiles and comments—changing the place in those eleven days from a little fishing village to a fashionable seaside resort, for naturally after the Prince's visit it was fashionable to visit Brighthelmstone; sea bathing became a craze; bathing machines lined the shingle; the strong men and women dippers made a fortune it was said; owners of the little houses in Black Lion, Ship, East, West, Middle and North Streets let lodgings, and there was a steady stream of carriages and other conveyances on the road from London.

'Nothing will ever be the same,' said the sages of Brighthelmstone.

They were right. Even the name was changed—to Brighton.

In Carlton House the Prince was entertaining. He was proud of Carlton House; and he had every reason to be when he considered the ruin it had been when it had come into his hands. It had not been lived in since the death of his grandmother, Augusta, the Dowager Princess of Wales, and he imagined that it was because his father had believed it to be uninhabitable that he had given it to him. Oh yes, the old man would have liked him to continue in his rooms at Buckingham House. But Carlton House had offered a challenge; it had given him a chance to show what he could make of a house, dilapidated though it might be.

And he had succeeded. It was by no means finished; he doubted it would be for years for he would always be thinking of some new improvement, but it was certainly very different from the Carlton House he had inherited. The architect, Henry Holland, had made an excellent job of the rebuilding, and that clever Frenchman, Gaubert, had decorated the interior with exquisite taste, superintended, of course, by the Prince himself. It was now beginning to look like a royal residence. His drawing room was hung with yellow Chinese silk; the dining room had been considerably extended; the ceilings heightened, the walls panelled and gilded, and columns of yellow and red granite added to give dignity. The ballroom in which he was now entertaining his guests was the most grand of all the rooms. Twelve lustres hung from the ceiling and the same number of branched chandeliers projected from the walls at intervals. There was an orchestra at either end of the room set up on platforms hung with crimson silk.

Members of the highest families of the nobility were present, including the Prince's special friends—Charles James Fox, Richard Sheridan, Edmund Burke, Mrs. Crewe and the Duchess of Devonshire. The Prince led his aunt, the Duchess of Cumberland, in the minuet and talked with her about his recent visit to Brighton.

'I vow,' he said, 'that as soon as the weather permits me I shall be there again.'

'Then I am delighted that I introduced Your Highness to sea bathing. Has it proved beneficial?'

'Undoubtedly. I find it invigorating. The place is small however. There is scarcely one building in it that is not a hovel. But I like the sea. Now if we could have the sea here in London . . .'

'Alas, even princes cannot divert the sea.'

'No, but they might divert the town. Why not?'

'A possibility.'

'I like that place. I like it even more now that it has changed its name.'

'Brighton. Charming. Well, if Your Highness decides to take advantage of the sea next summer, all the *ton* will do the same.'

The Prince danced with other ladies—including Lady Melbourne who was such a favourite at this time. He paid the usual compliments, but he was thinking of next year's sea bathing, and how amusing it would be to have a house in Brighton where he could entertain his friends. He talked to her of Brighton and she was as enthusiastic as he was.

He danced with Georgiana. How beautiful she was on that night, always so different from all the other women, the true leader of fashion.

'My dearest Georgiana,' sighed the Prince, 'how can you persist in being cruel to me?'

'My dearest Highness, I am in truth being kind to us both.'

'How could that be when you know that my most urgent wish is to have you love me as I love you.'

'I intend to be Your Highness's friend through life. It is so much easier to be a constant friend than a constant mistress.'

'I would be constant for ever.'

'Your Highness, I think Lady Melbourne is regarding you a little anxiously.'

'You have but to say the word and there should be no one but you.'

Georgiana laughed and did not take him seriously. Her husband the Duke was not interested in her, nor she in him; but Georgiana had no intention of becoming the mistress of the Prince of Wales. It was a position which she did not think any woman could hold for any length of time; and it was surely better not to set oneself on such a slippery perch. Their relationship was far more satisfactory as it was.

'I see Charles is there with Sherry and Amoret. What a beautiful creature she is. I'm not surprised that Sherry adores her.'

'All beauties pale before your own,' said the Prince.

And Georgiana laughed. 'Exactly what I would have expected my gallant Prince to say. Sherry would not agree with you.'

'He adores you, too.'

'Dear Sherry, he is my very good friend. And Charles . . . I do declare his frock-coat is threadbare. How dare he come to Carlton House dressed in such a slovenly manner.'

'Charles knows that he may dare what he will as far as I am concerned. It is not his coat I welcome here but the man inside it.'

'Right royally spoken. Fortunate Charles! I should have thought Lizzie Armistead would have taken better care of him.'

'You must admit that he looks a little cleaner since being in her care.'

'Let us come and talk to them. It is always such fun to talk to Charles. His great merit is his amazing quickness in seizing any subject. He seems to have a talent for knowing more of what he is talking about than anyone else. His conversation is like a brilliant player at billiards—the strokes follow one another—piff-paff.'

'And you suggest I should frown on his coat!'

'No, no, I do not. I merely wonder that he should wrap so much that is charming in such a disreputable package.'

The Prince and Georgiana had paused at the little group who bowed ceremoniously in recognition of royalty; and then immediately relaxed.

Sheridan, Georgiana noticed, had been drinking heavily. It saddened her; he was not as capable of carrying his drink as Charles.

'Sherry,' she admonished, 'if you drink so much you will destroy the coat of your stomach.'

'Then my stomach must just digest in its waistcoat,' retorted Sheridan.

Oh, yes, it was pleasant to be with these people who so amused him and flattered him with their attention. They talked politics, for they were all Whigs together, until it was time for supper. Five rooms were used for this purpose and the Prince with his special guests was accommodated in the grand escaglio room. He had Georgiana on his right and had arranged that Fox and Sheridan were not far away so that they could enjoy some enlivening conversation.

'Your Highness must be living beyond your means,' whispered Fox.

'I hadn't given the matter a thought,' admitted the Prince.

'Ah, what will be the end of this riotous living? Methinks we should see that the means fit the end.'

The Prince laughed. He could trust Fox. It was Fox who had tried to get £100,000 a year for him and no fault of his that he had had to be content with a miserable £62,000; it was Fox who had extricated him from that affair with Perdita when she had demanded he honour the bond he had given her and wanted £5,000 for those revealing letters.

Oh, yes, he could trust Fox.

Over supper the conversation turned to the eccentric conduct of Major Hanger at one of the balls at St. James's Palace a few evenings earlier. The Prince was telling Charles Fox about it.

'Stab me, but he came in the uniform of an officer of the Hessian service—and mighty strange he looked among all the satins and brocades. His short blue coat was ornamented with gold frogs and there was a band across his shoulders from which his sword hung. What a spectacle! Even the King could not suppress a smile . . . and it is no mean achievement, I do assure you, to make my father smile. But the Major did it when he put on his Kevenhüller hat with two huge feathers—black and white—and invited Miss Gunning to join him in a minuet. Poor lady! Such a graceful, beautiful creature, but what could she do? She simply gave up. We laughed. I was convulsed . . . and as I said the King smiled and my mother came as near to it as she's able. But that wasn't the end. You should have seen the gallant Major in a country dance.'

The Prince continued to laugh at the memory of it and stopped suddenly. 'Why should we not write a letter of congratulations to the Major. Say it was written in the name of the whole company who saw him perform. I will compile it and it shall be written in a handwriting the Major will not know.'

The Prince gazed round the table. 'You, Sherry. He does not know you. You shall be the writer of our letter.'

'It has always been my aim to write for Your Majesty's pleasure.'

'This will be as good as a play, I promise you.'

'Other men's plays, perhaps Highness. Not mine.'

'But other men's plays can be highly diverting sometimes, Sherry. And as you will have a hand in this affair you may lend us a touch of your genius.'

'How can I repay your graciousness, sir, but by complying with Your Highness's desires.'

'It shall be done after supper and delivered to the Major first thing tomorrow morning.' The Prince laughed, thinking of the Major's reactions when he received the note.

He talked of the Major through supper and as soon as it was over left his guests and taking Fox, Sheridan and a few favourite companions with him retired to an ante-room to write the letter.

Writing had always given him great pleasure and he could never see a pen without wanting to pick it up and compose flowery sentences. It was this habit which had proved so disastrous in the Perdita affair.

Now he sat down and with his friends looking over his shoulder wrote:

> 'St. James's, Sunday morning

'The company who attended the ball on Friday last at St. James's present their compliments to Major Hanger and return him their unfeigned thanks for the variety with which he enlivened the insipidity of the evening's entertainment. The gentlemen want words to describe their admiration for the truly grotesque and humorous figure which he exhibited; and the ladies beg leave to express their acknowledgments for the lively and animated emotions that his stately, erect and perpendicular form could not fail to excite in their delicate and susceptible bosoms. His gesticulations and martial deportment were truly admirable and have raised an impression which will not soon be effaced at St. James's.'

The Prince ended with a flourish.

'Now, Sherry, Hanger does not know your handwriting, and I flatter myself there is a touch of style about that letter which could be attributed to you. So, I pray you, copy it out and to-morrow it shall be despatched to our entertaining Major and I am sure from such a character we can expect some fun.'

Sheridan sat down and copied the letter.

'First thing in the morning,' chuckled the Prince, 'it shall be delivered; and soon afterwards I shall send him an invitation to dine with me. You, my dear Sherry, will not I trust take it amiss if for once you are not included in the invitation.'

Sheridan bowed: 'Always ready to forgo my greatest plea-sures in the service of Your Highness.'

The Prince could scarcely wait until morning for the delivery of the letter and its results.

Fox, watching the affair with a cynical amusement, thought: He must have his diversions, but he is young yet.

Dinner was a less glittering occasion than it had been on the previous evening and took place in the silver-walled dining room among the red and yellow granite pillars. The Prince had invited Major Hanger to sit near him and lost little time in bringing the conversation to the ball at St. James's.

'What an effect your appearance had on the ladies, Major. There we were all dressed like popinjays and you . . . in your uniform. You were indeed a man.'

The Major swallowed the bait; his eyes bulged and his face grew scarlet.

'Your Highness, I have had a most insulting letter. I have been held up to ridicule, it is more than mortal man can endure. Your Highness must forgive my anger but, Sir, I have been in-sulted.'

The Prince expressed concern. But how was this?

The Major brought the letter from his pocket. 'If Your High-ness would cast your eye over this you would see what I mean.'

The Prince read the letter with exclamations of sympathy. 'No doubt whatever,' he agreed, 'the writer of this letter means to insult you.'

At this corroboration the Major's anger increased. *'Blitz und Hölle,'* he shouted. 'I swear that if I could discover the writer of this letter I would demand satisfaction.'

The Prince agreed that in the Major's position he would feel exactly the same. 'How do you feel, Charles?'

Fox, playing up as was expected, replied that he considered it an insult to turn the Major's stately, erect and perpendicular figure to ridicule.

'I am determined to discover the writer,' cried the Major.

'I think we should try to help to bring this fellow to his deserts,' said the Prince. He picked up the letter. 'By God, this handwriting! I swear it is familiar to me. What say you, Charles? Does it not remind you of that mischievous fellow Sheridan? Come, Charles, you know his writing well.'

Fox took the letter and nodded. 'No doubt of it,' he said.

The Major's eyes bulged with indignation. 'Playwrights!' he said. 'They fancy themselves with a pen in the hand! By God, he shall regret this day.' He turned to Captain Morris who was sitting nearby. 'Sir, I wish you to take a challenge from me to Mr. Sheridan.'

'Major,' said the Prince, 'I know it is my duty to attempt to persuade you against the action and this I do, but I am bound to say were I in your position nothing would deter me. But do consider, Sheridan has written this in one of his mad mischievous moods and he is a mad and mischievous fellow.'

'Sir, I beg of Your Highness not to command me to forgo this duty. I have every wish to obey every command of Your Highness . . .'

The Prince bowed his head. 'My sympathies are with you, Major. I will keep silent and may luck go with you.'

'Now, Your Highness, having despatched this challenge to the fellow I will, with your permission, go to my lodgings and await the blackguard's answer.'

'I understand your concern. You should lose no time. If he accepts your challenge you will have preparations to make.'

As soon as the Major left a messenger was despatched to Sheridan asking him to report at Carlton House without delay so that the conspirators could plan the next move in what was to the Prince one of the most highly diverting practical jokes he had ever played.

It was daybreak in Battersea Fields. Captain Morris was with the Major, and Sheridan had chosen Fox as his second. In a carriage muffled up, hat well over his eyes, his face made up to resemble an older man, sat the Prince of Wales in the role of the surgeon who, Fox and Morris had agreed, must be in attendance.

The opponents faced each other; their seconds loaded the pistols; the signal to fire was given. The Major, a crack shot, aimed at the playwright but failed to hit him. The pistols were loaded a second time with the same result.

'God damn the fellow!' cried the Major. 'What's wrong? Should have got him first time.'

'The third time generally is effective,' said Captain Morris and glanced towards the carriage in which the 'surgeon' was seated trying to muffle his laughter.

The order was given to fire and Sheridan fell.

'By God, you have killed him, Major,' cried Captain Morris. 'Quick. We must get away while there is time.'

Before the Major could protest he was hustled into a carriage and ordered the coachman to lose no time. Away rattled the carriage and the Prince alighted and reeling with laughter went over to the fallen playwright.

'Well played, Sherry,' he said. 'Get up. By God, I'll swear you never had a better scene in any of your plays.'

The Prince drove back to Carlton House laughing hilariously with Fox and Sheridan; but suddenly he was serious.

'What can it feel like to have killed a man?'

'The first emotion would be gratification for having avenged an insult,' said Fox.

'Then remorse for having taken life, perhaps,' added Sheridan. 'But perhaps fear of the law would come first.'

'Remorse,' mused the Prince. 'I like the fellow in a way. He's grotesque but he amuses me. I shall let him know at once that you are not dead, Sherry.'

'Won't that spoil Your Highness's little joke?' asked Fox.

'My dear Charles, I have had my joke. I have rarely laughed so much. I have rarely been so diverted. But I am sure that when the Major recovers a little from his gratification remorse will set in. Also he might decide to flee the country. I shall send for him immediately and tell him that Sherry is not fatally wounded.'

'Your Highness has not only a sense of the ridiculous but a sensitive heart,' said Fox.

As soon as he saw the Major's remorseful manner the Prince hastened to reassure him.

'This is a bad business, Major, but I have some good news for you. Sheridan is not dead. I have had it from the . . . er surgeon. He will live.'

'Your Highness, I am indeed glad to hear that.'

'I thought you would be, Major. Alas our passions get the better of us and lead us to rash actions.'

'It's true, but it is a terrible thing to kill a man outside of war.'

'Well, you can assure yourself that the fellow will live. Come here to dine tonight and I will have here a gentleman who will give you the fullest information as to his condition.'

'I don't know how to thank Your Highness.'

'Believe me, Major, I have understood your actions all along.'

The Prince had the satisfaction of seeing the Major retire in a happier mood than that one in which he had arrived.

The Prince received Major Hanger yet again at Carlton House.

'Now,' he said, 'I shall send for the gentleman who can give you the information you need.'

He signed to a page and Sheridan came into the room.

'But . . .' stammered the Major, blinking at the playwright. 'What means this? I thought I had killed you!'

'Oh,' cried Sheridan, 'I am not quite good enough for the world above. I am not yet fully qualified for this one below. So I thought it better to postpone my departure a little longer.'

'But . . . I saw you fall. How could I have fired straight at you and you not . . .'

Sheridan turned to the Prince and said: 'I have no doubt His Highness will explain.'

'Major,' said the Prince, beginning to laugh, 'you have been the victim of a little plot of mine. It was I who conceived the idea and knowing you for the good sport you are I am sure you'll enjoy the joke.' He explained it all; how he had selected Sheridan to write the letter, how no balls had been put into the pistols, how both seconds were in the plot, and how the surgeon had been the Prince himself.

The Major listened in silence and then burst out laughing. His body shook with his guffaws and the Prince and Sheridan joined in.

'You see, we'll have this situation turning up in one of Sherry's plays. If so, Sherry, I claim credit.'

'If it should, Your Highness shall have it. It would bring people crowding to the theatre. Co-author—His Royal Highness the Prince of Wales . . .'

'Major, if you could have seen your face. I trust when you do fight a duel you will allow me to be present.'

'Your Highness shall certainly be there.'

'We'll drink to it. Come.'

They sat and drank and the Prince grew very friendly as the evening progressed. Major Hanger had provided him with the most amusing diversion of his lifetime; Sherry had made it all work out like a play; they were good friends; they would have many a laugh together in the future.

The Prince sang songs from Sheridan's plays and it was a very convivial evening.

After that Major Hanger was admitted into that very intimate circle of the Prince's friends which included Fox, Burke, Sheridan and Georgiana, Duchess of Devonshire.

With the coming of spring the Prince thought of the pleasures of sea bathing and how amusing it would be to repeat his visit to the little Sussex fishing village.

He sent for his major-domo, Louis Weltje—an odd little German who came from Hanover and was of a most unprepossessing appearance.

The Prince liked Weltje; he trusted the little German, and as he had picked him up himself, liked to feel he had made a discovery and found himself an excellent servant. He had come across Weltje during one of his adventures when he had roamed the streets incognito. Weltje had kept a gingerbread stall at which the Prince and his friends had paused to buy.

The gingerbread had proved to be excellent and the Prince declared it was the best he had ever eaten, and conversation with the owner of the stall disclosed him to be a native of Hanover.

'The place where the King comes from,' said the little man with a grin. 'What could be better than that? I thought to make a fortune but people over here don't know how to eat.'

'You mean you're a cook, do you?' asked the Prince.

Louis Weltje had nodded his great fishlike face and said: 'You liked my gingerbread didn't you, sir. I'm wasting my talents on gingerbread.'

'What else can you cook besides gingerbread?'

'You name it, sir, and I'll cook it as I'd be ready to wager you had never tasted it before.'

'Sauerkraut and sausages?' asked the Prince sceptically.

'If you'd a fancy for it, sir. But to my mind you don't look a sauerkraut man. Fond of fine delicacies, that's you, sir.'

'You may call at my house tomorrow and you'll be given an opportunity to cook, if you wish.'

'I've been waiting for an opportunity since I came here.'

'You can present yourself to the kitchens at Carlton House tomorrow, I'll see that you are well received.'

The Prince passed on, leaving Weltje staring after him. It was the sort of encounter which he enjoyed; and this had proved to be a worthwhile one. Not only was Weltje a first-class cook but he had other talents; he could manage the servants' hall, for in spite of his short broad body and his remarkably fishlike face, he had an undeniable authority and the Prince had soon made him his major-domo.

Now he told Weltje that he had a liking for a certain fishing village on the Sussex coast and would not object to spending the summer there.

'It will be difficult to find a suitable house for me to rent,' he explained. 'From what I saw of it the only possible one was that of Dr. Russell on the Steyne which the Duke and Duchess of Cumberland were using.'

'I will find a suitable residence for Your Highness,' promised Weltje.

'You will be a wizard if you do.'

'Your Highness,' said Weltje, with a clumsy bow, 'I *am* a wizard.'

That very day he was driven to Brighton, put up at the Ship Inn and in his usually efficient way took stock of the town. He examined all available houses; his progress was discussed in the streets and the lanes; this was going to make all the difference to the town. Royalty was going to adopt it. Louis Weltje at length found a residence which although not suitable would be adequate he thought for a short duration.

He went back to London to report.

'I have found a house for us, Your Highness, although it is not the residence I should wish.'

'I did not expect you to find a palace, Weltje.'

'No, sir. Nor have I. But I think when we have furnished it suitably and have the servants there it will suffice until we can build our own.'

'Build our own,' cried the Prince; and laughed, for the idea of building his own house in Brighton had been fermenting in his mind for a long time.

That summer the Prince was up and down from Brighton. The people on the route would hear his horses galloping by and rush out for a glimpse of him, a glorious sight in his fine blue or green coat, the diamond star flashing on his left breast; his beaver hat set at a jaunty angle on his frizzed hair.

They called a greeting as he passed which he never failed to return.

Of course his coming completely changed Brighton. It could

no longer be called a little fishing village. Prices shot up; the inhabitants went on complaining that things weren't what they used to be and secretly they all agreed that it was good for the town to have the Prince interested in them. Now that the Prince had shown that his liking for the place was more than a passing fancy came the fashionable world of London; the price of property was doubled and every little tradesman from the crab and lobster seller to the old cobbler seated in his window overlooking the Steyne put up his prices.

'We're fashionable Brighton now,' they said to each other. 'Brighthelmstone is gone. It's Brighton. Royal Brighton.'

There was an air of expectancy in every street. The local people grew accustomed to seeing fine ladies and gentlemen strolling about Brighton. Once a week there was a grand ball at the Castle Rooms and the people would stand outside to see the glittering jewels and the fine gowns of the ladies and the magnificence of the gentlemen, under the Prince's leadership, rivalled them. The Prince loved the play so therefore he visited the play house; but the local show, once he had become accustomed to its rural flavour, was not good enough for him, so companies had to come down from London. There was cockfighting in the Hove Ring; and boxing matches too, for the Prince greatly favoured this sport; and of course there were constant expeditions to the races.

Adventurers crowded into Brighton. Cardsharpers, strolling musicians, gipsies . . . they all believed they could make their fortunes in the town which the Prince had made his own.

Each day during the summer the bathing machines could be seen being pulled up and down the shingly beach; and the shouts of the bathers as they were seized and dipped by the stalwart attendants could be heard all along the front. Each morning when he was in Brighton the Prince went into the sea.

His friends were always thinking of some new practical joke, which might amuse him, some new form of gambling. They wagered on every conceivable occasion. They would command the local people to run races that they might wager together who would be the winner; they performed wild mad exploits if someone bet them they could not do them.

Brighton had certainly changed with the coming of the Prince.

But as he told Weltje, Grove House was all very well and his major-domo had undoubtedly found him the best available house in Brighton, yet still it was not quite a royal residence.

'We'll never get that, sir, till we build our own,' Weltje told him.

The Prince agreed it was true and began to think about a house of his own more seriously than ever.

Sometimes at dusk the Prince liked to take off his fine coat on which he wore the dazzling diamond star and, changing into an ordinary buff-coloured jacket such as might be worn by any noble gentleman, take a solitary stroll alone along the beach.

He was not sure whether on these occasions people did not recognize him or respected his privacy; but it was pleasant to escape now and then from the perpetually watchful eyes of subjects, however loving.

It was during one of his lonely walks that he saw a young woman sitting on the beach, her back against a groin, engrossed in the aimless pastime of throwing stones into the sea.

She wore a cloak, but the manner in which she lifted her arm to throw the stone was graceful and the Prince ever ready to investigate feminine charms, approached her.

'Good evening,' he said, 'Are you alone then?'

'Until this moment, sir,' she answered with a pertness which assured him that his identity was certainly unknown; even strange young women do not speak to the Prince of Wales in that manner.

'You are too pretty to be alone.'

'La, sir, and I see you are too forward to be.'

The Prince was amused. 'A very good reason why you should allow me to exchange a few words with you.'

'I could scarcely prevent it,' she retorted.

He sat down beside her and was delighted, for the hood had fallen back a little to disclose an extremely pretty face.

'Should you be out alone at this hour?'

'Clearly not, sir, since it enables strangers to believe that they can . . . accost me.'

She made as though to rise but he held out a hand and laid it gently on her arm. 'Please do not go . . . just yet. Stay and chat awhile. There is no harm done.'

She hesitated. 'If my guardian knew that I was out . . .'

'So you have escaped?'

'I cannot bear to be caged. I ran away . . . but only for an hour or so. I shall have to go back.'

'You live in Brighton?'

She shook her head. 'We are here because it is so fashionable to be here . . . now that the Prince of Wales favours it.'

'So your family is here because *he* is here.'

She nodded. He saw that she was very young. That was piquant; he had never been in love with a woman younger than himself before.

She grimaced. 'Oh yes, we must go to Brighton because His Royal Highness is at Brighton. *I* wish His Highness anywhere than at Brighton, I can tell you.'

'Thank you for the information. But why are you so set against His Highness's coming here?'

'Because if he weren't here I shouldn't be here, and if I weren't here I shouldn't have met . . .' She stopped.

'A chance stranger on a beach?'

She burst out laughing; she had very pretty teeth. 'Oh, I wasn't thinking of *you*.'

'How cruel of you!'

'Why should it be cruel? I don't know you.'

'We are going to change that, are we not?'

'Are we?' She was on her feet, for as he had spoken he had made an effort to take her hand. But she was too quick for him. She turned gracefully on her toes—not easy on the shingle, and poised for flight looked over her shoulder at him. He was on his feet.

'You are not going?'

'But I am. Goodbye . . . stranger.'

'But . . .'

'But I may be here tomorrow . . . at the same time . . . *if* I can get away.'

She ran off swiftly.

A rather amusing adventure, he thought, as he walked back to Grove House.

Her name was Lottie, she told him; but she would tell him no more. Where was she staying? Where did she live?

'Women,' she answered pertly, 'should be mysterious. I'm not very old, but I know that.'

'You succeed in being very mysterious.'

'Tell me, do you know the Prince of Wales?'

'I would say I was on reasonably good terms with that gentleman.'

'Then doubtless you know my guardian.'

'Tell me his name.'

She shook her head. 'Oh, no, I daren't do that.'

'Dare not? Why?'

She was mischievous suddenly. 'It would spoil the mystery.'
Then she was suddenly in tears. She was afraid they were going
to marry her to an old man . . . a rich old man. He was a suitable
match and she hated him and what was she going to do about
it? What could she do?

'You could run away,' said the Prince.

'How?' She was all excitement; and suddenly, so was he.

Why not? Her guardian was at Brighton. Someone in his
entourage? Suppose he set her up in a little house. There should
be no obstacle. He knew enough of her to realize that she was
not of the nobility; perhaps her guardian as she called him—or
her, perhaps—had a post in his household. In that case the afore-
said guardian could be made to realize that the patronage of the
Prince of Wales could be as comforting as marriage with a rich
old man.

'We could elope,' suggested the Prince.

'Oh, how, when?'

It would not be impossible. Suppose he had a post-chaise
waiting for her? All she would have to do was slip away as she
did when she came to the beach and into the chaise where her
lover would be waiting for her. He would give the order to drive
and they would go away . . . together. She would be out of
danger.

She was excited about the plan; but, she declared mournfully,
her guardian would be watchful of her; she would never escape.

He would have a footman's uniform procured for her; she
could put it on and leave her guardian's residence disguised in
it.

She was enchanted with the idea and clasped her hands with
excitement. She agreed to meet him the following night and
complete their plans.

But the next night she did not appear; and the Prince then
realized how diverted he had been by this adventure, and how
depressing it would be if it came to nothing. He was growing a
little weary of Lady Melbourne; Mrs. Billington had long since
begun to pall; Mrs. Crouch, another actress, was a real beauty
but she drank to such excess that she smelled like a wine shop
and the Prince did find this repulsive, particularly after Major
Hanger had said that her throat smelt like a smoking chimney.

But this little nymph of the beach was fresh and lovely, and
he would be wretched if he lost her.

For two nights she did not come, but on the third she was there. She sobbed against him and told him that she had been forbidden to leave the house. Her guardian was so suspicious, and she dreaded that she would not be allowed to make the escape.

They would arrange it, he said, for the very next night; she had the footman's uniform; she must put this on and slip out to where the carriage would be waiting; he would be inside and they would go to London together.

'I will be there,' he said, and embraced her tenderly.

Soon, of course, he would have to confess who he was; but that would only add to her delight, he was sure.

He was excited and absentminded the next day; he had decided that he would dine early and alone, and let it be known that he was leaving for London immediately after dinner.

He was dressing when Major Hanger was announced. As he received his intimate friends without formality, and since the affair of the duel Major Hanger had been one of them, the Prince ordered that he be brought to him.

The Major came and while the Prince explained the new method of wearing the neckcloth to him the Major listened with absentmindedness.

'I can see, my friend,' said the Prince, 'that you are somewhat distraught.'

The Major admitted that this was so and that he had come to ask the Prince's advice.

'Talk to me over dinner,' said the Prince, 'for I have business in London which means I must leave early.'

'Knowing Your Highness's success and experience with the fair sex, I believe you to be the one to advise me.'

'I am interested to hear what has gone wrong for you.'

'Everything . . . everything . . .' groaned the Major.

And when they were seated at the dinner table he told the story.

'I met the girl, Your Highness, in London. She wanted to come to Brighton. All of 'em want it. They want to have a chance of seeing Your Highness, I swear. So I brought her here . . . set the lady up in a pleasant little apartment, and what does she do? She starts an intrigue with a fellow of Brighton.'

'This is sad news, Major. You mean she prefers this fellow to you?'

'Stab me, if I could lay hands on him I'd douse him in the

sea. He'd have had enough of sea bathing by the time I'd done with him.'

'You don't know who he is?'

'No, but I shall find out. I'm determined on that. I've had her followed . . . meets a fellow on the beach, and is planning to go off with him.'

'What's this?' said the Prince.

'She goes to the beach. I've had her followed. Some fellow . . . from the household, I believe . . . meets her there. Oh, yes, I've had her watched; I've had her spied on. And she's eloping with the fellow, I hear. Not sure when but I'll find out. I'll let her know that I'm not paying for apartments for her to use while she goes out to meet this fellow.'

'What sort of a . . . woman is she?'

'Damned pretty. And up to tricks. Not so young as she looks and she knows a thing or two, my Charlotte does.'

'Charlotte?'

'Little Charlotte Fortescue . . . Blue eyes . . . black hair and the prettiest little figure . . .'

'One moment,' said the Prince. 'Describe her to me . . . in detail.'

The Major did describe her and before he had finished the Prince knew. His Lottie and the Major's Charlotte Fortescue were one and the same woman. So she had pretended she was an innocent girl, when all the time she was kept . . . yes kept . . . by the Major.

'Major,' said the Prince, 'I am your fellow.'

'What's that sir? What's that?'

The Prince explained.

'Well, stab me!' cried the Major. 'So she's been playing us both. And Your Highness is the, the . . .'

'The fellow you are going to douse in the sea.'

'Why, sir . . . The wicked creature! No wonder she's been looking so smug lately.'

'You mean . . . she *knew* who I was?'

'There's little Charlotte doesn't know.'

'When I think of her sitting in my carriage . . . in my footman's uniform . . . waiting for me . . .'

'Very pleased with herself, Highness, having hooked the Prince of Wales.'

The Prince was irritated. It was not pleasant to have been so duped by a slip of a girl. He had only been mildly involved. She was not really his type; she was far too young. And the fact that she had deceived him had completely changed his feelings towards her.

But she should not be allowed to get the better of him. He had an idea. It would be almost as good a joke as the duel.

'Listen, Major. The carriage will be waiting to pick her up. She will be expecting me inside it. You shall put on the coat and hat I wore for my meetings with her and be there in my place. Madame Lottie will trip along, enter the coach . . . See how long you can keep up the deception. Then you can take her to London and enjoy the little jaunt which was to have been mine.'

The Major slapped his thigh.

'By God, sir, trust you to think up a first-class joke. I'm ready to choke with laughter in anticipation.'

They started to laugh together; then the Prince was sober. It was rather an anti-climax to what was to have been a pleasant adventure.

After the Major had gone, he started to think how pleasant it would be if he could meet a woman who was good and beautiful, who was his ideal, who loved him tenderly and whom he could love.

There is no satisfaction in light love affairs, he told himself.

In due course the Major reported the consternation of Charlotte Fortescue when she discovered that her deceived lover had taken the place of the Prince of Wales; and the incident made the two men even closer friends. The Major's eccentricities were very diverting and he could always be relied on to think up some original trick to amuse.

On one occasion over dinner at Carlton House the Major became involved in an argument with Mr. Berkeley over the merits of turkeys and geese and which could travel the faster. Major Hanger was sure the turkeys would; Mr. Berkeley was equally certain that it would be the geese. Other conversation around the dinner table ceased and all attention was concentrated on the argument between Hanger and Berkeley.

The Prince joined in and said there was only one way of settling the matter. They must have a race. Because this was the Prince's idea it was taken up with enthusiasm. It was in any case another opportunity for a gamble.

Bets were taken and the stakes rose high.

The Prince was on the Major's side and backed the turkeys, declaring that he would be in charge of the turkeys and Mr.

Berkeley should be the gooseman. The preparations were in the Prince's mind, hilarious.

'Now, George,' he said to Hanger, 'you must select twenty of the very best turkeys to be found in the land.'

Hanger said he could safely be trusted to do that.

Mr. Berkeley was equally determined to find twenty of the finest geese.

It was not possible for the Prince to do anything without a great many people knowing of it; and the proposed match between turkeys and geese was no exception.

What will they be up to next? people asked themselves; and they came out to watch the race which Berkeley had artfully decided should take place in the late afternoon.

There was great hilarity when the birds were set on the road leading out of London for the ten-mile race. The Prince and Major Hanger were with their turkeys carrying the long poles on which pieces of red cloth had been tied with which to guide the birds if they decided to stray; and Mr. Berkeley and his supporters were similarly equipped to deal with the geese.

The turkeys got off to a good start and the betting was in their favour; in the first three hours they were two miles ahead of the geese; and then as dusk fell the turkeys looked for roosting places in the trees and finding them would not be dislodged; in vain did the Prince and the Major endeavour to do so; they were engaged in this when the geese came waddling into sight prodded by their supporters and went on past the roosting places of the turkeys to win the contest.

This was all very childish apart from the fact that enormous sums of money had changed hands and the Prince's debts were thereby increased because of it.

But although he spent lavishly on gambling, clothes, entertaining and improvements to Carlton House—in fact anything that took his fancy—he was not without generosity. He could never pass a beggar without throwing a handful of coins; he liked to scatter them among the children in the Brighton streets; and on one occasion borrowed eight hundred pounds from the moneylenders to give to a soldier just returned from the American wars whom he discovered living in penury; and not only did he give money but made it his personal duty to see that the soldier was reinstated in the Army.

In fact he wanted to enjoy life and others to enjoy it with him; he had not yet lost the pleasure he found in freedom; the shadow of the restricted life he had led at Kew under his parents' supervision was not far enough behind him for him to have forgotten it. But he was becoming a little palled. Light love affairs, ridiculous practical jokes, absurd gambling projects—they were lightly diverting for the moment; and that was all.

He longed for a stable relationship.

He was in this frame of mind when during a visit to Kew he strolled along the river bank with a little group of friends and met Maria Fitzherbert.

The encounter was so brief; she was there; he bowed and she was gone; but the memory of her lingered on.

'By God,' he said, 'what a beauty!'

His friends agreed with him; but they had no idea who she was.

And there she was in Lady Sefton's box in Covent Garden.

What a goddess! She was different from everyone else. It was not only due to the manner in which she wore her hair—and what glorious hair! It was all her own, not frizzed nor powdered, but dressed naturally with a thick curl hanging over one shoulder; and her bosom—full, white as marble, was almost matronly. Her complexion—and it was untouched by art—was clear and dazzling. And how delightful it was compared with the uniform red and white of rouge and white lead.

'I never saw a face I liked better,' he said to his companions. 'Who is she? For God's sake tell me. I shall not have a moment's peace until I know.'

'She is a Mrs. Fitzherbert, Your Highness. A cousin or some distant relation of the Seftons. A widow . . .'

'Adorable creature!'

'Your Highness wishes her to be presented?'

He was thoughtful. There was something about her manner which warned him. She was no Charlotte Fortescue—not even a Perdita. She was unique; and he knew from the start that he would have to go carefully.

'Leave this to me,' he said.

He had decided that for the duration of the opera he would content himself with looking. By God, he thought, there is plenty to look at.

She seemed unaware of him. That was what was so strange. Everyone else in the house was conscious of him—except Maria Fitzherbert.

'Maria Fitzherbert.' He repeated the name to himself. He wanted to know everything about Maria Fitzherbert. Just to look at her gave him infinite pleasure. No silly young girl this—a glorious goddess of a woman. No coy creature, no giggling companion. A mature woman, already a widow; a woman who was serious and in her lovely way mature. After the opera he would send someone to her box; he would say that the Prince of Wales desired to be allowed to visit her there. Impatiently he waited for the curtain to fall—and then it was too late. She had slipped away.

But it was not too late. He would follow her. He would take a chair as any ordinary gentleman might and he would follow her to her home.

How flattered she would be at this honour! She would invite him in for a delightful tête-à-tête; he would express his admiration; he would tell her that he knew something had happened to him tonight which had never happened before.

So to Park Street by chair in the most exciting manner.

But she had arrived there before him; and although she looked from the window and saw him standing in the street, she did not ask him in.

He was not seriously disturbed. Of course she was not *that* sort of woman. Nor, he told himself sternly, would he wish her to be; nor had he expected her to be.

He went home and all night he dreamed of Maria Fitzherbert.

In the morning he said to himself: I have fallen in love at first sight with Maria Fitzherbert.

Drama at Carlton House

The Prince had always lived publicly; his affairs could not be hidden, so he made no attempt to hide them. He was passionately in love with Maria Fitzherbert and he could not have kept that secret had he wished to. He made it clear that if any of his friends wished to please him, they must invite Maria Fitzherbert to their houses and him at the same time; they must make sure that at their dinner tables he was seated next to her; he wanted to talk to Maria Fitzherbert, dance with her, be with her every moment that was possible, and he wished no one to attempt to prevent this.

His friends reminded each other of Perdita Robinson. So it had been in the early days of that affair; and that hadn't lasted very long. Of course Maria was different from Perdita, Maria was socially acceptable; she had been twice married and she was a poised society woman; she was not very rich, but on the other hand she was by no means poor. She had a house at Richmond and a house in Town; she did not entertain a great deal, but then she had no need to. Every fashionable hostess knew that unless she invited Maria Fitzherbert she would not have the Prince of Wales.

And Maria herself? She was not honoured; she was not delighted. She could not see how any good could come from the Prince's infatuation. Maria was sensible; she knew that she was no beauty but that she was a great deal more attractive than many who were; there was about her a dignity, an almost maternal air; she was not even very young, being twenty-eight; and she did not see how there could be any honourable relationship between herself and the Prince of Wales, and she was not the woman to indulge in any other.

The Prince was very soon declaring his admiration.

'Never in my life have I met anyone who had moved me so deeply,' he told her. 'I could be perfectly happy in a world which contained no one else but you.'

She smiled serenely and said he was very charming to her, and she knew that she owed her welcome into society to him.

He tried to explain. He wanted her to owe everything to him; he wanted her to know that it was his greatest desire to serve her . . . not only now, but for the rest of his life.

She smiled her placid smile, which really meant that she believed he had made similar declarations many times before; and although she found him charming and it was pleasant to know that he enjoyed making them to her, she did not take them at all seriously.

'I don't doubt you have heard stories of my adventures with women,' he said ruefully.

'The affairs of a Prince of Wales must always attract interest, of course.'

'But you don't understand, Maria . . . Oh what a beautiful name. Everything about you is perfect. What I feel now is something entirely new. I realize now that I was never seriously involved with anyone before.'

But she did not believe him. She was gracious and charming, completely unruffled; she liked him; she thought him amusing, charming, a delightful companion; but she refused to consider him as a lover. She had been twice most honourably married, and she did not consider it an honour to be any man's mistress— even that of a Prince of Wales.

He was frustrated. He did what he always did in moments of stress. He took to his pen. He wrote to Maria, pouring out his feelings for her. She did not always answer the letters, but when she did she did so in the manner of a friend and he could not break through the barrier she had set up.

He was interested in nothing. In vain did his friends try to tempt him. The Duchess of Cumberland would give an entertainment to outshine any she had ever given before. He was not interested. Georgiana would invite all the most interesting people in London—all those who had most delighted him. Was that going to make Maria consider him seriously? Major Hanger would think up some delicious practical jokes. Maria thought them childish, said the Prince; and so they were. He was finished with such amusements.

'Mrs. Fitzherbert is a Tory and a Catholic,' Fox reminded him.

'I'd be a Tory and a Catholic if that would give me any headway with her,' was the Prince's retort.

That was an alarming statement. 'For God's sake,' said Fox to Sheridan, 'let the woman give in before real damage is done.'

The Prince could not eat; he lost his good humour; he wanted Maria, but Maria, while ready to be his friend, would not become his mistress.

Lady Sefton called on Maria. Maria received her in the drawing room at Park Street and Isabella Sefton studied her as people were studying Maria now, which made her smile.

'I know what you're thinking,' said Maria. 'It's what everyone thinks when they look at me nowadays. What does he see in her?'

'Well, Maria, you are very attractive.'

'That may be, but surely not attractive enough for so much fuss.'

'Too modest, Maria. You could have accepted Bedford. Then you would have been a Duchess.'

'A title for which I have no great desire, Isabella.'

'No more than you have a desire to become the first lady of London society.'

Maria laughed. 'For how long? Remember poor Perdita Robinson. Her reign was of very short duration.'

'You're no Perdita. Yours could be for ever, perhaps.'

'I can see no honour in it, Isabella.'

'You must be fond of him. He is charming, is he not?''

'Charming yes . . . and modest for one in his position. He is interesting too when he is not talking in the most exaggerated terms of his feelings for me which, I am fully aware, are aimed at one object. No, Isabella, your charming Prince is not going to succeed.'

'Not mine, Maria. You mean yours.'

'Our Prince, then. He will soon be tired—have no doubt of that. He is far too young and impressionable not to discover someone more willing than I who will be the most beautiful woman in the world, who will embody all he looks for in women and so on.'

'He is gallant,' admitted Isabella. 'He has always been fond of women; but I . . . and others tell me the same . . . have never seen him in this state before. He is interested in nothing but you; he talks of nothing but you. He makes no secret of his passion. You cannot deny, Maria, that the young man is in love with you.'

'Oh, Isabella, I am too old, too experienced in life . . .'

'With two old husbands?'

'Thomas was not so old. He was only twelve years older than I.'

'But you were little more than a nurse to both of your husbands, Maria; is it not time that you began to enjoy life?'

'I enjoy it well enough, Isabella; and I certainly should not if I were doing something of which I was ashamed.'

'Other women . . .'

'I am not other women, Isabella. How could I go to confession if I were living in sin . . . which is clearly what he wishes. No, the best news you could give me would be that someone else has caught his fancy and that he is no longer interested in me.'

'I don't believe he will be satisfied until you give in.'

'Then he will have to prepare himself for a life of *dis*-satisfaction. I have decided to leave London. The less he sees of me the better. Pray do not mention the fact that I am going. I am leaving early tomorrow for Marble Hill.'

Isabella smiled sardonically. Did Maria think that by removing herself to Richmond she would escape from the Prince of Wales?

Isabella was right. Within a few hours the Prince had discovered where she had gone. He immediately called for his phaeton and rode out to Marble Hill.

She must receive him. She must listen to an account of his sufferings when he had heard she had left Park Street; he had thought at first that she might have hidden herself somewhere. It was a great joy to find that she had only removed her bright presence to Marble Hill.

She felt the need of a little country air, she told him. She lived very simply.

There was nothing like the simple life, he agreed. He too longed to get away from balls and banquets and everything that went with them. The glitter of society had no charm for him . . . since it had none for her.

'I'm afraid the simple life I prefer would have no charms for Your Highness.'

'There is only one life that has any charms for me, Maria— and that is life with you.'

She sighed; she begged him to change the subject and talk of other matters. Anything in the world she wished, he said; so they talked lightly of politics, of her gardens, of people they knew, and she laughed gaily and he was enchanted with all her views, with her quick spontaneous laughter, with everything she said and did; and when he left, reluctantly, for it was she who suggested that he should go, he was more in love than ever.

Every day he drove out to Marble Hill. He declared that he would not let a day pass without a glimpse of Maria. She would understand in time how much he loved her; she would realize that she could not go on being so cruel . . . and so on.

He was determined to become her lover; and she was equally determined that he should not. But she could not turn him away when he came to Marble Hill; she could not help being fond of him; but her answer was always the same.

Everyone was talking about the Prince's passion for Mrs. Fitzherbert and a new ballad had been written and was sung all over the town:

> 'On Richmond Hill there lives a lass
> More bright than May day morn,
> Whose charms all other maids' surpass
> A rose without a thorn.
>
> This lass so neat, with smile so sweet,
> Has won my right good will,
> I'd crowns resign to call thee mine,
> Sweet lass of Richmond Hill.'

In desperation the Prince rode out to Chertsey. Charles James Fox had helped him over the Perdita affair; he had known how to act when she threatened to present the bond he had given her and publish his letters. Very satisfactorily Charles had dealt with that matter—and had rounded it up in a characteristically cynical way by becoming Perdita's lover. Charles would help him with Maria. He was certain of it.

Charles received him with pleasure and so did Lizzie Armistead. A delightful woman, Lizzie; she reminded him in some ways of Maria—a pale shadow of Maria, of course; but that serenity, that poise! And Charles had changed since they lived together in an almost respectable manner. It showed what the right kind of woman could do for a man. Charles, he believed, was more or less faithful to Lizzie; he still drank too much and gambled heavily—but he had changed. He had mellowed; it was as though he had found something well worth while in life.

The Prince sighed. It would be the same with him and Maria. He had sown enough wild oats; he wanted now to reap the contentment which should be the right of any man who was capable of enjoying it.

'We are honoured, Your Highness,' said Lizzie, sweeping a graceful curtsey. She gave no hint that they had once been very intimate indeed. Admirable Lizzie!

He embraced her with tears in his eyes.

'I am happy to see you well, my dear. And Charles?'

Charles had heard his arrival and was coming out to greet him.

'My dear, dear friend.'

Tears, thought Charles. This means he wants me to do something. How can I induce the woman to throw aside her principles and jump into bed with him?

'Your Highness, you honour us.'

'And envy you, you fortunate pair! I would give up everything to know contentment such as you enjoy in this little cottage.'

Cottage! thought Lizzie. It was scarcely that. It was a comfortably sized house and she was very proud of it. Compared with Carlton House, of course . . .

'We are astonished that Your Highness should deign to visit such a humble dwelling,' she replied.

'My sweet Liz, it's not the dwelling I come to see but you two dear friends.'

'Your Highness will come into our humble drawing room doubtless,' said Fox, 'and perhaps partake of a little humble refreshment which will be served by our humble servants.'

The Prince laughed through his tears. Then he said appealingly: 'The humility is all on my side, Charles. I come to beg of you to help me.'

He sat in the drawing room, diminishing it by his dazzling presence. His large plump form weighing heavily on the chair he had selected—feet stretched before him, glittering shoe buckles almost vying with the magnificent diamond star on the left side of his elegant green coat.

When wine had been brought he looked helplessly from

Charles to Lizzie. 'What am I going to do?' he demanded. 'She receives me. She is kind; she laughs; she is gracious; but she will not allow me to as much as kiss her cheek.'

'Mrs. Robinson held off for a very long time,' said Lizzie. 'I remember how she used to pace up and down her room and declaim: "His wife I cannot be. His mistress I will never be." It is a quotation, from some play most likely. She was full of such quotations. But all the time she had a firm intention to give in. She was being reluctant in order to make you more eager.'

'You cannot compare Mrs. Robinson with Mrs. Fitzherbert.'

'Except that they are both women. Mrs. Robinson had one husband and Mrs. Fitzherbert has had two.'

'Perdita's husband was living. He was somewhere in the background. Maria has been twice widowed.'

Lizzie knew when to be silent. Charles said: 'Has Your Highness tried offering her estates . . . er . . .'

The Prince laughed bitterly. 'You don't know Maria. She does not want money. She has made it clear to me that she is perfectly happy with her income. Moreover, she knows how to live within it which is more than we do within ours.'

'If she were not such an *admirable* woman,' said Charles, 'we should not be confronted by this impasse. Virtue can have its drawbacks. A little sin is very convenient now and then.'

It was Lizzie's turn to flash a warning at Charles.

'We must try to find some solution to His Highness's problem,' she said. 'He knows we would do anything . . . just anything . . .'

'My dear, dear Lizzie, I know it well.' The tears were in his eyes; he covered his face with his hands. 'But what . . . what . . . *what*?'

'Has Your Highness explored every approach? Is there anything that would make the lady relent?'

The Prince looked hopeful. 'She is fond of me. I am certain that the objection has nothing to do with my person. But she is a strict Catholic and this is at the heart of the matter. How lucky those of you are who are not born royal. You can marry where you will. You do not have to be dictated to. You are not at the beck and call of an old tyrant. The State does not decide with whom you shall spend your life, who shall bear your children. Oh, you most fortunate people. They will soon be trying to marry me to some hideous German woman. I know it. I shall be expected to fawn on her and pretend to be in love with her.

I tell you there is no one I want but Maria . . . Maria . . . Maria!'

Charles said: 'There must be a way. We will find it, Your Highness.'

The Prince's smile was immediately sunny. 'You will, Charles, I know you will, my dear good friend. I don't know what I should do without you, and you too, Lizzie. God bless you both.'

The Prince rode away from Chertsey in a happier state of mind from that in which he had come, but Charles was grave.

'The Guelphs,' he said, 'have always been able to turn on the tears at the least provocation; but this is a perpetual flow. I don't like it, Liz. He's getting desperate. God knows what he will do. He's capable of the utmost folly. Why can't he have the sense to fall in love with a nice sensible whore. Why does he have to choose this respectable, deeply religious, highly virtuous matron?'

'What are you going to suggest to him?'

'God knows. I saw marriage in his eye. You heard what he said about the hideous German. It shows which way his thoughts are turning. This will give Papa a hundred sleepless nights where he suffered but twenty before.'

'He can't marry Maria Fitzherbert. What about the Marriage Act? It wouldn't be a legal marriage.'

'No, and the woman's not only a Catholic. She's a Tory.'

'He surely would never go over to them. It would mean being on the side of the King.'

'I think his desire for Maria is greater than his hatred of his father. Most definitely we are up against a tricky situation. Action will have to be taken in a very short time.'

'At least,' said Lizzie, 'sorrow does not affect his weight. I thought he was going to break my chair when he sat there creaking on it.'

'Your very humble chair, Liz.'

'At least,' said Lizzie with an air of pride, 'it is paid for.'

'Oh, admirable Lizzie. If only H.R.H. were as lucky in love as I!'

Charles was going to help him and that was something; but this was a devilishly tricky situation and he decided to call in the help of his dearest Duchess.

Georgiana received him with great sympathy and when he had wept a little in her beautiful drawing room at Devonshire

House, which was very different from that in Chertsey, he demanded of Georgiana what he was going to do.

Georgiana shook her head. 'Maria seems adamant.'

He covered his face with his hands.

'Dearest Highness, there must be a way out of this.'

'What, Georgiana, what?'

Georgiana was silent. Why had the woman come to Court? Why had she not married another old husband and stayed in the country nursing him? That was the life which would suit her. She was beautiful in her way, thought Georgiana, but there was nothing especially wonderful about her. Her nose was too long and prominent anyway . . . quite an aggressive nose. Georgiana wondered that the Prince couldn't see it. When she thought of her own rather pert and pretty nose, her own beauty . . . she could not understand it. Why should he have to be so enamoured of this . . . matron? There was no other word for her. She had not borne children but she was like a mother. She would be fat in a few years time, Georgiana prophesied. And she must be nearly twenty-nine. Thirty, possibly, and he was twenty-two! It was a ridiculous situation. It was not that Georgiana disliked Maria Fitzherbert. Far from it. She was an interesting and pleasant creature. But she was a little tiresome in her virtue. After all, a love affair with the Prince of Wales would not have impaired it all that much, and what she lost in virtue she would have gained in prestige.

Poor dear Prince, he was so distrait and he was such a darling spoilt boy who was bewildered because here was a woman who did not fall to his grasp as soon as he held up his pleading hands.

She, Georgiana, had refused him, and that had kept him eager for her; but this was different; he was obsessed with Maria Fitzherbert as he never had been for the Duchess of Devonshire.

Still, she must not allow her pique to interfere with her friendship because she was discovering that she really was genuinely fond of him.

'I have an idea.'

'Yes, yes . . .'

'I am fond of Maria . . .'

The Prince seized her hands and covered them with kisses. His dearest Georgiana! Such good sense . . . ! So clever . . . ! Besides being beautiful she was the wisest, best woman in the world . . . next to Maria.

'I think I could talk to her. I could discover if there is anything that can be done. If there is a way out . . . I could perhaps speak more frankly on this rather delicate matter than you . . . and if you would give me your permission . . .'

'My dearest, *dearest* Georgiana, you will be my saviour, I know it.'

'You know that I will do everything in my power to help you.'

'I know it. God bless you.'

He was in tears again.

The Duchess's carriage had taken her to Richmond.

Now, she thought, to talk with the Sweet Lass of Richmond Hill. Not such a lass. It would be easier if she were.

'My dear Maria!'

'Welcome, Duchess.'

The Duchess surveyed her appraisingly. It is because she is different, she thought. That must be the answer. Those eyes are good and her hair is lovely, of course; her complexion clear and fresh and the bosom . . . well it's very fine. Marble hills indeed. But soft and billowy. He'll be able to weep on that in comfort.

'Maria, you know what I have come about. The Prince has been to see me.'

Maria sighed. One had to admire her. She is genuine, thought Georgiana. She really *means* she will not become his mistress.

'His Highness is in a very sad state.'

Maria had taken the Duchess to her drawing room, which was very elegant though of course very small and by no means to be compared with Devonshire and Carlton Houses.

'I have been thinking of what will be best for me to do and I have come to the conclusion that if I went away for a while he would turn his attention to someone else.'

She spoke in a matter-of-fact voice. What a calm and sensible woman! How different from that dreadful actress who had imagined herself on a stage all the time. Georgiana remembered how that vulgar little upstart had tried to wrest from her—Georgiana—the title of leader of fashion. The thought infuriated her even now, to think of that woman parading herself in the Mall or at the Pantheon and the Rotunda in her outrageous costumes . . . all in an endeavour to make people look at her instead of at the Duchess of Devonshire.

Georgiana smoothed the velvet of her skirts made specially to her own design. No fear of Maria Fitzherbert being so foolish. She was really what one would call a very nice, sensible woman. No airs—complete sincerity. Georgiana had seen that her mission would be in vain; she had had a lurking suspicion that if

Maria were offered a large enough reward she would have succumbed and she would have been the one to discover it and so
bring happiness to the Prince. But no. Maria was sincere in her
determination not to enter into an irregular relationship with the
Prince.

'Wherever you went he would follow,' said the Duchess.

'Not if I went abroad. He cannot leave the country without
the King's consent. I have lived a great many years of my life in
France. I was educated there and when my second husband was
ill I took him to Nice. We lived there for almost a year. I have
friends in France. I speak French as well as I speak English. So
. . . it seems a natural choice.'

'And when do you propose to go?'

'Within the next few days. I have in fact made all my arrangements.'

'Heaven knows what the Prince will do.'

Maria smiled, a little sadly Georgiana noticed, and she said
quickly: 'You are fond of him?'

'How could I help it?' Maria was by nature frank. 'This has
all been so . . . flattering. And he has been charming to me. I
have been surprised that one in his position could be so . . . so
humble . . . so modest . . . and so kind.'

'You sound as though you are a little in love with him.'

'If circumstances were different . . .'

'Ah,' said the Duchess promptly. 'If he were in the position
Mr. Weld or Mr. Fitzherbert had been in . . . you would not
hesitate.'

'No,' said Maria, 'I would not hesitate. Yes, I am fond of
him. It is impossible not to be. He has great charm. He is so
young . . . and I . . .'

'And your husbands have been so old. Oh, Maria, how cruel
is fate. If only he were Mr. Guelph with a pleasant estate in the
country all could end happily.'

'My dear Duchess, how kind you are to concern yourself with
our affairs.'

'Is there nothing that can be done?'

'Nothing. The Prince is pressing me to become his mistress.
I could never agree to that. It is against my beliefs . . . my
religion. I could never be happy in such a position and therefore
nor would he be. I have thought a great deal of this. It saddens
me. I shall miss him sorely, but I know that my best plan is to
leave the country. In time he will turn his attentions to someone
else . . . and then I shall return.'

'My dear Maria, what a noble creature you are! How I wish that you were a Protestant German Princess. Then I think His Highness would be the happiest man alive.'

Georgiana went straight to the Prince.

'I have seen Maria. I have very bad news for Your Highness. I had better tell you at once. Maria is planning to leave the country.'

The Prince wailed in his anguish.

'She is leaving in two days' time. That gives us a very short space for some action.'

'Georgiana, she must not be allowed to go. She must not.'

'We'll have to think of something. Never fear, we shall. Charles and I will put our heads together. But one thing I have discovered; she will never be your mistress. You'll have to have some sort of marriage.'

'I'd marry her tomorrow.'

Oh dear, thought Georgiana, I'd better see Charles at once.

'Don't go to her today,' pleaded Georgiana. 'You might drive her into leaving earlier. We have a day or so to think of something.' He looked so desperate that she said: 'But she is in love with you. That much she has admitted.'

'Georgiana!'

'Oh yes. She couldn't hide it from me. She is very unhappy to leave you. But it's this religion of hers. She can't live in sin. She'd rather be miserable for the rest of her life than that. That's the situation.'

'But she loves me! She loves me! She had told you this, Georgiana, dear, dear Georgiana. What did she say?'

'That you were charming and modest and irresistible. In fact I suspect that is why she is running away . . . because she is afraid that her reserves might break down.'

'But this is the best news I have heard for weeks.'

'She is leaving, remember, for France.'

'She must be stopped.'

'How? You cannot stop one of His Majesty's subjects from leaving the country unless you have a very good reason for doing so.'

'A very good reason! I shall *die* if she goes.'

'His Majesty would not consider that a valid reason,' said Georgiana tersely, 'because Your Highness would not die. You would only be brokenhearted.'

'And you think that is not a good reason?'

'I . . . I would change the laws of this country to make you happy. I was talking of the King.'

'Damn the King!'

'Treason! And His Majesty's damnation has nothing to do with our problem. We have two days in which to think up a plot. And I believe we are going to succeed. There is one indisputable fact which brightens the whole situation to my mind.'

'Georgiana, dearest friend, what is it?'

'Mrs. Maria Fitzherbert is in love with His Highness the Prince of Wales.'

'Oh, Charles,' cried the Duchess, 'how good of you to come so soon. I am distracted. I fear that the Prince is capable of anything . . . simply anything.'

'By which, dear Duchess, you mean marriage?'

'That is exactly what I mean.'

'It would have no meaning. You've forgotten the Marriage Act. Besides, the woman's a Catholic. That in itself is enough to lose him the throne.'

'I know. And so does he. But he does not care.'

'He behaves like a child.'

'Or a very romantic lover,' said the Duchess softly.

Fox burst out laughing. 'You know, do you not, that the woman is a Tory.'

'I know it,' said the Duchess sadly.

'A Tory and a Catholic. My God! It might be a plot of His Majesty's to plague *us* if it wasn't even more plaguing to him.'

'Do you think he knows what is happening?'

'He successfully manages to shut himself away in his Palace of Purity at Kew, and is more interested in how his farmers make butter than how his son makes love. The Fitzherbert must become his mistress by some means. Then in the natural course of events the affair will come to its logical conclusion.'

'But she holds out for marriage.'

'That's the point. We've got to make her give in.'

'She is adamant, Charles. I've spoken to her. It's her religion. I really think he is capable of following her to France.'

'He can't do it. It's impossible for the Prince of Wales to leave the country without the King's consent.'

'He's capable of anything. He has never been so mad about any woman before, Charles. Let's face it. Perdita was the nearest, but he never talked of marrying Perdita.'

'She didn't hold out long enough. Perdita was a fool.'

'Well, Maria Fitzherbert is not. And the fact that she really means what she says enslaves him more than ever. He senses her inherent virtue, Charles. It confirms his belief that she is the only woman with whom he can be happy. You know the Prince. Gambling, jokes, racing, prizefighting . . . he enjoys them all; but his dominating passion is for women.'

Charles nodded gloomily. 'What about a marriage . . . a marriage that was not really a marriage. Some sort of ceremony to soothe the lady's scruples.'

'A mock marriage?' murmured Georgiana.

'You could call it that.' Charles began to laugh. 'My God,' he cried, 'this is demanding as much of our time as the Declaration of Independence.'

'I'm sure the Prince feels it to be a matter of far greater importance.'

Charles shrugged his shoulders. 'Let us lose the North American Colonies. Let France and Spain come against us. Let the throne tremble and let the Whigs go to hell. What matters it as long as George, Prince of Wales, goes to bed with Maria Fitzherbert.'

'I am sure, Charles,' said the Duchess, 'that you are voicing His Highness's own sentiments.'

'I think I will go and see some of the Gentlemen of His Household. Something could be arranged perhaps. Who are they? Southampton, Bouverie and . . .'

'There is also Onslow. You could rely on him.'

'I will have a talk with them. I have a faint idea beginning to form. It seems wild but perhaps it will fit the situation. I will keep you in the picture.'

Maria was ready to leave her house in Park Street. In a few hours' time she would be making her way down to the coast; her bags were already packed. She had been rather surprised to receive letters from her Uncle Henry and her brothers Walter and John and while they did not actually advise her to give way to the Prince they managed to hint that they thought there was nothing dishonourable in doing so. How could they be so deluded, so blinded by the dazzle of royalty! The boys were young, of course, and they had missed a father's steadying influence, but Uncle Henry should have known better. Dear Uncle Henry had always been kind to her but she had always known him for a worldly man.

It was a good plan to go to France. There she would be able

to confide in her dear nuns and to talk frankly of her feelings. The more she saw of the Prince the stronger her feelings grew, and she was realizing how painful it was for her to leave him. It would be so easy to love him—far easier than it had been in the case of Edward and Thomas—although she had believed herself to be happily married to both of them. It was as well that she was leaving, not only to elude the Prince but so that she might not become the victim of her own feelings. She must face the truth. She would be very sad without him. But she had made up her mind. In less than an hour she would leave.

She heard the sound of carriage wheels in the street below. It was early yet. She went to the window. The royal carriage was pulling up outside the house. She drew back, shielding herself by the curtains. It was not the Prince who alighted but four members of his household. She knew three of them by sight; they were Lord Southampton, Lord Onslow and Mr. Bouverie; she did not recognize the fourth man.

She heard their voices addressing her footman.

'Pray conduct us to your mistress without delay. The matter is of utmost urgency.'

She faced them resolutely. 'I am just about to leave . . .'

'Madam, the life of the Prince of Wales is in the greatest danger.'

'Danger . . . ?'

'He has attempted suicide. He is asking for you.'

She looked at them suspiciously and Lord Southampton said: 'This is Mr. Keate, His Highness's surgeon. He will tell you that the Prince is on the point of death. He is calling for you, Madam. We fear the consequences if you do not go at once to him at Carlton House.'

Maria was alarmed, but a hideous suspicion had come to her. What plan was this? She was to be taken to Carlton House. What would happen when she arrived there? Was it a trick? How could she be sure? And what if he really had attempted to take his life?

She stammered: 'I cannot come alone. I must have a . . . a lady whom I could trust to accompany me. If you will call at Lady Sefton's house I am sure she will agree to come with me.'

Southampton and Onslow exchanged glances.

'I feel the Duchess of Devonshire would come. She is a great friend of the Prince and of you too, Madam. Would you agree to come if she was with you?'

'Why . . . yes,' said Maria.

'Then we beg of you to lose no time. The Prince's condition is serious.'

The Duchess hastily joined Maria in the coach, her face grave.

'But my dear Maria, this is terrible. What can have happened?'

'I know very little. They tell me that he has attempted to take his life.'

'How fearful! How dreadful! It can't be true.'

'It is true,' said Southampton. 'The Prince in desperation has stabbed himself.'

'Then he is . . .'

'His physicians are with him. Mr. Keate came along to urge the importance of bringing Mrs. Fitzherbert to his bedside.'

'Are you telling us that he is . . . dying?' gasped the Duchess.

'Your Grace,' said Keate, 'we may yet be in time.'

When they reached Carlton House the women were hurried into the Prince's apartment on the ground floor where he was lying on a couch, his face very pale and his clothes bloodstained.

'Maria!' he cried when he saw her; and she ran to him and knelt by his side. She took his hand which he grasped with fervour; and then he lay back, his eyes closed.

'Oh, my God,' whispered Maria, 'what have you done?'

'Maria . . .'

'Yes . . . yes . . .'

'Come closer.' He spoke in a whisper, his breath laboured, 'Please do not exert yourself.'

'I . . . am better . . . now you are here.'

Maria looked helplessly at the doctors.

'Comfort him, Madam,' said Keate, 'He is in a very low state.'

Maria put her lips to his forehead and a slow smile touched his lips. She heard him murmuring her name once more.

The Duchess of Devonshire said: 'He . . . will live?'

The Prince heard her for he murmured: 'Of what use to live . . . without Maria?'

'Please do not talk in that way,' said Maria, deeply agitated.

'How else can I talk when you . . . reject me.'

'Perhaps,' she said to the doctors, 'I disturb him. Perhaps it would be better if I went.'

The grip on her hand tightened and the doctors shook their heads gravely.

'I wish to die,' murmured the Prince.

'You see,' whispered Keate to the Duchess. 'He has no will to live.'

'There is only one thing that would make me want to live . . .' went on the Prince. 'Maria . . . Maria . . .'

'I am here,' said Maria.

'But you go away . . .'

'I am here beside you.'

'Nothing will induce me to live unless you promise to be my wife.'

'But . . .'

'No, it is useless. Goodbye, Maria. There is no reason for living . . . no hope . . .'

'Maria cannot refuse Your Highness,' said the Duchess, coming to the couch. 'Whatever she says I can see how deeply disturbed she is. Your Highness must get well. Maria, you will marry the Prince.'

'I will pledge my word with a ring . . . and she shall pledge hers to me,' said the Prince.

The Duchess took a ring from her finger and pressed it into the Prince's hand. She nodded to Maria. 'You cannot refuse a dying man.'

Maria thought: How he loves me! He has done this because he cannot live without me. Such passion was something she had never discovered in either of her husbands before. Lying back on the couch, so pale, he looked very handsome. It would be cruel to refuse to allow a dying man to put a ring on her finger.

'You will promise, Maria . . .'

She bowed her head and held out her hand, and the Prince slipped the Duchess's ring on her finger.

'Now,' said Keate, 'His Highness should rest. He has lost a great deal of blood but I believe that he is at peace.'

The Prince nodded but kept Maria's hand in his.

'Maria,' he murmured. 'You are my wife, Maria.'

Once more Maria bent over and kissed his forehead and a smile of triumph curved his lips.

As she was leaving Carlton House with the Duchess, Southampton came hurrying after them. 'His Highness demands to see a deposition drawn up and signed by Onslow, Bouverie, Keate and myself.'

'What deposition?' asked Maria.

'What has happened is tantamount to a marriage ceremony. It must be recorded and signed by witnesses. It is the only thing that will satisfy him. We daren't cross him and he is demanding it.'

'Let us go to Devonshire House,' said the Duchess, 'and there we will draw up a document and all sign it. That should satisfy him. You will do this, I know, Maria, for we have seen what a state His Highness is in. We must give him every opportunity to recover.'

So with the four men and the Duchess, Maria returned to Devonshire House where the deposition was drawn up and signed.

It was then taken to the Prince at Carlton House while Maria went back to Park Street.

When his friends returned with the deposition the Prince had discarded his bloodstained clothes and was drinking a whiskey and soda.

'You have it?' he cried.

'Here, Your Highness.'

'Let me see. Let me see. Ah . . . yes. She will not go back on her word. We have it here in writing.'

'Your Highness, if I may say so, played the part to perfection.'

'I should have done well on the boards, Keate, if I had been born into a different station. My dear Maria, she was deeply distressed.'

'And small wonder!' said Southampton. 'The idea of a Prince's falling on his sword because she had rejected him must have been alarming.'

'I would have done it,' said the Prince. 'Yes, I would have done it for Maria. So it is not really a great deception.'

He smiled complacently. The ceremony would satisfy Maria, and in no way inconvenience him. Not that he would not have gone through a true marriage ceremony with her if that had been possible. Most willingly would he have given up everything for her; but since it could be done this way and Charles thought so—and Charles was invariably right—how much more satisfactory it was than making the great upheaval through the country which an ordinary marriage would have done.

He was madly in love with her, enough to fall on his sword. He had brandished his pistols and declared he would shoot himself. And when he had been blooded because the doctors said the violence of his passions could give him a stroke and there had been so much rich red blood and he had splashed it all over his beautiful coat . . . he had really *felt* as though he had—in a sudden access of despair—fallen on his sword.

And the effect had been to bring her to his bedside, chastened, loving, tender, ready to give way as she had never been before.

Maria would soon be his.

Back in Park Street Maria considered the strange events of the last hours and the more she thought of them the stranger they appeared.

The Duchess of Devonshire had been waiting in Devonshire House when they called. Well, she might easily have been at home at that hour. She had handed over the ring as though she had brought it with her for the purpose. Maria twisted it round and round on her finger. It was a symbol. It meant she had promised to be the Prince's wife. But how could she be the Prince's wife? It was not possible. Their marriage, even if it were valid, would be forbidden. It was simply not possible for the heir to the throne to marry a commoner; and even if she were a Princess the marriage would not be allowed because of her religion. Sovereigns of Britain were simply not allowed to marry anyone of the Catholic Faith.

Why had she been so foolish as to sign the deposition?

Because one could not oppose the wish of a dying man.

A dying man. He had been very prompt with his answers.

And the deposition? She had been too agitated to read it properly, but it was, she realized now, a document which declared that she was the wife of George, Prince of Wales. But how could there be a marriage without a priest? The whole thing was a mockery.

She did not blame the Prince. He had declared many times that he would willingly forgo everything to marry her. No, he genuinely loved him and she loved him—the more because of what he had done today. He had tried to kill himself for love of her. It was a gesture that she would remember with tenderness all her life. If he were free to marry her . . . if there were no obstacles between them willingly would she give her promise to love and cherish him for the rest of her life.

But she would not accept a mock marriage.

Her bags were packed. She could leave the next day, for if she left the country she would make it clear that she was determined not to be trapped into dishonour by any mock ceremony.

She wrote a note to Lord Southampton telling him that she realized she had been the victim of a trap and that she blamed him and his friends. They had prevailed on her to sign a document which had no meaning. She therefore did not consider herself to be in any way committed, and she had decided to carry out her original intention and leave the country.

Early next morning she set out on her journey.

The Prince's Dilemma

The loss of blood sustained by the Prince together with all the excitement he had undergone had weakened him considerably and Keate said that a few days' rest were needed. Moreover, Maria would not expect him to recover too quickly.

'A few days in the country, sir,' said Keate, 'and you will be completely recovered.'

And then, thought the Prince, Maria.

Southampton said: 'Would your Highness care to come down to my place in the country for those few days?'

'I would indeed, Southampton,' replied the Prince.

'We can promise Your Highness fresh air and good nursing. And then in a few days time . . .'

'Maria,' whispered the Prince.

Pale and certainly a little feeble, the Prince set off for the country in the company of Southampton and Onslow and a few others of his suite. Jogging along in the carriage he made plans. As soon as he was feeling completely well—and that would be in a few days' time, for with his youth and good health he was very resilient and had really only suffered from his too violent passions and rather more blood-letting than that to which he was accustomed—he would be with Maria.

She should come to Carlton House. It would be no little love nest such as that he had provided for Perdita in Cork Street. Maria and he would live together openly. And if the King raised objections—to hell with the King.

In a few days' time they would be together. How affected she had been when she had seen him lying there on the couch! He could have no doubt of her feelings then.

At last he was happy. Maria could not hide her love for him. The most happy time of his life was about to begin.

When they arrived at Southampton's place a messenger from London was there.

He had come, he said, with a letter for Lord Southampton and had been instructed by Mrs. Fitzherbert to put it into no hands but his lordship's.

The Prince smiled happily. He thought: She is writing to Southampton to thank him for the part he played in our little ceremony. My dearest Maria is as happy as I am.

'Read it now, Southampton. Read it now,' he said, smiling blandly.

As Southampton read he turned pale; as he opened his mouth as though to speak, and yet said nothing, a sudden fear touched the Prince. 'What is it? What is it?'

'Sir, she has left the country. She reproaches me for . . . for taking advantage of the situation . . .'

The Prince snatched the letter. Maria's handwriting danced before his eyes. She had been the victim of a hoax, she had written, but she had not been deceived. She did not admire Lord Southampton for attempting to delude her, nor for imagining she was such a fool that she could be deluded. She was therefore reverting to her original decision to leave the country, and by the time he received this letter she would be on her way.

The letter dropped to the ground. The Prince's face had grown scarlet with anguish; he stalked into the house, past the members of the household who, having been warned of his coming, were waiting to give him an appropriate welcome.

He paced round the hall not seeing anyone. In vain did Southampton try to comfort him. He shouted; he wept.

'Pray remember your weak state, sir . . .' murmured Southampton.

But the Prince could only think of one thing: He had believed she was about to be his and she had gone—he did not even know where.

The King in his bedroom at Kew Palace awakened at five in the morning as was his custom and got out of bed to light the fire which his attendants had laid overnight. Then he returned to bed to allow the room to warm up before he rose and attended to the State papers which were on a table awaiting his attention.

Since young Mr. Pitt had taken office he had consoled himself that the Government was in good hands. Mr. Pitt was like his father had been, a trifle arrogant but courteous in his conduct to the King, yet somehow conveying the fact that while he was Prime Minister he intended to manage the country's affairs without royal interference. He might ask for the King's approval, but this was a formality and the King realized it. How different from Lord North was Mr. Pitt! But then if he had been like Lord North the country's affairs could not have been so skilfully managed.

The American Colonies . . . The King groaned at the thought of that major disaster. Rarely had Britain suffered such a humiliating setback. It would be remembered against him and North for ever. Any good he had done for his country—and he had given it a lifetime of service—would be weighted against that tragedy.

Never, never shall I forget it, thought the King. Where did we go wrong? At what stage could some action of mine make it turn out differently?

Back went his thoughts over the past. Little incidents chased themselves in and out of his mind, leering at him suddenly, mocking him, laughing at him until he thought they were mischievous pages who had broken into his bedchamber to play a game called Mocking the King.

What ridiculous thoughts came to him nowadays.

But once he had been strong. He had believed that a king should rule. In the days of his youth when he had been greatly in awe of his destiny and had believed that he would never be able to mount the throne without Lord Bute behind him, his mother had continually admonished him: 'Be a king, George.' Those words had haunted him in his dreams and when he had in fact become a king, when he had begun to take a grasp of State affairs, he had said: 'Very well, Mother, I will *be* a king.'

And he had tried to be.

When the country had been against continuing the war with the Colonists and he had wished to go on he had wanted to choose a cabinet and set himself at the head of it. That aroused even docile North to protest.

'Your Majesty is well apprised that in this country the Prince on the Throne cannot, with prudence, oppose the deliberate resolution of the House of Commons. Your Royal predecessors have been obliged to yield to it much against their wishes in more instances than one.'

That was the situation. In this country one was a king but no King. One was governed by a body of men called the Parliament and the King could be plagued by them. There were men like the Pitts. Old Pitt had been a brilliant statesman; to him could be accredited the founding of the Empire. Looking back that was plain enough; and his son Pitt the Younger was such another.

Poor old fool that some would think me, mused the King, I have sense enough to see that.

But these men of integrity such as the Pitts made up for their honesty with their arrogance. Young Pitt was an able man; he knew it; and he was determined to govern with concessions to none. Pitt blamed North's subservience to the King for the loss of the Colonies, and would have no interference with *his* Ministry.

'Young puppy,' thought the King and was immediately sorry. Mr. Pitt was no puppy: he was a brilliant statesman. Age had nothing to do with it. He had noticed that touch of genius from his father and he, the King, should be glad of it.

Moreover, Mr. Pitt was in opposition to Fox and any one who was in opposition to that man was a friend of the King's. Fox! The King's eyes bulged at the thought of that man. He more than any other was responsible for the sins of the Prince of Wales. He had heard that wherever the Prince was, there was Fox. The Prince doted on Fox; he confided in Fox; he treated Fox like a father; and there was that arch villain always at his son's elbow, teaching him to drink, to gamble and to live an immoral life with women. Mr. Fox thought this was the way a gentleman should live and the Prince was eager to learn.

Merely thinking of the Prince of Wales made the King's brain whirl. 'What next, I wonder,' he said aloud. 'What next, eh, what?'

He rose from his bed. The room was warm enough and he would start brooding on the activities of the Prince of Wales if he stayed there in bed. Better dress and look through the papers on his desk and be in time to take a dish of tea with the Queen.

He dressed thoughtfully. There were no ceremonies of the bedchamber at Kew. He was glad to escape from all that and it was the reason why he so enjoyed being at 'dear little Kew' as Charlotte called it.

Here he lived like a squire in a country village, and at the same time like a king of a little German Court whose law was absolute. Neither the determination of Mr. Pitt nor the villainies of Mr. Fox could interfere with life at Kew. If the King made some regulation then the household must obey, and no carping politicians could remind him that the King must submit to the rule of Parliament.

So at Kew he would make his rules.

He was horrified when he looked at himself nowadays. In spite of all the exercise he took and the careful manner in which he watched what he ate, he was growing fat. It was a curse no members of his family seemed to be able to avoid. It was unfair. After all his efforts to keep his body supple and agile, there was that disgusting paunch. His eyebrows had turned white and they were the more conspicuous because of his high colour. He was always depicted in the cartoons as being fatter than he was and he would be seated at a table laden with such foods as he had denied himself all through his life.

'It's the family tendency to grow fat,' he said; and he made more rigorous rules in the nursery.

And while the people sneered at him and lampoons and cartoons were circulated in the streets about him they admired the Prince and cheered *him*. That gambler, that drinker, that frequenter of prizefights, that *puppy* who was always chasing some woman or other—and in the most public manner—was admired.

And here he was back at the Prince of Wales.

But, he reminded himself, here at Kew it is different. Although he was not able to control the Prince of Wales he would see that those members of the family who were still under his control should toe the line. Frederick was in Hanover, learning to be a soldier; William was at sea; Edward would soon be going to Germany to study soldiering. That left only Ernest, Augustus and Adolphus among the boys at home—and the girls, of course, from Charlotte the Princess Royal who was eighteen to the adorable baby Amelia who was one, six girls in all. Quite a family, and he was going to see that they did not go the way of their eldest brother.

Though where I went wrong I fail to see. Perhaps I should abdicate. I lost the Colonies. Am I fit to be King? I sired the Prince of Wales. Am I fit to be a father? Well, the Princesses were a credit to him; they always sat so meekly in a little row and spoke when spoken to. They would be his comfort, and particularly his adored Baby Amelia. They must take care of her, he had told the Queen; the deaths of little Alfred and Octavius had been a terrible blow to them both. But there were thirteen left to them. Charlotte had been a good mother and a good wife, so he must not think of other more beautiful women. He wished he could get Elizabeth Pembroke out of his head.

She was a beautiful woman, and she was at Court, which made it rather more important not to think of her.

He came to Kew for rest and relaxation. He liked being at Kew; he liked Windsor too; both places were a refuge. At Kew and Windsor the people came out to see him when he rode past their houses. They dropped curtsies to him as though he were a country squire; and he would stop and ask how the crops were this year, and he could talk knowledgeably about the land, too. He ought to have been a farmer, some said.

But what was the use of trying not to think of the Prince of Wales. His son was in debt, and now there was some talk of his infatuation for a widow. The whole town was talking about it, singing songs about it.

It was no use trying to think of State papers. He would go and see the Queen.

The Queen was at breakfast with her daughters.

Charlotte, the eldest and Princess Royal, looked healthy enough; the others were a trifle pale. He looked at them anxiously for some sign of the family plumpness. He supervised their nursery diet in person; it was the same which had been in force when the Prince of Wales was lord of the nursery. Meat only on certain days and then all the fat was pared off; and if a fruit pie was cooked the pastry was not served to the children—only the fruit; but they could have as many greens as they wished. And they must take fresh air in plenty; they must walk, for exercise was good for them.

He was fond of them, but they were wary of him. It seemed he had gone wrong with his children as well as with his ministers.

'Good morning,' said the Queen and the girls stood up and curtsied.

He smiled at them. 'Having breakfast, eh, what? Eh? And not over eating, I hope. Don't want to be fat. Family tendency.'

The Queen said that it was not a tendency of her side of the family to be fat, and it might well be that the girls would take after her. 'Will Your Majesty take some breakfast?'

'Nothing but a dish of tea for me,' said the King.

'It is not enough,' scolded the Queen as she scolded regularly each morning and no one took the remark seriously.

The King drank his dish of tea and the Princess Royal thought how boring it all was and wondered when they would find a husband for her and she could escape.

She knew that outside the family circle people laughed at the

King and Queen. They called them dull and boring; and to listen to their conversation one must agree.

'How time flies,' the King was saying.

'I am always quarrelling with time,' replied the Queen. 'It is so short to do something and so long to do nothing.'

'It is long when we are young and short when we grow old.'

The Queen was looking pointedly at her daughters: 'Nothing angers me so much as to hear people not know what to do. For me I have never half enough time to do things. What makes me more angry still . . .' A sterner look at Princess Charlotte this time—'is to see people go up to a window and say ''What a bad day it is! What shall we do on such a day as this?'' ''Do?'' I reply. ''Employ yourselves and then what signifies a bad day?'' '

How dreary it all is! thought Princess Charlotte. No wonder George went wild when he escaped. Who wouldn't? And now he's chasing that widow and everyone is talking about him. Lucky George! I wish he would come here more often. I wish he would talk to us. The only time he ever came to see us was when he imagined himself in love with Mary Hamilton and that was because she happened to be one of our attendants.

What was the latest news of George? Perhaps the King and Queen would talk of him and forget their daughters were present.

But they did not, of course. They were talking of the festivals which the King had started this very year and which meant that everyone must be as enthusiastic about music as their Majesties. And I am not, thought the Princess. She was still a little resentful because the King had said she must have a concert for her birthday celebrations when she would rather have had a ball. 'Not like music,' the King had said. 'Well, Papa,' she had replied boldly, 'I do not think I have an *ear* for it.' 'No ear for it! What's that mean, eh? what? You'll have to *grow* ears for it. Music is something you have to learn to like.' And the Queen: 'His Majesty is quite right, Princess Royal. He expects every member in the family to love music!'

How wonderful to be married! As soon as they find a bridegroom for me, she thought, I will start making my wedding dress. I will put every stitch into it myself and all the time I sew I shall be telling myself: I shall soon be free.

She looked at her sister Augusta, who talked too much when their parents were not present and was impatient with the ceremonies of dressing; she allowed her women to dress her exactly as they wished and indeed were it not for them would look a positive scarecrow. As for Elizabeth she did not feel so irked by their restricted lives as the others; she could shut herself away in her room and write poetry. Mary and Sophia were too young to know very much about what they were missing.

The King was talking about the concerts in the Abbey which had been such a success and the box he had had set up there for himself and the Queen and another for the rest of the family. He mentioned Mr. Bates who had played the organ so admirably; and he personally had made arrangements that those who attended the concert should be able to see the organist.

He is so interested in little things, thought the Princess. No wonder everyone says he's an old bore.

'I've been speaking to Dr. Burney about the new arrangement of the *Messiah*. Dr. Burney is a most excellent man . . .'

How many times had she heard of the excellencies of Dr. Burney? How many times had she heard the arrangements for the concerts discussed? And Handel's name was constantly on his lips.

Well, I am eighteen, thought Charlotte, so surely they will find a husband for me soon. Six girls for whom to find husbands. It's quite a number.

'I should like to take a walk,' said the King to the Queen, which, thought the Princess, meant that they were going to discuss the latest pranks of George, for clearly the King wished to speak to the Queen alone and as he never discussed State matters with her—considering women unable to understand such weighty problems—quite obviously they were going to discuss that most fascinating of topics: the sins of George.

Oh, why could she not be there! Had he really gone through a mock marriage with The Widow? How exciting! And how typical of George! He was promising to give them as much fun over The Widow as he had over the actress Perdita.

'Princess Royal,' said the Queen, tapping her fingers on the table, 'my snuff box.'

Princess Charlotte rose hastily; she had forgotten this most important duty: to see that Mamma's snuff box was filled and ready for use. The King looked pained; the Queen continued to tap her fingers.

Really, thought the Princess, they care more about silly details like filling a snuff box than the loss of the Colonies.

They were now ready to go out.

The Princesses stood in a row, dropping curtsies, all remembering that they must not forget their dignity and behave as it

was called in the household *en princesse*, which meant that one
must never forget that one was a King's daughter and curtsey to
some and uphold one's dignity with others.

Lucky George, to have escaped this constant parental surveillance.

In the gardens the King walked with the Queen and for some
few minutes discussed the flowers, the paths, the planting of
shrubs and trees; then he came to the subject uppermost in his
mind.

'You have heard no doubt of the latest scandals created by our
eldest son.'

'I have,' answered the Queen. 'It is impossible not to hear.
Everyone speaks of it. Schwellenburg tells me that they are singing a song about him.'

'A ballad . . . not untuneful,' said the King, 'but it should
not have been written about a Prince of Wales.'

'I fear that he causes Your Majesty many sleepless nights.'

'I have had ten in a row.'

'Is there no way of curbing him?' The Queen spoke severely.
She had loved George best of all her children. She had been the
proudest woman on Earth, she had believed, on the day he had
been born; and when she had first seen the bawling lusty male
child that she had brought into the world that had been the happiest moment of her life. And she had doted on him. She still
looked at the wax image she had had made of him and which
she had kept on her dressing table for years. But this arrogant
dazzling young dandy was very different from that naked baby;
and because George had shown so clearly that he had little time
to give to his mother she turned against him now and then.
Sometimes she longed for him to come and confide in her, and
if he had she would have done all in her power to please him;
but since he did not, she gave way to her resentment in little
bouts of anger against him.

'Curb that young puppy? How, eh? How curb him, what?'

The Queen bit her lips nervously. She was terrified when the
King grew too excited because she remembered an illness he
had had some years ago when he had behaved in a very peculiar
manner, and she realized then that he was not quite sound in
his mind. Ever since she had been terrified that that illness would
recur.

When the King was worried, and she recognized this state of
mind by the rapid nature of his speech, her anxieties grew. One

subject which could bring the King to this state more than any other was the Prince of Wales.

'No, I suppose it is difficult,' she said soothingly.

'He's past twenty-one. He's got the people behind him. He's got that fellow Fox . . .'

Fox! Another dangerous subject.

'That man has something to answer for. I'd like to see him in the Tower.'

'If only you could order him to be put there.'

The King said testily: 'Kings in this country have no real power. They have to do what the Parliament says. How could I have Fox put away, eh? Tell me that? How? How? For what? For influencing the Prince of Wales in his drinking, gambling and fornicating habits, eh, what? Imagine them all getting up and screaming about that. Even Pitt would stand against it— much as he hates the fellow. No, we have to put up with Mr. Fox. The fellow is the biggest evil this country has ever known. He runs a gambling house, did you know that, eh, what?'

'I did not know,' murmured the Queen.

'Yes, Madam, a gambling house, and he is the boon companion of our son. He's living in sin I happen to know with a woman . . . a woman who was once our son's mistress, and they still visit and God knows what they do . . .' The King's eyes bulged as thoughts of the riotous living of his son, Mr. Fox and Mr. Fox's mistress came into his mind, and he imagined himself indulging in such practices with . . . women like Elizabeth Pembroke. 'Disgusting!' he cried. 'Eh, what?'

'Disgusting,' echoed the Queen.

'And he is in debt.'

'But you paid his debts.'

'That was some time ago. It does not take this . . . this . . . puppy long . . . to run up more debts. He gambles . . . gambles all the time. And Carlton House. Why, Madam, that is far more grand than anything you or I have, I do assure you. There is not a man or woman at this Court, I'll swear, who would not consider it a greater honour to be invited to Carlton House than to Buckingham House, St. James's, Kew, Hampton or Windsor.'

'Can it be so?'

'It is so, Madam. It is so. And now we have this Widow.'

'I have heard of her. They tell me she is a virtuous woman and has repulsed his advances.'

'A virtuous woman,' said the King; and wondered about her. He had heard that she was beautiful without being brazen, that she wore her hair unpowdered and her face unrouged and un-leaded. She sounded a good woman—and she had refused the Prince. 'H'm,' he continued. 'She is a good woman and I rejoice to hear it—but that young jackanapes is making a fool of himself by chasing her all over the place and telling everyone of his passion for her—talking of marriage, if you please.'

'That is sheer nonsense.'

'Everything he does is sheer nonsense. But I have asked to see his debts and I'll have a detailed account of everything he's spent before I see that they're settled.'

'Oh dear, what a trial he is. How could he have become like this?'

The King had the answer to that. It was: 'Fox.' He went on: 'Women chatter. If you hear anything about this affair you should let me know without fail.'

'Women chatter far too much.'

'That's true, and talk much nonsense, but this is an important matter. Nothing that comes to light should be ignored. I don't like these rumours of marriage. That's what makes me anxious.'

'It would be impossible for him to marry her. The Marriage Act would prevent its being legal.'

'I should not like him to go through a form of marriage with a virtuous lady.'

'He would never dare. He knows the law. Whatever madness he is capable of he knows that as Prince of Wales he dare not marry without the consent of you and the Parliament.'

'He should know that.' The King was silent; he was thinking of a youthful folly of his own. He wished he could forget it, but he doubted he ever would. Hannah Lightfoot, the beautiful Quakeress, with whom he had been in love when he was a younger man than the Prince was now, and with whom he had gone through a form of marriage, often came out of the past to remind him.

He dared not think of her. When he did he heard voices in his head. And he was as much afraid of those voices as the Queen was.

The Prince returned to Carlton House in a distracted state.

'What can I do?' he wailed. He summoned Georgiana and Charles James Fox. He demanded that they help him; they must advise him. Maria had fled. What was he going to do? He de-clared he could not live without her.

They sought to advise. Charles suggested a little patience.

Something would happen. Perhaps she would write. Georgiana offered comfort; but nothing could appease him.

'There is only one thing I can do,' he said, 'I must find her. I must cross to the Continent without delay.'

'You have forgotten,' Charles reminded him, 'that as Prince of Wales you cannot leave the country without the King's consent.'

'Then I must get that consent.'

'His Majesty will never give it that you may follow a woman you are hoping to make your mistress.'

'My wife,' cried the Prince. 'My wife.'

'Terms which, in this case, His Majesty would find synonymous.'

'I care nothing for His Majesty's opinion,' cried the Prince recklessly; which made Mr. Fox shake his head sadly, a gesture intended to remind the Prince, most tactfully, that His Majesty's opinion in this case was one which could not be ignored.

The Prince asked his father for an audience, and when the King received him the latter was pleased to notice that there was a new humility in his manner.

'Your Majesty, I have come to ask permission to go abroad.'

'Abroad. What for? The people won't have that. The Prince of Wales's place is in this country. Don't you know that, eh, what?'

'I have incurred many debts.'

'Natural enough . . . when you consider the way you live. Dashing all over the place . . . down to Brighton . . . Carlton House. And gambling too. What are your gambling debts, eh, what? And the money you spend on women. It does not surprise me that you have debts.'

'My expenses are great.'

'Must be . . . Must be . . . Gambling . . . women . . . they are very expensive pastimes.'

'Your Majesty cannot realize how expensive.'

There he was, the young rip. Sneering. What do *you* know of these things? No, thought the King, I have occupied my time with State matters. He wanted to shout that at the fellow, but he knew the sort of retort that would bring to those insolent lips. Perhaps it would have been better for the country if you had occupied yourself with gambling and women instead of politics. It might have been slightly less expensive than the loss of the Colonies.

They were always at the back of his mind—those Colonies. They and the Prince of Wales were the biggest anxieties of his life.

'And so,' said the King, 'you are in difficulties.'

'I owe money in all directions.'

'So you think you can run away and escape your creditors, eh?'

'I think it would be well to get away for a while.'

'And this is your reason for wanting to go?'

'Yes, sir.'

Liar, thought the King. You want to go in search of the widow who has run away and left you. Good sensible woman. To think that his subjects had to run away to escape the importunings of the Prince of Wales! A pleasant state of affairs!

'I could not give my consent to your going abroad,' said the King flatly. 'And I should like to have further details of your debts. I want an explanation of all details. And then we will see what can be done about settling them. And if this should be possible, I hope you will let this be a lesson to you.'

The Prince was not listening. He was frantic. Any other man could have been free to leave the country if he wished, but he was a prisoner.

He rode out to Chertsey. Fox was not at home but Lizzie was there to comfort him . . . if it had been possible to give him any comfort.

'Lizzie, Lizzie, what can I do?'

'There must be something,' she comforted. 'I will talk it over with Charles. There must be a way out.'

'I don't even know where she is. I've been to see the old buffoon and he talks about details of debts. How do I know how the money is spent? But he is determined I shan't go abroad. He knows why I want to go. Everyone gossips. And the sanctimonious old humbug preaches to me. ''Gambling and women,'' he says, and licks his lips because he's never had either.'

'Your Highness should plan calmly, I think.'

He seized her hands. 'How, Lizzie? How?'

'Well, let us think. If we could find out where she was, you could perhaps write to her.'

Letters! Soothing balm always! And he had a way with a pen which might move her. When she had thought he was dying she had relented so far as to allow him to put that ring on her finger, to sign the document. If he could move her with his pen. . . .

He looked hopefully at Lizzie.

'But where . . . where is she?'

'We shall have to find out.'

'And then I shall not be able to go to her. Then there are only letters. Oh, Lizzie, if you knew the *depth* of my feelings.'

'I do,' she said gently.

'You can't, I have never experienced this passion before during the whole of my life. I will never know another moment's peace until she comes back to me.' He threw himself on to a couch and covering his face with his hands, wept.

Lizzie Armistead told Charles Fox afterwards that although she had heard him express himself somewhat emotionally before she had never seen him act so violently. He was half laughing, half crying; he lay on the floor and rolled backwards and forwards; he struck his forehead and frightened Lizzie because she thought he was going mad.

'Your Highness,' she begged, 'I pray you get up and sit down. Nothing can be solved by rolling on the floor.'

'What can be solved standing up?' he demanded.

'Calm thinking might bring us to a solution.'

'Lizzie, I will tell you this: I shall forgo the Crown. If I cannot as heir to it marry where I will then I shall abandon my claim to it. I have my brothers. I shall sell everything I have—jewels, plates, everything. I shall find Maria and fly with her to America.'

America, thought Lizzie. A rather unfortunate choice. She wondered how the Americans would greet the son of the King who had been their greatest enemy.

But this was not the occasion to point it out to the Prince.

She had an idea. 'Your Highness cannot go abroad, that is certain since the King forbids it, but why should others not go and at least find out where she is. If you traced her you could write to her and I believe your letters would be most persuasive.'

'Lizzie,' he said. 'God bless you. You were always my good friend.'

There was one man who could find Maria if anyone could. That was the Duc d'Orléans, who was at this time in England. The Prince was certain that Maria had gone to France, because she knew the country well and it would be a second home to her. Orléans was living in London with Grace Elliott who, not very long ago, had been the mistress of the Prince of Wales.

Theirs had been a comfortable love affair—no protestations

of devotion on either side. Grace—known as Dally the Tall, because she had a tall and willowy figure and before her marriage to a Dr. Elliott she had been a Dalrymple—was a gay young woman who had had a host of lovers and she and the Prince had parted without regrets and therefore as the best of friends.

When the Prince invited Orléans to Carlton House and confided his troubles, the Frenchman was full of sympathy.

'She is in your country, I am sure of it,' cried the Prince. 'But I do not know where.'

'It should not be impossible to find out,' replied Orléans. 'Such a beautiful Englishwoman would create talk wherever she went.'

The Prince clenched his hands together at the thought of his infinitely desirable Maria in that country where men were noted for their gallantry. What if someone were able to offer her what the Prince was not . . . honourable marriage?

'I must find her,' he cried. 'I want to tell her that I will give up everything . . . simply everything in order to marry her.'

The Duc nodded sympathetically. He thought the Prince a fool who did not know what he was talking about. Give up a crown for this plump matron? Orléans had his eyes on another crown and from the reports he heard from his spies all over his country, and particularly those who prowled about the Palais Royale, affairs in France were working towards some sort of climax which could be very beneficial to the Duc d'Orléans.

He was a very ambitious man and although not yet forty, owing to the life he had led he had developed that revolting skin disease which made his hair fall out and his complexion hideous to behold; but these disabilities affected him little in society because they were offset by his fortune and his connection with the royal family of France.

It suddenly occurred to him that this might be a very propitious time to return to France, for if interesting events were about to take place it was as well to be on the spot.

He could go back to Paris, setting new fashions in his pink coat, top boots and leather breeches; he would have his English style carriage over there, introduce horse-racing; and at the same time let the people know how much better affairs were run in England than in France.

Here was an excellent excuse for returning. Not because affairs were taking an interesting turn; not because the news he heard from his spies was setting him on the alert; not because he wished to be at hand to help disconcert his cousin, the King, and the woman he hated most in the world, the Queen of France—but to help his friend and kinsman, the Prince of Wales, to find a woman who had run away from him.

'I doubt not that I could have her whereabouts discovered in a week or so.'

'Is that possible?'

'If I went to France and saw to this matter myself.'

'But . . . you do not wish to leave England.'

'In the service of my dear friend I would do anything.'

'You mean that you would . . .'

The Duc bowed gracefully. 'For you, my dear friend and Prince, I would do much.'

The Prince fell on to the Duc's neck and embraced him, forgetting for once that horrible skin disease.

And the Duc, full of plans, left with Grace for France where he set about introducing English fashions, undermining the throne of France and finding Maria Fitzherbert.

As he had predicted, this last was simple.

He discovered that Mrs. Fitzherbert had gone first to Aix-la-Chapelle, but because she did not wish to stay too long in one place and believed that it would be suspected that, in view of the fact that she knew that country well, she would have gone to France, had crossed the frontiers and was visiting The Hague.

So now he knew and he was all impatience to visit Holland. First, though, his debts must be paid before he could leave the country. The King had been brooding over those debts for weeks and had made no announcement. So he went to see him again.

The Prince had changed, and the King was quick to notice this. A little of the arrogance had disappeared; he looked pale—and, yes, he had grown a little thinner.

Some good has come out of this then, thought the King.

'Sir, you have promised to settle my debts.'

'I must first have a full account of how they were incurred. There is this item.'

Oh God, thought the Prince. What is he talking about?

'I want a full account of how this £25,000 is made up.'

'I have no idea.'

'But you must have an idea . . . a sum like this. How could you run up debts for that amount without knowing how, eh, what?'

'I tell you I have no idea.'

'Then you go away and think about it. I don't believe you can't know how such a large sum of money was spent. If it's a debt you're ashamed to explain then I ought not to pay it.'

'Sir, I wish to go abroad.'

'Well, *sir*, I should remind you that that is something you cannot do without my consent. And I do not give that consent. You understand me, eh? You understand, what?'

Miserably, his heart full of hatred towards his father, the Prince left.

But at least he knew where she was, and there was the comfort of pen and ink-pot. He wrote pages to her which gave him some pleasure. He would shut himself in his apartments and cover sheet after sheet. Although the Prince had been deeply affected by women since his adolescence he had never before been in love like this. The most surprising thing of all was that he remained faithful. No other woman could be of the slightest interest to him. All through the winter his only comfort was talking to his friends about his devotion to Maria, writing impassioned letters to her, keeping couriers running back and forth across Europe. These were often arrested as spies and only the help of the Duc d'Orléans saved them from imprisonment. When he explained that the mission of these men was love and not espionage they were immediately freed and given every facility to reach Maria.

But she stubbornly remained out of the country in spite of his appeals and everyone now understood that Maria Fitzherbert was not playing a waiting game in the hope of luring the Prince to indiscretion; she really was the deeply religious woman she had made herself out to be and she would not consider living with the Prince on any terms but marriage.

Sir James Harris, the English Ambassador to The Hague, came to London to report and the Prince seized the opportunity of sending for him.

Harris had been a friend of the Prince; and as ambassador in a country such as Holland over which the French and the English were fighting for control, he was often in the depths of intrigue. He was therefore in close touch with the King and his ministers, and understood many of the problems not only of State but of the royal family.

Like all those who wished the family well, he deplored the Prince's absorbing passion for a woman whom he could not marry and who had refused to live with him on any other terms.

If Mrs. Fitzherbert had given in, the problem would have been immediately solved; it was ironical, but it was Mrs. Fitzherbert's virtue which was causing such concern.

The Prince greeted Harris warmly at Carlton House and immediately came to the reason for his visit.

'I want to know whether it would be possible for me to go to The Hague as a private person, and if I did how would you, as the King's representative there, receive me?'

Harris was alarmed. So much depended on his answer, but he hesitated only briefly and said: 'I should be very sorry to see Your Highness in Holland otherwise than in a character which would allow me to receive you in a manner conformable with the respect and affection I bear Your Highness. Your coming abroad, however, without the King's consent, would imply that you came after having been refused it. You may rest assured that in this case I should have received orders as to how I should act on your arrival and however much these orders were in contradiction to my feelings, as the King's servant, I should be obliged to obey them.'

'I should be the last person to ask you to do otherwise. But what can I do? Am I refused the right of every other individual? Cannot I travel legally as a private person, without the King's consent?'

'It seems immaterial to know whether Your Highness can or not, since it is evident that you cannot with any propriety to the public or satisfaction to yourself, cross the seas without it.'

'Why not? I wish to travel economically, to be unknown and to live in retirement '

'I confess that no event would give me so much pain as an Englishman to see a Prince of Wales abroad under such a description.'

'But what can I do? The King suggests I put aside £10,000 a year to pay my debts at a time when, with the strictest economies, my expenses are twice my income. I am ruined if I stay in England.'

'Your Royal Highness will find no relief in travelling in the way in which you propose. You will be slighted or the object of intrigue.'

What can I do? The King hates me. He has hated me since I was seven years old.'

'His Majesty may be dissatisfied with Your Highness but surely he cannot hate you. I am convinced that nothing would make him and the Queen so happy as to restore their affections to you. This would be the greatest blessing to the nation and comfort to the royal family.'

'That may be so but it cannot be. We are too wide asunder.'

'I do believe Your Highness should try every possible means before you carry into execution your plan of travelling.'

The Prince sighed. 'I see I shall have to think it over.'

Couriers were leaving Carlton House for Germany as well as Holland, for the Prince was now writing not only to Maria but also to his brother Frederick. Frederick had been his close companion in youth and the affection between them had been great; they had helped each other out of many a scrape and the fact that they had been parted was an added grievance against the King. When the Prince had heard that his brother was to be sent to Germany to train for the Army, he himself had begged for a commission that they might continue to be together. Why could they not both serve in the English Army? Why must Frederick go to Hanover? All the objections had been ignored and the brothers parted. But they had declared they would be friends for ever.

Frederick had heard of the charms of Maria Fitzherbert and of his brother's devotion and how nothing would satisfy him but marriage with this lady; and he, who had been at his brother's side during the affair with Perdita, who had attended those clandestine meetings on Eel Pie Island to be at hand to give a warning if needed, now declared himself entirely at this brother's service over the matter of Maria Fitzherbert.

If necessary, wrote the Prince, he would give up the Crown, which would mean that Frederick would inherit it. Was Frederick agreeable to make this sacrifice?

Frederick replied that he would make any sacrifices for his brother.

Dear, dear brother, how cruel to keep them apart! Frederick must realize, the Prince reminded him, that at some time he himself might want to marry someone who was not acceptable as a future Queen of England.

Frederick's reply was characteristic of him. In that event there was William, Edward, Ernest, Augustus or Adolphus to step into the breach. There was one thing for which they must be grateful to their parents; they had been generous in providing substitutes should they feel unable to accept the Crown.

They could always laugh together. The Prince was a little more hopeful and the people in the streets were singing more than ever, with sympathy and interest in their emotional, love-sick, but never boring Prince of Wales:

> 'I'd crowns resign
> To call thee mine,
> Sweet lass of Richmond Hill.'

Maria wrote to him. He must forget her, she told him. It was no use his talking wildly of marrying her and giving up the Crown. This she appreciated but even if he disobeyed his father and was so imprudent as to follow her abroad, she could never marry him. She implored him to try to forget her.

She would always remember his devotion to her and be grate-ful for it; the memory of his fidelity and devotion sustained her in her exile; but he must not think of leaving England. It would be a fatal mistake which he would regret for the rest of his life—and she would never forgive herself if she allowed him to do this.

She thought of him often; she would not deny that she loved him. Yet if he came abroad she would never stay with him, but would make sure that he could not find her. This she meant and she begged him to be calmer, to wait a while, to see if his feelings changed in the next months.

He read and re-read that letter. It seemed to hold a gleam of hope; and at last he began to see that it would be impossible for him to leave the country and that no good could come of it.

That brilliant young man who had the appearance of having been born old, called on the King: William Pitt, the younger, whose great claim to the King's loyalty was that he was in opposition to Charles James Fox.

The Prime Minister had come to talk to the King about that disturbing subject the Prince of Wales, a subject equally dis-tasteful to both of them.

'His Highness,' said Mr. Pitt, 'has incurred many debts which Your Majesty feels should be discharged.'

The King grumbled about the follies of youth. Not that Mr. Pitt was very old, but being of an entirely different temperament from that of the Prince of Wales he would understand the King's meaning. There had been little time for youthful follies in the life of a young man who had become Prime Minister of England at the age of twenty-four: and to Mr. Pitt the so-called pleasures of the Prince were childish pastimes; how could the pursuit of a woman compare with his own quest for the Great Seal? Pitt was at the head of the country and there he intended to remain. He had no fears of the Prince's animosity; but he did fear Fox. There was a man brilliant enough to unseat him, one of whom he must be ever watchful. And the Prince had made it perfectly clear that Fox was his friend and Fox's politics his.

'Yes,' said the King. 'I feel these debts should be discharged. The Prince is living beyond his income and there are some members of the Government who feel that the income he receives is not adequate for a Prince of Wales.'

'Sentiments most forcefully expressed in the House by Mr. Charles James Fox,' said Pitt grimly. 'Has it occurred to Your Majesty that if we gave the Prince of Wales a sum of money with which to discharge his debts, a large amount of this might possibly be used for the advancement of the Whigs?'

The King looked startled. His brows bristled and looked whiter than ever because his face had flushed scarlet with rage. His eyes bulged and he cried: 'Eh, what?' three times while Mr. Pitt regarded him coldly. The King was rather incoherent sometimes and made Mr. Pitt very uneasy, for what if he were to become incapable and it was necessary to appoint a Regency? He saw the figure of the Prince grown powerful and beside him the shadow of a wily Fox.

No, the King must keep his place. He was after all a young man yet. He could not be more than forty-seven. Yet he had seemed to grow old during the last years.

Pitt went on: 'I think that the Prince's debts should be discharged on one condition.'

'Condition, eh? What condition?'

'That he breaks with the Whigs and Mr. Charles James Fox.'

The King smiled slowly. Nothing would please him more than to see that break. It was a good idea. Trust young Mr. Pitt to come up with the right answer.

The King decided to use Sir James Harris in his negotiations with the Prince and, sending for him, told of his conversation with his Prime Minister.

'Now, my dear Harris, you will go to the Prince and acquaint him with the conditions with which he must comply before his debts are settled.'

When Harris arrived the Prince burst out before he could say anything: 'If you have come to dissuade me from travelling, let me anticipate your kind intentions by telling you that I have put that idea out of my mind. My friends, as well as yourself, are against it, and I subscribe to their opinion.'

Harris expressed his satisfaction and told him that he had in fact come to speak about the Prince's debts.

The Prince listened horrified. 'Abandon my friends! How could I do that? Give up my opinions for the sake of money!'

'It would, Your Highness, bring about a reconciliation between you and your father. His Majesty is more distressed by your connection with the Whigs and Mr. Fox, than by anything else; and I believe that if you were no longer devoted to them there would be a basis for building up strong family affection.'

'No, no, my dear Harris, even if I would do this, there would never be a reconciliation. The King hates me. I will show you our correspondence over the last six months when I first asked his permission to go to Holland. You will see how I have attempted to be friendly with him and how he rebuffs me.'

'Sir, do you think it wise for me to see this correspondence?'

'Yes, I do, so that you may know how the King treats me. I wish the people knew what I have to endure.'

'I should be sorry indeed, sir, if the enmity between the King and yourself were public knowledge.'

'Read those letters,' commanded the Prince; and when Harris had done so he had to admit to the harsh uncompromising attitude of the King.

'If you would only marry,' sighed Harris, 'then I think there would be a happier relationship between you and your father.'

'I will never marry . . . as my father wishes. I have taken my resolution on that. Moreover, I have settled this with my brother Frederick.'

'Give me leave to say, sir, that you *must* marry. You owe it to the country, to the King and yourself.'

'I owe nothing to the King. Frederick will marry and the Crown will descend to his children. As for myself I do not see how that affects me.'

'Until you are married, sir, and have children, you have no solid hold on the affections of the people even while you are Prince of Wales; but if you come to the throne a bachelor and His Royal Highness the Duke of York is married and has sons to succeed you, your situation when King will be more painful than it is at the moment.'

The Prince turned away in anger, but hastened to assure Harris that it was not directed at him.

Sir James Harris could see that it was no use trying to persuade the Prince of Wales. He was bemused by his affection for this woman. In time, thought Harris, it will pass. It must, for she is abroad and he is here . . . and she seems to mean that she will not go to him.

But the Prince of Wales retired to his apartments to write to Maria, to swear eternal fidelity and to reiterate the words of the ballad. He would his crown resign to call her his. It was true. He wanted nothing but Maria.

Maria in Exile

During her first week or so abroad after her flight from England, Maria settled down in Aix-la-Chapelle where she took the waters and lived quietly while she considered the events which had led up to her departure.

She was unhappy, far more so than she had believed possible. In ordinary circumstances she would have enjoyed a brief stay at the spa—a brief stay, ah! That was the point. She had not come for a holiday, but as an exile.

She thought a great deal about the Prince and wondered how he had taken the news of her flight. He would be heartbroken and how sorry she was to inflict such suffering on him. She almost wished that she had not been brought up with such a stern religious outlook. So many women would have been able to reconcile themselves to the situation. If he had been anyone else but the Prince of Wales . . . But how stupid to think along such lines. He *was* the Prince of Wales, and there was an end to the matter. But was it an end to the matter? Was she to spend her life wandering round Europe, an exile from her native land? Nonsense, he would forget her in time. One day she would hear the news that he had fallen in love with someone else—someone more amenable than Maria Fitzherbert.

She revolted against the idea.

What has come over me? she asked herself. I am just a stupid woman who hates the thought of being alone.

One day when she was seated in the Assembly rooms after having taken the water a party of people came by talking in English. They paused and looked at her, and she pretended not to notice. But they were aware of her and she believed they knew who she was.

She left the Assembly rooms and hurried to her own suite. No doubt these English visitors were telling their friends that Maria Fitzherbert was in Aix-la-Chapelle.

She knew what it would be like. Everywhere she went people would stare at her; they would whisper about her behind her back. 'That's Maria Fitzherbert who fled from England to escape the attentions of the Prince of Wales.'

So, she thought, it has followed me here.

Visitors here on returning to England would spread the news; he would hear of it and might do something foolish such as coming over to be with her. What trouble that might cause she could not imagine. And now that she was so lonely, would she continue to resist if she had to listen to his pleading in person?

He must not know. He must never come here. She must not forget that he was the Prince of Wales and what he did could affect the whole country. Travelling through France she had noticed certain signs which had alarmed her. There was a shortage of bread in some towns and the people were murmuring against the aristocracy. She had seen pictures of the Queen portrayed in a most unflattering manner. At home there were lampoons and cartoons about the royal family, but these suggested a good humoured mockery. Here in France there was a sinister undercurrent which was perhaps more apparent to one who had come fresh to it—particularly after having known the country—than to those who had seen it gradually grow.

Maria did not wish to be the cause of trouble to the English royal family.

She must remain abroad for the good of them all.

But not, she had decided, in Aix-la-Chapelle where, because of its proximity to England, many English people came to take the waters.

She would go over the frontier to The Hague where it might well be that no one had ever heard of Maria Fitzherbert.

She had not been in Holland many weeks when she began to wonder whether her move had been a wise one.

The country, like France, was in a state of conflict, only it was different here. In Holland it was known that the republic was independent of the Stadtholder, and there was open enmity between them, whereas the feeling in France was subversive and all the more alarming because of it.

The Stadtholder wished to preserve good relations with England and was in favour of an alliance with that country. The influence of France, however, had been responsible for the break between the Stadtholder and the people of Holland, for the French wished to establish a state which relied on them and was completely under French influence.

One thing that pleased Maria was that here at The Hague no one seemed to have heard of the affair between the Prince of Wales and Maria Fitzherbert, so that she could enjoy a quiet anonymity which had been denied her in France.

She took a house not far from the palace and as a visitor of obvious wealth was soon drawn into a social circle. There were few English people in the town and those who were there had been there for some time so that they were unaware of events outside Holland; and it was not long before she had an invitation to attend the palace, for the Stadtholder, being a grandson of George II, was very ready to welcome any English visitors to the town.

Maria had always liked company and eagerly accepted the invitations. She found the Stadtholder charming; his wife no less so; and their daughter, a young girl in her teens, very interested indeed in all things English.

She gradually learned that the royal family were in a sad plight, that daily they expected a revolution which could mean the Stadtholder's losing his title and being banished from his country. He was a weak man and could not make up his mind as to which action to take which was, Maria thought, no doubt responsible for his present disastrous position. His wife, who was a niece of Frederick the Great, was talented and charming, and although she was fully aware of the precarious situation of her household, seemed able to dismiss the ugly problem. She wanted to hear about England and the manners of the Court there; and Maria told her, as best she could, leaving the Prince of Wales out of the conversation as much as possible.

The young Princess of Orange always expressed great pleasure when Maria visited the Court and it was not long before she discovered why.

One afternoon she received an invitation and when she arrived it was to find the young Princess waiting for her.

'Oh, Mrs. Fitzherbert,' she said, 'I want to speak to you alone.'

Maria was surprised and the Princess hurried on: 'I never get the opportunity. And I will speak to you in English. I have learned it and worked hard at it because I have a very special reason for doing so.'

'It is not easy to learn, I fear.'

'It is the most difficult language in the world. But I must learn it. I practise every day. And now that you are here, Mrs. Fitzherbert, it gives me an opportunity to practise on *you*.'

Maria laughed. 'Pray practise all you wish.'

'I will. Now please tell me about the English Court. Tell me about the King and Queen and *all* their children.'

'That would take a long time,' said Maria, 'if I knew very much about them. There are so many of them.'

'Very well I will be contented to hear about the Prince of Wales. Pray tell me of him. You have seen him, of course.'

Maria flushed slightly. 'Oh, yes, I have seen him.'

'I have heard he is very good looking. Is he?'

'Yes. He is good looking.'

'And charming?'

'Yes, charming.'

'He dances and sings like an angel. Is that true?'

'I have never seen an angel dance nor heard one sing.'

'Ah, but have you seen the Prince of Wales sing and dance?'

'Well, yes, I have.'

'That is good enough then. I hear he is kind, very clever and witty and wears dazzling clothes. Is this all true?'

'I suppose it is.'

'I think he must be the most *perfect* man in the whole world. Do you think so, Mrs. Fitzherbert?'

She was overcome with embarrassment. She wanted to ask permission to leave. She had an appointment; she had a headache; anything to get away.

'Do you, Mrs. Fitzherbert?'

She heard herself answer almost defiantly: 'Yes, I believe I do.'

The girl was smiling ecstatically. 'I was sure it was true. Now I know. The fact is, Mrs. Fitzherbert, I am going to marry him.'

'Your Highness is . . .'

The Princess nodded. 'Papa is determined on it. It's so important to him. He needs a strong alliance and he is determined that it shall be with England. So if the Prince of Wales will have me . . .'

She looked charmingly shy and Maria thought of phrases in those passionate letters with which he had bombarded her. 'I shall never marry anyone but you.' 'From now onward to the end of my life there shall be no one for me but my Maria.'

And yet, she thought looking sadly at the young girl, it was not impossible. It was far more likely that he should be this girl's bridegroom than her own.

Oh, how foolish she had been to come here! This was more embarrassing than Aix-la-Chapelle.

'I want you to come here often,' the Princess was saying, 'and then you can tell me all you know of the English Court and most of all of the Prince of Wales.'

When Maria left she was very disturbed. How could she tell this young girl that she was only here because she was eluding the pursuit of that same Prince? She felt so sly listening to these confidences; and yet how could she tell the truth?

She was not made any happier by the fact that as she left she noticed a man standing near her carriage. She had seen this same man loitering close to her house, and she had fancied that he was watching it. It seemed strange that he should be waiting near her carriage. Her coachman looked a little uncomfortable. It occurred to her that the man might have been asking questions about her.

Could it be that rumour had followed her as far as The Hague?

During the next few days she was summoned to the Palace on several occasions and there the Princess again plied her with questions.

'I have talked often,' said the Princess, 'to Sir James Harris. He is a very charming man and I believe very much in favour of the marriage. I want to discover whether he has given the Prince of Wales a good account of me. But of course I have to be very careful. Everything must be so diplomatic. But I am sure my father would have suggested he find out whether I would be welcome as the future Queen of England. Queen of England! What a grand title! Do you not think so, Mrs. Fitzherbert?'

Mrs. Fitzherbert thought it a very fine title.

'And married to the most charming prince in the world as well. It seems a great deal, does it not, Mrs. Fitzherbert?'

'Indeed it is a great deal.' Maria spoke wistfully. She thought: Yes, doubtless he will marry this girl . . . Or someone like her. And although at first he will think regretfully of me he will grow away from his sorrow. In a few years he will have forgotten how once he longed for Maria Fitzherbert. He is more suited to this girl. He a royal prince, she a royal princess—they are distantly related to each other, and both young. It is so suitable. Yes, it will undoubtedly be arranged; and when it is, I can safely return to England.

She felt a great sadness in her heart; she wanted in fact to talk of the Prince of Wales and his virtues. Surely the greatest of these was his fidelity.

'Sir James Harris will be arriving very soon,' said the Princess. 'I cannot wait for him to come. He may bring news. Who can say?'

Maria went back to her house and felt very lonely. How sad it was to be exiled from one's home! She was longing for the bustle of London and the charm of Richmond. What would she not give to be in her house at Park Street? She thought of the Prince standing there as he had that night when he had followed her home from the Opera. What outrageous adorably mad things he did! The idea of a Prince of Wales following a woman home and standing there in the road pleading for admittance, and then when it was refused feeling no rancour, only a great and abiding love.

She thought of Marble Hill—that wonderful view of Richmond Hill—and of the Prince driving up in his phaeton, having come with dashing speed from Carlton House.

I want to go home, she thought. I want to see him again. It was cruel to go away as I did.

Someone had ridden up to the house. She heard her servants talking; a great excitement possessed her and she went to the door of her room to listen.

The servant came to her. A courier had arrived from England. He had letters for her. She knew from whom those letters came; she seized them eagerly. He had discovered where she was. He had good friends on the Continent. He wanted her to know that he was steadfast unto death, that he would marry no one else but her, that he was exploring all possibilities; he might meet her in Hanover where they would live quietly together for the rest of their lives; he might fly with her to America; he wanted her to come back because he could not live without her; but whatever happened of one thing she could be sure: he would be faithful unto death.

She read through the letters. She felt alive again. Had she been obliged to travel so far to learn the true state of her feelings?

She shut herself in her room and kneeling by her bed she took her rosary in her hand and prayed for courage.

She knew what she must do. She must not answer those letters. She must leave The Hague. Not only could she no longer listen to the confidences of a young girl who herself hoped to marry him, but she must hide herself afresh, for the English

Ambassador, Sir James Harris, would soon be arriving in The Hague and she did not want him to find her here.

Maria left Holland and a few weeks later arrived in Paris. There she stayed for a while in the convent in the Faubourg St. Antoine with the English Blew Nuns of the Conceptionist Order with whom she had been educated. For a short while she was at peace there, living the days of her childhood over again, her life regulated by the ringing of bells. She confessed that she had fled from England to escape the Prince and was applauded for having taken the only step possible to a good Catholic.

Then she began to feel restive and would leave the convent and wander into the streets of Paris. She liked to watch the city come to life in the mornings when the streets were full of noise and commotion; she found pleasure in watching the barbers covered from head to foot in powder, the practitioners of the law, black clad like so many crows making their way to the Châtelet, and the lemonade sellers and the coffee women who stood at the street corners with their tin urns on their backs. And in the afternoons when the din in the city was intensified and vehicles of all kinds jammed the narrow streets, people crowded into the cafés to chatter of inequalities, of differences between rich and poor, the price of bread and of the new ideas which were being circulated. All men are equal; why should the rich live in luxury while the poor man could not find the price of a loaf of bread? Liberty and Equality were the watchwords of the day. In the carriages the quality rode by, splashing pedestrians with the mud of the Paris streets—the worst mud in the world, Maria remembered, for if it touched a garment it would certainly in time burn a hole there. It was foul smelling and sulphurous and people cursed as it splashed them. But the ladies, rouged and patched, their hair dressed fantastically high in the fashion set by the Queen of France, did not notice the murderous glances which followed them.

When she returned to the convent Maria discovered that the peace which she had at first found there was missing. She was not meant for the secluded life. It was not that she wished for the luxury of a court; if the Prince had been a country gentleman such as Mr. Weld or Mr. Fitzherbert she would have been delighted. She pictured their living in the country, entertaining their friends. Would he be content? How many times had he said that all he needed for contentment was to be with her? She had been a little sceptical in the beginning; but then she had doubted his fidelity which had now been proved.

He loved her. She believed that. Had he not tried to take his life because of her? What a dilemma—and was she solving it by running away?

The Paris streets which had once so delighted her now began to depress her. On one occasion she hired a carriage and rode out to Versailles. All along the road was the familiar noise and bustle: the great *carrabas* drawn by eight horses—the Versailles omnibus—carrying in its wickerwork cage some twenty people, and beside it the little '*pots-de-chambre*' gambolled along— more comfortable than the *carrabas* but exposing the occupants to all weather. Maria in her carriage was aware of the resentful glances cast her way. There was no way of escaping the growing animosity between the people with money and those without. How different it had been on that day when her parents had taken her there to see King Louis XV at dinner; she still had the dish which had contained the sugar plums. It might be that she would be invited to Court. This would most certainly be the case if it were known she were here. If the Duc d'Orléans should return to Paris, which was very likely, he would hail her as an old friend. Then her hiding-place would be disclosed once more.

Perhaps she should not stay in Paris; perhaps she should leave France altogether. She decided that she would go to Switzerland and very soon was on her way.

But after a brief stay there she was eager to return to France, which being like a second home to her seemed to offer a less cruel exile. Not Paris this time but somewhere quieter, in the country perhaps. She decided on Plombiers in Lorraine and there she took a fine old house and attempted to adjust herself to the life of the town.

It was not long, however, before her whereabouts was discovered, and letters from the Prince began arriving regularly. He kept her informed of everything that was happening between the King and himself regarding their future; and she was a little exasperated but entirely satisfied because he seemed to regard it as a certainty that in time they would be together.

Since the King had refused him permission to travel abroad, and everyone had convinced him that this was impossible, he had been taking other steps. He had already arranged with his brother Frederick to take his place.

Maria thought of the consequences of such an act. It would

have to be a solemn renunciation. And what if in the future he should regret?

There were thirty-seven pages in his flourishing handwriting telling of his devotion to her, how his only comfort was in writing to her, begging her to come back because if she did not he would die without her.

It was very touching, very appealing. Had any one woman, Maria asked herself, ever been so devotedly loved? He would give up his crown for her sake.

If I had not been brought up in this stern belief . . . She dismissed the thought; but she was thinking more and more of surrender.

Driving in her carriage one day she passed a man on horseback who bowed gallantly. He was extremely handsome and had the manner of a nobleman; and the next day she met him again. On the third day he pulled up beside the carriage and she had no alternative but to order her coachman to stop.

'Forgive me, Madame,' he said, 'but I felt I must stop to say what pleasure it gives me to see such beauty in our country lanes.'

Maria inclined her head and replied: 'You are very kind, sir. Good morning.'

'But I believe we must be neighbours . . . or at least not many kilometres separate our estates.'

'Is that so?'

'You are impatient to continue with your drive, I see, so I will introduce myself. I am the Marquis de Bellois and I know you to be the English lady who has honoured us by liking Lorraine enough to visit us and stay with us. I doubt not that we shall meet again.'

As her carriage drove on Maria was a little uneasy. The man had a very bold expression and she had no wish to become involved with him.

But the Marquis proved to be a man of purpose and it was not long before Maria found herself drawn into the social life of the surrounding country. It would have been churlish to refuse to know her neighbours and since she accepted invitations to the houses of the neighbouring gentry she must return those invitations. It seemed to her that in a very short time she was entertaining as frequently as she and Thomas used to do at Swynnerton. And always at her elbow was the Marquis de Bellois.

She was enchanting, he told her; she was like no one else. All other women were of no interest to him since he had set eyes on the incomparable Mrs. Fitzherbert.

She learned a little about this man. His reputation was far from good; he had all the graces that could be learned at Court— and the French Court at that; but he was an adventurer and she was a woman of fortune. Maria was no fool. She knew very well what was going on in the mind of the Marquis. He had debts; he was looking for a wife; and this beautiful young English widow would suit him very well. Moreover, there were rumours of the Prince of Wales's passion for her which was an added fillip.

Did he think, Maria asked herself, that she would accept him when she had refused her faithful, adoring and disinterested Prince? When she thought of her own fortune and that of the Prince she laughed aloud. Her income would not keep him in . . . shoe buckles. Yet he did not think of money. He thought only of his devotion to her. She had run away from him, caused him great pain, and yet he continued to love her.

When the Marquis asked her to marry him she refused immediately.

'But I do not take no for an answer,' he told her.

She smiled wanly; and was again reminded of her Prince.

But she was disturbed by the persistence of the Marquis, who was constantly in her house. He was determined, he said, quite determined; and she began to be a little afraid of him for there was something rather sinister in his persistence. She heard stories of his adventures with some of the village girls. What if he should attempt to trap her?

She gave orders to the servants that no one was to be admitted whom they did not know and when the Marquis called she arranged that one of her maids should be in the next room to come at once should she receive a signal.

And finally she decided that she could no longer endure this vague uneasiness. So one day, having made her arrangements, she very quietly left Plombiers for Paris.

Back to the convent and there to live the unsatisfactory life again. Paris was growing more and more uneasy. Everyone was talking about the strange affair of the Diamond Necklace. The Cardinal de Rohan had been arrested and there was a strong suspicion that the Queen was involved in the fraud.

In the streets, in the cafés and the lemonade shops they were discussing this affair; and there were horrible pictures passed round of the Queen—always wearing a diamond necklace—in revolting positions with her favourites, male or female.

The scene was growing uglier and the longing for London was almost too intense to be borne. In the streets men were wearing the jacket in the English fashion, in the shops they were drinking *le thé*; they were going to the horse-racing; all customs which the Duc d'Orléans had brought over with him from England, and to which the French took with a certain perversity because they hated the English and were constantly in conflict with them.

But this reminded Maria poignantly of home and as she had been away for almost a year she was longing to be back.

The Prince had one again discovered her whereabouts. What a good espionage service he had! she thought indulgently. She should come back to him. There should be an honourable marriage. All that she was holding out against could be dispensed with. If he were no longer the heir to the crown he could marry the woman of his choice.

But what of the Royal Marriage Act which stated categorically that a member of the royal family under twenty-five could not marry without the Sovereign's consent? And this was not just an ordinary member of the family. This was the Prince of Wales.

The Dukes of Gloucester and Cumberland had married without the King's consent, and their Duchesses were not received at Court but they were recognized as Duchesses. Yes, but they had married before the Bill was made law.

He could marry her (just as she wished, with a priest, he had said) but the State would not consider it a marriage. It was not the State that she was thinking of. It was the Church. If she and the Prince made their vows before a priest in the eyes of the Church they would be married.

In was, in fact, the laws of the Church that concerned her, not those of the State.

The Prince believed, he wrote, that his father would not frown on the arrangement. He had always hated him and Frederick was his favourite son—doubtless because he had not seen him for a long time; but the fact remained that the King would rather see Frederick the heir. Frederick had always been his brother's great friend and would make any sacrifice for his sake. He would marry the woman chosen for him, produce children and live amicably with the King and Queen, which could be the greatest trial of all.

What was Maria waiting for? She only had to return and the life of bliss would begin.

She was thinking of it perpetually. For a whole year she had lived in exile; and all that time he had never wavered. Surely that was proof enough of his devotion?

And if marriage could be arranged that would not offend the laws of the Holy Church . . .

But it would, of course it would.

Two voices argued within her. She knew that one was prompted by her head, one by her heart; and it was the first to which she should listen.

But she was lonely; she was homesick; and this year away from him had taught her one thing: she loved the Prince of Wales.

It was winter in Paris and the slushy mud of the streets had turned to snow. The air of tension in the streets was growing; there were rumours about the trial of the Cardinal de Rohan and his accomplices which would take place next spring.

Maria wanted to go home. She wanted the comfort of her house in Park Street, the rural beauties of Richmond Hill. She wanted the excitement of Carlton House.

Then she read in a Court Circular that the Marquis de Bellois was in Paris.

She wrote to the Prince of Wales. She was coming home. She could no longer live in exile and . . . without him.

The jubilant reply to this sent her into such ecstasies that she could no longer listen to the voice of reason.

She was going home; she was going to her lover—the man who was known throughout the country as the irresistible Prince Charming.

How could she—the woman who loved him more deeply than anyone else—refuse him?

Fox's Warning

Charles James Fox was very anxious. He discussed the new turn of affairs with Lizzie Armistead in their home at St. Anne's Hill, Chertsey; and she had rarely seen him so disturbed.

'It can only mean one thing, Liz,' he said. 'The lady would not have come home without a definite offer of marriage.'

'That's impossible. How can he marry her?'

'Knowing His Royal Highness I'll swear he has put up a good case to the lady. There is no one who can fit the case to suit his own personal needs like H.R.H.'

'Mrs. Fitz is no fool. He would have to offer a real marriage. No ring slipped on the finger at the point of death would suffice. He has tried that once and she wouldn't have it.'

'That's true, and it is what worries me. And there is something else, Liz. He did not tell me that she was coming home. He has kept the matter secret, it is true; but previously I have shared his secrets. He is planning marriage and he knows I can only dissuade him from it . . . so, characteristically, he doesn't tell me.'

'Perhaps it is not a real marriage he is offering her.'

'It cannot be a real marriage, but it is something she—and no doubt he—are deceiving themselves is. I see the most fearful disaster ahead, Liz. If he goes far enough he could lose the Crown.'

'What are you going to do?'

'I cannot let this pass. I cannot pretend I don't know what is going on. He is keeping his plans secret from me, which is very significant, but I must let him know how he stands. Damn it, Liz, I have always advised him in the past. I have guided him in

125

his political life. Where would he have been without me? And in those most important steps of all . . .'

'But he is only not consulting you because he fears that you will persuade him of the folly of what he proposes to do.'

'Princes like those who agree with them and applaud all their actions, however foolish. But I never did that. I have advised him honestly and he has had the good sense to appreciate this. I must let him know what danger he is in.'

'What do you propose?'

'To write to him. I will do it at once. He must be made aware of the consequences of such an act as he proposes.'

Lizzie nodded and brought out pen and paper.

> 'The Right Hon. C. J. Fox, M.P., to H.R.H. the Prince
> of Wales.
> December 10th, 1785.

'Sir,

'I hope that Your Royal Highness does me the justice to believe that it is with the utmost reluctance that I trouble you with my opinion unasked at any time, much more so upon a subject where it may not be agreeable to your wishes. I am sure that nothing could ever make me take this liberty but the condescension which you have honoured me with on so many occasions and the zealous and grateful attachment that I feel for Your Royal Highness and which makes me run the risk even of displeasing you for the sake of doing you a real service.'

Fox paused. It was indeed a delicate subject; and was he presuming too much on the friendship he believed the Prince had for him? Here was a spoilt boy just ready to grasp a long awaited treat. How would he feel about the friend who was attempting to spoil his enjoyment by explaining in detail how bad it would be for him? But I must, thought Fox. It could be ruin for him and the party.

He took up his pen resolutely:

'I was told just before I left Town yesterday that Mrs. Fitzherbert was arrived; and if I had heard only this I should have felt most unfeigned joy at an event which I knew could contribute so much to Your Royal Highness's satisfaction; but I was told at the same time, that from a variety of circumstances which had been observed and put together, there was reason to suppose that you were going to take the very desperate step . . .'

Again Fox paused. Could he refer to the Prince's cherished dream as a 'desperate step.' But what else could he call it? And indeed a desperate step was a mild way of expressing it. It was disaster.

'. . . (pardon the expression) of marrying her at this moment. If such an idea be really in your mind and it be not now too late, for God's sake let me call your attention to some considerations, which my attachment to Your Royal Highness, and the real concern I take in whatever relates to your interest, have suggested to me, and which may possibly have the more weight with you when you perceive that Mrs. Fitzherbert is equally interested in most of them with you.

'In the first place you are aware that a marriage with a Catholic throws the Prince contracting such a marriage out of the succession of the Crown. Now, what change may have happened in Mrs. Fitzherbert's sentiments upon religious matters I know not, but I do not understand that any public profession of change has been made; and surely, sir, this is not a matter to be trifled with; and Your Royal Highness must excuse the extreme freedom with which I write. If there should be a doubt about her previous conversion consider the circumstances in which *you* stand; the King not feeling for you as a father ought, the Duke of York professedly his favourite, and likely to be married agreeably to the King's wishes; the nation full of its old prejudices against Catholics, and justly dreading all disputes about the succession. In these circumstances your enemies might take such advantage as I shudder to think of; and though your generosity might think no sacrifice too great to make to a person whom you love so entirely, consider what *her* reflections must be in such an event, and how impossible it would be for her ever to forgive herself.

'I have stated this danger on the supposition that the marriage should be a real one, but Your Royal Highness knows as well as I that according to the present laws of this country it *cannot*; and I need not point out to your good sense what uneasiness it must be to you, to her, and above all to the nation, to have it a matter of dispute and discussion, whether the Prince of Wales is, or is not, married. All speculations on the feeling of the public are certain; but I doubt much whether an uncertainty of this kind, by keeping man's mind in perpetual agitation upon a matter of this moment, might not cause a greater ferment than any other possible situation. If there should be children from the marriage, I need not say how much the uneasiness (as well of yourselves as of the nation) must be aggravated. If anything should add to the weight of these considerations it is the impossibility of remedying the mischiefs I have alluded to; for if Your Royal Highness should think proper, when you are twenty-five years old, to notify to Parliament your intention to marry (by which means alone a *legal* marriage can be contracted) in what manner can it be notified? If the previous marriage is mentioned or owned will it not be said that you have set at defiance the laws of your country; and you now come to Parliament for a sanction for what you have already done in contempt of it? If there are children, will it not be said that we must look for future applications to legitimate them and consequently be liable to disputes for the succession between the eldest son and the eldest son *after* the legal marriage? And will not the entire annulling of the whole marriage be suggested as the most secure way of preventing such disputes? If the marriage is not mentioned to Parliament, but yet is known to have been solemnized, as it certainly will be known if it takes place, there are the consequences—First, that at all events any child born in the interim is immediately illegitimated; and next, that arguments will be drawn from the circumstances of the concealed marriage against the public one. It will be said that a woman who has lived with you as your wife without being so, is not fit to be Queen of England; and thus the very thing that is done for her reputation will be used against it: and what would make this worse would be, the marriage being known (though not officially communicated to Parliament) it would be impossible to deny the assertion; whereas if there was no marriage, I conclude your intercourse would be carried on as it ought, in so private a way as to make it wholly inconsistent with decency or propriety for anyone in public to hazard such a suggestion. If, in consequence of your notification, steps should be taken in Parliament, and an Act passed (which considering the present state of the power of the King and Ministry is more than probable) to prevent your marriage, you will be reduced to the most difficult of all dilemmas with respect to the footing on which your marriage is to stand for the future; and your children will be born to pretensions which must make their situation unhappy, if not dangerous. Their situations appear to me of all others the most to be pitied; and the more so, because the more indications persons born in such circumstances give of spirit, talents or anything that is good, the more they will be suspected and oppressed, and the more will they regret the being deprived of what they must naturally think themselves entitled to.

'I could mention many other considerations upon this business, if I did not think those I have stated of so much importance, that smaller ones would divert your attention from them rather than add to their weight. That I have written with a freedom which on every other occasion would be unbecoming, I readily confess; and nothing would have induced me to do it, but a deep sense of my duty to a prince who has honoured me with so much of his confidence, and who would have but an ill return for all his favour and goodness to me if I were to avoid speaking truth to him, however disagreeable, at such a juncture. The sum of my humble advice, nay, of my most earnest entreaty, is this—that Your Royal Highness should not think of marrying till you can marry legally. When that time comes you may judge for yourself; and no doubt you will take into consideration, both what is due to private honour and your public station. In the meanwhile, a mock marriage (for it can be no other) is neither honourable for any of the parties, nor, with respect to Your Royal Highness, even safe. This appears so clear to me that if I were Mrs. Fitzherbert's father or brother I would advise her not by any means to agree to it, and to prefer any other species of connection with you to one leading to so much misery and mischief.

'It is high time I should finish this long and perhaps Your Highness will think, ill-timed letter; but such as it is, it is dedicated by pure zeal and attachment to Your Royal Highness. With respect to Mrs. Fitzherbert, she is a person with whom I have scarcely the honour of being acquainted, but I hear from everyone that her character is irreproachable and her manners most amiable. Your Royal Highness knows too that I have not in my mind the same objections to intermarriages of princes and subjects which many have. But under the circumstances a marriage at present appears to me to be the most desperate measure for all parties concerned that their worst enemies could have suggested.'

Fox threw down his pen and frowned at the paper. Then he called: 'Liz. Come here, Liz.'

When she came he handed the sheets to her. She opened her eyes very wide. 'So much?'

'It has to be fully explained to him.'

She sat down and read the letter. 'He won't like it,' she said.

'It can't be helped. I must put the case to him. There'll be disaster if he marries this woman.'

'He won't thank you for being the prophet on this occasion.'

Fox shrugged his shoulders. Lizzie remembered that he had always been a man of integrity where politics were concerned. It was no doubt the reason for his feud with the King.

This could mean, thought Lizzie shrewdly, the end of friendship with the Prince of Wales. Charles was right, of course; but he was advocating a course of action which was completely contrary to the Prince's desires; and although the future would doubtless prove Charles right, the Prince would not thank him any more for that.

No need to point this out to Charles who knew it already.

As a politician and a friend Charles was doing his duty.

She watched him seal the letter and send for the messenger.

When the Prince received the letter he took it to his bedchamber so that he might be quite alone to read it.

So Charles had ranged himself with those who would disapprove of the marriage. What depressing reading! The more so because in his heart the Prince realized the wisdom of Charles's comments.

Charles was a rake. He could not understand a woman like Maria; he did not in his heart believe that the only way she would live with the Prince was if a marriage was performed. There *must* be a marriage. Without that he would lose her. He wanted to shout at Charles: Do you think I don't know all that you say has some truth in it? Of course I do. But it's no good. There *must* be a marriage ceremony and I am going to see that there is one. I have promised Maria. She has come back to England for this purpose. The next step *is* a marriage ceremony—and it is inevitable.

Why must Charles plague him? It was not like Charles. His friendship had always been amusing as well as instructive; they had had such gay and pleasant times together; and in this, the most important event of his life, Charles was against him.

If Charles was going to preach against the marriage, then he must not be in the secret. He must not know what was taking place. In fact very few people were going to be in the secret, the fewer the better. He would not, of course, show Fox's letter to Maria. He would show it to no one. He must try to placate Fox, allay his suspicions, and at the same time go ahead with the arrangements for his marriage to Maria. But Charles was too shrewd to be put off with anything but a denial.

He sat down and wrote:

> 'H.R.H. The Prince of Wales to the Right Hon. Mr.
> Charles James Fox, M.P.
> 'My dear Charles, Your letter of last night afforded me more satisfaction than I can find words to express; as it is an additional proof to me (which I assure you I do not want) of your having that true regard and affection for me which it is not only the wish but the ambition of my life to merit. Make yourself easy, my dear friend. Believe me, the world will soon be convinced that there never was any ground for these reports which of late have been so malevolently circulated . . .'

He paused. And that, he admitted, was a deliberate lie. But what can I do? he asked himself. How can I admit to Charles that I am determined to go through a ceremony of marriage with Maria because it is the only thing that will satisfy her. Maria will believe in our marriage . . . and so shall I and if necessary I will resign the Crown.

He took up his pen to write a political acquaintance—a Whig who had recently changed sides and become a Tory.

> 'It ought to have the same effect upon all our friends that it has upon me—I mean the linking of us—closer to each other; and I believe you will easily believe these to be my sentiments; for you are perfectly well acquainted with my ways of thinking . . . When I say my ways of thinking, I think I had better say my old maxim, which I ever intend to adhere to; I mean that of swimming or sinking with my friends. I have not time to add much more except to say that I believe I shall meet you at dinner at Bushey on Tuesday; and to desire you to belive me at all times, my dear Charles, most affectionately yours.
>
> George P.
> 'Carlton House, Sunday morning 2 o'clock.
> December 11th, 1785.'

As he sealed the letter he felt uneasy.

Then he demanded of his reflection in the mirror on the wall: 'But what else could I do?'

The Ceremony in Park Street

Much as he tried to forget Fox's letter, the Prince could not. Phrases from it kept coming into his mind. It could not be a real marriage. There was that obnoxious Marriage Act haunting him; it might have been designed by his father especially to plague him. His uncles, Cumberland and Gloucester, had escaped it, although it was due to their actions that it had been brought into force. Why should not a man be allowed to marry where he pleased?

On one point the Prince had made up his mind: nothing was going to stop his union with Maria.

When he was with her he was in such transports of delight that he forgot mundane necessities. He could only think of the arrangements that must be made quickly so that she could consider herself his wife. The Maria who had returned from her travels was more enchanting—if that were possible—than the one who had left England; for now in her serious way she admitted her love for him.

'I don't deserve it. I don't deserve the love of a pure good woman like you, Maria,' he cried.

He looked back on the man he had been—at all those sordid intrigues with women. He regretted them; he confessed to them with tears to Maria. He was unworthy of her; but she embraced him and said that it was the rest of the world who would consider *her* unworthy and she would never forget all he was prepared to give up for her.

'You will see,' he cried. 'Maria, there is nothing in the world I will not do for you. I cannot wait for the ceremony to be performed. Why does there have to be this delay.'

133

'We have waited so long,' replied Maria tenderly, 'that a week or so is not much more.'

'It seems an age to me . . . as every minute does away from my beloved White Rose. Ah, Maria, so you are a Catholic and therefore a Jacobite, I believe. An enemy of the House of Hanover!'

'There is one member of that house to whom I will be faithful unto death do us part.'

He repeated the words ecstatically. He could not wait to say them before a priest.

'Gardner has not yet succeeded in getting an undertaking from Rosenhagen to perform the ceremony,' he commented grimly.

She was anxious. 'Do you think we shall be unable to *find* a priest to marry us?'

'I'll find a priest. Have no fear of that.'

'Still, Colonel Gardner does seem to be having difficulty. So you think . . .'

She paused and when he tenderly urged her to continue she said: 'Colonel Gardner is not only your private secretary but your very good friend. He may think it in your interests *not* to find that priest.'

The Prince was alarmed, remembering Fox's letter.

He grew a little pink and said: 'He had my instructions. He will obey them.'

'Then perhaps it is Rosenhagen who is reluctant.'

'Rosenhagen will do what is required of him, my dearest.'

A particular phrase from Charles' letter occurred to him: 'If I were Mrs. Fitzherbert's father or brother I would advise her not to agree.'

Her father was still living but more dead than alive having suffered a paralytic stroke some years before, so he would not be in a position to raise any objections; but she had brothers and an uncle who had taken a particular interest in her. What if they should write to her as Fox had written to him?

'Your family should be present at our wedding. Do you think so, my love?'

She turned to him all eagerness. How lovely she was when animated. It was something she had hoped for but had hardly dared to suggest.

'You had dared not suggest it! Oh, am I such an ogre then? Do you so fear to offend me . . . you who did not hesitate to break my heart when you ran away and left me?'

'How could I believe that it would be broken merely because I went away? And I promise most faithfully to do such a skilful job of repairing it that you will never notice the cracks.'

He laughed; he embraced her; and then he said that her family should be presented to him. Her brothers, her uncle—he wanted to ask them in person to their wedding.

She was pleased, so he was happy.

He sang for her and what better choice than that popular ballad.

She listened fondly. Each day she grew more attached to him. She wanted this wedding as eagerly as he did; and what more appropriate song than that which was so popular throughout the town.

> 'I'd crowns resign
> To call thee mine,
> Sweet lass of Richmond Hill.'

Colonel Gardner reported with some concern that the Reverend Philip Rosenhagen had written that it would be against the law for him to perform a ceremony of marriage between the Prince of Wales and Mrs. Fitzherbert.

'Did you tell him,' demanded the Prince, 'that I pledge myself to keep the matter a deep secret?'

'I did, sir, and his reply was that he dare not betray his duty to you.'

'What! Rosenhagen! When has he developed such a sense of duty? He has performed many a shady trick in his life, I can tell you. Why has he suddenly become so virtuous? Did you hint that there might be preferment for him if he obliged us on this occasion?'

'I did, sir. But I think he was after some specific offer.'

'Bribery?'

'I think so, sir.'

'Try someone else.'

'I thought of that, Your Highness. There is the rector of Welwyn in Hertfordshire, the Reverend Johnes Knight. He is no ordinary parson as you know, but a man of wealth—not particularly ambitious. He doesn't need to be. He has been to Court now and then. Your Highness may not remember but he is a friend of friends of Your Highness's. I have ascertained that he is at this moment visiting Lord North at Bushey and I propose—with Your Highness's permission—to write to him there and ask him to come to Carlton House. I think he might be willing to perform the ceremony.'

'Do it, Gardner. I confess I find all this delay irksome.'

It was more than irksome. It was faintly alarming. Fox's letter had done it. If Fox felt so strongly, so might others. One could never be sure who was going to hold up hands of disapproval. And if all these arguments against their union were to reach Maria's ears, who knew what she would do? He simply must not allow her to leave him a second time.

In the meantime he was going to meet her family; he was going to persuade them of the advantages of this marriage in case these disturbing impediments were put to them.

The Reverend Johnes Knight was playing a round game in the drawing room of Lord North's house in Bushey when a messenger arrived from Carlton House with an invitation for the clergyman to dine with the Prince of Wales.

Lord North looked a little startled that his guest should have received such a letter and agreed that he should set out without delay for Carlton House; but the gravity of his lordship's expression set the Reverend Johnes Knight wondering what it could mean, and when Lord North drew him aside and whispered that if he were wise he would tell no one of the summons to Carlton House until he had ascertained what was required of him, he was a little uneasy.

'I am merely to dine with the Prince,' he said.

Lord North raised his eyebrows. 'I should imagine that something more will be asked of you than your company at dinner.'

It was possible. When previously had the Prince invited the Reverend Johnes Knight to dine with him? The answer was: Never before.

With some trepidation he presented himself at Carlton House where he was conducted to a waiting room, and when he had been there a very short time one of the Prince's gentlemen, Edward Bouverie, came to say that the dinner party was cancelled. The Prince, however, would see him if he would present himself at Carlton House on the following morning.

Somewhat bemused the Reverend Johnes Knight left Carlton House and feeling hungry went into the Mount Coffee House to have a meal.

As he stepped inside he heard his name called and there saw an old friend of his, a Colonel Lake, who asked what he was doing in London at this time. Remembering Lord North he prevaricated for a while but let out that he had called at Carlton House, at which the Colonel grew very alert. He was to have dined there, the clergyman proudly explained, but the dinner had been cancelled and he had looked into the coffee house for something to eat.

'Why not dine with me?' suggested the Colonel, and the clergyman was delighted to have company, for he was a man who was not fond of being alone.

Over dinner they talked of friends and politics and at last the subject of the Prince's infatuation for Mrs. Fitzherbert was mentioned.

'I would not have believed he could have been so affected. Why, when she went away he was well nigh demented. There is no doubt about it, he is deeply enamoured of this woman.'

'What a pity that she is not a German Princess. What a happy situation that would be! But alas, life does not work out as conveniently as that.'

'Unfortunately not. The Prince is a charming young man and I should like to see him happy. I see no solution to his problem. She won't live with him without marriage; and how can he marry her?'

'Alas, it seems that they are faced with an impossible situation.'

The Colonel gave his companion a shrewd look. 'There is no way out. They may seek some clergyman misguided enough to perform the ceremony.'

'Do you think they will?'

'I should hope not. What would your opinion be of a member of your profession who so far forgot his duty to the Crown and to the State as to do such a thing?'

'It would be quite wrong, of course.'

'I trust no clergyman would do such a thing. I am sure that if such a request were made to you you would refuse. That is so, is it not?'

'Why—yes, yes of course I should refuse.' The Reverend Johnes Knight felt a little sick; he had lost his appetite.

When he left the Colonel he went to his parents' house in Stratford Place where he spent the night; to their questions as to his business in town he was evasive, and the next morning presented himself at Carlton House.

There he was not kept waiting long but was conducted to the Prince's bedchamber where His Highness, wearing a dressing gown as though he had just risen from bed, was waiting for him.

'My good friend . . .' he began, his eyes warm with affection, and the Reverend Johnes Knight felt in that moment that he would do anything to please such a charming Prince.

'I must offer my apologies for bringing you up from Bushey and being unable to see you last evening. Circumstances . . . circumstances . . .'

The Reverend Johnes Knight murmured that it was such an honour to be received by the Prince at any time and he would make a hundred journeys up from Bushey for such a pleasure.

'For a very long time,' said the Prince confidentially, 'I have been deeply in love with a good and virtuous lady. I shall know no peace until she is my wife. At one time I was so desperate that I attempted to take my life and should have done so had my doctors not saved me in time. I have suffered greatly by the attitude of my father towards me. I should tell you, my dear friend, that he hates me, that he greatly regrets that my brother Frederick is not his eldest son. I have suffered . . . how deeply I can never explain.'

The Reverend Johnes Knight expressed his sorrow at the Prince's sufferings.

'I knew you would,' went on the Prince, 'because I believe that you are deeply attached to me. Is that so?'

'It most certainly is, Your Highness.'

'Then I am going to ask you to give proof of that attachment. I am going to ask you to perform a marriage ceremony between myself and Mrs. Fitzherbert.'

'Your Highness, I could not do it. It is against the law. The Marriage Act stands in the way, sir. It would be criminal of me to perform such a ceremony.'

'As soon as I am on the throne that iniquitous Marriage Act will be repealed.'

'I am sure it will, sir, but now it is in force and I cannot therefore . . .'

The Prince paced up and down the room, a look of blank despair on his face.

Then he turned to face his visitor. 'So you refuse me?' he said plaintively.

'Your Highness it is with the deepest regret, but I must.'

'If you refuse I must find a clergyman who will.'

The Reverend Johnes Knight was torn between his desire to serve the Prince and what he knew was his duty. He might, it was true, find someone to marry him, but what sort of clergyman would he be? Someone who would ask for preferment for performing the task; someone who would have to be bribed, someone who might betray the Prince's secret to Mr. Pitt if he were offered a bigger bribe to do so.

He pointed this out to the Prince who grew more and more melancholy. 'It is for this reason that I wished you to help me. I wanted an honest man to come to my assistance. Ah, so many people swear they will serve me . . . but only when it pleases them to do so.'

The Reverend Johnes Knight was young and impressionable and the Prince was well aware of this. He went on talking of his sufferings, of the manner in which the King had ill-treated him, of his enduring love for the most virtuous of women; and at length the Reverend Johnes Knight cried out: 'I will do it. For Your Highness I will do it.'

At which the Prince embraced him and said that never never would he forget his very good friend.

At the house in Park Street the Prince of Wales met Walter and John Smythe and Henry Errington. Dressed soberly by his standards in a green coat of the finest cloth and white leather breeches he looked quietly elegant; but the diamond star on his left breast and the diamond buckles on his shoes made it impossible to mistake him for any but the Prince of Wales.

He greeted the men with a warm friendliness which implied that this was for him a very solemn occasion. His emotions—superficial as they often were—were constantly displayed for everyone to see. Tears would fill his eyes when he spoke of friendship and at the sentimental words of a ballad. It was one of the reasons why he drew people to him; he made them feel in the short time he was with them that they were of importance to him.

Henry Errington had come with some misgivings. Seeing himself as a guardian of the family since his brother-in-law was incapacitated he felt it was for him to look after Maria's interest and he was a man of the world enough to know that a marriage with the Prince of Wales could not be recognized by the State because of the Royal Marriage Act.

'Pray be seated,' said the Prince. 'I am delighted to make the acquaintance of my dearest Maria's family. I want to explain this situation to you for it will grieve me deeply if I cannot dismiss your concerns . . . which, believe me, I fully understand.'

He crossed his legs gracefully; John Smythe's eyes were dazzled by the diamond shoe buckles but more so by the easy manners of the Prince. He kept telling himself that this glittering personality was proposing to become his brother-in-law. His sister Maria was the most talked of woman in England; and when the Prince of Wales spoke of her there were tears in his eyes.

She was, the Prince went on to say, all that he asked in life. He would willingly give up the crown for her sake; this marriage that was about to take place would be in the eyes of the Church a true marriage. He, who respected Maria as he could no one else on Earth, was determined on this. He was in an unfortunate position. He spread his hands deprecatingly—very white hands adorned by a few fine diamonds—and the star on his breast flashed as though in defiance of this statement. But he was going to marry Mr. Errington's niece, Walter and John Smythe's sister. If he could make her the Queen of England that would be the greatest joy of his life. Who knew . . . When he became King he would instantly repeal the Marriage Act. What he wished to impress on his dearest Maria's family was that his intentions were entirely honourable. He respected Maria as a pure good woman and he was going to see that everyone else did the same.

John stammered that this was a great honour to their family; and he trusted that Maria would be worthy of such a Prince.

John was won over; Walter quickly followed. The uncle was not quite so ready; so the Prince turned his attention to him.

He need have no fear, he assured him. He understood of course, his misgivings. He himself would have had them in similar circumstances; but if he would but trust him . . . 'well, I shall be your nephew by marriage, shall I not? . . . If you will but trust me, you will not be disappointed in it. I promise you.'

How could Henry Errington hold out against such charm? How could he—a humble country gentleman—resist the honour of becoming uncle to the Prince of Wales?

'I see,' he said, catching the Prince's emotion, 'that my niece must be a very happy woman to have inspired such . . . such disinterested devotion.'

The Prince was all smiles. That battle was won.

'I shall expect you at the ceremony,' he said. 'Uncle Henry, you must give the bride away.'

He rose, thus dismissing them. He was eager to be back with Maria.

When he left the Prince the Reverend Johnes Knight walked through the streets of London deep in thought.

What had he done? He had promised to perform a marriage between the Prince of Wales and Maria Fitzherbert, an act which he knew to be illegal. Moreover, he had given his word to Colonel Lake, who had suspected rightly that this was the reason why he had been summoned to Carlton House, that he would have nothing to do with the affair.

Not only had he committed himself to an illegal act but he had lied to a friend.

As far as performing the ceremony was concerned he would not have been so worried. After all, this was the Prince of Wales who could at any time be the King. He did not believe he would come to much harm through the act. But what had Colonel Lake said to him? Had he not asked him if he would do such a thing, and had he not given him his word that he would not?

If only the Prince of Wales had received him when he had arranged to. If only he had not gone into the Mount Coffee House he would not have given his word to Colonel Lake.

But he had and he *had* given his word and he would be not only a clergyman who had failed in his duty—but a liar into the bargain.

Moreover, why should Colonel Lake have been so insistent? He was one of the true friends of the Prince of Wales. It would only have been because he knew that the marriage could bring harm to the Prince that he was so much against it.

'I cannot do it,' he said.

Back at Stratford Place the Reverend Johnes Knight sat down to write a letter to the Prince of Wales.

It was difficult, but he knew he had to do it.

He took up his pen and began. He was a devoted servant of the Prince's, he explained. He wished to please him. He would have sustained any loss that might have been his; he would have suffered any punishment that he might have incurred by breaking the law; all this he was ready to do for the Prince's sake. But before his interview with the Prince he had given his word to a friend that he would not perform the marriage ceremony and this promise had—because of the Prince's eloquence—slipped out of his mind. He was in a most unhappy state, but he could only crave His Highness's pardon while being sure he would understand the position in which his humble servant found himself.

After having written and despatched the letter, Knight waited the answer with trepidation.

It was not long in coming. The Prince's reply was kind; he did not reproach Knight but commanded him to present himself at the house of Colonel Gardner which was in Queen Street.

Colonel Gardner was waiting for him on his arrival. He received the clergyman coolly and remarked that it was regretful he had not recalled his promise to a friend before the Prince had told him of his intentions.

'I admit it,' said Knight. 'I cannot tell you how deeply I regret my conduct.'

The Prince arrived and was cordial though disappointed. He did not believe that it would be impossible to find a clergyman who would comply with his wishes, although the first two had defaulted.

'I should like to know,' said the Prince, 'who this friend is who extracted this promise from you.'

'Your Highness, I could not tell even you that and I beg of you not to ask me.'

'It was Lord North, I'll swear. You were at his house when I sent for you.'

'Sir, I do assure you that it is not Lord North.'

'Well,' said the Prince, 'you have shown us that you are a man to respect a promise. Now I shall ask one of you. I want you not to speak to anyone of what has passed between us and to destroy any correspondence concerning this matter.'

'Your Highness,' cried Knight fervently, 'I give you my word.'

'I accept your word,' replied the Prince.

It was dismissal, and thankfully the Reverend Johnes Knight came out into the cold December air.

When he had gone the Prince turned mournfully to Colonel Gardner.

'So,' he said, 'we are still without our officiating clergyman.'

But this was soon rectified. Colonel Gardner had discovered a man who would do what was asked.

'Your Highness,' explained Colonel Gardner, 'I have on this occasion taken a different approach. I believe that had we offered Rosenhagen a sum of money in the beginning we should not have had these unfortunate incidents. I am therefore offering £500 to this man and Your Highness's promise of preferment.'

The Prince nodded. 'And he has accepted?'

'With alacrity, sir. He is not a worldly rogue like Rosenhagen, nor an honest man like Knight. He is a young curate, ambitious, eager to marry, and looking for honours in the Church. Just the man to be prepared to take a risk in the hope of getting them.'

'And you think there'll be no hitch this time?'

'None at all. He is the Reverend Robert Burt who has but recently taken Orders. I am sure that it is now safe to go ahead with our plans. I have impressed on this man the importance of secrecy.'

'Importance indeed!' agreed the Prince. 'You know, Gardner, that if this got to Pitt's ears he could have it stopped.'

'Yes, sir. But I do not think we shall have trouble from Burt. He is most eager to serve Your Highness and for . . . preferment. He will have to be given a living after the ceremony.'

'He shall have it.'

'And a good one, sir.'

'There is one at Twickenham . . . a very comfortable one . . . in Mrs. Fitzherbert's own parish there. That would be most appropriate, Gardner. He shall have that.'

'Then I am sure we need have no fear. If Your Highness's enemies had wind of the affair and tried to bribe him they could not give as much as that.'

'I would have preferred to deal with a man like Knight.'

'It is difficult to find men like Knight who will act in circumstances like this.'

'That infernal Marriage Act. By God, that will go as soon as I'm on the throne.'

Colonel Gardner was silent. The Prince, by marrying a Catholic, might very well have forfeited his right ever to mount the throne.

'I will give him his instructions, Your Highness. The ceremony will take place at night. That will be safer, I'm sure.'

'At night,' agreed the Prince.

'Say between seven or eight o'clock . . . at Mrs. Fitzherbert's house in Park Street.'

The Prince nodded.

'I will tell Burt that he must be walking along the street with an air of casualness. He will be met by a gentleman who shall make a comment . . . as yet to be decided . . . and who will bring him to the house where we shall be waiting for him.'

'That is good. Ah, Gardner, my dear friend, we are moving at last. It will not be long now.'

On the evening of the 15th December the little party was gathered in Park Street.

The Reverend Robert Burt walking slowly down Oxford Street and turning into Park Street was stopped by a man who greeted him as he had expected, and together they walked down Park Street to the house of Mrs. Fitzherbert which they unostentatiously entered. Assembled in the drawing room was Mrs. Fitzherbert with her brother John and her uncle Henry.

As soon as the clergyman had been ushered into the drawing room the Prince arrived. He had come very quietly on foot from Carlton House and with him was his friend Orlando Bridgeman. He had chosen Orlando who was about the same age as he was himself and had been a friend of his for some time; he was the Member of Parliament for Wigan and therefore one of the Prince's more serious friends. Moreover, being a Shropshire man he was acquainted with the Smythes, and Maria knew him well, so he seemed an admirable choice.

The Prince had explained to him that it was a friendly act to take part in this ceremony and that he was not allowing Colonel Gardner to be present because if it were discovered later that he had been party to it, it could jeopardize the Colonel's relationship with the King.

'As for you, my dear Orlando, I shall ask you to wait outside the house while the ceremony is performed, then you will not be directly involved. Also, we must be warned if anyone attempts to come into the house. It is a possibility, for if this should reach Pitt's ears, as Prime Minister he would have the right to stop the ceremony. I have waited so long, my dear friend, that I should go mad I am sure if anything happened to prevent my marriage now.'

Bridgeman replied that nothing should if he could help it. He would take up his stand in the shadows at the door of the house and would immediately report if any stranger came near and sought to enter.

'Then let us waste no more time,' said the Prince.

He went into the house declaring that he was there and that the ceremony should proceed without delay.

In that drawing room of the House in Park Street the Prince and Maria made their vows; and after the ceremony the Prince wrote the certificate which confirmed that on the 15th day of December of the year 1785 Maria Fitzherbert was married to George Augustus Prince of Wales.

* * *

He embraced his Maria with rapture. He had decided where the honeymoon should be spent.

Marble Hill, of course. Was she not his sweet lass of Richmond Hill? Had he not been ready to renounce a crown for her sake?

This was going to be the beginning of such happiness as she had never known. Maria believed him. This romantic marriage was so different from the others she had experienced. As the coach took them out of Park Street to Oxford Street and along the road to Richmond he told her what he would do for her. Every hostess would have to receive her if they wished to see him. She was the Princess of Wales and he would know how to deal with anyone who attempted to deny this. All that she wanted should be hers. He would give her a carriage with the royal arms on it; he would give her priceless jewels. None of which she wanted, she told him; all she wanted was his love.

An enchanting reply which delighted him. But then when did his Maria not enchant him?

He was happy; he was in love; he was married to the most beautiful woman on earth; he had eluded the fat German Princess they would have chosen for him. He had his sweet lass.

How slow the coach was! But he did not greatly care; she was there beside him, with her perfect complexion, her cloud of curly fair hair and that pure white bosom to be caressed and wept on.

The coach stopped. He looked out. Where were they?

'Hammersmith, I believe, my dearest.'

'Why have we stopped?'

The coachman was at the door.

'Begging Your Highness's pardon, the roads are so blocked with snow, the horses have broken down. It will be necessary to rest here for a while, sir. There is an inn here, sir, where you could stay while we see what can be done.'

So they alighted and by candlelight they supped at Hammersmith.

It mattered not where they were, said Maria, since they were together.

And fervently the Prince agreed.

Prince William's Indiscretion

The Court was at Windsor where it was housed most uncomfortably. The Castle itself was in a state of deterioration and as repairs were done now and then the King and Queen with their elder children stayed in what was known as the Upper or Queen's Lodge while the younger ones were housed in the Lower Lodge. These Lodges were gloomy and cold, the rooms small and old fashioned; there were numerous cupboards and small alcoves; the staircases were steep and dangerous; and there were so many pairs of stairs and so many passages that attendants new to the place were constantly losing their way. The fires in the small rooms during winter overheated them but the blast through the corridors was icy. Most of the household suffered from colds; and every morning during the coldest weather they were expected to attend a service in the unheated Castle chapel which was colder even than the corridors.

Still the King and Queen preferred Windsor to St. James's, and Buckingham House which had, not so long ago, been made into a home for them at great cost. 'Dear little Kew' was of course the favourite residence, but as both the King and Queen liked living in the country they were often at Windsor.

One knew exactly what was going to happen each day, said some of the bored members of the Court. No one would believe this was a royal household for it was conducted as many houses were in remote districts throughout the country. There was no *ton*, no excitement, nothing royal. The Queen examined her household accounts with a fervour she showed for nothing else except her habit of taking snuff; the King walked about the neighbourhood like a squire, interesting himself in what crops his tenants were growing and had even been known to take a hand at the butter-making. They were parsimonious both of them, and no one was ever allowed to be late for meals or the King wanted to know the reason why. Every evening there was music—and even this varied very little. There was always some composition by Handel and all the Princesses had to be present—even baby Amelia who must, said the King, be brought up to appreciate the *right* kind of music—which was of course the kind which appealed to him.

The Royal Court was in the greatest contrast to the Prince's entourage at Carlton House. Often the King and Queen heard their son's establishment spoken of almost reverently. *There* was the centre of gaiety; *there* the fashionable, the erudite and the witty gathered. The Princesses listened eagerly for news of their brother; they envied him; they wished he would come to Windsor or Kew or wherever they were. But he rarely did; he was too busy living his exciting life.

The King thought about him constantly and disliked him more intensely every day. The Queen fretted about him. Why had he made this gulf between them? Why could he not be the dutiful son she longed for him to be? She was torn between her love and pride in him and her resentment towards him, and she thought of him more than she did the rest of her children put together. There were very disturbing rumours about him and the Catholic widow, Mrs. Fitzherbert. The only pleasant thing about those rumours was the good opinion everyone seemed to have of the lady.

The Queen discussed him with Lady Harcourt, one of her closest friends as well as one of her Ladies of her Bedchamber.

'I think it is a very good friendship . . . nothing more,' she said. 'I remember he had such a friendship with one of the Princess's attendants—Mary Hamilton. She was a pure girl and I hear that this Mrs. Fitzherbert is the same.'

'I've heard it too, Your Majesty,' agreed Lady Harcourt, 'but . . .'

Yet how could she disturb the Queen who had so much to disturb her? Lady Harcourt knew how anxiously the Queen watched the King for a return of that strange malady which had attacked him once and in which he had rambled so incoherently that both he and the Queen had thought he was going mad.

Lady Harcourt—who was devoted to the King as well as to the Queen—sincerely hoped that the Prince would not provoke his father so much that he made him ill.

On one cold morning early in the year 1786 the Queen arose as usual, and when she had undergone the ceremony of the early toilette, which took about an hour, had been to the service in the icy chapel and had taken breakfast in the company of the King and her elder daughters she returned to her apartments for the morning toilette, a lengthy matter for her hair had to be dressed and powdered and this was one of the two days in the week when it had to be curled, and this took an hour longer than usual.

She sighed because no matter what attention was paid to her appearance it made little difference. She wished these ridiculous hair styles were not fashionable. They came from France where Marie Antoinette had so exaggerated them as to make them ridiculous.

She sat watching her women as they set the triangular cushion on the crown of her head and, frizzing her hair, built it up over the cushion. Now they would curl it and set it into waves one either side of her head before they wrapped her in her powdering robe and the business of powdering began.

While her hair was dressed her women read to her; she liked to hear what was being written in the papers; and when they had finished those she enjoyed a novel. The readers were constantly passing over little items about the Prince and Mrs. Fitzherbert which could make an awkward pause now and then and the Queen knew the cause of it, and while she wanted to know what was being said of her son was afraid to ask unless it should be something vulgar, ridiculing or informative—something which her sense of duty would tell her she ought to pass on to the King.

Her hair dressed, her toilette completed, she would send for the elder Princesses and spend a quiet hour with them, sewing or knotting while one of the ladies read aloud to them. The Queen always listened attentively to what was read; she had made a habit of this and it was one of the main reasons why she had mastered the English language so well and spoke it fluently with only a trace of a German accent.

She was pleased to see the girls waiting for her, and that the Princess Royal had remembered to fill her snuff box.

She took a pinch and called for her work; and set them all their duties. The Princess Royal should thread her mother's needles; Augusta should be responsible for bringing in the dogs and taking them out again when the sessions were over; Sophia should hand her her snuff box when she needed it. In the meantime they should sew of course. The others should continue with their sewing or knotting *all* the time and Miss Planta, the governess, who was a good reader, should read aloud to them, and Miss Goldsworthy who was the sub-governess and who was affectionately known as Gooley by the royal family should take over from Miss Planta when the latter was tired.

The party were busy with their tasks as they had been so many times before when suddenly the door was flung open and a young man burst into the room without ceremony and, looking wildly about him, dashed to the Queen and flung himself on his knees before her.

The Princess Royal jumped to her feet, treading on one of the dogs which had been nestling there so that he gave a loud yelp and went on yelping.

Princess Augusta cried: 'William! Brother William.'

'William?' stammered the Queen.

'Yes, Mamma,' said the young man. 'It is I, William. I have to see you. I have made up my mind. Nothing will deter me. I have come to tell you that I want to marry Sarah and you must make my father agree to the match. I have given my word . . . I . . .'

'One moment,' said the Queen, seeking for her dignity, staring with dismay at her son. What was he talking about? It was George and Mrs. Fitzherbert who had been in her mind . . . not William and this . . . Sarah.

'Pray get up, William,' she said.

But he would not do so. He continued to kneel, catching her knees.

'You must help me, Mamma,' he said. 'I have made up my mind. No one is going to stop me.'

William was shouting; the Princesses and their governesses were looking on with round inquisitive eyes. This was very extraordinary. They were all expecting they knew not what concerning the Prince of Wales—and here was William . . . also in love and wanting to marry someone of whom the King and Queen would not approve. Sarah . . . who was Sarah and where had William who had been stationed at Portsmouth met her?

The dogs were barking; one of them had become entangled in Augusta's knotting string; Sophia had let the snuff box fall to the floor; and William went on shouting.

'Stop!' cried the Queen. 'Miss La Planta, Gooley, conduct the Princesses to their apartments. They may take their work with them and you may read to them.'

The governesses curtsied and the Princesses did the same, leaving the Queen alone with her son.

William seemed a little sobered now, and the Queen said to him: 'Now, William, you had better tell me exactly what all this is about.'

It was amazing what the effect of a little regal authority had on William; he had grown considerably calmer.

'I have come to ask you to speak to the King about my engagement,' he said.

'Pray sit down and tell me what this is all about.'

William meekly obeyed.

'Now,' said the Queen, 'what was it that so induced you to forget your duty as to leave Portsmouth, and your manners as to burst in upon me and make such a scene before your sisters and their governesses?'

'This is a very serious matter.'

'It is indeed. Desertion is punishable in the Navy by . . . I know not what. But I am certain that it will be severe. But let me hear what this *engagement* is.'

'Mamma, I am in love.'

'My dear William, have you not yet learned that love and marriage do not always go together in the lives of princes?'

'Are you suggesting that I should indulge in an immoral relationship with Sarah?'

'Indeed, I am not. I am suggesting that you should never have been so foolish . . . and so wicked . . . as to become involved with her.'

'Sarah is the most beautiful of girls. She is completely suited to the rank of Princess.'

'But she is not, I imagine, of such a rank?'

'Of course she is not.'

'Then pray tell me who she is.'

'She is Sarah Martin—daughter of the Commissioner of Portsmouth in whose house I lodge.'

'I see. And you imagine yourself to be in love with her.'

'There is no imagination about it. I am.'

'And you propose to marry her. You must know, William, that without your father's consent and that of the Parliament such a marriage would not be legal.'

'George does not seem to think so.'

'George! You are referring to the Prince of Wales, I suppose. Let me tell you that this Royal Marriage Act applies to you all . . . George included, even though he may be the Prince of Wales.'

'Mamma, we may be princes but we are still men.'

The Queen looked with exasperation at her son who hurried on: 'If you do not approve of my marriage to Sarah I am ready to abandon everything to be with her. I shall be happy enough as Lieutenant Guelph. In fact that is what I am known as in the Navy. I prefer it. I would rather be a commoner and free than a prince and a prisoner.'

'No one is suggesting that you should be a prisoner, William. Only that you should observe the laws of your country as we all have to do.'

'All men—except the members of our family—may marry as they please. That is the greatest freedom of all. Mamma, I *will* marry Sarah. I must make Papa see. Where is he now? Perhaps I could go to him and explain . . .'

'My dear William, His Majesty is greatly worried by your brother's conduct. I pray you do not add to his anxieties.'

'And what of George? I suppose he will have his way. I suppose he will find some way out of his . . . his . . . *cage.*'

'I will not listen to such foolish talk. Your brother will marry as you will, which is as the King wishes.'

'Oh, I can see that it is important to George. His son would be the King. But surely it cannot be so important for me. There is Frederick to come before me. Mamma, will you speak to the King?'

The Queen was silent. She imagined the King's reaction to this news. She pictured his coming in now and finding his son in Windsor when he should be in Portsmouth. The shock would be terrible; and she was afraid of these shocks. Heaven knew what the Prince of Wales was doing. They must expect shocks from that direction. But that William, their third son, should suddenly present them with his problem was quite unexpected.

It would never do for the King to find his son here. It would be much better if she could break the news gently.

'I will speak to your father, William,' she said.

'Oh, Mamma.' He took her hand and kissed it. How affectionate they are, she thought, when they want something.

'You will plead with him? You will tell him how important this is to me? Tell him that he need not be ashamed of welcoming Sarah into the family circle. She is good . . . and beautiful, and would be an asset to any family.'

'I am sure she would,' said the Queen. 'I will speak to your father on condition that you return immediately to Portsmouth.'

The Prince stared at her in dismay.

'I will see that you hear the King's decision there. But if you stay here I can do nothing. For one thing His Majesty will be so enraged when he sees that you have deserted your post that he will not listen to you. Go back as quickly and quietly as you can to Portsmouth and I will take the first opportunity of speaking to your father.'

He took her hands and looked earnestly in her face.

'You will speak *for* me.'

'Yes, my son, I will speak for you.'

He kissed her hands fervently.

She thought: If only George would ask me to do something for him. But George was different from William. He went his way without needing any help from his mother. He was after all Prince of Wales.

'Thank you, Mamma. I will return to Portsmouth at once . . . and you will speak to the King.'

'At the first opportunity,' the Queen promised.

The King came in from hunting the stag in Windsor Forest, looking tired; but then he almost always did nowadays. The Queen thought: He takes too much exercise. He forces himself to, because he thinks it is good for his health and will reduce his weight. But he was growing fatter in spite of all his efforts; his face was a deeper shade of red and there was a tinge of purple in it, but perhaps that was due to those white eyebrows. His eyes seemed to bulge more than they used to.

I watch him too critically, she thought. I am too anxious.

She asked him if she could have a word alone with him. He looked surprised. 'Eh, what?'

'At Your Majesty's convenience.' She did not wish to make it sound too important. She had no wish to worry him in advance.

In due course they were alone and she said to him: 'A disturbing thing happened today. William came here.'

'William.' The white brows shot up; the blue eyes bulged; the colour in the too colourful face deepened. 'William! Left Portsmouth! Eh? What for? What did he do that for? Why did he leave Portsmouth, eh, what?'

Oh dear. The rapid speech, the repetitions. Always a bad sign.

'He has one of these notions which young people get. He's fallen in love with the Commissioner's daughter and wants to marry her.'

'Marry her. Is he mad, eh?'

The Queen shivered. She hated that word.

She said quickly: 'He is young. Your Majesty knows what young men are. I think some action will have to be taken and Your Majesty will know what.'

'Action, eh, I should think so. What is this? How far has it gone? What is the girl? Commissioner's daughter? He lodges in the Commissioner's house. So that's it! Well, it will have to be stopped, of course. Young fool. Will have to stop being a . . . a young fool. And he came here. How dare he? Desertion, that's what it was. Does he think because he's my son he can flout the rules of the Navy? We'll have to teach that young puppy a lesson or two.'

The Queen thought of the 'lessons' which had been taught the boys when they were younger. This had been the application of the cane—often by the King himself. He had declared to the Queen, 'Only way . . . only way you can train young puppies.' And she had hated to hear the screams of the boys and had been a little frightened by the fury and resentment she had seen in their eyes towards their father . . . and this applied particularly to the Prince of Wales. Of course William could not be allowed to marry this Sarah Martin, but she was sorry for William—and she hoped the King would not be too severe.

'He is in love with this Sarah . . .' began the Queen.

'Sarah!' cried the King; and his thoughts immediately went to another Sarah. Lady Sarah Lennox, with whom he had been in love, whom he had given up to marry Princes Charlotte of Mecklenburg Strelitz, this plain old woman who was sitting there now and was the mother of the troublesome William and that other even more troublesome one, George, who had given him so many sleepless nights. He wondered what his life would have been like if he had married beautiful Sarah Lennox—and he could have married her, for there was no Marriage Act in those days to prevent him and in any case, as the King, he could have given his own consent to whatever marriage he had wanted to make. Yet he had done his duty—a fact of which he had been proud all those years but which nevertheless continued to rankle.

'Sarah?' he repeated.

'Her name is Sarah Martin . . . this Commissioner's daughter.'

'He must be mad.'

The Queen flinched.

'He is only twenty.'

'Old enough to know better. Where is he now?'

'He has gone back to Portsmouth. He will stay there until he hears Your Majesty's decision.'

The King grunted.

'What is Your Majesty going to do?'

The King hesitated and looked at her cautiously. Usually he kept her in the dark. He had always said that he would not have women interfering in State matters. But this was scarcely a State matter. It was a family matter—and he was going to see that that was what it remained. In this case he could take Charlotte into his confidence.

'I will order the Commissioner of Portsmouth to transfer Prince William to Plymouth without delay.'

The Queen sighed.

'And there this . . . this . . . young woman will not accompany him. I doubt not that in Plymouth he will find someone else to take her place . . . but this, this little adventure will have taught the young rip that he should not take these ladies too seriously.'

The Queen nodded and the King said angrily, 'Sarah . . . Sarah . . . what was it?'

'Martin,' answered the Queen a trifle sadly, for she knew what memories the name recalled. There had been plenty to let her know when she had arrived in England that the King had been deeply enamoured of Sarah Lennox and reluctantly was taking Charlotte to be his Queen. That, thought the Queen, was the fate of princesses—and of princes too. This William would discover.

In a few days he was transferred from Portsmouth to Plymouth.

Family Conflict

The Prince was happy. He was seen everywhere with Mrs. Fitzherbert. Whispers circulated throughout the Court and the Town—Are they married? Or is she his mistress? It was obvious from the Prince's manner that either one or the other of these conditions were true. If anyone wished to entertain the Prince of Wales they must entertain Mrs. Fitzherbert also. If there was no invitation for the lady, then the Prince of Wales regretfully declined. He would dance with no other but Mrs. Fitzherbert; he must be placed next to her at table; and after each ball, banquet or evening engagement he could be heard saying to her with the utmost gallantry: 'Madam, may I have the honour of seeing you home in my carriage?'

She did not take up her residence in Carlton House, but continued to live at Richmond and in Park Street. She was, however, constantly in the company of the Prince of Wales, and the change in him was remarkable. He was extremely affable to everyone; he was constantly bursting into song; he moderated his language and rarely used a coarse expression; he drank less; he liked to retire early on some evenings. He was undoubtedly a newly married husband deeply in love with his wife and domesticity.

He took a box at the Opera for her and was frequently seen with her in it; they rode together in the Park. His habits had changed considerably; he no longer sought the company of others. Mrs. Fitzherbert was all he asked.

The friendship with Charles James Fox had clearly weakened. There had been a time when he had been constantly in that man's company, had accepted his news, laughed heartily at his wit and called him his greatest friend. But Mrs. Fitzherbert was inclined to view the politician with disfavour.

'He is both coarse and unclean,' she commented; and there was a distinct coolness between them.

'He is a brilliant fellow,' the Prince told her. 'My love, I think you would enjoy his conversation.'

'He is undoubtedly very witty and a brilliant conversationalist, and I am sure a very clever politician,' agreed Maria, 'but he certainly does not change his linen often enough and his wit is inclined to be cruel.'

'Everyone cannot be like my angel,' commented the Prince.

'Who likes only those who are worthy to be the friends of hers.'

The Prince was enchanted by that reply and began to feel less friendly towards Fox from that moment, and when he remembered that Fox had tried to prevent the marriage he felt some resentment. How dare Fox preach to him! Fox who had led just about the most immoral life any man could lead! But Fox had not preached. He had only pointed out the facts—and they were true enough. All the same, much as he respected Fox, he did not want to see him. To tell the truth he wanted no one but Maria.

He walked into Maria's drawing room where she received him with open arms and a demeanour which was almost regal. What a queen she would make! If he could make her so. Why not? When the old man died he would alter that Marriage Act with a stroke of the pen. He would have powerful ministers behind him. Fox! There he was back at Fox. No matter! His Maria was beautiful, worthy in every way to be a queen. He told her so.

'But this place is not good enough for my dearest.'

'My darling, it is ideal for me.'

'No, no, Maria. I want to see you in a setting worthy of you.'

'Settings are unimportant.'

'Of course. What setting does the brightest jewel in the kingdom need? You don't *need* it, my precious love; but you should have it. I see you in a white and gilded drawing room with Chinese silk lining the walls.'

'It sounds like Carlton House,' she said with a laugh.

'But this shall be yours. And there we shall entertain. You must admit, my dearest Maria, that this place is a trifle small.'

'It is big enough for the two of us. I care only to entertain you.'

He embraced her and wept on that wonderful bosom, so soft, so voluptuous yet so maternal. Oh, Maria, perfect woman, with all the attributes, everything that he needed to make him happy!

'Why . . . real tears,' she said, stroking his frizzed hair.

'Tears of joy,' he cried. 'Tears of wonder and gratitude. What have I done to deserve you, Maria? Tell me that.'

'You have been good and kind to me, faithful to me, you have sacrificed much for me . . . '

He lay against her listening. It was true.

> 'I'd crowns resign
> To call thee mine . . . '

But it had not been necessary to resign the Crown. This sort of marriage did not interfere with the succession in the least. It was a secret marriage, a morganatic marriage, if one cared to call it that. And it was secret; therefore what harm could come of it? As soon as he was the King he would get the Act repealed and marry Maria; and any children they might have before that happy event would be legitimized. It was really very simple. He could not imagine why there had had to be the fuss.

So now listening to Maria enumerating his virtues he was very happy indeed.

But she must entertain now and then, and since whenever she entertained he would be present, she must have a worthy establishment in which to do it.

'Lord Uxbridge's place in St. James's Square is to let,' he told her.

'My dear, dear George, you cannot mean that *I* should take such a place?'

'But why not. It's reasonably habitable.'

She threw back her head and laughed. The most musical laugh in the world, he thought, raising his head to kiss her throat before settling down once more on that magnificent bosom.

'Well?' he said.

'Far, far too expensive for me. It would cost all of three thousand a year to maintain it.'

'That does not sound a *very* large sum.'

'Not to you, my extravagant Prince. To me it is one thousand more than my income.'

'Your Prince is not without intelligence, you know.'

'Indeed I know that he possesses that very useful asset in abundance.'

'Then . . .'

'Then what, my dearest?'

'Supposing you have an income of six thousand a year, that intelligence tells me that you would not then find Uxbridge's place too expensive.'

'The logical answer to that is that I have not an income of six thousand a year.'

'And the logical answer to that is that you *shall* have.'

'Listen to me. I have no intention of taking an income from you.'

'Why not?'

'It is unnecessary. I have considered myself very comfortably placed. I have two fine houses . . . well, fine enough for me . . . but then I do not judge them by royal standards.'

'But you now have raised your standards, my love . . . my queen . . .'

She smiled tenderly. 'Fine houses . . . jewellery . . . these gifts which you are constantly trying to bestow on me are of no importance. What matters is that we are together, not where.'

'I know it. I know it. But I wish you to have everything that is worthy of you and that is the best in the world. I want you to have Uxbridge's House. I will pay the rent and with your six thousand a year you will, I know, keep the creditors at bay.'

'Six thousand!' she cried. ''But my dearest, what of *your* creditors.'

'Money! Other things are far more important. Don't you agree?'

'Yes, that is why I suggest that I continue as I am here in Park Street and that no new expenses are incurred on my account.'

But the Prince was determined. 'This house,' he said, 'was Mr. Fitzherbert's. Is he to be allowed to present you with a house and I not?'

That was a different argument and Maria was perplexed. After that it took very little persuasion to make her agree.

'The truth is,' said the Prince roguishly, 'I have already told Uxbridge that we are taking it.'

'Of course the Prince married her,' said some of the gossips. 'She would never have succumbed otherwise.'

'He can't have married her,' said others. 'It would be illegal. What of the Marriage Act? She is his mistress. She was only holding out to make him the more eager.'

Whichever theory was supported there was no doubt that the

Prince and Mrs. Fitzherbert were lovers; and everyone watched them with interest.

The gossip reached Windsor. Madam von Schwellenburg who considered herself head of the Queen's household—and was in fact the most disliked member of it—muttered to herself as she went about her apartments feeding the toads which she kept in cages about her room. Her little pets she called them; and she was far more gracious to them than she was to the maids of honour who were under her sway.

'Herr Prince vos up to no goot,'' she told the toads. She had come to England with the Queen twenty-six years before but had never bothered to learn English properly. She despised the English, hated their country, so she said; and was furious when attempts had been made to send her back to Germany. 'Dis is vere I lifs,' she had said, 'and dis is vere I stays. Novon villen me move.' But she showed her dislike for the country, to which she clung, in every way and it was apparent in her atrocious rendering of the language.

She disliked everyone except the Queen, whom she looked upon as her charge. Charlotte herself did not like the woman but kept her with her from habit. In the first place, when her mother-in-law, Augusta the Dowager Princess of Wales, had tried to get rid of Schwellenburg soon after Charlotte's arrival, she had clung to the woman on a matter of principle. But there were times when she wished her back in Germany.

So Schwellenburg had grown old in the Queen's service and none the more attractive for that. She disliked the King and the Queen's children; she disliked everyone and everything except herself, the Queen and her toads. She delighted in the misdeeds of the Princes and the gossip concerning the Prince of Wales was in particular a great joy to her.

'Herr Prince von bad vicked,' she told her favourite toad, the one who croaked the loudest when she tapped his cage with her snuff box. 'Has vedded von bad voman.'

She had seen that the cartoons in the papers were brought to the Queen's attention by setting them out with the appropriate pages in evidence on the royal dressing table. She had tried to tell the Queen about the rumours, but the Queen had shrugged them aside.

'There are always these stories about royal people, Schwellenburg.'

'Of veddings?' asked Schwellenburg maliciously. 'Dis vomen ist von Cadolic. Von bad ding.'

'It is of no importance, Schwellenburg. I have heard that the lady whose name is being coupled with the Prince's is a very virtuous one. I am sure it is quite a pleasant relationship.'

'Like Vilhelm vis Portsmod Sarah.'

Really the woman was intolerable. 'Go and attend to your toads, Schwellenburg. I no longer need your services.'

The very mention of her toads made Schwellenburg forget everything else, and the Queen was delighted to be alone.

It was a different matter when Lady Harcourt spoke to her. Lady Harcourt was a trusted friend. Charlotte was very fond of the Harcourt family, for it was Lord Harcourt, the present Lady Harcourt's father-in-law, who had come to Strelitz all those years ago to arrange for her marriage to George, who was then the Prince of Wales. She could trust Lady Harcourt and had only a year or so before appointed her a Lady of the Bedchamber. To Lady Harcourt as to no other could she confide her innermost thoughts; it was a great comfort to have such a friend.

Lady Harcourt said, when they were sitting together with their knotting in their hands: 'Your Majesty, I am distressed about the rumours . . . and I have hesitated whether or not I should speak to you about them.'

'My dear, you know you may speak to me on any subject you think fit.'

'But I did not wish to add to your anxieties.'

'Have you heard something dreadful?'

'It is alarming.'

'About William? That was a distressing affair. I do hope he is behaving sensibly. The King has sent him to Plymouth, but he may well take it into his reckless head to go back to Portsmouth. What a trial one's children are.'

'I was not thinking of His Highness Prince William but . . . of the Prince of Wales.'

The Queen's fingers faltered on her knotting.

'You have heard something . . . fresh?'

'I do not think it is fresh, but it is so . . . persistent. I greatly fear that there may be some truth in the rumour.'

'What is the rumour?'

'That he is married to this woman, Mrs. Fitzherbert.'

'I have heard that rumour. It is simply not possible. How could he be married to her? It is against the law. The Royal Marriage Act forbids any member of the family to marry without the King's consent.'

'But, Your Majesty, that need not prevent the Prince's doing so.'

The Queen said piteously: 'Oh, my dear Lady Harcourt, what have we done—the King and I—to be so plagued by our sons.'

'They are young men, Your Majesty . . . lusty young men. They wish for independence.'

'He is the heir to the throne. He could not be so foolish.'

'He is undoubtedly in love with this woman, and the Prince when he does anything does it wholeheartedly. He is, I have heard, wholeheartedly in love with Mrs. Fitzherbert.'

'But I have heard that she is a good and virtuous woman. She would never allow this.'

'It is because she *is* a virtuous woman, Your Majesty, that it has happened.'

The Queen was silent for a while and then she said: 'What can I do?'

'Should Your Majesty not speak to the King?'

Charlotte turned to her friend. 'I can say this to you though I would say it to no other. I am afraid . . . for the King.'

Lady Harcourt nodded.

'This affair of William and the Portsmouth girl. It has upset him more than the Court knows. I have heard him talking . . . talking endlessly at night. He . . . he rambles. He goes on and on . . . and sometimes I do not know what he is saying. He has grown very melancholy. He talks of his sons and how he has failed with them, how the Prince of Wales hates him, how William flouts him.'

'Has he been bled and purged?'

'Constantly. Far more than is generally known. I dare not speak to him at this time of this affair.'

'It may not be true,' said Lady Harcourt.

'No,' replied the Queen gratefully. 'It may not be true. But I think we should know whether it is or not.'

Lady Harcourt nodded.

'If it were true,' said the Queen, 'it could imperil the succession; it could shake the throne. I could not tell the King in his present state of health.'

'Your Majesty is the Prince's mother. Perhaps you could yourself see him . . . find out if this rumour is true. He would not lie to you if you asked him for a direct answer.'

'I will do it,' said the Queen. 'But my dear Lady Harcourt, should it be true, I tremble to contemplate the effect it would have on the King.'

'Perhaps Your Majesty could keep it from the King . . . until he is recovered.'

The Queen smiled brightly. It was a pleasant idea; but she knew in her heart that he never would recover. She laid her hand momentarily over that of Lady Harcourt.

'It is good to talk . . . with friends,' she said. 'I will summon him to Windsor and demand he tell me the truth.'

On receiving the Queen's request that he should come to Windsor to see her, the Prince drove down from Carlton House in his phaeton.

The Queen was moved when she saw him—so elegant in his dark blue coat, his silk cravat and the diamond star glittering on his left breast. He towered above her. How handsome he is! she thought. If he would only kneel at her feet and beg her to intercede for him with the King as William had! But of course he did no such thing. He stood before her, arrogant, caring nothing for her and showing by his manner that he quite clearly had no love for her. Her mood changed, for since he would not let her love him, her feelings were so strong that they bordered on hatred. She had never felt this strong emotion towards any of the others—it was only for George, her adored first-born whom she had worshipped in the first years of his life.

'You wished to see me, Madam.' His voice was cold containing no affectionate greeting, but merely implying: Come let us get this business finished so I can get away.

'I have heard rumours,' said the Queen, 'rumours which greatly disturb me.'

'Yes, Madam?'

'Concerning you and a lady named Mrs. Fitzherbert.'

'Indeed?'

'Rumours,' continued the Queen, 'that you have married the lady. Of course I know this to be an impossibility but . . . '

'Why an impossibility, Madam? I am capable of going through a marriage ceremony.'

'I did not doubt it, but you would not be so foolish . . . or so wicked . . . as to deceive a lady of good character into believing that it was possible for you to marry her.'

It was the wrong approach. She had seen that when his face flushed angrily.

'Madam, I am married to a lady whom I love and honour above all other people.'

'Married! You are certainly not married.'

'I should have thought, Madam, that I was the best judge of that.'

'Evidently you are not if you can delude yourself into thinking you are this woman's husband. It is quite impossible for you to be. Have you never heard of the Marriage Act?'

'I have heard so much of that criminal measure that I never want to hear of it again. In fact my first act when I mount the throne will be to repeal it.'

She stared at him aghast. How could he talk so? And the King was only forty-eight years old—a comparatively young man. One would think his father was in his dotage. She shuddered.

'Please do not talk in that way. I am not sure that it is not . . . treachery.'

The Prince laughed. 'Madam, I thought the reason why I am treated like an imbecile or an infant in the nursery was because it was well known that I should one day be king. Is one supposed not to mention this fact as though it were something shameful?'

'The King is still a young man.'

'He looks and behaves like an old one, so you cannot blame people for thinking of him as such. But you asked me here because you had heard rumours that I was married. Well, I tell you that I am, that the lady I have married is worthy to be the Queen of England; she will not disgrace your drawing room . . .'

The Queen burst out: 'She will never have an opportunity of proving that.'

'So you will not receive her at Court?'

'Certainly I shall not.'

'Why not? Why not?'

'Because I do not receive my son's . . . mistresses . . . in my drawing room.'

'Madam, this is my wife.'

'You know very well that cannot be. You may have gone through a form of marriage with her but she is not your wife. And I repeat, I will not receive your mistress in my drawing room.'

The Prince was white with anger. 'Very well. But every other drawing room in London will think itself honoured to welcome her. And Madam, let me tell you this: *your* drawing room is as dull as a mausoleum and the conversation there about as lively as at a funeral gathering. In *my* drawing room, Madam, where the wittiest and most brilliant people of the country foregather, my *wife* will receive the honour due to her. So, let me inform

Your Majesty that it will be no hardship to my *wife* that she is not received in the Queen's drawing room when she is the hostess in that of the Prince of Wales.'

He gave a curt bow and walked briskly from the room.

The Queen stared after him, her heart heavy; her eyes blank with misery.

She thought of William's raging against his family in Plymouth, of the Prince of Wales in his glittering drawing room at Carlton House, doubtless making fun of his parents; and the King, growing more and more melancholy, talking to himself, addressing everyone with that repetitive rapidity which frightened her.

There was Frederick in Germany. Frederick had always been of a sunny nature. He had been devoted to the Prince of Wales in their childhood, of course, and the two of them had always been together . . . loyal to each other, helping each other out of mischief.

He would be nearly twenty-three now.

Perhaps if Frederick came home there would be one son to comfort them. And it might well be that Frederick would be the future King of England, for would the people accept a King who refused to marry—for this marriage with Mrs. Fitzherbert was no marriage in the eyes of the State, and when it came to State affairs it was the State that mattered—and had gone through a morganatic marriage with a Catholic.

Perhaps she could hint to the King at some time when he was in the right mood that perhaps it was time Frederick came home.

After the interview with the Queen nothing would satisfy the Prince than that Maria should be received in every drawing room in London—and not only received but treated as though she were Princess of Wales. Any hostess who did not immediately acknowledge her as such was ignored by the Prince and, as to be cut by the Prince of Wales was social suicide, the desired homage was paid to Maria.

She had seen that it was useless to protest against the extravagance of the young lover. He would come to her all excitement because he had a surprise for her. The surprise would be a 'trinket'. A trinket indeed—a brooch, a necklace, a locket . . . set with diamonds, sapphires or emeralds of which she would alarmingly calculate the cost as she expressed the delight which he expected. How could one tell a Prince of Wales that he must try to live within his means? He had no idea of money. He saw an ornament. It was beautiful. Then his Maria must have it.

She was alarmed by the extravagance of the entertainments she was obliged to give at Uxbridge House. It was not that she was in the least incapable of playing hostess. Entertaining as she had at Swynnerton with Mr. Fitzherbert had given her all the experience she required in that field; and she had a natural dignity and regality which was denied to people such as the Duchess of Cumberland.

When the Duke and Duchess of Cumberland returned from abroad they immediately were aware of the situation and the Duchess hastened to welcome Maria as her 'dearest niece'. The Duke was equally effusive. Not only was this necessary to retain the friendship of the Prince of Wales but it also offered a good opportunity of flouting the King—and therefore it was quite irresistible.

So Maria entertained as the Prince wished while she counted the cost and confided in her companion, Miss Pigot, an old friend whom she had brought with her as chaperone and companion when she set up in Uxbridge House, her anxieties concerning the cost of it all.

'Dear Pigot,' she said, 'the Prince cannot understand how much happier I should be in Park Street . . . or if he does not like me to be in that house since I inherited it from Mr. Fitzherbert, some smaller establishment.'

'The dear Prince is so anxious that every honour shall be yours,' replied Miss Pigot.

And Maria had to agree with her. How could she spoil his pleasure? He was such a boy—not yet twenty-four, and in his enthusiasms young for his age. She would be thirty in July. Six years. It was quite a difference at their ages. So she must remember his youth, and his enthusiasms were so enchanting, especially when they were all directed at giving her pleasure.

With the coming of the spring he said they must go down to Brighton. He wanted Maria to enjoy the place as much as he did. With him went the most brilliant section of London society and the inhabitants of the once obscure little fishing village came out to gape at the nobility. But most of all they gaped at the glittering Prince of Wales.

Nothing, said the people of Brighton, will ever be the same again.

The Prince took up residence in Grove House. This was the third year he had rented it; and Mrs. Fitzherbert took a house behind the Castle Inn—which was as close to Grove House as could be.

There were balls and banquets and the people would stand outside Grove House and the Assembly Rooms to watch the people through the windows. Ladies and gentlemen took to strolling through the streets in the warm evenings and the Prince would be there always with the same fair plump lady on his arm. They were a magnificent pair. Like a king and a queen, said the people of Brighton.

Every morning the Prince took his dip in the sea superintended by Smoker Miles, a strapping old sailor who was more at home in the water than on land. He was the autocrat of the bathing machines, and if he said no swimming that day there was no swimming. One morning the Prince of Wales came down as usual but old Smoker looked at him and shook his head.

'No, Mr. Prince,' he said, 'no bathing for you this morning.'

'But I have decided to bathe this morning, Smoker,' said the Prince.

'Oh, no you don't,' retorted Smoker.

The Prince, amazed that anyone should so address him, attempted to brush the man aside, but Smoker set his great bulk between the Prince and the bathing machine and said: 'No. You'll not bathe this morning, Mr. Prince.'

'And who gives this order?'

'I do, Mr. Prince, and no matter what princes say I give orders here.'

The Prince attempted to mount the steps into the machine, but Smoker caught him by the arm.

'I'll be damned if you do,' shouted Smoker. 'What do you think your father would say to me if you were drowned, eh? He'd say: "This is all your fault, Smoker," he'd say. "If you'd taken proper care of him, poor George would be alive today." '

The thought of the King so addressing Smoker made the Prince roar with laughter. Smoker looked hurt.

'It's true what I say,' he said. 'And I'm not having the King of England tell me I don't know my duty. This sea don't behave for anyone . . . not even the Prince of Wales.'

'Not even for the King of Brighton?' asked the Prince.

'You mean me, Mr. Prince. Ho, that's good that is. The King of Brighton.'

Smoker clearly liked the title and the Prince bowed to him ironically. 'I am merely a prince and irksome as it is princes often have to obey the will of kings.'

Smoker repeated the story often and was soon known as the King of Brighton; and more and more people came down to the sea to be dipped or watched over by King Smoker.

Maria bathed on the ladies' side of the Steyne under the care of old Martha Gunn, the big strong woman who was the female counterpart of Smoker.

Those were happy days in Brighton.

The Prince said to Maria as they strolled along by the sea in the cool of the evening: 'Grove House is a poor sort of place and I should like to build a house for myself here. Don't you agree, my dearest, that that would be a very excellent idea?'

Maria, who had by this time realized the futility of trying to curb his extravagance, agreed.

Then a most unprecedented incident occurred.

Returning to Carlton House from Brighton he found strangers seated in his hall and his servants bewildered and uncertain how to explain to him. It was the strangers themselves who had to do that.

'Your Highness's pardon, sir, but if you will settle this little matter of £600 we'll go quiet as lambs. No disrespect to Your Highness, sir. It's just orders, sir . . . all in the matter of business.'

The Prince was aghast.

The bailiffs had come to Carlton House.

The Prince immediately went to see his friend, Sheridan. It was true since his marriage he had neglected his friends, but he knew that he could trust Sheridan to help him. Charles too, but he hesitated to go to him since Maria had driven a wedge between them.

Sheridan received the Prince in his house at Bruton Street with expressions of pleasure.

'Sherry, I am in the most extraordinary and humiliating dilemma.'

'Your Highness?'

'The bailiffs are in Carlton House. And all for a paltry £600. Sherry, what am I to do?'

'But Your Highness, who will deny you £600 should you ask for it? I can think of a thousand people who would willingly give it.'

'You, my dear friend?'

'Your Highness knows that all I have is at your service but I doubt whether I could lay my hands on £600. I myself am expecting a visit from your intruders on any day now. But Your Highness should have no difficulty. Why, there is your uncle, Cumberland, who would be only too honoured.'

'He calls me Taffy. And I don't greatly care to be under an obligation to him.'

'But what of Georgiana? Or the Duke of Bedford? There are a score of them.'

The Prince agreed. 'But it is undoubtedly humiliating when one must borrow from one's friends, Sherry.'

Sherry agreed, but he also pointed out that the bailiffs must be ejected as soon as possible.

He was right. There were many eager to lend the Prince of Wales £600 for the purpose; but when the matter was settled and Sheridan returned with the Prince of Wales to Carlton House and they sat drinking together, Sheridan said: 'Your Highness's debts should be settled. This situation may well occur again; and as Your Highness pointed out it is a humiliating position for a Prince of Wales to find himself in.'

The Prince nodded and looked expectantly at Sheridan. He was very fond of Sherry, who was so charming and handsome, although beginning to look a little jaded. When he had first met him, only a few years ago at the time he was involved with Perdita, Sheridan had not been the politician he was today—merely manager of Drury Lane. But he had had an enviable reputation, having made his name with *The Rivals* and *The School for Scandal.* They had been a trio—he, Fox and Sheridan; and Burke was a friend of theirs too. How he had valued those friendships! And how he had delighted in their wit and erudition! They had stood together for the Whigs. Those were good old days, but the coming of Maria had changed them. For one thing he was too devoted to Maria to have as much time as he had had in the past for his old friends, and Maria's definite antagonism to Fox had affected the Prince's feelings.

But now Sheridan was an influential politician and such a close associate of Fox that the Prince's diminishing affection for the latter seemed to touch Sheridan too.

Yet on this day when he had gone to Sheridan for help, he felt as affectionate towards him as he ever had.

Sheridan looked into his glass and said: 'It must be ended . . . with all speed.'

'How so?'

'Does Your Highness know the extent of your debts?'

'I have no idea, Sherry, and the calculation of them would so depress me that I have put off making it.'

'Parliament should settle them.'

'Is it possible?'

'It would not be the first time.'

'No, and I am really kept very short.'

'I think it should be talked over with Fox.'

The Prince nodded gloomily. It seemed now as always that he could not manage without Fox's help.

When Maria heard that the bailiffs had been to Carlton House she was aghast.

'My darling, what are you going to do?' she demanded.

'Oh, it will be settled, never fear.'

'But, dearest, we will have to consider in future. You spend far too much on me.'

'I could never spend too much on you.'

'I should be most unhappy to be an encumbrance.'

'The most delightful encumberance in the world,' he assured her.

'But, my dearest, what are you going to do?'

'Fox is coming to see me. You can trust that wily old fellow to come up with the answer.'

'Fox.' Her long aquiline nose wrinkled in disgust.

'Dearest, I know you don't like him but he'll know what should be done.'

'May I be there when you speak to him?'

The Prince hesitated, but she looked so appealing that he agreed.

Thus when Fox came with Sheridan to discuss the Prince's debts he found Maria present.

'Maria is fully aware of the situation,' explained the Prince.

Fox bowed and Maria returned his greeting coolly. Sheridan she accepted more graciously. She thought he was a bad influence for the Prince because he was a drinker and a gambler and had numerous affairs with women, but he was at least clean and so more tolerable.

'Maria thinks the debts must be paid at once,' said the Prince, looking at her fondly. 'She has been lecturing me on my extravagance and says that at the earliest possible moment my creditors must be paid and economies made.'

'A view,' said Fox, 'with which I am in entire agreement.'

The Prince smiled from one to the other rather wistfully. He would have liked them to be good friends—these two whom he loved more than any other human beings.

'The question,' put in Sheridan, 'is how?'

'Has Your Highness a rough estimate of the amount?' asked Fox.

The Prince thought that somewhere in the neighbourhood of £250,000 might see him through.

Fox was taken aback. It was a very large sum.

'There are two alternatives,' he said. 'Your Highness can either approach the King or the Parliament.'

'Neither appeals,' replied the Prince. 'The Parliament means Pitt—and he has never been a friend of mine. And the idea of going to my father and asking him for money is completely repulsive to me.'

'It may be the only answer,' warned Fox.

'He'll crow. He'll jeer. Eh, what? What? You've no idea what an old fool he has become in the heart of his family. I would do a great deal to avoid going to him and begging for his help.'

'That leaves Parliament.'

'And Mr. Pitt.'

'It's worth a try,' said Sheridan.

And so it was agreed.

When Pitt received the request to settle the Prince's debts, he decided that he would do nothing about it.

Why should his Ministry help support a young man who was clearly the tool of the Opposition? The Prince was extravagant. Very well, let the public know how extravagant he was, but that was no concern of Mr. Pitt and his Ministry.

To tell the Prince of Wales—who might very well be King at any time—that he would do nothing to help him would have been a foolish and reckless act; and Mr. Pitt though a young man could not be accused of folly or recklessness.

He prevaricated; he asked for details; he shelved the matter for a few days, a few weeks. It was a large sum of money, he pointed out. It was a matter which could not be settled overnight.

Meanwhile the creditors were growing impatient, and the Prince fearing that the bailiffs might return to Carlton House, went again to Fox.

'There is no help for it,' said Fox. 'Your Highness will have to ask the King. After all, it is your due. Your allowance is not large enough. As Prince of Wales you are not expected to live like a pauper.'

So the Prince wrote to the King telling him that he had debts and that a sum of £250,000 would cover them.

The King replied that he was considering the matter. Nothing happened for a few weeks; then the Prince wrote again.

The Prince must understand, replied the King, that before the money could be advanced to him, it must be known how it was spent. There was one item for £54,000. What could have been the reason for spending such a large unspecified sum?

The money had been spent on furniture, plate and jewellery which the Prince had insisted on giving Maria and he was not going to give the King details of that.

The King wrote a curt note that he would not pay the Prince's debts nor would he give his sanction to an increase in his son's allowance.

When the Prince received this letter he was so angry, realizing now that all the time neither the King nor Pitt had any intention of paying his debts, that he declared he would make his own arrangements. He would shut up Carlton House; he would live like a private gentleman and he would pay £40,000 a year out of his allowance to his creditors. And the country should know how he was treated by his father and his father's Government.

When the King received this letter from the Prince he was disturbed. If the Prince shut up Carlton House the people would soon know it. It was not becoming for a Prince of Wales to live like a private gentleman. The people had always been on the Prince's side; they would be so now; particularly as the King himself had had debts which the Parliament had had to settle.

He summoned Pitt to ask his advice.

Pitt read the letters and did not like the tone of them.

'It would not be good,' he said, 'for the Prince to become a martyr.'

'I agree,' replied the King, 'I will write to him without delay and let him know that I have not given him an absolute refusal.'

'I think that an excellent idea, Your Majesty,' said Pitt. 'I suppose these debts should be paid, but at the same time His Highness should be made to realize that Your Majesty's Government does not look with pleasure on his extravagant way of life.'

'He shall be made to understand that, Mr. Pitt, I promise you.'

When Pitt had left the King immediately wrote to the Prince.

He had not made a complete refusal, he explained, but if the Prince proposed taking any rash steps he should remember that he himself would be the one who would be obliged to take the consequences of them.

On receiving his father's letter the Prince cried: 'Very well. I'll show him.'

Maria was with him. She was delighted by his resolution and that made him all the more determined.

'You are right,' she cried. 'I know you are right.'

She did not realize, dear Maria, that nothing could have put the King into a more unfortunate position; to her it was just a matter of economy.

'I shall sell all my horses,' he told her. 'I shall shut up Carlton House, except a few rooms. You and I will go down to Brighton. It is cheaper living there. By God, I can imagine my father's pique when he hears I have put up my horses and carriage for sale. And I shall do so . . . publicly. It is time everyone knew how I am treated.'

Fox was gleeful.

'This,' he declared to Sheridan, 'will be a defeat for the King and Pitt. We must see that everyone views it in that light. If the Prince suggested going abroad for a spell for the sake of economy it would do no harm. My God, this is going to make old George wish he had paid young George's debts. Depend upon it, he will try to do so now. But we don't really want him to . . . not yet.'

Fox was very merry. Oh, clever Mr. Pitt, who had prevaricated a little too long. Oh, stupid old George, who did not realize that the people were asking themselves and each other why it was that he quarrelled with all his family.

Fox set his writers working on their pamphlets and cartoons. 'We must make the most of the situation, Sherry,' he said. 'A little discomfort won't hurt young George. In fact, I believe he is enjoying it.'

And so it seemed. The Prince of Wales, like other members of the royal family, was finding the game of baiting the King highly diverting.

In the coffee houses people talked about the quarrel between the Prince and the King; it had taken the place of the Fitzherbert affair. What an amusing and fascinating personality they had in the Prince of Wales! There was always some excitement going on about him. God bless the Prince of Wales, cried the people.

As for the King, he was an old bore, he and his fertile Charlotte. The Prince and his Maria Fitzherbert were more pleasant to look at and their story was so romantic.

Fox and his friends talked of the impossibility of the King to get along with any member of the royal family. He had quarrelled with his brothers, Gloucester and Cumberland, because of their marriages. Was it not time the bones of those old skeletons stopped rattling? Gloucester was forced to live in Florence because he found it undignified that his wife, a royal duchess, should not be received at Court; the Cumberlands were not received either because they had married without the King's consent. Prince Frederick, Duke of York, was in Hanover learning to be a soldier (the King did not think the English Army good enough for his sons), William was at sea, Edward was in Geneva, and the younger Princes were to be sent to Göttingen because the King did not consider the standard of Oxford and Cambridge as high as that of the German university.

What a ridiculous old man this king of theirs was! No wonder his family quarrelled with him. And now he had treated the Prince of Wales so badly that he had to give up Carlton House and had been forced to sell all his horses and carriages in order to pay his debts.

Was it not a disgrace to the nation that the Prince of Wales did not possess his own carriage?

When the Prince and Mrs. Fitzherbert drove down to Brighton they went by hired post-chaise. This was the first time Royalty had ever had to travel in a hired conveyance and the Prince took a delight in allowing Mrs. Fitzherbert to pay whenever they hired a conveyance.

The nation was shocked, and at Windsor the King was sadly aware of his growing unpopularity.

The Prince had successfully turned the tables. He was clearly enjoying his spell of penury, whereas the King was finding it most embarrassing.

Attack at St. James's

'Dear Haggerdorn,' said the Queen, 'how I shall miss you when you have gone.'

Mrs. Haggerdorn, faithful attendant for twenty-five years, turned away to hide the tears which filled her eyes. For so long now she had dreamed of going home and now that the time had come she felt this reluctance to go—but her only real regret was leaving the Queen.

'Your Majesty has been so good to me,' whispered Haggerdorn. 'That is why I am sad to go.'

'Twenty-five years is a long time,' said the Queen.

'Ah, Madam, I shall never forget the day we left. And that dreadful sea journey when Your Majesty set such an example to us all by playing the harpsichord when we were all so sick.'

'I happened to be a good sailor, Haggerdorn; and I expect I was a little defiant. It is a terrible anxiety to come to a country one has never seen . . . to a husband who is a stranger . . .'

'Ah, Your Majesty, I know it. In my small way I too suffered. But Your Majesty has been a blessing to His Majesty and the English people. You have given them so many sons and daughters.'

'Too many, perhaps, Haggerdorn. We have had our troubles. But cheer up. You will soon be in Mecklenburg. Think of that. You will see my family, my old friends. Do you think they will remember me, Haggerdorn, after twenty-five years?'

'They could never forget you, Madam.'

'Perhaps not. They will have heard news of the Queen of England from time to time. I expect they hear of the scandals my son has a talent for creating.'

174

There was a hint of dislike in her voice which startled Haggerdorn. She remembered how at one time the Queen's voice had softened every time she spoke of the Prince of Wales.

Perhaps, thought the mild and peace-loving Haggerdorn, it was indeed a good thing that she was going home. There had always been trouble with the Prince and now that he was growing older those troubles would grow with him; and the other boys were growing into the trouble-making age. Madam von Schwellenburg had always been so arrogant and demanding. Then there was His Majesty the King. Only those close to the Queen realized how anxious she was on his account and how oddly he could behave at times.

He entered the Queen's apartment at that moment, brows furrowed, eyebrows bristling, his face that unhealthy brick red.

The Queen said: 'Your Majesty, dear Haggerdorn is saying goodbye to me. You know she is leaving us.'

The King looked at Haggerdorn, his eyes softened by sentiment.

'Ah yes, yes, good Haggerdorn. Pleasant journey. Sorry to see you go. Very sorry.'

Haggerdorn curtsied as elegantly as creaking knees and rheumatic pains would allow. Oh, yes, it was time she left draughty Windsor Lodge. She needed a little comfort in her old age.

'I shall miss her,' said the Queen.

'Yes, we shall miss her.' The King was at his best on such an occasion. He was kind and showed an interest in Haggerdorn's plans. No wonder, thought the Queen, that it was said he was more like a country squire than a king.

He made Haggerdorn tell him what she intended to do; and assured her that he would see that she went off well provided for.

Yes, thought the Queen, a very good squire.

How critical she was becoming—of the King, of her sons, of her life!

Haggerdorn's impending departure had made her think of that day twenty-five years ago when the dazzling prospect of being Queen of England had been revealed to her. And what had it amounted to? She had become a breeder of children. Fifteen children in twenty-five years. There had not been a great deal of time when she had not been either pregnant or giving birth. Two little boys had died—Octavius and Alfred—but thirteen were left to her; and now that they were growing up, they for whom she had lived and suffered were turning against her. Her eldest son despised both her and his father; and never before had she been aware of such friction in the family. She was anxious about the Prince; she was anxious about the King. Lucky Haggerdorn who had no responsibilities, no ties, who would go home to Mecklenburg-Strelitz and enjoy a peaceful old age!

When Haggerdorn had been dismissed the Queen said to the King: 'I have been thinking about the replacement of Haggerdorn.'

'Yes, yes,' said the King, now as always deeply interested in household matters.

'I have an idea. I wonder what Your Majesty will think of it.'

The change in him was miraculous. She thought: If he could be shut away from State affairs and his troublesome sons, he could be a happy family man. He should be concerned with only small matters. Poor George, to have been born heir to a crown!

'I am eager to hear,' he told her.

'Do you remember the authoress we met at dear Mrs. Delaney's . . . the famous Miss Burney? I was thinking of giving the place to her.'

The King's face lit up with pleasure. 'Dear Mrs. Delaney,' he said. 'I remember well.'

That was a pleasant memory. He had set Mrs. Delaney up in a house close to Windsor Lodge; he had supplied all the furniture himself and had even seen to the stocking of the kitchen cupboards. She remembered his great glee when he brought Mrs. Delaney to see it and tears of pleasure now came into his eyes at the memory.

'Miss Burney,' said the King. 'A very clever young lady, so they tell me.'

'There can be no doubt that she is clever. I should like to hear her read her own books. We are in need of a reader and it seems to me an excellent plan to have a famous authoress in the household.'

The King was nodding. Such a pleasant encounter. Miss Burney had been so *overcome* by royal condescension and both he and the Queen had talked to her of her books.

'Yes, yes, yes,' went on the King. 'I think you should give the place to Miss Burney.'

It was ten o'clock on a hot July morning when the carriage containing Miss Burney and her father left St. Martin's Street for Windsor. Dr. Burney was delighted with this honour bestowed on his daughter; Fanny herself was less certain.

What was she, a famous novelist, the darling of London literary society, accustomed to enlightened conversation, going to do in what she knew must be the stultified atmosphere of the royal household?

Perhaps it was not such a fortunate day when she had gone to stay with Mrs. Delaney and had made the acquaintance of the King and Queen. Who would have thought from that meeting that this would have happened?

But one did not apparently decline what was undoubtedly looked upon as an honour.

Oh dear, thought Fanny, there is nothing to be done but submit.

And she thought of the Queen—the squat ugly little woman with the German accent; and the big alarming King with those fierce eyebrows and that disconcerting habit of shooting questions at one which perhaps did not need an answer. 'Eh, eh? What, what?' And speaking so quickly that if one were a little nervous—and who would not be speaking to the King?—one just could not understand what he was talking about.

But Father, dear Father, was delighted; and so were the family. She could imagine them all boasting: 'Fanny, you know our famous Fanny, is now in the royal household, on terms—but the most *familiar* terms—with Her Majesty the Queen.'

Dr. Burney was now looking as pleased as though he were taking his bow on a concert platform after the most successful performance of his career.

How, Fanny asked herself, in these circumstances, can I reveal my true feelings?

Her eyes rested on her bag. In that were her clothes which she was sure would be most unsuitable. She had no feeling for clothes and never would have. But in that bag was her diary and that should be her comfort, her solace, and in it she would write frankly of her feelings and impressions; she would also write to her sister Susan. Yes, whatever alarms and discomforts, she would always be able to write.

Dr. Burney was talking of the King with respectful awe. The King, whatever people might say of him, loved music, so Fanny should hear some good music in the royal household. There were concerts every night.

Yes, I know, thought Fanny. But what conversation will there be?

She thought of the old days when she had listened to dear Dr. Johnson and James Boswell and Mrs. Thrale.

Oh dear, thought Fanny, I feel like a nun about to be incarcerated in a monastery—or a bride who is going to a husband who is a stranger to her. Thus must the poor Queen have felt when she came here from Mecklenburg-Strelitz all those years ago. At least my plight is not as bad as hers. It is not for ever. Fanny giggled to herself. And I shall not be expected to bear the royal children.

Her father smiled at her. Fanny was realizing the honour which was hers.

They came into Windsor and there was the Castle—grand and imposing.

''You will not live in the Castle, of course,' her father reminded her, 'but in the Upper Lodge.'

'Less imposing,' said Fanny, and added hopefully: 'But perhaps more comfortable.'

The carriage had arrived at Mrs. Delaney's house and here they alighted. Mrs. Delaney welcomed them into her house, beaming with pleasure, for she regarded this appointment of Fanny's as her doing.

While the luggage was being taken out Mrs. Delaney sent a message to Upper Lodge to say that Miss Burney had arrived. Then Fanny, Dr. Burney and their hostess sat together in the little drawing room while Mrs. Delaney gave Fanny a grounding in Court etiquette.

'I am certain to do something wrong,' declared Fanny. 'I know it.'

'My dear,' said Mrs. Delaney, 'you will find Her Majesty very kind.'

'She will need to be,' said Fanny grimly.

'Remember, my dear, that you are a famous novelist and that the Queen has enjoyed your books. In fact she is hoping that you will read them aloud to her and the Princesses.'

'But you know my voice. It is low, and when I raise it it . . . it squeaks. Oh, dear Mrs. Delaney, I shall be the most dismal failure.' Fanny brightened. 'But then I shall be dismissed and go home again. So perhaps that will not be such a bad thing.'

'It is a *good* thing,' said Dr. Burney, 'that Her Majesty cannot hear you talking in this way.'

A message was delivered at Mrs. Delaney's that the Queen had heard of the arrival of Dr. and Miss Burney and was ready to receive them.

'So,' said Mrs. Delaney, 'you may go and good luck go with you.'

Fanny put her arm through her father's and they crossed the short distance between Mrs. Delaney's house and the Upper Lodge.

In the Queen's drawing room Her Majesty was seated, and standing beside her was a large and extremely ugly woman to whom Fanny took an immediate dislike.

Forward, thought Fanny, remembering Mrs. Delaney's instructions. Kneel, look suitably humble, do not speak until spoken to.

'Dr. Burney . . . Miss Burney.'

The Queen was smiling. 'It gives me great pleasure to see you. Miss Burney, we hope you are going to be happy with us.'

'Your Majesty is very gracious,' murmured Fanny.

Dr. Burney, at ease, said something about his daughter's being overcome by the honour done to her.

'It is delightful to have a novelist with us who has given such pleasure with her books,' said the Queen. 'This is my Keeper of the Robes. She will tell you what your duties will be. Schwellenburg, pray take Miss Burney to her apartments. I daresay she is a little tired and perhaps would like to rest before she begins her duties.'

The cue to depart, thought Fanny, her spirits which were never downcast for long, beginning to rise.

She walked out backwards—a necessary procedure, Mrs. Delaney had told her, and a most awkward one, Fanny decided. Oh dear, I'm sure I shall trip and if I have to wear high heels how shall I manage it?

At last the door had shut and she was able to walk naturally.

She smiled up at the grim face of Madam von Schwellenburg and thought it extremely unpleasant.

'This vay com,' were the words which came from that excessively ugly mouth.

I do not think, thought Fanny, as she was led to her apartments, that I underestimated the trials of life in the royal household.

Fanny's apartments were on the ground floor of the Queen's Lodge. She had a drawing room, which gave her a view of the Round Tower and a small bedroom which looked out on a garden. Not exactly commodious, she thought, but adequate. Less comforting was the door next to that of her drawing room which led up to the apartments of Madam von Schwellenburg.

She was given a man- and maidservant and momentarily thought that she might be about to enjoy a life of ease, but was quickly disillusioned.

Madam von Schwellenburg took pains to impress on her that, as Keeper of the Robes, she was Fanny's superior since Fanny bore the explanatory title of Assistant Keeper of the Robes.

'*I* make rules,' Schwellenburg informed her. 'I . . . selfs.' And did Fanny like toads because to Madam von Schwellenburg they were the most delightful of creatures. Hers were especially clever toads. They croaked when she tapped their cages with her snuff boxes.

Fanny was revolted by the creatures and showed it.

'So . . . you do not like?' Schwellenburg was offended. She was not going to have upstart novelists turning their noses up at her precious pets. And from then on she decided to make Fanny's life burdensome to her.

'Novels,' she declared to her pet toad, giving Fanny a venomous look over her shoulder. 'I von't haf nuddink vat you call novels, vat you call romances, vat you call histories. I might not read vat you call . . . *stuff*.'

Fanny felt an irrepressible urge to giggle, but restrained it. She had quickly perceived that Madame von Schwellenburg was going to be one of the trials of her Court life.

There were others—rising at six every morning and putting on a cap and gown so as to be ready to fly to the royal apartments as soon as the summons came from the Queen, which could be at any time between seven and eight. The Queen rose earlier but never sent for Fanny until her hair had been dressed by Mrs. Thielky, who was a German, but who spoke English as well as the Queen and with less of an accent.

Schwellenburg, Fanny had heard, stayed in bed until midday. Soon after her arrival in England she had proclaimed herself to be too important to take part in any work; her post was to superintend the maids. This she insisted on, which pleased Fanny, since one did not have to see so much of the disagreeable old woman if she were absent during the morning. When summoned, Fanny and Mrs. Thielky between them dressed the Queen—Mrs. Thielky as the more experienced handing the garments to Fanny who put them on.

Fanny could not help smiling to herself and imagining the

disaster that would have occurred if she had had to decide which went on first.

She would tell Susan that she would run a prodigious risk of picking up the gown before the hoop and the fan before the neck kerchief.

Soon after eight there were prayers in the Castle Chapel at which all the royal family in residence attended. Then back to breakfast—the most pleasant time of the day when she could sit over the meal for an hour with a book. There followed what could be a leisurely morning if it was not one of the Queen's curling and crimping days which she discovered occurred twice a week and at which ceremony she would be required to assist.

But the Queen's dressing for the day did not take place until a quarter to one and this was the real ceremony with Schwellenburg in command. Fanny was grateful for the consideration of the Queen who never commented on her little mistakes, but looked at the newspapers while the operation was in progress and often read out little paragraphs. After she had done so she would glance at Fanny to see if she had liked that little piece, and Fanny was touched by this little attention to her literary tastes and felt that, but for the nature of her immediate superior, she could have settled in to her new life happily enough.

Being at Court Fanny had her own toilette to attend to—something to which previously she had not given a great deal of thought. But at five o'clock the biggest trial of all—she must dine with Madam von Schwellenburg—a horrible ordeal with the old German woman showing with every gesture and almost every word she spoke her disapproval of her new assistant. Coffee was taken in Schwellenburg's drawing room while the King and his family paraded on the terraces; the Princesses liked to make quite a ceremony of this and, dressed elaborately, they walked up and down twirling their fans and bowing and smiling at the people who had come to look at them.

Poor creatures, thought Fanny, they were like birds in cages, and these terrace parades are their only chance to spread their wings a little . . . but very little.

At eight o'clock it was one of her duties to make tea for the equerries or any gentlemen who had received a royal invitation to attend one of the nightly concerts.

Between nine and eleven, while the concert was in progress, Fanny must sit with Schwellenburg; then there was supper and the last attendance on the Queen. After that Fanny would fall into her bed and be asleep almost immediately.

It was a tiring day and, as each day was very like those which had preceded it, very monotonous.

But Fanny had her diary and she looked forward to her encounters with the Princesses—who being young and eager to escape the monotony interested her more than anyone else at Court, and she was sorry for them because although etiquette would forbid her renouncing a post which so many had coveted and which had been bestowed upon her by the Queen, she knew that in due course she would escape—whereas the poor little Princesses had endured this state all their lives and would continue to do so until they married.

During her leisure hours she wrote in her diary and letters home. This was her greatest pleasure.

The King had had a word or two with Miss Burney when he passed through the Queen's apartments. His eyes twinkled every time they alighted on her; he evidently thought it most odd that she should have written a novel. But he always spoke to her kindly and if he had not spoken so quickly and she could have understood what he meant she would not have been in the least afraid of him.

As he came out of the Lodge on an August morning he was thinking of the Prince of Wales and the spectacle he made of himself pretending to economize. Something would have to be done about that sooner or later. He would have to speak to Pitt again.

As his carriage drove from Windsor to St. James's he was aware of the sullen looks which came his way; there was silence too. No loyal shouts. Quite a number of people passed the carriage without a glance. There was one cry of 'Long live the Prince of Wales'.

Sad, thought the King, when a loyal shout for the son meant a disloyal thought directed against the father.

He was tired. There were occasions when he felt ill, when he wished that he could shut himself away if not at Windsor at Kew and never have to see a politician again and to forget that he had ever begotten a son named George.

As soon as the levee was over he would return to Windsor. He would hunt, for exercise was so good for one of his ever-increasing weight; and on horseback he could forget his trouble.

His carriage was approaching St. James's Palace where a little knot of people—not more than half a dozen—had paused to watch him. He stepped out of the carriage and as he did so a woman disengaged herself from that little crowd and ran towards him waving a paper in her right hand.

Oh dear, thought the King, a petition. Still he must pay attention when his people wished to call attention to some imagined injustice.

He put out a hand to take the paper and as he did so the woman's left hand shot up; in the same second he saw the gleam of the knife and felt the dull thud in his chest.

There was a scream from the crowd. The King's attendants had seized the woman.

'Let me go,' she cried. 'I am the true Queen. The Crown is mine.'

The poor creature is mad, thought the King, and his eyes filled with tears.

'Treat her gently,' he commanded. 'I am unharmed. But tell me is my waistcoat cut?'

'Your Majesty . . . you are feeling . . .'

'I am unhurt,' said the King. 'Take the poor creature away. Come, we have a levee waiting for us.'

The Queen with the Princesses and some of the ladies were sitting at their needlework. Miss Burney was present with Miss Planta and Gooley, and the three of them were taking it in turns to read.

The Queen listened while she watched the Princesses and hoped that they were taking advantage of having a novelist as a companion. She was a little disappointed in Miss Burney's reading. It seemed strange that one who could write so admirably should not be able to read equally so. But no, Planta and Gooley were really so much more *audible* than Miss Burney; but Miss Burney was very popular with the Princesses, particularly baby Amelia who had really taken to her; and as Amelia was the King's delight and the darling of the household, for the little girl could by an imperious demand lure His Majesty's mind from bothering State matters, Amelia's approval was of great importance.

The Princess Royal had filled the snuff box and Augusta had threaded the Queen's needle and handed it to her; and it was Miss Burney's turn to read.

'Mary,' said the Queen, glancing severely at the youngest of her daughters present who had just dropped her thimble, 'pray do not fidget so, for Miss Burney has the misfortune of reading rather low at first.'

Fanny blushed and tried to speak more loudly and the Queen plied her needle, listening attentively, sewing and keeping her eyes on the company at the same time.

Suddenly there was a commotion outside the room and everyone was alert. They could hear one of the ladies shouting at the top of her voice and all recognized that voice as belonging to Madame la Fite, the Frenchwoman, one of whose duties was to read in French to the Queen and Princesses.

'I must see Her Majesty. It is *nécessaire*. I tell you. It is *trés important*.'

French phrases always crept into Madame la Fite's English when she was excited and quite clearly she was excited now.

'Gooley, pray go and see what is happening,' said the Queen.

Miss Goldsworthy rose at once, but before she could reach the door it was flung open and Madame la Fite came in; she ran to the Queen and threw herself at Her Majesty's feet.

'Oh, *mon Dieu*. Have you heard. What an *horreur*.'

'Madame la Fite, pray calm yourself,' said the Queen. 'What is it? What have you heard?'

'Oh . . . I cannot say. It is the King . . . I cannot . . . '

A not unfamiliar sick fear gripped the Queen. In her imagination she had lived through scenes like this. He had done something which would make them say he was mad. So often he seemed to be clinging with all his might to his sanity and she always feared to hear that he had let go.

She heard herself saying very quietly: 'What has happened, Madame la Fite?'

She was aware of the round awestricken faces of her daughters. She would like to send them away, but it was too late now. If what she feared had happened, it was no use attempting to keep it from them; they would know sooner or later.

'He has been stabbed. Twice!' Madame la Fite threw up her hands in a dramatic gesture. 'Twice the assassin has struck. This is what I have heard.'

The Queen stood up. Odd that she should have felt relieved. Now she could take charge of the situation.

'I have no doubt that His Majesty is safe,' she said.

The news that His Majesty was safe was brought to the Queen almost immediately. He was quite unharmed. He had been attacked by a table knife which was quite blunt and had not even cut his waistcoat. His Majesty had behaved with the utmost calm and had gone on to his levee. He would be returning soon to Windsor.

Rumours were of course flying round, but there was no need to take any notice of them. The Queen could be assured that the King was safe.

In the streets the people were saying that the woman who had attempted to take his life was one of the maidservants from Carlton House who had lost her job because the King refused to pay the Prince of Wales's debts. Another rumour was that she loved the Prince and was determined to make the King pay for treating his son so badly. Others said that it was a general discontent with the King and the longing for a new one.

The woman, however, had been proved to be a lunatic, for she kept declaring that the Crown was hers.

When the King arrived at Windsor the Queen greeted him with obvious relief.

'It was nothing,' he said. 'The poor creature was mad. I told them to treat her with gentleness.'

The Queen nodded.

'Poor soul,' she said.

And the King solemnly echoed those words.

The news was brought to Grove House in its exaggerated form.

The King had been twice stabbed outside St. James's Palace. He was dying, but they were trying to make light of it.

'I must go to Windsor with all speed,' said the Prince of Wales.

His phaeton was brought and he drove it himself, and in record time arrived at Windsor.

There was a flutter in the Princesses' apartments at the Upper Lodge.

'George is here,' cried the Princess Royal, clasping her hands in an ecstasy of excitement.

'He's come because there has been an attempt on Papa's life,' replied Augusta.

'Perhaps,' said her sister, 'he's hoping it has proved fatal, because then he would be the master of us all.' Her eyes grew dreamy. 'I'll swear everything would be different then. George would let us mix in society. This dull life would be over.'

'Charlotte, how can you say such things!'

'I will say what is true, Augusta.'

'I'd like to do a portrait of George,' sighed Elizabeth. 'He would be a most interesting subject.'

'He's very good looking,' sighed Charlotte. 'And he does such exciting things. Oh, Miss Burney, wouldn't you like to put him into a novel?'

Miss Burney laughed. 'Well, one doesn't write novels about real people, Your Highness. I think it would be *lèse majesté* or something like that.'

'Your Highness is embarrassing Miss Burney,' said Gooley reprovingly.

'Dear old Gooley, you're as bad as Papa and Mamma. I believe you *approve* of the way we're treated.'

'Now,' retorted Miss Gooley, 'we must obey His Majesty's orders and there's an end to it, as Your Highnesses all know well.'

Three-year-old Amelia had escaped from her nurses and run into the room. 'I am here. *I* am here.'

'Where you have no right to be,' said the Princess Royal affectionately reproving.

Amelia laughed and began running round the room. 'I'm a horse. I'm Papa's horse.'

There was the sound of carriage wheels in the courtyard, and all the Princesses ran to the window.

'He's going. He's going already. Oh, look. Is he not handsome?'

'He looks angry.'

'Oh dear, there must have been another quarrel.'

'But why . . . *why*? He only came to see how Papa was.'

'To see if it would soon be his turn to wear the Crown.'

'Oh, he is wicked, our dear brother. Charlotte, move over, I can't see his shoe buckles.'

'Melia wants to see George.' The child turned imperiously to Fanny. 'Miss Burney lift me up. I want to see George.'

Nothing loth, and wanting to see George as eagerly as Amelia did, Miss Burney lifted the youngest Princess into her arms and stood at the window watching an angry Prince drive off in his phaeton.

During his angry ride to London from Windsor the Prince decided that he would report exactly what had happened. He had gone down to Windsor full of good intentions; he had heard that his father had been shot at; he had gone to assure himself that the rumours were false and if they should not be, to offer what help he could. And the King had refused to see him.

How the old fellow must hate him!

He must talk to Fox and Sheridan immediately; moreover, something must be done about his debts. He could not go on living in this state for ever.

As soon as he returned to Carlton House he sent for Fox and Sheridan.

'I have been most ignobly treated at Windsor,' he told them. 'Naturally I went down as soon as I heard the news.'

'It was the only thing Your Highness could do,' replied Sheridan.

'In the event of the King's death Your Highness should be at hand,' agreed Fox.

'This turned out to be the attack of a mad woman with a dessert knife. I can tell you, gentlemen, the Queen received me very coldly.'

'On orders from the King, no doubt.'

'And he was in the next room. I even heard his silly old voice at one point. "Eh, what? Eh, what?" He was well . . . and he knew I was there. I said to my mother: "I wish to see the King that I may assure myself he has suffered no ill effects from this unfortunate affair." And do you know what she replied? "That may be, but His Majesty does not wish to see you. And I can assure you that your visit here is having more ill effect than the attack by this mad woman." My own parents! Is it not time the people knew how I am treated?'

Fox was silent for a few seconds, then he said: 'Yes, it is time . . . time to bring this matter into the open. I think we should now make our plans.'

'Plans for what?'

'For having the matter of Your Highness's finances discussed in Parliament whether Pitt is agreeable or not.'

The Prince looked delighted. He could trust Fox. Sheridan was in agreement. Fox had brought him into politics, he owed his advancement to Fox. So naturally whatever Fox suggested seemed to him the wise thing to do.

'We need time,' said Fox. 'We must make sure of our support. But the time has come for us to take the initiative.'

Fox radiated energy. Nothing pleased him more than a parliamentary conflict. This was a gamble of sorts. The public was naturally a little shocked that a prince could spend so much money he did not possess; but he had sold his horses and carriages; he had even paid off some of his debts and had lived economically, even riding in hired chaises—so he did repent of his follies. Whereas the King was determined not to help his son. He was an unnatural father; the people were beginning to realize that the King really hated the Prince of Wales. Besides, he was an unattractive old man, a boring old man, who preferred living in the country like a squire than in St. James's and Buckingham House like a king.

Fox said: 'I do not think the King has ever been so unpopular. This is clearly the time to take action. Now we must plan carefully how best we can outwit the King and clever young Mr. Pitt.'

Parliament would not reassemble until the autumn and then there were the formidable forces of Pitt to consider. Fox was eager not to go into battle until he was absolutely sure of victory and he believed that the Prince should make some bigger show of paying off some of the debts through his economical way of living. If he were not in Town—and how could he entertain there if he had shut up his reception rooms—the people would grow restive. They enjoyed watching the junketings that went on in his mansion, the fine carriages lining the Mall, the stories of his romance with Mrs. Fitzherbert. But that winter London must lose its Prince. The royal family must be content with the dreary King and Queen and occasional glimpses of the Princesses who were kept so shut away that they had no opportunity of bringing their personalities to the notice of cartoonists and the people.

'Then,' said Fox, 'in the spring we should be ready to go in and confound Mr. Pitt and His Most Ungracious Majesty.'

Marine Pavilion

Louis Weltje was a man of ideas and he had long been turning over in his mind a plan which he felt was a good one. On his trips to and from Brighton in the service of the Prince of Wales he had had time to survey the possibilities of that fishing village and he found them exciting.

Sea bathing he believed had come to stay. More and more of the fashionable world were spending long periods of the summer there. Old Smoker was a character; so was Martha Gunn; and stories of their salty conversation were repeated in the ballrooms of the great houses. Everyone must go to Brighton. The sea bathing was so beneficial to the health that it set one up for the winter; there was as much elegance in Brighton as in London because the Prince of Wales was there, and everyone knew that where the Prince of Wales was there was the *ton*, the high society, the only place where the fashionable could possibly exist.

So Herr Weltje began to make plans.

For three years the Prince had rented Grove House, but no one was going to say that Grove House was a worthy residence for the heir to the throne. Yet, reasoned Weltje, where else could the Prince stay? Quite obviously if there was no house in Brighton worthy of him, one must be provided.

No one could be unaware of Herr Weltje; he was as outstanding in his way as the Prince was in his. But whereas the Prince was remarkable for his good looks and his glittering elegance, Weltje stood out in his ugliness.

He had a face like a cod fish, some said, his short nose had an exaggerated tilt; his head was too big for his short fat body and he waddled like a duck.

To make up for his unprepossessing appearance Weltje had an alert mind. One did not rise from gingerbread peddler to major-domo in a royal household without intelligence; one was not known as the best cook in London without reason; one did not own a confectioner's shop in Piccadilly, which, it was true, was managed by one's wife, and a club which was patronized by the Prince and his friends if one was not a very clever business man.

The gingerbread seller was determined to make a fortune before he retired from business and then perhaps return to his native Hanover to spend it . . . or perhaps by then he would be content merely to remain in England.

But now . . . Brighton. Herr Weltje saw possibilities in old Kemp's Farm which stood on the west side of the Steyne. At this time few would give it a second glance, but that was all to the good. Its position was excellent; the name could be changed to Marine Pavilion; and with such a name and certain renovations it could be a more worthy dwelling for a Prince than Grove House.

Herr Weltje believed he had another winner. He would take a lease of the place, and when it was ready let it to his royal master.

When the Prince heard of the project he was delighted. Building was one of his passions and he threw himself wholeheartedly into turning Kemp's Farm into Marine Pavilion. They must have, he told Weltje, the best of architects and he would have Henry Holland brought down to Brighton. The house must be ready for occupation by Easter as he had no intention of taking Grove House again and as Carlton House was shut up he intended to come down to Brighton as soon as the weather was warm.

Work started immediately. The Prince would never suffer delay and in a few weeks there was not a sign of Kemp's Farm. In its place an elegant mansion began to take shape. It was dominated by a rotunda in its centre, with a shallow cupola. Ionic colonnades connected this with the two wings on either side; and a gallery, on which forbidding looking statues had been placed at intervals, surrounded the rotunda. The north wing, with the rotunda, had been added to what had been Kemp's Farm, and which formed the basis of the south wing, so that Holland had more than doubled the size of the place and had arranged that almost every window should have a view of the sea. He had made it a very pleasant residence with verandas and balconies; and the gardens before the Pavilion were delightful. The front lawns were surrounded by a low wall and some trellis so that it was easy for people to see over and watch the Prince and his guests enjoying the sunshine in the gardens.

It was a pleasant summer villa, the Prince decided; not ostentatious, but suited to his present mode of living. His passion for building made him dream of what alterations might one day be made to the Pavilion—but for the time being, with its two wings on either side of the rotunda, it must be adequate.

Maria, who had refused to live openly with him, took a little house very near Marine Pavilion—just a small villa, made charming by its green shutters, and it was particularly convenient because only a narrow strip of garden separated it from the Prince's house.

During that winter while Fox was urging loyal Whigs to support the Prince's request that his debts be considered a State matter and he be enabled to maintain an establishment suitable to his rank, he lived as simply as he could. Since living at Carlton House was too expensive he accepted the loan of several country houses. Lord North lent him his at Bushey and his uncle the Duke of Gloucester wrote from abroad that his mansion at Bagshot was at His Highness's service.

Maria was delighted with his economies and he delighted in pleasing Maria. Brighton took to her; she never gave herself airs, but at the same time had such a regal presence that she won immediate respect. All the well-known hostesses received her as though she were indeed the Princess of Wales. The Duchesses of Cumberland, Devonshire and Rutland, Ladies Clare, Clermont and Melbourne, were all at Brighton—they must be if they would be fashionable; there they entertained and unless they could induce the Prince and Mrs. Fitzherbert to head their guests they were most despondent. The Prince was seen going everywhere with Maria. Martha Gunn openly called her Mrs. Prince; and people took up the name. It was clear that they accepted Maria as the wife of the Prince of Wales, and the stories that a marriage had taken place between them as true.

The good people of Brighton would not have had it otherwise. The building of Marine Pavilion had brought prosperity to Brighton builders. Everyone was wanting villas put up—and grand ones too.

The people of Brighton cheered the Prince wherever he went. They did not forget what they owed to him—and of course to Mrs. Prince.

* * *

The popularity of the Prince was never so high as it was during that summer. His extreme affability and his free and easy manners won the hearts of the people of Brighton. He was sorry he had run up such debts, they said; and how had he? On setting up home for Mrs. Fitzherbert. A reasonable and romantic reason. What right had the King to be so hard on his son? They remembered that the Parliament had paid the King's debts before this. And why was that? How did he run up debts with *his* cheeseparing. They knew. It was because the Queen was spending money abroad on her needy family, that was what it was! And in the meantime the charming Prince of Wales—who it was admitted had lived extravagantly but understandably so—had to live in penury.

Penury was scarcely the word to describe the way of life at Marine Pavilion—but the Prince was undoubtedly economizing.

Under the influence of Maria, he drank less and that made him more affable still. He was interested in his servants; when a boy was dismissed for dishonesty the Prince found him weeping bitterly and asking the cause, and discovering it, said to the boy: 'If I gave you another chance would you promise me never to steal again and be my good and faithful servant?' The boy swore it and the chance was given and ever after no one dared say a word against the Prince of Wales in his hearing. Thus he was popular with the townsfolk and particularly in his own household. It was said of him that no one was ever adored so wholeheartedly by his servants as he was. He could always be relied on to help anyone in financial difficulties. It was true that he had no notion of money but quite a proportion of his debts had been incurred through his generous help to those in distress.

Maria, knowing this, rejoiced in her prince and she declared more than once that economizing in Brighton was no real hardship. In fact she had never been so happy in her life.

The Duc d'Orléans, that lover of Grace Elliott and all things English, was naturally at Brighton. He was known to be out of sympathy with his cousin the King of France and the enemy of the Queen of that country; he loved the English way of life. He was always to the fore at any race meeting; he gambled extravagantly; and he declared himself to be one of the best friends of the Prince of Wales.

One day when he found himself alone with the Prince he broached the subject of the Prince's financial difficulties and told him that it grieved him very much to see such an elegant gentleman, such a natural leader of fashion, forced to submit himself to such a bourgeois state as economy.

The Prince laughed. 'Oh, I am not so extravagant as I believed myself to be.'

'I don't like it, cousin. In fact I feel ashamed to have so much and to see you with so little.'

'Monsieur le Duc, you have a kind heart, I see.'

'I should have a happy one if you would allow me to offer you a loan which would wipe out a good proportion of your debts.'

The Prince thought how pleasant it would be to snap his fingers at his father and Mr. Pitt and avail himself of this offer.

He hesitated and Orléans was quick to see this.

'Come! What is a little money, between cousins?'

'I would not wish to inconvenience you in the least.'

'Inconvenience! It would give me the greatest pleasure.'

Sheridan came riding down to Brighton to call on Maria.

'Did you know that the Prince is about to accept a loan from the Duc d'Orléans?'

'Why, no!' cried Maria.

'I see that you realize the importance of this. He must be persuaded not to accept this. It's a political move on the part of Orléans.'

'The Prince will be calling shortly. Wait here and see him with me.'

When the Prince arrived he was pleased to see his dear friend Sherry and glad that he got on better with Maria than Fox did.

'Sherry is anxious about this money you are proposing to borrow from the Duc d'Orléans,' said Maria.

The Prince laughed. 'Is it not an excellent idea to allow the Frenchman to help me out of my difficulties? Imagine my father's rage when he knows that I have not to beg to him any more.'

'Your Highness,' said Sheridan, 'this is a member of the French royal family. I have already heard of the money he is now raising in France. This would be taken to amount to a loan from France. Your Highness will see that it would be quite impossible for you to take it.'

The Prince was startled and Maria, watching, thought he looked like a child who has had a promised toy suddenly snatched from him.

'Why?' he demanded.

'Because, sir, the Duc of Orléans is a political figure. He does not offer you this money entirely out of friendship. There is a great deal of unrest in France at this time and it would seem that there is trouble ahead. It may be that the Duc has plans . . . plans which might involve this country. Your Highness is apt to forget, if I may be so bold as to say so, the importance of your position. I must tell Your Highness that both Fox and Portland consider it most unwise of you to accept this loan.'

'So it is being discussed already?'

'In France, Your Highness, as well as in this country. I know now that with your sound good sense you will see the danger of putting yourself so deeply in debt to France through the Duc d'Orléans.'

Maria said: 'Sherry is right, I feel sure.'

The Prince smiled and nodded. 'Of course. I see it all. But . . .'

'Your Highness,' said Sheridan hastily, 'Charles has sent a message to you. Be patient for a little longer. He plans to bring your affairs up in Parliament very shortly. He is ready for the attack and he says the signs are good. There is victory ahead.'

'I will write at once to Orléans and thank him for his generosity while I tell him that I shall be unable to take advantage of his goodness.'

Sheridan sighed with relief.

The Prince was amenable. He would go to Chertsey without delay and tell Charles that Maria Fitzherbert was the best possible influence the Prince could have and that he, Charles, and she should lose this distrust they had for each other.

Betrayal in the House

Charles James Fox had been doing his best to persuade the Whig Party to support the Prince in his plea to Parliament for a settlement of his debts; but, with the exception of Sheridan, he had found little support. There was one question which Fox knew was making his friends hold back, and that was the all-important one of the Prince's marriage.

Only those who had actually been present when the officiating clergyman had pronounced the Prince and Maria Fitzherbert man and wife could swear that the marriage had taken place. These were the Prince and Maria, her brother, her uncle and the Reverend Robert Burt; all these had pledged their secrecy, and in any case by assisting at such a ceremony they were guilty of the vague but serious crime of præmunire. So no one could be absolutely certain.

Fox believed he was, however, because he had in his possession a letter from the Prince categorically denying that the marriage would ever take place; and it was on this that he based his case.

He wanted to bring up the matter in Parliament because he was certain that he could win. The Prince's debts must be paid; the Prince's allowance must be increased; and the King must be shown up for the mean old skinflint that he was. The country must understand that the King was a foolish and disagreeable old gentleman who quarrelled with every member of his family. The Prince was the hope of the future. Pitt was the King's man; Fox was the Prince's; and a wise electorate would choose the gay and charming Prince with Fox, rather than Pitt and the stupid unpleasant old King.

Never had the King been so unpopular. This was the time to strike; and Fox believed he was ready.

He knew, of course, why Portland and the others were holding back. They were unsure whether or not the Prince was married. If it came out that he was—and since his financial affairs would be under discussion it might well do so—then the Prince's popularity would be immediately lost. At the moment the affair was wrapped in mystery and the people loved a mystery. The papers were full of the love affair between Maria and the Prince. But what if it were admitted that the Prince of Wales had in fact married a lady, twice widowed, six years his senior . . . well, that might be accepted. But she was a Catholic; and ever since the Smithfield fires the people of England had determined never to have a Catholic on the throne. James II had lost his crown because of this; the Hanoverian succession had come into force because of it; the recent Gordon riots showed without a doubt that the feeling was as strong as ever.

It was clear to Fox that the reason the Whigs as a party would not support the Prince was because of the fear that he had married Mrs. Fitzherbert and that this would be disclosed; and if it were so, and he was associated with the Party, then the Party would suffer great harm and perhaps for years to come be linked with the Catholic cause.

The marriage was not mentioned because the Prince was present at most of the discussions and it was considered too delicate a matter and one of which he had no wish to talk. Everyone who knew him well knew also that he greatly disliked discussing anything which was unpleasant to him.

Fox, however, was not disturbed. He believed he knew what had happened; and he felt confident.

If the Prince would only state openly to his friends that there had been no ceremony, then there would have been no difficulty in persuading them to support him; but this he would not do.

Fox believed he understood. The Prince was romantic; he was deeply in love with Maria Fitzherbert. If people believed that there had been a ceremony of marriage, let them go on believing it. It was doubtless what Maria wished. She preferred people to believe that she had gone through a ceremony of marriage; and the Prince wished to please her.

It all seemed clear enough to Fox.

The Duke of Portland, however, was adamant. He declared that he—as head of the Whigs—could not allow the Party to bring up the matter of the Prince's debts.

The Prince was angry and cut Portland when next they met. Portland shrugged his shoulders. He was sorry to displease the Prince but he had the Party to think of.

'I am determined,' the Prince told Fox, 'to have the matter brought up in Parliament. Quite clearly I cannot continue in this state.'

Fox said: 'Certainly it shall be brought up. Never fear, we shall do without Portland. Sherry and I are worth the rest of the Party put together. We'll get an independent member to bring up the subject. I know the man: Alderman Newnham. As a rich city merchant he carries weight. I think he's our man.'

Within a few days Fox was able to report to the Prince that he was indeed the man.

Alderman Newnham would bring up the matter of the Prince's debts in the House of Commons during the next sitting.

On April 20th Alderman Newnham addressed Mr. Pitt, Chancellor of the Exchequer, which office he held in addition to that of Prime Minister.

'Is it the design of His Majesty's ministers to bring forward any proposition to rescue the Prince of Wales from his present very embarrassed condition? His Royal Highness's conduct during these difficulties has reflected greater honour and glory on his character than the most splendid diadem in Europe, yet it must be very disagreeable to his Royal Highness to be deprived of those comforts and enjoyments which so properly belong to his rank.'

Mr. Pitt rose and replied: 'It is not my duty to bring forward a subject of such nature as that suggested by the honourable gentleman except at the command of His Majesty. I have not been honoured by such a command.'

Mr. Pitt sat down and Alderman Newnham was immediately on his feet to announce that he would bring up the matter again on the 4th May.

Fox was amused. 'We have begun,' he told Lizzie. 'Pitt has been taken by surprise. He did not believe the Prince would allow the matter to be brought up.'

'Why not? He knows the Prince cannot continue as he is.'

'This is really a question of Is the Prince married or is he not? Pitt thinks His Highness daren't risk an enquiry into his affairs.'

'But surely His Highness does not wish for such an enquiry?'

'His Highness wishes his debts to be paid—and I intend to see that they are.'

Pitt sprang a surprise on the House by referring to the matter before Alderman Newnham brought it up again. He chose an opportunity when the House was full to ask whether the honourable magistrate, Alderman Newnham, intended to persevere with the motion and what scope and tendency it would take.

Newnham replied that it was simply to rescue the Prince of Wales from his present embarrassing position.

Pitt's reply was threatening.

'The principal delicacy of the question,' he remarked, 'will lie in the necessity for enquiring into the *causes* of the circumstances.'

Fox knew what that meant.

Ever since Maria's return from the Continent there had been cartoons and paragraphs about her and the Prince in the papers; but just at this time, when the question of the Prince's debts was about to be brought up in the House, John Horne Tooke, a politician who also enjoyed writing pamphlets and was renowned for his eccentricities, produced one of his papers entitled *The Reported Marriage of the Prince of Wales*. His motive seemed to be to expose the iniquities of the Marriage Act and to pour ridicule upon it, for since as he believed the Prince had married in spite of it, what use was it? He ended by writing:

'It is not from debates in either Houses of Parliament that the public will receive any solid information on a point of so much importance to the nation, to the Sovereign on the throne, to his royal successor and to a most amiable and justly valued female character whom I conclude to be in all respects both legally, really, worthily and happily for this country, Her Royal Highness, the Princess of Wales.'

This pamphlet caused a stir throughout London and the Court. Is he or isn't he? everyone was asking. Bets were taken on. Everything else now seemed to have taken second place to the all important questions: Is the Prince married? Can the Prince be married? What about the Royal Marriage Act? Is the marriage legal? But first of all: Did an actual ceremony take place?

Fox was alert.

He said to Sheridan, 'It seems that one of us must always be in the House in case Pitt should bring up the matter at any moment. You know what this is going to mean. It's not going to be a question of the Prince's debts—that is just the cover. It's going to be Is he married or not?'

'Does His Highness grasp this fact, do you think?'

'He grasps it. But he has to have his debts settled. This is the price Pitt is asking. Damned clever. He's not going to let us show the King for the mean old devil he is. He's going to try and show up the Prince and possibly attempt to have him cut out of the succession. We must be on our guard. You and I are the only defenders. You can be sure that Portland won't allow the Party to be involved.'

Nevertheless Fox was taken off his guard. Perhaps he had underestimated the effect Horne Tooke's pamphlet would have. There was one section of the House which was very much opposed to any encroachment on the Established Church of England; these were the country squires who were determined that they would never have a Catholic on the throne—nor should any monarch have a Catholic consort. This group had been very influential in driving James II from England and establishing William of Orange on the throne; and if the Prince of Wales had indeed married a Catholic they saw—not the same danger, of course, which had arisen in 1688, but what could be the beginning of a similar situation. Wives influenced husbands; they were anxious that the heir to the throne should be solidly Protestant, and if he had been so foolish as to marry a Catholic wife—even morganatically, they wanted to know it.

So they met and appointed as their spokesman John Rolle, a squire from Devonshire. Rolle was a blunt and honest man; his accent betrayed his Devon origin and he was slow of speech but forthright; no one had ever been able to bribe John Rolle; he was no respector of persons and he did not care if his frank speaking offended royalty. As a sturdy noncomformist he was not prepared to support any Catholic influence on the throne; and if the Prince of Wales had married a Catholic he was determined to know it.

On the 27th April, Alderman Newnham rose, as had been arranged, and suggested that an address be made to His Majesty the King, begging him to consider the present embarrassed financial position of the Prince of Wales and to grant him such relief as he should think fit, that the House might make good whatever sum was considered necessary to restore the Prince to a reasonable state.

Pitt was about to reply to this when John Rolle forestalled him.

His words, uttered in that burred accent, sent a shock through the House, for it was realized that from the moment the Devonshire squire had spoken there could be no more prevarication.

If ever there was a question which called particularly upon the attention of that class of persons, the country gentleman, it would be the question which the honourable Alderman had declared his determination to agitate, said Rolle, because it was a question which went immediately to affect our Constitution in Church and State. Whenever it was brought forward he would rise the moment the honourable Alderman sat down and move the previous question, being convinced that it ought not to be discussed.

Sheridan was disturbed. The moment was at hand. And where was Fox? On this most significant occasion Fox was not in the House. The burden therefore must fall on Sheridan.

What could he do? He must play for time. It was Fox who must deal with this. On the impulse of the moment it seemed there was only one thing he could do and that was to pretend not to understand Rolle's meaning.

He jumped to his feet. He failed to see, he said, what the matter had to do with Church and State. The motion had been brought, he believed, merely to free the Prince from financial embarrassments.

But Rolle was not the man to be so easily set aside. He was immediately on his feet. If the motion were introduced, he said, he would do his duty.

The wily Pitt was immediately aware of Sheridan's dismay and took his advantage.

He rose to his feet. 'I am much concerned,' he said, 'that by the perseverance of the Honourable Member I shall be driven, though with infinite reluctance, to the disclosure of circumstances which I should otherwise think it my duty to conceal.' The atmosphere of the House had become tense. 'Whenever the motion should be agitated I am ready to avow my determined and fixed resolution to give it my absolute negative.'

Sheridan was quickly aware of Pitt's indiscretion. He had made an announcement to the effect that he would refuse something which had not had the privilege of debate. This was unparliamentary; and uneasy as he was, Sheridan was politician enough to be obliged to discountenance his opponent by making him aware of his indiscretion.

He must attempt to hide his concern in his attack on Pitt. 'Some honourable gentlemen have thought proper to express their anxious wishes that the business should be deferred,' he pointed out, 'but Mr. Pitt has erected an insuperable barrier to such a step. It would seem to the country, to all Europe, that the Prince had yielded to terror what he had denied to argument. What could the world think of such conduct, but that he has fled from the enquiry and dare not face his accusers? But if such was the design of these threats, I believe they will find the author of them has as much mistaken the feelings as the conduct of the Prince.'

There was excitement throughout the House.

Sheridan sought to hide his dismay, but he knew that the question of the Prince's marriage would now most certainly be brought forward.

He went with all speed to Carlton House and there gave the Prince a detailed account of what had happened in the House.

'There can be no hope now,' said Sheridan, 'that the question will not be brought up in the House. We have to have an answer.'

The Prince grew pale with rage and scarlet with mortification.

'Rolle!' he cried. 'Who is this fellow? Some country yokel! What have my affairs to do with him? Why cannot he keep his silly mouth shut? The only thing I am asking is the payment of my debts. What has any other matter to do with it? What concern is it of theirs?'

'Your Highness,' replied Sheridan, 'the question will be asked. What we have to concern ourselves with, is how it is going to be answered.'

The Prince was silent. He was well informed enough to understand the issue at stake. To admit to the marriage was disaster. Maria . . . a Catholic! It was enough to put an end to the Hanoverian dynasty. Why should the Hanoverians be the rulers if they were tainted by Catholicism? It was the sole reason why the Stuarts had been spurned.

Was ever a man in such a predicament? He had to deny his marriage or run the risk of losing his crown!

The silly words of the ballad kept ringing through his head:

> 'I'd crowns resign,
> To call thee mine . . .'

But Maria was his; he could have Maria *and* the Crown; and in his heart he knew he had no intention of losing either if he could help it.

'Sherry,' he cried, 'for God's sake tell me what to do.'

Sheridan looked at him steadily. It was clear that he was worried. It was no use calling on his Irish charm, his witty flattery now; this was a matter of a stark Yes or No.

'I can only hope,' he said, 'that it is possible to deny the marriage, for if it were not I think Your Highness would be in a very perilous position indeed.'

The Prince could not look into Sheridan's eyes. He despised himself. He had sworn that he would stand by Maria; that they would go abroad and live if necessary; he would do anything for her. But the Crown! How glittering it seemed at that moment. He saw a picture of himself going from one European country to another—a private gentleman, an outcast in a way, stripped of the glitter of royalty. Who would pay his debts then? And how was it possible for one brought up as he had been, one who had known from his nursery days that he would be King of England, to give up all that he had looked on as his right?

As for Maria . . . he loved Maria; he would always love Maria. He *thought* of her as his wife and to all intents and purposes she *was* his wife. Surely that was enough? Maria herself, he told himself triumphantly, would not *wish* him to make the sacrifice. That was the answer. Maria would be most unhappy if he admitted to the marriage.

Yet he could not deny her completely.

'Sherry,' he said, 'how would it be possible for me to marry Maria? The Marriage Act makes it illegal.'

Sherry was relieved. He had made the right answer. Sherry was as ready to prevaricate as the Prince himself. They would not discuss the fact that a marriage could be a true marriage in the eyes of the Church if not in those of the State and that any marriage which the Church considered a true one, was a marriage.

But no, this was easy. They must glide safely over the facts. There was so much at stake.

'Sherry,' said the Prince, 'Maria must be warned.'

Sheridan agreed that this must be so.

'You are my very good friend. You have a way with words. Haven't we always said so? You, my dear Sherry, will be able to explain.'

Sheridan was uneasy; but he saw the point. Fox would have

to be warned; and from now on Fox would have to take over in the House. But Maria Fitzherbert disliked Fox and he Sheridan, was the one who must set about placating her.

A delicate task, but since the Prince insisted, he must do his best.

He went at once to Maria's house and told her that he had something of the utmost importance to say to her. He then explained what had happened in the House and how through the actions of Rolle and Pitt the question of her marriage to the Prince of Wales would be raised.

Maria was alarmed. She had sworn to the Prince that she would tell no one of the ceremony which had taken place; so she could not explain the truth to Sheridan.

'We all know that you are virtuous,' said Sheridan, 'and the Prince has shown by his conduct that he regards you as his wife. But it is, of course, of the utmost importance that no *ceremony* should have taken place . . . no ceremony with a priest that is. There was a ceremony we know when the Prince attempted his life and he put a ring on your finger . . . such a ceremony while full of significance to yourself and the Prince is not one which the country would frown on . . .'

I'm getting involved, thought Sheridan. How difficult it is to meander round and round the point in order to avoid it!

'Sherry,' she said, 'I feel like a dog with a log tied round its neck.'

'Maria, I would do anything in the world to protect you. But if it were admitted that a ceremony has taken place I should fear the consequences to His Highness.'

She was silent. She thought of the ceremony, the solemn words she had spoken, the vows she had taken. To her it was a true marriage—and she had believed it was so to the Prince. She trusted in him; he had sworn so often to stand by her, to face his father and the whole country for her sake. Why then should he be afraid of Mr. Pitt and the House of Commons? But of course he was not afraid. She believed that when he was called upon to answer that question he would tell them that she was indeed his wife; that they had made their vows before a priest; that the marriage ceremony had been performed.

Sheridan was looking at her expectantly. But she would not tell him. She had sworn herself to secrecy; she could not betray Robert Burt and let him be submitted to the results of præmunire.

It was for the Prince to stand up and make the avowal; it was for him to protect them all.

And he will, she thought. Of course he will.

'I am sure,' she told Sheridan, 'that the Prince will know how to act.'

Fox listened to Sheridan's account of what had taken place. He heard of the interview with Maria.

'She did not say there was a ceremony?'

'She did not,' replied Sheridan. 'I believe the Prince has made her swear to secrecy.'

Fox was thoughtful. 'No doubt she is thinking of the ceremony with the ring at the time of the false suicide. That is what it must be. A hundred curses on this man Rolle and a thousand more on Pitt. But never fear, I shall know how to deal with this.'

'I thought you would,' said Sheridan. 'I wish to God you'd been in the House on the 27th.'

'I couldn't have done anything more than you did, if I had.'

'It's that devil Pitt.'

'Yes, it is often that devil Pitt. Cheer up, Sherry. You'll see the Fox at work. I always liked a fight; and believe me there's no one I'd rather have for my opponent than clever Mr. Pitt.'

'Are you seeing the Prince?'

'No. I have what I need.'

Fox was smiling slyly. Had there been a marriage ceremony? That was not exactly the point as he saw it. What he believed was that there had to be a denial of the ceremony. That was imperative or the succession would be imperilled. A fine thing after all the work he had done in bringing up the Prince to support the Whigs if Pitt attempted to divert the succession to the Duke of York, which he might well do if it were disclosed that the Prince of Wales had married a Catholic—for that was exactly what Fox would have done in Pitt's place.

The denial—a categorical denial was necessary, and he was going to make it. He had every reason to make it because he had in his possession a letter from the Prince of Wales dated 11th December 1785 in which His Highness most definitely stated that he had no intention of marrying Mrs. Fitzherbert. And as that letter had been written only a few days before the Prince and Mrs. Fitzherbert had quite clearly become lovers, that was all he needed for his case.

* * *

Alderman Newnham had announced that he would bring forward his motion concerning the debts of the Prince of Wales on April 30th; and that day saw a crowded House of Commons.

Fox was in his place and with him Sheridan; and there was an air of excitement as members waited for the expected duel between those two great politicians Pitt and Fox, and more than anything for the revelation which must inevitably be made.

Alderman Newnham rose and began: 'On Friday last much personal application was made to me from various quarters of the House to press me to forgo my purpose, and much has been said of the dangerous consequences which might result from the discussion of such a subject. One gentleman has gone so far as to contend that it would draw on questions affecting Church and State . . .'

Members leaned forward in their seats; eyes were turned towards Fox and Sheridan; and when Newnham had finished speaking Fox was immediately on his feet.

Fox began by asking the House's indulgence for his absence on the previous Friday. He had not heard, he said, that a subject of so much delicacy and importance was to be alluded to.

'I should like the House to understand,' he went on, 'that I speak from the immediate authority of the Prince of Wales when I assure the House that there is no part of His Highness's conduct that he is afraid or unwilling to have investigated.'

He then went on to speak of the Prince's debts. His Highness had been amiable towards his father to whom he had been both dutiful and obedient; and he was prepared to give a general and fair account of his debts although the House would readily see how impossible it was for him to give details of every single item. He could assure the House that there was not a single case in His Highness's life which he would be ashamed to have known.

'With respect to the allusion to something full of danger to Church and State made by the honourable gentleman, one of the members for Devonshire, until that gentleman thinks proper to explain himself, it is impossible to say to what that allusion refers. I can only suppose it refers to that miserable calumny, a low malicious falsehood. In this House, where it is known how frequent and common falsehoods of the time are, I had hoped that a tale only fit to impose on the lowest persons in the street would not have gained the smallest portion of credit; but when it appears that an invention so monstrous, a report of a fact which has not the smallest degree of foundation, a report of a fact actually impossible to have happened, has been circulated with so much industry as to have made an impression on the minds of members of this House, it proves at once the uncommon pains taken by the enemies of His Highness to propagate the grossest and most malignant falsehoods to deprecate his character and injure him in the opinion of his country. When I consider that His Royal Highness is the first subject in the Kingdom, and the immediate heir to the throne, I am at a loss to imagine what species of party it was which could have fabricated so base and scandalous a calumny . . . a tale in every particular so unfounded and for which there is not the shadow of anything like reality.'

Mr. Pitt watched his opponent without betraying his feelings; he was, as usual, the calmest member of the House. Fox went on stressing his point, his eyes flashing with contempt and indignation.

'His Royal Highness has authorized me to declare that as a peer of Parliament, he is ready in the other House to submit to any, the most pointed questions, which can be put to him, or to afford His Majesty or His Majesty's ministers the fullest assurance of the utter falsehood of the fact in question, which never has, and which common sense must see never could have, happened.'

When Fox sat down Pitt had little to say. He had achieved his purpose; the matter of the Prince's marriage had been brought up and denied by Fox, on, so said Fox, the Prince's authority. Rolle however, had something to say. He replied that he knew and they knew that there were certain laws of Parliament which forbade a marriage such as that which they had been discussing, but it was absurd to say that it could not have taken place. Therefore it was desirable that the matter should be elucidated.

Fox was immediately on his feet. 'I do not deny the calumny in question merely with regard to the effect of existing laws, but I deny it *in toto*, in point of fact as well as in law. The fact not only never could have happened legally, but never did happen in any way whatsoever, and has from the beginning been a base and malicious falsehood.'

Rolle retorted: 'Has the Right Honourable gentleman spoken from direct authority?'

'I have spoken from direct authority,' replied Fox.

It was enough.

Fox, friend and confidant of the Prince of Wales, had 'on

direct authority' denied the Prince's marriage to Mrs. Fitzherbert.

Fox left the House of Commons with the feeling of a man who has done what had to be done in the best possible manner.

Passing Brook's Club he decided to look in for a gamble before going to Chertsey to tell Lizzie about the day's proceedings.

No sooner had he entered the club than Orlando Bridgeman came up to him. Bridgeman's face was rather flushed and the young man looked extremely mortified.

'Charles,' he said. 'I've just heard your speech in the House.'

'I daresay. Every member must have been present. I've rarely seen the place so crowded.'

'But you were *wrong*.'

'Wrong? What do you mean?'

'They *were* married.'

'Nonsense.'

'Oh yes, they were. I was at the wedding.'

Fox looked sceptical.

'I assure you I was. It was on the 15th December. I went to Park Street with the Prince and waited outside to make sure that no one came into the house while it was taking place.'

'Ah, but you weren't an actual witness.'

'I tell you, Charles, it did happen. I swear it.'

'You had better do no such thing. Your best plan is to forget all that happened on that night.'

'But what of Maria . . . Mrs. Fitzherbert?'

'If it took place . . . she might as well forget it too.'

'You couldn't have had the Prince's authority . . .'

'I have the Prince's authority,' said Fox. 'Look here, my dear young man. This is a delicate matter . . . a dangerous matter. You heard our friend Rolle. This could put the throne in danger . . . or could have. I have dealt with it in the only way it is possible to deal with it.'

'But what of that lady?'

'The Prince's mistress? Well, that's considered a very fortunate position for a young lady.'

'Not Maria!'

Fox shrugged his shoulders. Then he was stern suddenly. 'I should advise you not to tell anyone else what you have told me. Weren't you sworn to secrecy?'

'Why, yes.'

'Well then, keep your own vows and don't worry about anyone else's.'

Fox did not go on into Brook's but decided to go straight to Chertsey. So the deceitful young romantic had gone through a ceremony after all; and he had not told Fox. Well, it was fortunate he had not, because that declaration had had to be made; and it was easier making it when one believed one might be speaking the truth and far more difficult if one knew one were lying. So, a few days after he had written that letter—four days to be precise—he had gone through a ceremony of marriage!

Put not your trust in Princes, thought Fox. But that he should have deceived me so utterly!

Now he will have to face the fury of his lady; and it is no use his asking kind Mr. Fox to help him escape from that.

Fox had left it to Sheridan and Earl Grey to go to Carlton House to give the Prince an account of what had taken place in the House.

He received them eagerly and was by no means put out when he heard how Fox had denied his marriage.

In fact he was relieved. That matter was settled then. And that other? What of his debts?

Sheridan replied that he did not think there would be much difficulty about that. It was almost certain that a sum of money would be granted for their settlement; all that remained was for them to see it was adequate.

When they had left him, the Prince wrote to Fox telling him that he had heard through Sheridan and Grey an account of the proceedings in the House, and that he felt more comfortable because of this. He believed that some terms were likely to be proposed and if Charles would call on him on the next day at two he would find him at home. He signed himself 'Ever affectionately yours, George P.'

But when he had despatched the letter he thought of Maria who would now know what had happened in the House of Commons because everyone would be talking of it.

It was not so easy, not so *comfortable* as he had been thinking it. Something would have to be done about Maria.

He must go to see her without delay. He must be the first to tell her what had happened.

When she came to greet him her hands outstretched, he grasped them both and embraced her.

She could not have heard. Thank God, he was here in time.

He laughed suddenly—a little unnaturally. 'What do you think Charles Fox has done? He has been to the House and denied that you and I are man and wife. Did you ever hear of such a thing?'

Maria released herself from his embrace and stood very still, looking at him questioningly. He felt the colour flood his face; he knew that he had betrayed himself. Maria believed that Fox had been authorized to do what he had done and she guessed on whose authority.

Still she did not speak. She stood as though she were a lifeless statue.

'Maria!' he cried. 'Maria!'

She had known that Newnham had raised the matter in the House of Commons; she knew the issues which were at stake. She had believed in him, this young gay romantic lover who had declared so many times that he would resign his crown for her sake; she had talked to him of her beliefs, her religion, that in her which had made her leave the country to escape him. He knew full well her principles; she had thought he understood since he had arranged that ceremony which was a true marriage in the eyes of the Church and therefore in hers and—she had believed—in his.

But he had denied it . . . denied it ever had taken place! She, a deeply religious woman, who believed in the sanctity of the marriage tie had agreed to live with him only if she were married to him, and he had wished the marriage to take place; he had wanted a true marriage as she had!

And now he had denied it. He had betrayed her. He had allowed that man whom she had always looked upon as her enemy to get up in the House of Commons and tell the world that she was not the Prince's true wife; she was his mistress. He had had many mistresses, the most famous of them the notorious Perdita Robinson—and she, Maria Fitzherbert, would now be said to be one of them.

'Maria,' he continued, 'listen to me. Fox has done this . . . Fox. He has said this. I did not know he was going to say it. If he had consulted me . . .'

'He has said it.' Her voice sounded quiet and calm. 'He has dishonoured me . . . publicly.'

'But Maria, it is only Fox . . .'

'Only Fox! Only the man whose word carries more weight than any except Pitt's!'

The Prince's eyes filled with tears. 'Maria, my beloved, can you blame me for Fox's misdeeds?'

'But you knew. You must have known.'

'I swear it, Maria. I did not know. He did not mention the matter to me.' He began throwing his arms about in dramatic gestures; he threw himself on to a couch and wept. 'That you should believe this of me! Haven't I *sworn* . . .'

'Yes,' said Maria, 'you have sworn.'

'And can you believe that I would forget my vows?' He was on his feet, embracing her. 'You cannot break my heart, Maria. You know I won't live without you. Don't you trust me? Oh, Maria, how can you treat me like this? You doubt my word. You believe *Fox* . . . rather than me. What of *your* vows, Maria?'

'So you did not know? You are not in this . . . *plot* to betray me?'

'Maria!'

He looked so appealing with the tears on his cheeks; he cried so elegantly; he had had so much practice in the art of weeping and he never did it ungracefully. His conduct since the ceremony had given her every reason to believe that he was devoted to her. He had even reformed his wild ways a little to please her. He was young; her maternal feelings were aroused; she was relenting.

It was Fox who had done this. She had always known he was an enemy. How wrong of her to blame the Prince for Fox's misdeeds.

She kissed his cheek lightly.

It was enough. He flung his arms about her.

'Now I am happy,' he said.

But it was only a respite. The next day she had a full report of Fox's speech. 'On direct authority,' Fox had said. That could mean only one thing. Fox would never have dared stand up in the House of Commons and declare he had direct authority to deny the Prince's marriage if that authority had not come from the Prince himself.

When the Prince called on her he was surprised by the change in her and he knew it was not going to be easy to explain this to Maria.

'So it is true,' she said. 'You have conspired with your friends to betray me.'

'I can explain . . .'

'There is nothing you can say which will explain it.'

'Maria, it makes no difference to us.'

'It makes every difference to us. I think you had better leave me now. I do not wish to see you again.'

'You don't mean that.'

She was fierce suddenly. 'I certainly mean it. Do you think I wish to live with a man who denies his marriage to me? If you are ashamed of it—that is an end to it. Go back to Mr. Fox. Drink with him on the success of your plan. I have my marriage certificate. What if I sent that to Mr. Pitt? But you need have no fear, I gave my word that as far as I was concerned it should remain a secret. I keep my word. And now, I wish to be alone.'

The Prince stared at her, dumbfounded. 'Maria, what has happened? I have never seen you like this before.'

'You know full well what has happened. And I have never before been betrayed in this way. Did you hear me? I no longer wish you to remain here.'

'Now, Maria, please . . . I can explain.'

'I daresay you can think up further lies. You are very skilled in that.'

'Oh, that you could speak to me like this!'

'I have told you I have no wish to speak to you at all. I have finished with speaking to you.'

'*You* can say this to *me* . . . who would do anything in the world to please you?'

'The only way in which you could please is by leaving me . . . this moment.'

'Oh, my fierce Maria!'

She threw him off impatiently. The charm, the tears, the protestations of undying affection—they were no good now. She did not believe in them any more.

'Maria, I will do anything in the world for you . . .'

'Except acknowledge me as your wife?'

'Fox made that declaration in the House . . . because . . . because he had to. It was Pitt who was making trouble. Don't you see . . . if they had admitted to the marriage, on account of your religion there would have been trouble . . . about the succession, Maria.'

'That was an aspect I pointed out to you *before* our wedding.'

'This was in the House of Commons.'

'Of course it was the House of Commons. Where else would such an issue be brought up? You knew it when you married me and now you pretend to be surprised. I want to hear no more. Go . . . I will not listen.'

'You *shall* listen, Maria. Very soon I may be King and my first action will be to abolish the Marriage Act. I will make you a Duchess. We will have another ceremony, and then . . .'

'You talk like a child or a fool. Do you think a Catholic Queen would be more acceptable than a Catholic Princess of Wales? But that is not the point. You have denied our marriage. This is an outrage to my honour and to my religion. I have nothing more to say, except that I shall do nothing to betray your perfidy. Your secret is safe with me. But I do not wish to see you again.'

'Maria,' he cried piteously, but she had gone.

The Prince went back to Carlton House and summoned several of his friends, among them Sheridan, Grey, Sir Philip Francis and Lord Stourton.

When they arrived they found him pacing up and down in a distraught manner.

'It's Maria,' he cried. 'I have never seen her like this before. She is like a tigress. She has said she won't see me again. What am I going to do?'

Sheridan said: 'It will pass. In a few days she will be ready to be friends again.'

The Prince shook his head. 'I know Maria. She is determined. She has these damned principles. I know she means what she says.'

'She is devoted to Your Highness. She will never refuse to see you.'

'I know Maria,' said the Prince blankly. 'You remember how she left England . . . and stayed away for a year? Oh, my God, what if she goes away again. What am I going to do? Some of you must see her. *Explain* . . .'

'Explain what, Your Highness?' asked Grey. 'The only explanation she will accept is your repudiation of Fox's statement. Your Highness will see that that is impossible.'

'I did not give him authority . . .' cried the Prince.

Grey was a man who spoke his mind. He said: 'Fox had a letter from Your Highness four days before the marriage was alleged to have taken place. That is his defence for speaking as he did.'

'A letter . . .' said the Prince, his dismay apparent. He remembered now. He frowned at Grey. That man had always been too frank for him. Not like Sherry, who always said the pleasant thing whatever he was thinking.

'Your Highness had to make the choice,' said Grey bluntly.

'Acknowledging your marriage or facing the threat of losing the Crown. Fox chose the only course.'

'I did not direct him to do so. That's what Maria must be made to understand. One of you must explain to her. You, Francis . . . You go . . . You go now . . . Now, this minute . . . and come straight back here.'

Sir Philip Francis looked uneasy but could not very well disobey the Prince's command.

He went, and during his absence the Prince and his friends discussed the affair; the Prince, seeking loopholes, by which he could persist in keeping quiet about his marriage and so keep his chances of the succession, storming and weeping, telling his friends how he could not live without Maria and that something would have to be done.

They listened with apparent sympathy, but there was not one of them who did not know that to own publicly to the marriage would be fatal to the Prince and the Whigs—however much that party had attempted to dissociate itself from the affair.

The Prince must see reason; he must get over this mad infatuation for a religious woman; or she must cast aside her principles and allow herself to be accepted as his mistress.

In due course Sir Philip Francis returned to Carlton House.

'Well, Francis, well?' cried the Prince.

'She is furious. She says she has no wish to see Your Highness ever again.'

The Prince wailed and threw himself on to the couch, covering his face with his hands.

'She said that Fox has rolled her in the kennel like a street walker and that he has lied. Every word he had said was a lie.'

'She *believes* every word Fox said was a lie,' said the Prince hopefully.

'Even so,' Grey pointed out, 'Your Highness would have to make a public declaration that this was so to satisfy her.'

Trust Grey to dash all hopes to the ground.

'What am I going to do? I must do something. Sherry, what can I do?'

Sheridan said soothingly: 'I doubt not in time it will blow over. She will forget it. She will realize that this is the only way . . .'

The Prince was looking trustingly at Sheridan.

Then he said: 'If it was brought up in the House again. If it could be *modified* . . .'

Lord Stourton said that he did not see how it could be modified. It was a statement which unfortunately could only have one answer: Yes or No.

'There must be some way. Touch on the marriage lightly . . . and make sure that Maria is spoken of with respect. Charles went too far. There was no need for him to go so far. Grey, you could explain it to the House.'

'Your Highness, it would be an impossibility.'

The Prince's eyes were angry. Grey frustrated him at every turn. 'It seems you are determined to make difficulties,' he said coldly.

'Your Highness, the difficulties are already made.'

'You could do it. You could modify . . .'

'Modify,' cried Grey. 'Will Your Highness explain what you mean by modify? I fear I cannot see how this could be done.'

'But you will *think* of something.'

'I regret, Your Highness, that I cannot do so and I think it a grave mistake to bring this matter up in the House again.'

'You seem determined not to help, Grey,' said the Prince coldly.

He turned to Sheridan who, during the altercation between Grey and the Prince, seemed to have been trying to shrink further into his chair.

'You'll do it, Sherry?'

Oh, God, thought Sheridan. What am I let in for now?

'Your Highness, let us consider the matter.'

The Prince brightened. 'Dear Sherry, I knew I could rely on you.' A snub to Grey, but Grey was not a man to fawn on Princes. Not like poor old Sherry, thought Sheridan, who has come up in the world, from theatre manager to Prince's crony on Irish blarney and an ability to juggle with words. He had to think quickly now: Face the House on this matter which was already concluded or lose the friendship of the Prince of Wales, who would one day be King. Grey had already chosen. Well, Grey was a man of background and political ambitions; Grey could doubtless afford to throw away the friendship of the Prince. Sheridan could not. He was a born gambler in any case. He would back the Prince.

'I will do what I can,' he promised.

'Dearest Sherry!'

'But I think Your Highness will agree with me that the matter should not be brought up until *after* Fox has secured the payment of your debts.'

The Prince reluctantly agreed to this. He knew his dear friend

Sherry was right; and no one had such a way with words as he had.

When Sherry had spoken in the House, Maria would feel happier. She would see him again. She would give him a chance to explain. All would be well between them. They would go down to Brighton together; and if his debts were paid he would give her a fine house of her own; he would make some alterations to the Marine Pavilion.

It would be wonderful to live like a Prince again . . . with Maria.

Mr. Pitt called on the King.

'Your Majesty will share my relief,' said the Prime Minister, 'that this unfortunate matter of His Royal Highness's affairs has come to an end. He has, through Mr. Charles James Fox, given us a complete denial of the marriage with Mrs. Fitzherbert. Therefore he has not, as we feared, acted in defiance of Your Majesty's own Royal Marriage Act.'

'It is a relief, eh?' replied the King. 'I feared he might have married the woman. He's capable of it, Mr. Pitt. Quite capable.'

'I feared so, too,' said Pitt. 'And now this matter of his debts. They amount to £161,000 which I propose shall be paid by Parliament; and £60,000 shall be set aside for His Highness's expenses at Carlton House. If Your Majesty is agreeable to this, I feel the time has come to raise His Highness's income and suggest an additional £10,000 a year.'

The King said he thought this was very generous and the young rip ought to be satisfied with that.

'There is another matter which I wished to discuss with Your Majesty,' went on Mr. Pitt, 'and that is the discord which exists between Your Majesty and His Highness. This is undesirable and it seems that now is a good moment to change it. It has been publicly stated that the Prince, contrary to rumour, has not defied Your Majesty's Marriage Act. You have sanctioned the payments of his debts and increased his income. There is therefore no reason for discord in the family. There should be a reunion—a making-up of differences. This, I think, sir, is very important and the moment is ripe for it.'

The King looked proudly at his Mr. Pitt, and silently thanked God for him. Momentarily he compared him with dear old North—good friend, but what a blunderer!—and what the King felt he needed more and more as the weeks passed was a good steady prop. Mr. Pitt enabled him to get away to Kew and Windsor. Mr. Pitt was fast becoming a power in the land. Mr. Pitt kept the Fox at bay. Good Mr. Pitt!

'You are right I am sure, Mr. Pitt. There shall be a family reunion. The Prince shall come to Windsor and I will make sure that the family receive him with friendship.'

Mr. Pitt bowed and took his leave.

Parliament had agreed to settle the Prince's debts and Alderman Newnham rose to say that he was happy that the motion he had been proposing to bring forward—that of the Prince's debts— was now no longer necessary.

Members of the House expressed their satisfaction.

'I readily concur in the joy the honourable gentleman has expressed,' said Mr. Pitt.

'We must all feel the highest satisfaction,' added Mr. Fox.

Mr. Rolle, however, while commenting on his satisfaction, added: 'But I temper that satisfaction by making it clear that if it should hereafter appear that any concession has been made, humiliating to the country or dishonourable in itself, I would be the first man to stand up and stigmatize it as it deserves.'

There were groans through the House. Why could not the blunt old countryman leave the matter alone.

Mr. Pitt, however, suavely rose to assure the honourable member that this was not so and he need have no fears.

Sheridan knew that this was his only opportunity. He must speak before the matter was closed. How much better, he thought, to let it alone. But he dared not. He must speak. His friendship with the Prince was at stake.

He stood up. He was aware of Fox watching him warily. Fox would know exactly why he was doing this.

'I cannot believe,' began Sheridan, 'that there exists on this day but one feeling and one sentiment in the House, that of heartfelt satisfaction at the auspicious conclusion to which the business has been brought. His Royal Highness wishes it to be known that he feels perfect satisfaction at the prospect before him and he also desires it to be distinctly remembered that no attempt has at any time been made to screen any part of his conduct, actions or situation . . .'

The members were looking askance at Sheridan. This had all been said before. Why repeat it? Sheridan himself hurried on to the purpose of his speech.

'While his Royal Highness's feelings have been doubtless considered on this occasion, I must take the liberty of saying, however much some may think it a subordinate consideration, that there is another person entitled in every honourable and delicate mind to the same attention. I will not otherwise attempt to describe this person except to affirm that ignorance or vulgar malice alone could have persevered in attempting to injure one on whose conduct truth could fix no just reproach and whose character claims, and is entitled to, the truest and most general respect.'

Eyebrows were raised; lips were curled in cynical smiles. What was Sheridan suggesting? Mrs. Fitzherbert was the Prince's mistress, yet at the same time she was a paragon of virtue, an example to all women?

Even the jaunty Sheridan could not hide the fact that he was embarrassed as he sat down to silence.

But when he presented himself at Carlton House the Prince embraced him.

'My dear friend,' he cried. 'I knew I could rely on you. I have had a report of your speech in the house. Maria will be delighted, I know. I but waited to see you and thank you in person before I go to call on her.'

Sheridan went home in high spirits. He had made a bit of a fool of himself in the House, but that could not be helped. He stood higher with the Prince than ever before; and that was good because Fox's influence was waning fast.

Meanwhile the Prince was calling on Maria; and he had the discomfiture to be told that Mrs. Fitzherbert was not at home.

Not at home to the Prince of Wales! It was incredible. But she had meant it when she had said that she would not live with him. A few words spoken by Sheridan would not influence her. She thought they were absurd. Did they really think that Sheridan's getting up in the House and referring to her as a pattern of womanhood could affect her when Fox had stated on *direct authority* that she was living in sin with the Prince?

No, Maria was wounded. She had been betrayed.

The Prince was mistaken if he thought he could treat her so and be forgiven. She had made it clear in the first place that she would not live with him without marriage; and since by his action he had shown that he considered himself not married to her, she could not live with him.

Fox at Chertsey was in a mood of resignation.

'What a mess, Liz! What a mess!'

'You regret having denied the marriage?' asked Lizzie.

'It was the only thing to do. If it had come out that they had actually gone through a ceremony the Commons would be in an uproar. God knows what would have happened. The people always fancied the Stuarts more than the Guelphs, though our Prince is more popular than most of them have been. But they would never have accepted a Catholic marriage. No, it had to be said; and it was my lot to say it.'

'Our Little George is something of a coward, is he not?'

'You know him as well as I, Liz.'

Lizzie smiled, remembering that time when she had briefly been the Prince's mistress and had accumulated quite a little fortune out of the adventure which was now helping to keep a home together for herself and Charles.

'Perhaps not quite,' she said. 'He has a kind heart but he hates trouble. He'd help anyone out of a difficulty if he could without too much trouble, but he'd go to a great deal of trouble to protect himself.'

'He's no fool. He realizes what's at stake. He knows that what has happened was the only way to get him out of a dangerous situation.'

'But he has, by all accounts, lost his Maria.'

'A temporary loss. She'll come round.'

'She's no ordinary woman.'

'A paragon of virtue according to Sherry.'

'He did very well in the circumstances.'

'Poor Sherry. I'm glad it was his job and not mine. Yes, he did well too . . . considering the position. How he kept a straight face I can't imagine.'

'He was thinking of his own future, that was why. He has to keep the Prince's favour . . . for what is he going to do without Mr. Fox there to support him.'

'Eh?'

'Well, Mr. Fox will, I prophesy, no longer be the close associate of His Royal Highness. Maria would think it rather strange, would she not, that one who had so displeased the Prince should continue to enjoy his friendship.'

'You're too clever, Liz.'

'How can one be too clever? I merely state the obvious. If he wants to keep Maria he has to be displeased with Mr. Fox—and you can bet even higher than your usual stakes that Mrs. Fitzherbert, who never did love Mr. Fox, will now regard that gentleman with loathing. And since His Royal Highness must placate Maria . . . well, you don't need me to go on, do you?'

He took her hand and smiled at her.

'No need at all,' he said. 'That is why I propose leaving the country. A change of scene will be very desirable.'

She tried to hide her fears and he held out his hand to her.

'Liz,' he said, 'how would you like to go to Italy? We could study the art treasures of that country. I'll show you the Sistine chapel. We'll sit in the sun and drink their wine.'

She was smiling; intensely happy.

'Oh, my God, Liz,' he said. 'You didn't think I would go without you . . . anywhere?'

The Prince in Despair

The King was pacing up and down the Queen's drawing room. How I wish he would stay still! thought the Queen. This excitement is bad for him.

'Although I am receiving him,' the King was saying, 'I shall expect deference from him. He'll have to drop that arrogance, eh? He may be a little king in Carlton House but I'm the King here at Windsor.'

'He'll remember that,' said the Queen. 'I'm sure he has learned his lesson.'

'What's that, eh, what? His lesson? Do you think he'll ever learn? But we'll show him that if he's going to be received back into the family he has to deserve it, eh, what?'

It was not the right attitude perhaps, thought the Queen. Oh dear, she did hope this was going to be an end to these family quarrels.

'Mr. Pitt seems to think that it is a bad thing that there should be enmity in the family.'

The King frowned at her. Charlotte should know by now that he never talked State matters with her. She was not supposed to mention the name of Mr. Pitt. But there was gossip, of course. There was chatter. He was talking to her about the return of the Prince of Wales to the heart of the family simply because it was a domestic matter and these were the only matters he discussed with her.

'I think it's a good thing that there should be no enmity in the family. Anyone would agree to that, eh, what?'

'But certainly. Oh, how pleased I am that he did not marry

220

that woman. I am surprised in a way because I have heard that she is a very pleasant creature.'

A very pleasant creature, thought the King; and a very beautiful one by all accounts. They had all found beautiful women for themselves, except the King. He had Charlotte. How old she looked! Poor plain little Charlotte. Yet he had been faithful to her, in deed if not in thought, since their marriage.

Well, he was getting old now and he was glad he had been a good husband.

'Have you warned the Princesses?' he asked.

What a way to talk of the return of a brother! thought the Queen. Warned!

'Yes, I have told them that they may expect a visit from their brother.'

'Hm, and what did they say to that?'

'They are delighted. Amelia was so excited that she bounced up and down in her chair and shot her milk all over the table.'

The King's face creased into a smile. 'Oh, she did then, eh, what? I must go and ask her if she is equally excited by a visit from her Papa.'

The very mention of Amelia's name soothed the King. He doted on the child; in fact the stern rules which the others had to obey were not in force for Amelia. She could imperiously climb on to her father's knee and ask him ridiculous questions and make him sing songs to her—and he merely obeyed her, the love shining from his eyes. She was doubly precious because they had lost Octavius and Alfred—and Sophia the next youngest was six years her senior. It was small wonder that Amelia was his pet.

He rose, the prospect of seeing his youngest daughter temporarily wiping away the anxieties he felt by the impending reunion with his eldest son.

'She will be in the nursery now,' said the Queen.

'Then I will call on Her Royal Highness.'

His good humour was completely restored and when he arrived at the nursery he found his youngest daughter sitting on the floor playing with her toys and kneeling there with her was Miss Burney to whom he had heard Amelia had taken a great fancy.

'Hello, Papa,' said the Princess, scarcely turning her head, while Miss Burney stood up and curtsied.

'Come, Miss Burney,' said Amelia. 'It is my turn. Watch. Watch.'

'His Majesty is here, Ma'am,' whispered Fanny to the little girl.

'I know, but it is *my* turn.'

'You cannot play while His Majesty is waiting to speak to you, Ma'am,' said the agitated Fanny who was never quite sure how to behave in a situation which she had not visualized happening, and about which she had not been able to consult that doyen of court behaviour, Mrs. Delaney.

The little girl looked surprised. 'Can I not?' she asked. Then: 'Go away, Papa. Go away.'

'What?' cried the King. 'Eh, what?'

And Fanny stood up, blushing and mortified.

'Papa, I said: Go away. We want to play. So Papa . . . go. Go.'

The King looked at Fanny and smiled and then picked up the child in his arms.

'Why not a welcome for your old papa?' he asked.

'But it is my *turn*,' she explained.

How beautiful, he thought. Youth! The little nose, the soft skin with just a freckle or two, the fair hair, the blue eyes of her race. This child makes everything worth while for me. Charlotte produced her . . . not Sarah Lennox. Sarah could not have given him a lovelier child than this one.

'Papa,' said Amelia sternly. 'It is my *turn*.'

'It is my turn to kiss my little Amelia.'

'Then do so and be quick,' she cried imperiously. 'Now, Miss Burney. Take me. Come here, Miss Burney. Take me, I say. Oh, Miss Burney, come here.'

She was kicking and struggling while Fanny stood there uncertain how to act when the King put his daughter down.

He smiled at Fanny. He liked her. He was amused by her. She had had her book printed because she had thought it would look well in print, she had told him. He had always remembered that. Very fair indeed, he had said at the time. That's being very fair and honest.

'Well, Miss Burney,' he said, 'the Princess Amelia seems to approve of you, eh, what?'

'I . . . yes, Your Majesty.'

'And that,' he said, 'is very fair and honest, eh?'

There was great excitement in the Princesses' apartments.

'Just fancy,' said the Princess Royal, 'he is our brother and yet it's as though we are to receive a call from visiting royalty.'

'I wonder how he and Papa will get on,' added Augusta. 'I wonder if they will start quarrelling immediately or wait a while.'

'They will have to be very polite just at first,' said Elizabeth. 'Mr. Pitt's orders.'

'Is Mr. Pitt so very important?' asked Sophia.

'Very! The most important man in the country: He's not married, you know.' That was the Princess Royal, who thought a great deal about marriage. She was twenty-one and most Princesses had been found a husband at that age.

'Well,' laughed Augusta, 'you don't think they'll let you marry him even if he's not, do you?'

'I often think it would be helpful if we were allowed to marry commoners—our own countrymen. Then there wouldn't be all this difficulty in finding husbands for us. It's well-nigh impossible when they must be foreign royalty and Protestant. And there are so many of us, some of us are sure to be left out.'

'Sometimes,' said Elizabeth, 'I think that Papa won't let *any* of us marry.'

'What do you mean?' cried Charlotte.

'Well, he is strange, is he not? He talks so quickly and goes on and on repeating himself. Don't say you haven't noticed that he seems to get worse instead of better. I think he feels strangely about *us*. He wants us to be virgins all our lives.'

'Oh, no,' wailed Charlotte.

'We shall have to have secret lovers,' said Augusta, her eyes sparkling.

'Or be like George and marry in secret,' said Elizabeth.

'But George didn't marry. That's what all the fuss has been about. Mr. Fox denied it in Parliament. They thought he had but he hadn't all the time.'

'It will be wonderful to *see* George. Such exciting things always happen to him. Do you remember when he was always in our apartments and sending those long letters to Mary Hamilton?'

'At first I thought he'd come to see us.'

'I think,' said the Princess Charlotte enviously, 'that it must be the most exciting thing in the world to be George.'

'All you need to have done,' said Augusta, 'was to have been born four years earlier and a boy. Then you would have been the Prince of Wales. That would have suited you, Charlotte.'

Charlotte admitted that it would have suited her very well indeed.

Then they began to talk of the stories they had heard of the

Prince of Wales until Charlotte, remembering the presence of Mary and Sophia, signed to them to change the subject—which would of course be taken up again with relish as soon as the younger girls were no longer with them.

There was an air of excitement at tea-time with the equerries. Everyone was aware of it—the charming Colonel Digby of whom Fanny was growing more than a little fond; pleasant and careless Colonel Manners who never paused to think what he might be saying; and Colonel Goldsworthy who was constantly gossiping. This was one of the most enjoyable hours of Fanny's day, but only on those occasions when Madam von Schwellenburg was too tired or indisposed to take charge. At such times as this the Colonels would vie with each other to poke fun at the disagreeable old woman which, decided Fanny, she fully deserved, and as she was quite unaware of their suppressed amusement—there was no harm done.

But this was a happy evening, with the gentlemen all paying attention to Fanny—and in particular Colonel Digby—and the conversation running on the Prince's imminent visit.

Colonel Goldsworthy of course knew all the gossip, and Colonel Manners told some amusing stories about the Prince's exploits and Colonel Digby was flirting to such an extent with Fanny that she really thought that he might be considering making a proposal of marriage.

It was all most diverting.

Colonel Goldsworthy was warning Fanny what she must expect when winter came to Windsor.

'Ah, you are well enough now, Miss Burney, in your lilac tabby and your little jacket, but wait until the autumn. There is enough wind in these passages to carry a man o' war. So on no account attend early prayers after October. You'll see Her Majesty and the Princesses and all their attendants soon start to cough and sniffle and then . . . one by one they disappear. You'll find that after November not a soul goes to the chapel but the King and the parson and myself. And I only go because I have to. I'll swear it's the same with the parson.'

'So His Majesty is the stoic, Miss Burney,' Colonel Manners added.

'I am sure His Majesty would always do his duty.'

'Even to letting the whole family perish with the cold.'

'They seem to have survived a great many winters, Colonel

Manners. But I do declare it must be most trying if one wished to sneeze in the royal presence.'

'That one must never do, Miss Burney. It is forbidden.'

'What happens if one does sneeze? A sneeze will on occasions creep on one unawares.'

'Is that so, Miss Burney? Is there not a slight tickle in the nose . . . a few warnings? They do say that if the forefinger is placed under the nose, so, and the breath held, the sneeze can be suppressed.'

'Oh dear, I do hope that if I ever feel a need to sneeze I shall remember that.'

Colonel Digby said that if he were at hand she need only ask him. His finger was always available to be applied beneath Miss Burney's charming nose.

Fanny giggled. 'But Colonel Digby, how could I *warn* you in time?'

'Never mind. Should you commit this most serious offence I should take the blame.'

'Colonel Digby, you are too good.'

His eyes were fervent. Oh dear, thought Fanny, what a good thing we are not alone . . . or is it?

Then Colonel Digby asked Fanny what she was reading and the conversation turned to literary matters which did not please the others; so Colonel Manners talked of the King and the coming visit of the Prince in order to lure Miss Burney and Colonel Digby from the subject which interested them both so much. If he did not, he knew that in a short time they would be talking about Dr. Johnson and James Boswell and the literary set of which Fanny had been a member until she came to Court.

'They'll never understand each other,' Colonel Manners was saying. 'You wait. H.R.H. won't be in the Lodge more than an hour or so before the fur starts to fly. Like to take a bet on it, Digby? What about you, Manners?'

'Make your bets,' said Digby. 'I'll give them a few weeks. But both of them will be on their best behaviour for a while, at any rate.'

'Is it possible?' asked Manners.

'Mr. Pitt's orders,' added Goldsworthy. 'His Highness has to be grateful for his windfall; somewhere in the region of £200,000, I've heard. Wouldn't you expect affability for that? As for His Majesty, well as I said, he has had his instructions. Family devotions is the order of the day.'

'Can they keep it up?' asked Manners.

'They'll manage . . . for a while. The King is a stoic.'

Goldsworthy cut in: 'You've no idea. Why, yesterday I was hunting with His Majesty. He doesn't spare himself . . . nor his attendants. There we were trotting . . . riding . . . galloping. The er . . . I beg your pardon, I fear, Miss Burney, but I was going to say a strange word. The er . . . perspiration . . . was pouring from us so that we were wet through, popping over ditches and jerking over gates from eight in the morning till five or six in the afternoon. Then back to the Lodge, looking like so many drowned rats with not a dry thread among us, nor a morsel within us, sore to the bone and . . . forced to smile all the time. And then His Majesty offered me refreshment. "Here. Goldsworthy," he said, "have a little barley water, eh, what?" And there was His Majesty taking his barley water from a jug fit for a sick room . . . the sort of thing. Miss Burney, you would find on a hob in a chimney for some poor miserable soul who keeps his bed.'

They were all laughing, visualizing Goldsworthy's discomfiture.

'And what do you think,' went on the garrulous Colonel, 'the Prince of Wales will say if he is offered *barley water*?'

They were all laughing. And that was how it was on those evenings when Fanny was mistress of the tea table and Schwellenburg delighted them all by her absence.

And soon they, like everyone else at Windsor, were back to the subject of the Prince of Wales.

All the way to Windsor the Prince was thinking of Maria as he drove his phaeton at frantic speed to relieve his feelings. With any other woman he would not have worried. Well, with any other woman it would not have been of vital importance. But he had not seen Maria since she had closed her doors on him and he was getting desperate.

Now he had to go through this silly farce of reunion. As if there ever could be a true reunion? As if he and his father could ever agree, or see anything from the same point of view. The King was an old bigot, a silly old despot without even the strength and the power to be one. He had no taste for art; and the only culture he possessed was for music; and even that was mainly confined to Handel.

God help me! thought the Prince. What will it be? Evenings of Handel; lectures on the duty of princes; a game or two of backgammon; the dullest conversation in the world; services in that freezing chapel; more lectures on princes who must not act so as to be talked about; diatribes about Mr. Fox, Mr. Sheridan and the Whigs; more on the virtues of Mr. Pitt and the Tories.

And Maria? Where was Maria? What if she attempted to leave the country? He had given orders that he was to be told at once if she proposed any moves like that. He had given instructions that close watch was to be kept on her.

How happy he would be if he were driving out to Richmond instead of Windsor . . . if only Maria, beautiful, desirable Maria were waiting for him instead of his doddering old father, his stupid mother and his simpering sisters. Well, perhaps he was wrong to condemn the Princesses. He had nothing against them. They, poor creatures, were what they were because they were forced to live like nuns in a convent. Poor Charlotte—twenty-one, she must be. His Maria had had two husbands before she was that age. Not that he cared to think about Maria's previous husbands, except of course that it was her experiences which had made her the mature and fascinating creature she was—and of course they had both been older than she was and must have been dull creatures compared with her third—the Prince of Wales.

Her third husband . . . that was the point!

Would she ever forgive him? What could he do? Sherry must help him. It was no use calling on Fox. She hated Fox more than ever and who could wonder at it? Really Charles had gone too far!

And here was Windsor and why was it not Marble Hill and how could he live without Maria? She must come back to him. Something must be done . . . or he would have no wish to live.

The King received him formally, the Queen beside him. The Princesses were lined up and presented to him as though he had never met them before.

The girls clearly adored him; it was obvious in their faces. Not so the King and Queen.

He could see the irritation he always provoked; it was apparent in the King's bulging eyes and the twitching of his brows; and the Queen's resentment was there too. She wanted to be part of his rich and exciting life. As if that were possible!

But there was a pretence of affability; and later he attended a drawing room which was very public; many of his own attendants were present and the King chatted to him most of the time to show the company that all was well between them.

But all was not well, thought the Prince. It was some months since he had seen the King and it might have been that he was therefore more aware of the change than those who saw him every day.

By God, he thought, the old man's changed. He talks too much and the repetition is greater than it used to be. He seems to lose the thread of what he's saying. What does it mean?

He wished that Fox were available so that he could report to him. If the King were going to be . . . ill, that could present a new and dazzling prospect. He wondered whether Pitt had noticed the alarming changes in his father.

Yet even with such a prospect before him he could think of little but Maria. He would know no peace until he had explained to her that the fault was not his. Charles James Fox had gone too far. That must be his theme.

Maria must come back to him. Whatever the world thought, to him she would always be his wife.

So he went through the farce of friendship with the King; he was affable to the Queen; he talked to the Princesses, noticed that Charlotte was inclined to be bandy, thought what dull creatures they were—but then all women were dull when compared with Maria—and then was sorry for them because they would be prisoners for longer than he had been. He at least had made a part escape at the age of eighteen when he had set up Perdita Robinson in Cork Street.

He thought of those days with pity. Had he really believed himself in love with Perdita? How could any emotion he would ever feel compare with his love for Maria? And Maria had left him . . . sworn she would never see him again.

So there he was back at Maria.

As soon as he could conveniently leave Windsor he was on his way back to London, to write to Maria, to appeal to Maria, to beg her, implore her to come back to him.

Maria would not see him. She was staying in the house of a friend who was also a distant connection of her family, the Honourable Mrs. Butler, and with her was Miss Pigot—and both these ladies acted as her guardians.

The Prince called; alas, she would not see him. It was unprecedented. Who else but Maria would not be at home to the Prince of Wales? He stormed and raged; then he pleaded; but it was no use. Maria was not to be seen. What could he do?

He demanded to see Miss Pigot. She was an old friend of his

as well as Maria's and she told him at once that Maria had repeatedly said that she would not see him and there was nothing Miss Pigot could do to persuade her.

'But she can't mean it, dear Pig.'

Dear Pig assured him that she did.

'I have never seen her so distressed, Your Highness, as she was when she heard what Mr. Fox had said.'

'But she knows Fox.'

'Yes, but he spoke on Your Highness's direct authority. That's what broke her heart.'

'Her heart broken. What about mine. Sheridan spoke well of her. Did she hear that?'

'Oh, yes, sir, she heard of it; and she was mollified to some extent, but it didn't alter what Mr. Fox had said.'

'Dearest Pig, tell me what I can do to convince her that I adore her.'

'Well, there's only one thing, and it seems it's the only thing you can't do. Admit to the King and the Parliament and the world that she's your wife.'

'There'd be trouble . . . great trouble . . . if I did.' He thought of the King as he had last seen him. That peculiar look which was sometimes in his eyes. What could it mean? Glittering possibilities! And what disasters could follow if he admitted to marriage?

'She's a Catholic, that's the trouble.'

'It's a sad state of affairs, Your Highness. And it seems there's no way out.'

'Pig, you'll do what you can for me?'

'You can be sure I will.'

'Remind her of what a good husband I've been to her, will you?'

'She doesn't need to be reminded, sir. She remembers . . . She says so.'

'She says I've been a good husband?' he asked eagerly.

'Yes, right up to the time you denied you were.'

'*I* did not. It was Fox. Oh, he went too far. There was no need to go as far as that.'

Miss Pigot shook her head at him sadly. 'I'll do my best. I talk to her, but at the moment it's no use. If I saw that it was, you can trust me to let you know at once.'

'Bless you, dearest Pig.'

'I'll tell her how downcast you are.'

'Downcast! I'm broken-hearted. Honestly, Piggy, I shall do something desperate if she doesn't come back to me.'

'I'll tell her. She's still fond of you, of course.'

But although she told Maria, it was no use. Maria was adamant.

He had denied he was married to her; and if that ceremony had not been a solemn one to him, then her conscience would not allow her to live with him as his wife.

The Prince was very ill. He suffered a violent paroxysm and had to be bled almost to the point of danger. Rumours spread through the Court that he was seriously ill.

Miss Pigot brought them to Maria. She looked at her friend and mistress sadly.

'He has brought this on himself because you won't see him,' she said.

'He is too violent,' said Maria. 'He should learn to control his feelings.'

'Perhaps they are too strong to be controlled.'

'They weren't strong enough for him to claim me as his wife.'

'Oh, Maria, are you not a little hard on him? Consider his position. He could lose the throne.'

'I told him that many times. I told him to consider carefully. You know I went abroad to escape him but he would not have that.'

'He loves you, Maria. You forget that.'

'I do not forget that he loves me in his way . . .'

'In such a way that he is brought near to death because of you.'

'You are a good advocate, Piggy. Has he asked you to plead his cause?'

'I speak as I see,' said the blunt Miss Pigot. 'And I see this, Maria: If he admitted he was married to a Catholic he would have put the succession in danger. There might even be a war. Have you ever thought of that? You say you love him; he says he loves you. He cannot give up his crown. There is too much involved. It is like asking you to give up your religion. Why should all the sacrifice be on one side?'

'Piggy, what are you saying?'

'I'm telling you the facts as I see them. You want him to tell the world that he has married you—that's just for your satisfaction, to make things right for your religion, you say. All well and good. Well he is asking you to give up your pride, your religious convictions . . . not all of them, only those that concern the open acknowledgement of the marriage. He can't and you won't . . . or perhaps you can't either. But I don't see how one is being more self-willed than the other. For obvious reasons he can't proclaim you his wife.'

'He made his vows to me.'

'And you to him.'

Maria was silent.

'And now,' said Miss Pigot, 'he's ill because of you . . . fretting for you.''

''If it's one of his paroxysms,' said Maria, 'it's a fit of rage and anger because everything he wants doesn't fall into his lap.'

'I've had it on very good authority . . . from his doctors no less . . . that his condition is very dangerous.'

Maria turned away and went out of the room.

Miss Pigot, watching her, thought: Perhaps this is the time. A message to His Highness? Perhaps she could explain to him that if he were very careful . . . there might be a chance.

The Prince of Wales called at the House of the Honourable Mr. Butler.

He was very pale and looked a little thinner. His doctors had advised him that he should not go out but he had insisted.

Mrs. Butler received him with great respect and he was delighted to see that she was shocked by his appearance.

'Your Highness is well enough to be out?'

'I have managed to get here,' he said feebly.

'I beg of Your Highness to be seated.'

He sank gratefully into the chair.

'And I beg of you, my dear friend, to tell Mrs. Fitzherbert that I am here and to say that I wish to see her. It may be for the last time.'

'Your Highness . . .'

He waved a delicate white hand. 'That is what I wish you to tell her.'

Mrs. Butler said she herself would go to Maria, which she did, and shortly afterwards conducted the Prince to Maria's sitting room where she gently shut the door on them.

When he saw Maria he was so overcome by his emotion that he felt dizzy and as though he would faint. Maria ran to him and caught his arm. Oh, to be touched by Maria again! He leaned against the chair, prolonging the moment.

'I . . . I have been very ill,' he said. 'I am still weak.'

'Pray sit down,' said Maria.

He allowed her to put him into the chair and sat there, his eyes closed.

'You should not have come out,' she said.

'I wanted to see you. I felt . . . it might be my last chance.'

'What do you mean?' she demanded almost angrily.

'You may not have heard, Maria. But I have been very ill. I have been profusely bled and it has weakened me. My doctors despaired of my life.'

He was delighted to see the concern in her eyes.

'You will be distressed when I am gone, Maria.'

'This is nonsense,' said Maria, 'to talk of dying. Why should you?'

'Because I have lost all that is worth living for.'

'But you have not lost your hope of the Crown,' she told him with some cynicism.

'Oh, Maria, Maria . . . what is that to me if you no longer love me.'

'It seems a good deal . . . since you betrayed me for the sake of it.'

Still angry, still hurt, still unforgiving!

He sighed. Then he covered his face with his hands and sobs shook his body.

'What can I say to you, Maria? If you wish it to be goodbye then I shall go back to my bed and . . . die. For there is nothing to live for.'

'I have already reminded you once that there is a crown.'

'A crown! It is others who care for that, Maria. You must listen to me. Yes, yes, I insist. Fox . . . you know what Fox is. Haven't you always known? I have been deceived by the fellow. He's clever. I don't deny it. But he it was who made the announcement . . . without telling me, Maria. What could I do?'

'Denied it.'

'And started a possible conflict? Think of that, Maria. Don't think I haven't *implored* them to put this right. Sherry will tell you. I spoke to Sherry. I begged him to do something and, God bless him, he did his best. But Fox had already done the mischief. What could we do? Maria, my beloved, don't blame me for the sins of others. You know Fox. My God, didn't you show me that you had no liking for him?'

'I heard he had a letter from you . . . written just before the ceremony . . . saying that there would not be one.'

'Fox would say anything. I may have written a letter. I have been forced to do so many things. They were on me like a pack of wolves. Oh, Maria, let's forget them all. If you would love me again I should be completely happy. We will go to Brighton together; everything you want will be yours.'

'All I wanted was to live in peace and happiness with the man I thought was my husband.'

'You shall, Maria. You shall.'

'No,' she cried. 'You should go. It is over. I understand everything. You should have listened to me in the first place. Perhaps it is my fault. I wanted us to be together so I pretended all would be well.'

'Oh, Maria.' He had flung himself at her feet. 'Love me, Maria. It's all I shall ever ask again.'

'Pray get up,' she said. 'You will do yourself an injury.'

'So much the better. I have been the victim of wily politicians and I am now the victim of love.'

She sat down on a sofa and he was immediately beside her.

'It was wrong of you to come out,' she said. 'You look so pale.'

He closed his eyes; his heart pounding with hope.

She touched his brow. 'You should rest awhile before you go. You should never have come.'

She was concerned, alarmed for his health.

'Maria,' he said, 'if you would love me I would get well again . . . quickly.'

'You are going to get well,' she said briskly.

'I am beginning to feel alive again.'

He clasped her in his arms. He wanted, he said, to lay his head on that magnificent bosom which had so long been denied him.

She was weeping. Maria was not one to weep easily so it showed how deeply moved she was. He had been right to come. This was going to be the reconciliation. He would not go out of this room until he had Maria's promise that all was well between them.

He wanted, he said, to stay close to his Maria for ever. He wanted her to know that he would die if she would not return to him.

He embraced her; she returned his embrace. He was forgiven.

Return of the Duke of York

They are together again. Society could talk of nothing else.

The Prince's recovery was miraculous. The very next day he was well enough to drive Maria down to the Epsom races in his phaeton, singing as he went, the healthy flush back in his cheeks, the radiant Mrs. Fitzherbert beside him.

He kept declaring that he had never been so happy in his life. And indeed there was every reason why this should be so. His debts were paid; he had a grant for Carlton House; there had been an addition to his income; his succession to the throne was no longer in peril—and crowning glory, he had his Maria back, as loving as she ever was, admitting that the separation had been as painful to her as to him and that he, Prince Charming, had been in no way to blame. It was all the fault of the villain Fox.

Poor Charles! The Prince felt he had been rather unjustly treated, but he was enjoying life in Italy with the very charming Lizzie and he guessed Charles wouldn't grudge him his happiness.

That evening the Duchess of Gordon gave a ball and naturally she craved the honour of the Prince's company and that of Mrs. Fitzherbert. They came together; he danced almost every dance with her, only leaving her side when duty demanded it. Everyone smiled on them, implying pleasure in seeing them together and happy again. And at the end of the ball the Prince was heard to say, as he had said so many times before: 'Madam, may I have the honour of taking you home in my carriage?'

And regal, dignified Mrs. Fitzherbert graciously gave her permission.

All was well. The balls and banquets would start again. The

Prince was the leader of Society and Princess Fitz, as they called her, shared that honour with him. It was realized that if one wished to entertain the Prince of Wales one must be on terms of friendliness with Mrs. Fitzherbert.

The Prince took a house for her in Pall Mall; and the carriages of the nobility were seen constantly stopping at her door. At dinner parties she was put at the side of the Prince in the place of honour; it was as though everyone was determined to treat her as the Princess of Wales, in spite of Mr. Fox's denial—because it was quite clear that that was what the Prince wished.

He would make up for that denial by making sure that she received every honour which would have been hers had she been his wife; he could not of course make the King and Queen receive her, but who cared for the King and Queen? The Prince of Wales was the leader of society—and his 'wife' with him.

Whig hostesses were eager to show their loyalty; and Tory ones were even more ready to accept her as the Princess of Wales because that would show that Fox had lied.

The Duke and Duchess of Cumberland hastened to pay their respects and show their affection for Mrs. Fitzherbert and to treat her as though she was their niece of marriage. Her triumph seemed complete when the Duke of Gloucester—Tory that he was and more friendly to the King than his brother Cumberland was—wrote to her from Florence where he preferred to live since his wife was slighted in England by not being accepted at Court. He sent her a present to show his cordial feelings and Maria was delighted when she read it.

'H.R.H. The Duke of Gloucester to Mrs. Fitzherbert
Florence, May 24th, 1787

'Dear Madam, I take the opportunity of a private hand to desire your acceptance of a Cestus, done in oyster shell. I hope you will think it pretty. Pray send us some account to trust to of the present negotiation. I hope the Prince will be made easy in his affairs. I sincerely hope you are happy and well for I know you deserve it. I remain, dear Madam, your humble servant.

'William Henry.'

So since the Gloucesters and Cumberlands accepted her, surely this implied that although Fox had emphatically denied that she was married to the Prince and nothing had been done to contradict it, the world believed in the marriage and were determined to accept her as the Prince's wife.

She would not have believed a short while ago that this would have been possible.

It was true there were some who whispered against her. Gilray's *Dido Forsaken* was insulting, yet that in a way implied that she had been ill used and that Fox had lied. There she was on a funeral pyre on the shore, the Crown and the Prince of Wales's feathers floating away from her; making off from her was a little boat on the prow of which was written the word 'Honour'. Pitt was steering the boat and in it were the Prince and Fox. From the Prince's mouth came a balloon in which were the words: 'Never saw her in my life.' And from Fox's: 'No, damme, never in his life.'

Well, of course every well-known figure was a target for the cartoonists and lampoonists and Maria dismissed the insults with a shrug.

They left London for Brighton—the Prince to inhabit his Marine Pavilion, and she to the house with the green shutters which was almost in the Pavilion gardens; and there society was gayer than Brighton had ever known it. London was deserted. The centre of the fashionable world was Brighton. The inhabitants of that town, delighted with the prosperity which the Prince's preference had brought to them, cheered him and Mrs. Fitzherbert whenever they appeared. The Prince could be seen strolling along by the sea in the company of Maria and a group of friends, riding through the town, taking his morning dip under the surveillance of Smoker, walking in his gardens, dancing there in one of the houses of his noble friends—almost always in the company of that lady known by some as 'Princess Fitz' or by the name Smoker had given her—'Mrs. Prince'.

Humble houses were hastily transformed into mansions. Not only were the builders of Brighton making fortunes but so were the lodging houses and shop-keepers. Everywhere the Prince of Wales's feathers were displayed; and the theme was 'God Bless the Prince of Wales'.

The Prince constantly reiterated that he had never been so happy in his life and Maria echoed those sentiments. The Prince was full of high spirits yet Maria was having a decided influence on him. Her dignity was undeniable. She might not have been the most beautiful woman in Brighton but her grace and regality were unique. No one could doubt which of the ladies bore the title of Princess Fitz; Maria, said the people of Brighton, looked like a queen. Seated on a garden chair in the Pavilion grounds she was indeed like a Queen on the throne. There she would watch the Prince play cricket in his flannel jacket, trimmed with blue ribbon, and very tightly fitting white trousers, his face under the white beaver hat beaming with pleasure in the game while his eyes were constantly going in Maria's direction to make sure she was not missing any part of his performance. He was proud of the costume which he had designed himself, proud of his game, proud of Maria, proud of the way he had arranged skilfully his life so that he could keep his place as the prospective King and at the same time his hold on Maria and the people's affections.

That was doubtless a glorious summer.

Throughout troubled France there was sweeping a wave of admiration for the old enemy England, and the aristocracy from across the Channel must come to see Brighton. So not only was Brighton visited by the fashionable world of London but that of Versailles was also in evidence.

The people of Brighton were amazed by the French fashions. The English had been startling enough; but now came the exaggerated headdresses, the enormous hooped skirts; and the latest 'simplicity styles' set by Marie Antoinette in her artificially created 'natural' village known as the *Hameau*. Ladies in muslin dressed as shepherdesses, even carrying crooks, appeared in the Brighton streets; but the men were the most extraordinary; they appeared to mince in a manner new to Brighton; they threw their hands and arms about and chattered wildly; and jewels scintillated on their persons, so that they glittered even more than the Prince of Wales himself.

There were no dull moments in Brighton that summer.

And the French nobility, no less than the English, did honour to Maria; she could be seen riding in her carriage, with the Princesse de Lamballe, kinswoman of the King of France and reputed to be one of the greatest friends of Marie Antoinette.

The Prince had quickly replenished his stables and now racing was one of his greatest pleasures; he loved his horses; in fact it was said of him that the two things which delighted him most in the world were women and horses. He was constantly going to the Lewes races—though it was said not as often as he would have gone if Mrs. Fitzherbert had really enjoyed it.

During the hot summer days along the seafront and away to the downs was one moving panorama of glitter and colour; and in the centre of it was the man who was known as the First

Gentleman of Europe, hardly ever seen without Maria Fitzherbert at his side.

In the Marine Pavilion one night at the beginning of August the
Prince was supping with a few friends. On one side of him sat
Maria and on the other the Princesse de Lamballe. The Prin-
cesse was chatting in her somewhat inconsequential manner of
Versailles and her dear friend the Queen when one of the foot-
men came in to announce that a message had arrived for the
Prince from Windsor. Would His Highness receive it now or
wait until after supper?

'Windsor!' cried the Prince; and he thought of the last time
he had seen his father. 'I will have it now.'

He turned to the Princesse and craved her indulgence. Then
to Maria, and did the same.

He read the message and exclaimed with joy. 'This is wonderful news. My brother Frederick has come home from Germany. I haven't seen him for seven years. I cannot tell you how
this news pleases me.' He smiled at Maria. 'I thought that I had
all I desired. Now I know that I wanted just this to make my
contentment complete.'

'This is your brother?' said the Princesse de Lamballe.

'My brother Frederick. One year younger than I. We were
brought up together . . . never apart. We are the best friends in
the world and it is seven years . . . think of that, Madame, seven
years since I have seen him. I remember the day he left for
Germany.'

'For Germany . . .' echoed the Princesse.

'You may well look surprised. He was to have Army training.
Why not in England? To answer that question, Madame, you
must not turn to me, but to my father.'

The Prince's eyes narrowed; but one did not of course discuss the King derogatorily with members of another nation. The
Prince shrugged his shoulders and was content to talk of the
friendship between himself and his brother.

As soon as supper was over—and Maria noticed that the
Prince, who set the pace, had hurried it somewhat—he told his
guests that he was all impatience to see his brother and that he
was going to lose no time in leaving for Windsor.

It was a hint. They left, Maria only remaining.

'You will go to Windsor in the morning?' she asked him.

'In the morning! A fine way that would be to greet Frederick.

No . . . no. I am leaving at once, my love. I shall drive to Windsor tonight.'

'What . . . in the dark?'

He laughed aloud. 'My dearest you cannot surely think that I'm afraid of the dark.'

She knew that it was no use trying to dissuade this self-willed boy, although she thought it would have been more dignified for him to leave next morning in befitting style.

He called for his phaeton and at once set out, driving himself at great speed through the night from Brighton to Windsor.

They embraced. They wept.

'My dear Frederick, is it indeed you?'

'It is, George. And is this the Prince of Wales whose adventures have been startling all Europe?'

They began to laugh suddenly. 'Frederick, this is a happy day. You must tell me of your affairs.'

'Oh, you admit I have some. Then you do not think the Prince of Wales is the only one to have . . . affairs?'

They were laughing again, embracing, weeping, examining each other.

'George, you've grown fatter.'

'So have you.'

'The curse of the family.'

'Never mind. It shows contentment.'

'You are contented George?'

'Never more in my life. You must come to Brighton. Wait till you see Brighton . . . and Maria.'

'I can't wait,' declared Frederick.

The King was delighted with his second son. He talked to the Queen about him. 'He's not like his elder brother. Oh, no. There's a difference. You've seen it, eh, what?'

'No one could be quite like George,' said the Queen half admiringly, half resentfully. And she added: 'I should hope.'

'Frederick is a good boy at heart. He'll be able to give us some tales of battle, eh? I'm glad I sent him to Germany.'

The Queen looked dubious. The people hadn't liked it; and she believed that the Prince of Wales might have behaved a little better to them if they had not robbed him of the brother he had loved. And wouldn't the Duke of York have been able to learn how to be a soldier as well in England as in Germany? Now he was returned to them—and although he was their son, they hadn't seen him for seven years and that did, in a way, make him seem like a stranger.

'Frederick,' mused the King, 'he's the Hope of the House. That's how I think of him. You understand . . . eh, what? Now that George seems bent on giving us trouble . . .'

'George seems to have reformed a little under the influence of that . . . of that . . .'

'He'd never reform. He's putting on a show. He knows how to act a part . . . the rip! No, Frederick is a good boy. He's done well in Germany; he'll do well at home. Come. We'll go to your drawing room. He'll be there now.'

It was not often that so many of the family were assembled. There were the six princesses, even baby Amelia, all standing solemnly about the Queen's chair awaiting the arrival of their parents; the equerries and some members of the household were there, and George and Frederick were together, deep in conversation, heads close, laughing as though no one else in the drawing room existed for them.

They all stood to attention at the arrival of the King and Queen; the Princesses curtsied prettily, including baby Amelia, who for once was too impressed by the glittering personalities of her two big brothers to assert her right to be the centre of attention.

The King and Queen took their places. Frederick stood by his father's chair, George by his mother's. The conversation was stilted. Why was it they never knew what to say to each other?

The Queen saw the glances which passed between her two sons—eyes raised to the ceiling, affecting to suppress yawns.

George was bored with his family. Could it be that Frederick—the King's Hope of the House—was going to be his brother's ally?

Oh why, why, thought the Queen, in this family is there always a state of war!

'We'll have some music,' said the King. 'I'll swear you've heard some good music in Germany, eh, what?'

The Duke of York said that he had heard excellent music in Germany.

'Well we will try to give you some here.' He raised a hand and his equerry was at his side. He asked that the musicians be sent for.

'I doubt you've heard a better pianist than Cramer,' said the King. 'And Fischer is a genius with the hautbois.'

'I look forward with immense pleasure to hearing these gentlemen, sir.'

'And the rest of the band,' said the King with a smile.

The concert started.

'Oh, God,' whispered the Prince of Wales to the Duke of York, 'did you think it would be so deadly?'

'The music's good. It's the company.'

'You should come to Brighton.'

'So I've heard.'

'You *shall* come to Brighton.'

'When?'

'As soon as we escape from this funeral gathering. Tonight . . . I'll drive you there in my phaeton. I'll take a bet with you. A thousand guineas. When you get to Brighton you'll find excuses why you must stay there.'

The King was frowning in their direction. Concert time was not the occasion for conversation.

But that evening the Prince of Wales drove the Duke of York down to Brighton.

'Frederick, this is the lady I want you to meet and love as a sister. Maria, my brother Frederick Duke of York and Bishop of Osnaburgh . . . Now Bishop!'

The two brothers were laughing. 'You remember those cartoons of you, Fred. Maria, he was made a Bishop before he took his first tottering steps and the cartoonists always drew him balancing a mitre that was as big as himself.'

'It is a great pleasure to meet you, Madam,' said the Duke of York, bowing.

Maria replied with the regality of a Queen receiving visiting royalty that it gave her the utmost pleasure to see him and she trusted that he intended a long stay in Brighton.

'We have a bet on it,' said the Prince. 'He's going to be as reluctant to leave Brighton as I always am.'

'My God, George,' said the Duke of York, 'you have made yourself a pleasant place here.'

'Nothing to what I intend to make it. I'm going to show you round. Come on . . . now. You shall inspect Marine Pavilion and I'll tell you of the schemes I have for the place.'

He slipped one arm through Frederick's and another through Maria's; but as they went from room to room and the brothers shouted and laughed together and recalled to each other the ridiculous and tragic scenes from their youth Maria began to feel that she was a little less close to the Prince than she had been.

Frederick's coming did put an end to the halcyon days. Maria was still the Prince's 'dear love'; he must know that she was there to return to; but that did not mean that he wished to be in her company all the time.

Frederick was full of high spirits in which George joined; and this meant driving madly about the country, drinking, gambling, playing practical jokes on each other. Maria's dignity did not fit into this; and while the Prince wanted the home atmosphere he also wanted the sort of horseplay so beloved by his brother.

Maria was realizing the difference in their ages; never before had those six years seemed to represent such a gap. He seemed to her very childish, such a boy, and she thought regretfully of the days immediately following their reconciliation when he had seemed more sober and as though he had really grown up. But he was after all a lighthearted boy; and he must, she supposed, have his fun.

They seemed to be surrounded by two different kinds of friends. There were some who shared the friendship of both of them, people like the Duchess of Devonshire, the Sheridans, the Dukes of Grafton and Bedford. But the Prince had his own set which consisted of people like Major Hanger, that eccentric fellow who was so fond of practical joking—a habit Maria deplored. She was never amused to be the subject of such jokes, although to please the Prince she accepted the role she was sometimes called upon to play.

Two people of whom Maria could never approve were Sir John and Leticia Lade. Sir John was celebrated for the manner in which he could handle horses, and was soon taking charge of the Prince's stables. His wife was an amazing woman who swore more colourfully than any soldier, a fact which was perhaps not surprising because before she had married Sir John she had lived in St. Giles's and had been the mistress of a highwayman known as Sixteen String Jack. When he was caught and hanged Letty married Sir John. She was an amazon of a woman and could handle a horse even better than her husband and had immediately called attention to herself by riding astride and by her management of a curricle and four.

They had a house near Brighton and at the races had made the acquaintance of the Prince of Wales, who was amused and intrigued by the free talk of Letty and the skill she shared with her husband in the management of horses. The Prince's love of horses drew him to the pair and they were often seen together.

Then there was the wild Barry family. Hellgate, Cripplegate, Newgate and Lady Billingsgate. Hellgate was Richard, Earl of Barrymore, who had such a quick temper that he was constantly flying into violent rages; hence his name. His brother Henry was club-footed and so was Cripplegate. A young brother, Augustus, had been so often imprisoned for debt that he was called Newgate, this being the only prison he had not stayed in: and their sister Caroline swore in such a manner that she was Lady Billingsgate. Hellgate explained to the Prince that their wildness was due to their having been left orphans at an early age and put into the care of a tutor which had taught them all a virtuous society would say they should not know.

'We called him Profligate,' said the Earl, which made the Prince roar with laughter. Although of course when he repeated the joke to Maria it brought only a forced smile to her lips.

Maria did not approve of the Lades, nor the Barrys.

Dear Maria was decidedly prim. Not that he would have her otherwise. She was perfect as she was. He would not have liked to see her swearing with Letty Lade or joining in the pranks he played with the 'Gates'. But she must remember that he was young—six years younger than she was—and that he wanted to enjoy all the fun that was to be had; so he wanted to be with these amusing friends and when he wearied of them to return to Maria's comforting bosom.

He had taken her brothers Walter and John into his circle, and they were in constant attendance. They clearly adored him and would do anything however wild to amuse him. This worried Maria a little; but what could she do? How could she tell her brothers that they must avoid the company of her husband, particularly when that husband was the Prince of Wales. They were getting into financial difficulties and could not understand why Maria did nothing for them. Why did she not procure some rewarding post for them in the Prince's household? It was true she extracted them from several financial embarrassments; but the Prince would have done anything for her. She only had to ask for some sinecure to be bestowed on her brothers and it would have been done in a flash.

But Maria was adamant. She would have liked them to go back to the country; she deplored the fact that their father had been unable to control them owing to his illness. Uncle Henry was far too easy going.

So Maria kept an eye on her brothers and longed for the days before the return of the Duke of York, who was always agreeable to her and ready to be her good friend; but she did deplore the practical jokes, the wild horseplay, the extravagance.

It was different from those lovely days at Brighton when the Prince had scarcely ever left her.

But he was still devoted; still determined that everywhere she should be accepted as the Princess of Wales.

In her house in Pall Mall where the walls of her drawing room were hung with puckered blue satin, and on the walls of the dining room hung full-length portraits of the Prince of Wales and the Duke of York, she entertained lavishly during the winter; and in the spring she rode down to Brighton with the Prince.

They were happily married—as she saw it; and she did not believe it would ever be otherwise.

Then there was disturbing news of the King.

The King's Madness

'The Queen,' said Miss Burney to the very gallant Colonel Digby who, others had noticed, was constantly at her side, 'seems to me to be obsessed by a most fearful apprehension.'

'Ah, Miss Burney,' laughed the Colonel, 'you are too fanciful. I believe you dream up all sorts of terrors—and possibly joys—for us all, Her Majesty no exception.'

'It is not true,' declared Fanny. 'But do you not sense this strangeness in Her Majesty? At the reading yesterday I am sure she did not hear a word. She was occupied with her own thoughts; which I fancy were far from pleasant.'

Colonel Digby remarked that the Queen no doubt had her problems. His Highness's conduct at Brighton was giving concern to the King—so perhaps that was the cause of her preoccupation.

'Yes,' agreed Fanny. 'But there is *something*. It is as though she expects some ghost to appear suddenly . . . some horribly menacing spectre.'

The Colonel laughed aloud; he did laugh frequently with Fanny, although he was of rather a melancholy turn of mind and his favourite topics of conversation were what happened after death and did Fanny believe in immortality. He enjoyed conversation more than anything else; for what else, he demanded, was there to do in the King's household than talk? Fanny listened, forever wondering what his intentions were, for he had only recently become a widower and being but forty-four years of age, he had told Fanny, he would like to marry again. They had much in common, for he had read widely and liked to discuss literature with her.

It was the tea-time hour—one of the best of the day as far as Fanny was concerned. Madam von Schwellenburg had not yet made her appearance and Colonel Goldsworthy had been dozing for the last twenty minutes.

'Oh yes,' went on Fanny, 'it is true. I have seen it in Her Majesty's face. She is afraid of something . . . and what she fears is *terrible*.'

Madam von Schwellenburg came into the room at that moment frowning and looking disapprovingly at Fanny who was always chatting with Colonel Digby. 'Miss Berners' as she called her, would have to learn that she had not come to Court to flirt with 'chentlemen'. She had come to perform duties for the Queen and that meant waiting on the Queen's chief Lady of the Bedchamber.

'Tea I vill haf, Miss Berners,' she said, and Fanny immediately served her.

The unpleasant woman made a face. 'Poof. Not goot. Too much time on talks . . .' She frowned at Colonel Goldsworthy who emitted a slight snore. 'Colonel Goldsworthy . . . he alvays sleeps vith me. Sleeps he vith you too, Miss Berners?'

Fanny said that the Colonel had been hunting with the King and his party and no doubt that had made him a little tired.

Madam von Schwellenburg tapped her foot impatiently on the floor and looked delighted when one of the pages appeared to say that His Majesty wished to see Colonel Digby.

The Colonel sighed, gave Fanny a languishing look and departed.

'Colonel Digby is too fond of talk. He likes too much the vimen. He look alvays for Miss Gunning.' Schwellenburg shot a mischievous glace at Fanny, but Fanny was pursuing her own thoughts: There *is* something which is disturbing the Queen, she thought. I *know* she is terrified.

Unable to achieve the required effect through her references to Colonel Digby's attentions to Miss Gunning, Schwellenburg scowled and said: 'You vill to me bring my snuff box, Miss Berners. I have it left near the first cage.'

Fanny rose obediently and went to get the snuff box, asking herself as she had a hundred times before, why she had given up a life among interesting people to be a servant to the most disagreeable woman she had ever met.

She was right when she had imagined that the Queen was disturbed. Charlotte was very worried indeed. Ever since the King's illness many years ago when his mind had become unbalanced she had been watchful, always afraid that there would be a recurrence of his illness. He had changed after that first bout, which must have been nearly twenty-three years ago, and she had never been able to forget it. She remembered how he had suddenly burst into tears for no reason at all; he had had a fever and the rash; and had believed that the whole world was against him. And after it he had developed that rapid manner of speech which was rambling and incoherent, interspersed with 'ehs?' and 'whats?' as though he were asking questions and could not wait for the answer.

Many times she had believed that a return of his illness was not far off. But it had never been so near as it was now. It needed only a little incident, she was sure, to drive him completely mad.

And if that should happen? She shuddered.

There were times when she was actually afraid of him, for now and then he looked at her so wildly that she thought he would do her an injury. It was as though he hated her. That was impossible. He was a mild man, a kind good man. Yet that wild look in his eyes was . . . terrifying.

Sometimes when he came into her bedchamber she wanted to call to some of her women and command them to remain so that she might not be alone with him.

Yes, she was afraid of the King.

Yesterday he had told her that he had a slight rash on his body. She had heard herself say coolly: 'And have you seen one of the doctors?' And she was thinking: Oh God, that was how it started on that other occasion.

'I wonder,' she had said, 'whether Your Majesty should go to Bath for the waters.'

'Fauconberg was saying that they are better at Cheltenham,' replied the King. 'But this is not the time to go to Cheltenham. There is too much to be done. And how do we know what that young rip will be up to next, eh, what? Brighton, eh? Changing the place. Building there. Marine Pavilion! Going round with bad companions. That fellow Sheridan. Rake! Libertine! Drunkard! Gambler! And married to that good woman. They gamble away fortunes on horses. They play practical jokes in the streets. He's surrounded himself with the worst possible people. Where's it leading to, eh? what? Won't obey his father. Gallivanting with people like the Lades . . . the Barrys . . . that man Hanger. Ought to be hanged . . . the lot of 'em, eh? what? He won't obey though. Do you think he gets round Lady Charlotte Finch, eh? Do you think he inveigles her to give him pastry with his fruit. Eh? Eh? Eh, what?'

The Queen looked at him in dismay. He had thought for a moment that the Prince was in the nursery under the care of Charlotte Finch. The King's protruding eyes were frightened . . . and his fear was hers—for he remembered too and the fear which haunted her was always at his side.

He had recovered. He said, 'Cheltenham . . . eh, what? Not the time. Another time perhaps, eh? what?'

The Queen took an opportunity of speaking to Lord Fauconberg, summoning him to her side during the soirée.

'I think the King is working too hard and a change of air would be beneficial to His Majesty. I believe you mentioned Cheltenham.'

'Yes, Your Majesty, an excellent spot. Not yet appreciated, I believe. The air there is as pure as you will find anywhere in England, including . . . this new fashionable Brighton.'

'His Majesty would, I am sure, have no wish to go to Brighton.'

'Cheltenham would, Madam, be more to His Majesty's taste I feel sure. And if you would honour me by using my place for your stay I should be delighted.'

'So you have a place there?'

'Bay's Hill Lodge, Madam—scarcely a palace, but if Your Majesties needed a quiet time and took but a few attendants it might suffice. There are good views across the Malvern Hills and the Pump Room is near by.'

'It sounds inviting,' said the Queen. 'I will speak with His Majesty and if it is possible to persuade him to accept your kind offer I will do so.'

'Why, Madam, the people of Cheltenham would consider themselves most honoured. Though I should warn Your Majesty of the smallness of the place.'

'It is such a place I am sure which would most appeal to the King.' She hesitated. 'Lord Fauconberg, perhaps you would speak to His Majesty. Make this offer to him. I think he might accept it.'

Lord Fauconberg replied that he would obey Her Majesty's instruction and gave no sign that he knew it was because the suggestion was more likely to be acceptable if it came through him than through the Queen. But Charlotte knew that he was aware of this and resentment flaring up in her, she felt a sudden anger against the King. Why should she have been constantly thrust aside? Why should her opinion always have been considered of no importance? How unfairly she had been treated since her arrival in England. She felt a wave of dislike for the man who had consistently shown her that he considered her advice worthless.

Why then did she live in this constant fear of a dreadful disability overtaking him?

It is not love, she thought calmly. Oh, no, not love.

When the Royal party set out for Cheltenham Miss Burney and Colonel Digby were in attendance.

The King was pleased with the place which was small and offered a peaceful existence. He was delighted to discover that there was a small theatre and declared he would visit this and perhaps hear some concerts.

The Queen, carefully watching him, believed that his health had improved a little. The quiet of Cheltenham was restoring his calm. Each morning he went to the Pump Room to drink the waters and later for walks in the company of the Queen and a few attendants; he was amused because the town was so small and that the same plump middle-aged woman known as Nanny the Bellman was postmistress, town-crier and tax-collector. He was amused too to learn that there were no carriages of any sort in the town and that the people had to rely on two very ancient Sedan chairs. It was a peaceful existence and by eleven o'clock at night the King liked everyone to be in bed.

Thus was life in Cheltenham; and there was no doubt in the Queen's mind that it agreed with the King.

But the respite was temporary. The King would come to the Queen and talk excitedly, his words spilling over each other as though they could not wait to get out; his eyes would bulge and his speech grow more and more rapid; and he would talk until his voice grew hoarse. The rash had broken out again; and the Queen grew more and more fearful with every day. This was the realization of the fears which had haunted her for so long.

She strove to keep the King's condition from those about him. Gossip would be unendurable; and she pictured the distortions of the newspapers. But it was impossible to keep the King's condition from his attendants; he embarrassed them; they did not know how to act when faced with one of his tirades.

One day Colonel Digby excused himself from attendance on the King. He was, he said, confined to his rooms with gout.

The King strode off without him for his 'exercise'. The Queen heard him talking to Colonel Goldsworthy, for the apartments were so close to each other in Bay's Hill Lodge that it was like living in a small house.

'Fresh air, Goldsworthy. Must have it, eh, what? Get fat without it. Tendency in the family. Plenty of exercise and attention to diet. I've always watched it. All the children . . . Cut out drink, Goldsworthy. No good to you, eh, what? Healthy life in the country. Peace . . . Not often a king can enjoy that. Matters of State . . . ministers . . . his family . . . Children become an anxiety, Goldsworthy. They run up debts, get involved with women . . .'

The Queen put her fingers into her ears.

I can't bear it, she thought. It will be useless to try and hide it much longer.

Colonel Digby scratched lightly on Miss Burney's door.

'Is there any hope of a dish of tea, Miss Burney?'

Fanny smiled a little coquettishly. There was no doubt in her mind that Colonel Digby was courting her. She thought of writing to Susan about the situation. Susan would be so amused and interested.

'Colonel Digby! And I heard you were laid low with the gout.'

'Say rather a surfeit of His Majesty's conversation.'

Fanny raised her eyebrows. 'I must say the King can be most . . . *alarming*. I confess I am at a complete loss for words when he speaks to me.'

'That need not worry you, Miss Burney. He has enough and to spare.'

'Yes but . . .' Fanny sighed. She was fond of the Queen and she did sense her anxiety. 'His Majesty is a little strange.'

The Colonel looked solemn and remarked that no doubt the King was contemplating the inevitable misery of mankind, which made Fanny laugh, while she disputed the fact that mankind was inevitably miserable.

The conversation grew animated when Miss Planta looked in and expressed some surprise to see Colonel Digby there alone with Fanny.

'Oh, do come in, Miss Planta. We are having such an *interesting* discussion.'

Miss Planta joined them for a while and then excused herself rather pointedly and the discussion continued between Fanny and the Colonel until Madam von Schwellenburg bustled in and throwing up her hands in horror cried: 'Wot this? Tea drinking again. Giv me von dish, Miss Berners. Ach . . . not goot . . . not goot.'

And she sat there with baleful expression until the Colonel took his leave.

She often said that Fanny must come with her to feed the toads—a task Fanny loathed. Horrid creatures, and their mistress was only one degree less ugly!

'Ladies come to serve Queen,' Schwellenburg audibly remarked to her pet toad, 'not to flirt wiz chentlemens.'

But Fanny was still thinking of the pleasant hour with Colonel Digby and as soon as the opportunity arose wrote to Susan:

'There is something singular in the perfect trust he seems to have in my discretion, for he speaks to me when we are alone with a frankness unequalled; and there is something very flattering in the apparent relief he seems to find in dedicating what time he has to dispose of to me in my little parlour.'

The Queen looked at her maid of honour.

'Colonel Digby took tea with you yesterday, Miss Burney.'

'Yes, Your Majesty, that was so.'

'But pray how did it happen? I understood he was confined to his room with the gout.'

'He grew better, Madam, and hoped by a little exercise to prevent a serious fit.'

So, thought the Queen, they were avoiding him. They found his conduct embarrassing. They risked royal displeasure rather than face those long diatribes. How can I blame them?

She could not attend to the reading. She realized that she had been sitting with her needle poised in her hand for some minutes.

They must not notice that she was acting oddly too.

It will be almost a relief, she thought, when it is *known*.

The King came out of the house laughing to himself. It was a pleasure not to be surrounded by equerries and attendants. Out into the lanes. The land looked good.

'How pleasant to be a farmer,' he said to himself. 'Growing the crops, making the butter. Should have enjoyed it. Nothing like fresh country air. Fresh air. Good for everybody. Fresh air

. . . simple food . . . no drink . . . no fat . . . have to be careful. Tendency in the family.'

He had forgotten that it was impossible for the King to wander out and be unrecognized. He had come to a few houses round a village green and some children playing there had seen him and hastened to carry the news that the King had come. In a short time he was being followed by a group of villagers and seeing them, he turned and greeted them.

'Pleasant, eh? Pretty country. Nothing like the country. Good clean country air. Not like London? Give me the country. Healthy, eh, what?'

The villagers did not know what to do; they looked at each other and giggled and the King went on talking about farms and the country and the peace of the quiet life—but so rapidly that they could scarcely hear what he was saying.

He came to a bridge.

'Hey,' he cried. 'What's this, eh? A bridge, eh, what?'

A man who was standing close to the King received the full glare of those protuberant eyes.

'If it please, Your Majesty,' he said, 'it is a bridge.'

'A bridge, eh, my boys? Then let us give it a huzza, eh, what?'

At which he took off his hat, waved it in the air and gave three lusty cheers.

It was while he was doing this that Colonels Digby and Goldsworthy found him and discreetly managed to conduct him back to the house.

The villagers looked after him, murmuring to each other that the ways of royalty were very strange.

Colonel Digby mentioned the King's odd behaviour to the Queen who listened intently.

'His Majesty,' she said, 'has always been interested in the country.'

And she thought: It can't be long now. He is very close to complete breakdown.

It was the very next morning when the King awoke in the early hours and chuckling with pleasure rose and went to the Colonels' quarters.

He banged on their doors and ran up and down the stairs shouting 'Tallyho!' and waking everyone in the near vicinity.

Once again Colonel Digby dealt with the situation and courteously conducted His Majesty back to his room.

* * *

Miss Burney was reading to the Queen. It was not a very affecting passage, but suddenly the tears began to fall down the Queen's cheeks.

Fanny stopped reading in dismay and the Queen vainly sought to repose her features. It was not possible. The tears flowed over, and the Queen put her hand to her face and wept.

It was over in a few minutes.

'How nervous I am,' she said. 'I am . . . quite a fool, don't you think so?'

'No, Madam,' replied Fanny quietly.

The Queen smiled at her gratefully, for she knew in that moment that Miss Burney understood the reason for her emotion.

'I think,' said the Queen, 'that we have had enough of Cheltenham. I will speak to the King.'

'Yes, Madam,' replied Fanny; and she went on talking which was not quite correct in the presence of the Queen but on this occasion Fanny believed it was what Her Majesty desired. 'Cheltenham, Madam, is now on the map because of Your Majesty's visit. The *Morning Post* says that all the fashions are completely Cheltenhamized throughout Great Britain.'

The Queen nodded. 'The people of Cheltenham will be very pleased.'

'Cheltenham will now rival Brighton,' said the irrepressible Fanny.

Brighton was synonymous in the Queen's mind with trouble. Trouble, thought the Queen. Trouble all around.

'Yes,' she said aloud, 'it is indeed time we left Cheltenham.'

Back at St. James's the King's strange behaviour continued. His ministers noticed it; there were whispers about it. It was not long before it was mentioned in the papers.

The Queen asked to see all the papers and Miss Burney took them to her and anxiously watched her peruse them.

With one comment she was extremely angry. Miss Burney did not dare ask what it was, but the Queen said: 'They should be sued for this. I shall not allow it to pass.'

Fanny listened quietly, thinking that since her arrival at Court Her Majesty had changed. She was not so aloof from affairs, nor so resigned.

The Queen shrugged her shoulders suddenly.

'Light the candle, Miss Burney,' she said.

Fanny obeyed and the Queen held the paper in the flame.

* * *

The King's conduct became stranger and stranger. At Kew he went out riding in the rain and came back so wet that when his boots were taken off water poured out of them. This gave him a chill and brought the rash out again. He liked to go out alone and would pace up and down talking to himself and beating time to music which no one else could hear.

One day out riding with the Queen he called for the carriage to stop that he might seize one of the lower branches of an oak and shake it as though it were a hand. When the postilion approached him he ordered him away because, he said, he was conversing with the King of Prussia.

When about to drive with the Princess Royal he got into the chaise and then got out again to give orders to the postilions; once more he got in and out again and continued to do this, all the time talking so rapidly that his voice was growing more and more hoarse and finally the Princess Royal burst into tears, alighted and ran back to her apartments.

This conduct could not be ignored.

The King was ill; many believed that he had not long to live. News of this reached the Prince in Brighton and brought him with all speed to Windsor.

On the way from Brighton to Windsor the Prince of Wales was thinking of the prospect before him. If rumour could be believed his father was very ill indeed, in fact near to death; and this meant of course that the Prince of Wales could shortly become the King of England.

It was a dazzling prospect; and yet the Prince felt uneasy. He wished that he could have shown more affection towards his father. Now that the poor old fellow was so ill he felt remorseful. All the same it *was* an exciting prospect. He had already spoken of it to Burke and Sheridan and with such close friends and allies there was no need for hypocrisy. They were delighted by the thought of a new reign; and in his heart so was the Prince.

'Your Highness will want to send for Fox,' suggested Burke.

Sheridan agreed that Fox would be needed; and the Prince fell in with their suggestion, although a trifle uneasily. Maria's dislike of Fox and the fact that he had been unfairly blamed for the denial of the marriage was disturbing, but he realized that in such a crisis they needed Fox.

'I've no idea where he might be,' went on Burke. 'Somewhere in Italy I believe. But I think Your Highness will agree that no time should be lost as it may be some weeks before we can find him.'

The Prince had agreed and the search for Fox was begun.

Oh, yes, indeed, it was a brilliant prospect. Fox would be the leader of the Whig Party, with the support of the Prince who would have become King. Although Fox had announced himself to be disgusted with English politics, although he had declared that he wished to hear nothing of what was going on at home in Parliament, although he wanted to receive no newspapers, no letters—this would bring him home.

The Prince arrived at Windsor and went immediately to the Queen.

He kissed her hand and looking into her face was immediately aware of the change in her. She was very anxious, certainly; but she was no longer the meek woman he had hitherto known; there was something almost militant about her.

'It is well,' she said, 'that you should be here.'

'I must see the doctors at once,' said the Prince. 'I shall want a detailed account from them.'

He imagines himself King already, thought the Queen. But it has not yet come to that.

'Pray do not allow the King to guess that you have come with such speed because you are waiting to take the throne.'

'Madam,' said the Prince coldly, 'I assure you good manners would prevent me from acting in such a manner.'

'I hope so,' she said. 'You will be shocked when you see him. His appearance has changed considerably. His voice has changed. He talks constantly . . . talks and talks until his voice is hoarse and in fact fails him altogether. The veins stand out at his temples and his eyes look like black-currant jelly.'

The Prince said sharply: 'What is his malady? There seems to be a great deal of mystery about it. Who is attending him?'

'Sir George Baker, who has always attended the King.'

'He's an old fool. The King himself once said he was an old woman.'

'He is reliable.'

'I will send a doctor of my own choosing to see him.'

Oh, yes, thought the Queen. He sees himself as the master of us all already. But it shall not be. He shall not ignore me.

What had come over her? This was her beloved son.

The Prince sought out his brother Frederick who had also arrived at Windsor.

'You have seen him,' said the Prince of Wales to Frederick. 'What is your opinion?'

'That he's very ill indeed. You should be at hand, George. He behaves so oddly. Of course our mother has been trying to hide this but she can't do it much longer.'

'She seemed like a different woman. I have never seen her like this before.'

'She's given up having children. Perhaps that accounts for it. She does not approve of your way of life, George.'

'Nor do I approve of hers.'

Frederick laughed. 'There may be conflicts in the family. Although I suppose we should not be surprised at that. It's the family tradition.'

'Fred.'

'Yes, George.'

'Whatever happens, I shall be able to rely on you?'

'To the death,' said Frederick.

The brothers clasped hands.

'By God,' said the Prince, 'I'm glad you came back from Germany in time.'

While the family dined together, Frederick was watching his father and elder brother very closely. The King did not address the Prince of Wales, in fact he had given no indication that he was aware of his being present, but he was disturbed and Frederick believed that this was due to the presence of the Prince.

The Princesses Charlotte, Augusta and Elizabeth were silent. Visits from their brother had always been exciting, but they knew why George was here this time and it was a frightening thought.

The King had started to talk and the subject of his discourse was so involved that none of the family could understand what it was all about. On and on he went, occasionally shooting out an eh, what?

The Queen sat clenching and unclenching her hands, feeling that at any moment she would cry out that she could endure no more. The Princesses' eyes were on their mother expecting she would give them the command to leave the table. The Prince of Wales was watching his father incredulously and thinking: He's not physically ill. He's *mad*!

The King glared at his son. 'Eh?' he whispered, for he had almost lost his voice. 'Eh, what?'

The Prince said: 'I cannot hear what Your Majesty says. You are whispering. If you will speak a little louder . . .'

The King stood up suddenly. There was a terrified silence as he walked to that chair on which the Prince of Wales was sitting.

The Prince was rising when the King seized him about the neck.

'Puppy! Insolent dog! You would tell the King of England that he should speak out . . . would you? By God, I'll kill you. I will . . . I will . . . I will . . .'

The Prince tried to drag the King's hands from his throat. Frederick sprang up and there was a scuffle which was joined by the equerries. The Prince of Wales fell back against the wall and stared at the King whose eyes were dark with rage.

The Queen put her hand over her mouth to prevent herself screaming; the Prince was weeping and Colonel Digby asked if it were His Majesty's wish that he should conduct him to his apartment.

The King looked puzzled, but after a little persuasion allowed himself to be led away.

Never had there been such a scene in the royal dining room. The Princess Charlotte ran to get Hungary water to bathe her brother's forehead and so revive him. In her own apartments the Queen could no longer restrain her fears; she threw herself on to her bed and gave way to violent laughter and tears.

The truth could no longer be hidden.

The King was mad.

The Regency Bill

The Prince rode out to Bagshot from Windsor where, in the parlour of a hostelry, he found Sheridan and Maria waiting for him.

He embraced Maria warmly and Sheridan almost equally so.

'This is going to be a very big change in our fortunes,' he said, looking earnestly at Maria.

'My only hope is that all will go well with you,' she answered.

'A Duchess first,' he whispered, 'and then, by God, you shall be acknowledged Princess of Wales.'

'You think too far ahead, my love,' said Maria gently; but she was pleased. He knew that the dearest wish of her life was not for fine titles and riches but to be acknowledged as his wife—though of course that acknowledgement could only mean that she had a right to the second highest title a woman could attain.

Sheridan said: 'We must act with care at this stage, Your Highness. It is to discuss our moves that I thought we three should meet.'

They sat down and talked.

Fox must come back as soon as possible, said Sheridan.

The Prince looked anxiously at Maria who was naturally not at all pleased at the thought of the return of the man who had, she had said, treated her as though she were a street walker, but she knew of his brilliance; she knew he was the natural leader of the Whigs and she knew too how important the Whigs were to the Prince. Yes, she reluctantly agreed, Fox must be brought back.

Both Sheridan and the Prince were relieved. But one could

258

trust Maria's good sense and her greatest concern really was for her husband's well-being even if this should be brought about at her own discomfiture.

'So we will pursue the hunt for Fox without delay,' said Sheridan, not mentioning to Maria that the hunt had already been in progress for days and that he—and the Prince—were disturbed because the statesman seemed difficult to find. He had been traced to Geneva but had left a week or so before the messenger arrived and none there knew of his next destination.

Sheridan, whose ambition was great, realized that the task before him was one for a practised politician; he was scarcely that, and to take a false step at such an important stage could ruin his political future. He loved the excitement of politics; he was deeply in debt all round, partly because he neglected the business of earning a living in the theatre for the sake of the excitement politics offered—and he was a drinker, a gambler and spendthrift. So he dared not take a wrong step; he needed Fox.

'There are two alternatives,' he said. 'Your Highness could in a few weeks' time be King of England . . .'

'The King seemed strong enough when he seized me,' replied the Prince. 'I don't think the trouble is his *physical* health.'

Sheridan replied: 'If the King were mad and still continued to live, there would be a Regency.'

'A Regent should have the power of a king,' said the Prince.

'It would depend, Your Highness, on what power the Parliament gave him. Your Highness should not forget that we shall have Mr. Pitt to deal with.'

The Prince's eyes narrowed. Mr. Pitt, the enemy! The man who had forced the denial of the marriage out of Fox!

'We can be sure,' he said grimly, 'that Mr. Pitt will do his utmost to deny me my rights.'

Sheridan nodded. 'That,' he said, 'is why we need Charles James Fox who, while he will serve Your Highness with all his power, will be mightily diverted to discountenance Mr. Pitt.'

Oh yes, even Maria had to agree that they needed Mr. Fox.

In an easy chair in his lodgings in the town of Bologna Mr. Fox stretched himself with ease. In a few moments Lizzie would come in with a dish of tea to revive him after his afternoon's nap. It was a pleasure to watch Lizzie move across the room. What a graceful creature she was! Italy suited her; and so did this wandering existence. She was never ruffled, and such an intelligent companion. Lizzie had all the qualities he looked for in a woman. Now if he had known Lizzie when he was a young man, and if at that time he had had the wisdom to recognize her qualities, he would never have led the life he had. But then it was due to his adventures with so many members of her sex that he was able to appreciate her. Perhaps, he thought, he would marry her one day. Why not?

This was the life. Politics? Well, yes, he had to admit that his greatest ambition had been to be Prime Minister; but that affair of the marriage and the Prince's deception had made him want to turn his back on Westminster. And so here he was in Italy—and what treasures of art, architecture and music he, and Lizzie with him, had discovered there! He believed this period of travel might well be the happiest of his life.

Where should they go from here? When Lizzie came in with the tea they would discuss the next move.

He yawned pleasurably and here was Lizzie although it was not quite time and she was holding letters in her hand.

Letters? he thought. But he had left no address in England, his sole purpose being to get away. He had not even wanted to know what was happening there so he had asked that no news sheets or papers should be sent to him. So what could Lizzie be doing with letters?

She was as unhurried as usual as she said to him: 'They have tracked you down.'

'London?' he said.

She gave him two letters. 'There is a messenger outside. He has been chasing all over Europe looking for you, he tells me. He has lately come from Geneva and somehow traced you to this place.'

'Good God!' cried Fox. 'What can this mean?'

He was opening one of the letters. 'Burke,' he said. He read it through and handed it to her. The other letter was from Sheridan.

There was a brief silence and then he said: 'The King is ill . . . seriously ill. So our young prince will soon be king. You know what this is going to mean for the Whigs.'

'That Mr. Fox will lead them to power?'

He was grinning at her.

'But Mr. Fox said only yesterday that he was done with politics.'

'Mr. Fox, Madam, can now and then talk nonsense.'

'So I thought at the time,' said Lizzie. 'When do you wish to leave?'

'I shall answer these letters to tell them I am returning with all speed, then go, while you make the necessary preparations to follow me to London as soon as possible. There must be nothing to detain me.'

'Nothing at all,' said Lizzie, and left him.

The messenger departed with all speed and shortly afterwards Fox set out on his journey, leaving Lizzie to settle their affairs and follow. He was travelling through France when the news reached him that the King was mad.

This, he thought, will mean a Regency.

His eyes were already sparkling with the light of battle. He must press on with all speed. Lizzie would have been concerned for his health had she been here, for he was too impatient to be back to pause long enough to rest adequately. He arrived in London on November 24th, which meant that the journey had taken only nine days. Remarkable speed—but when Lizzie arrived she would see the effect it had had on him. But that was nothing. Let him get to the House and he would show Pitt that he could not have all his own way while Fox was there to prevent him.

Mr. Pitt travelled down to Windsor. The Prince, who had returned from Bagshot, declined to see him, and Mr. Pitt therefore asked for an audience with the Queen.

Charlotte received him gratefully. It was the first time she had been included in any State matter and she was appreciative of Mr. Pitt's obvious respect for her.

He asked her questions about the King's condition and she answered as frankly as she could, for there was no possibility now of hiding the fact that the King was mad.

'Your Majesty,' said Mr. Pitt, 'the possibilities are that Parliament will decide that a Regency is necessary and the Prince of Wales will expect to be the Regent.'

'That, Mr. Pitt,' said the Queen firmly, 'is scarcely a state of affairs which would please me . . .' She amended that immediately to, 'which would please us.'

Mr. Pitt admitted this. 'I doubt that I should remain long in office.'

'And it is essential that you should, Mr. Pitt.'

The Prime Minister bowed his head. It was an acknowledgement that he and the Queen were allies and he decided to take the Queen into his confidence. 'If His Highness *should* attain the Regency,' he said, 'it will be necessary to restrict his power wherever possible.'

The Queen agreed that this was so.

'I had been thinking of a joint Regency . . . with perhaps Your Majesty as one of its members.'

The Queen's sallow face flushed a little. This was triumph such as she had never dreamed of. But she was not a fool. She did not believe for one moment that she would be allowed by Mr. Pitt or the Prince of Wales to exert her power over Parliament. But there was one way in which she could have perhaps as much influence as any; that was if she had the care of the King. Suppose this bout was like that other—as temporary as that. Why not! It was not impossible.

'I believe, Mr. Pitt,' she said, 'that it is better for me to take no part in politics but to devote myself to His Majesty. If I were his sole guardian for as long as this unhappy malady continues, I believe I could be of the greatest service.'

Mr. Pitt was pleased. The Queen was a woman of sound good sense. They could indeed be allies.

The Queen was frightened. She was never quite sure what the King would do. He terrified her because he called for her constantly. She had moved into a bedroom which was next to his and he seemed to have an obsession that his enemies were trying to separate him from her. All night long she would hear his rambling conversations, shouting at first, and then as his voice began to fail him growing hoarser and hoarser until just a vague whispering came from the other side of the wall. She would not forget that dreadful night when he had attempted to murder the Prince of Wales. He had always been a kindly man but there had been murder in his face that night, and after witnessing that violent scene she could no longer feel safe. What if he were to turn against *her*? That very night he had escaped from his equerries and come into the room she occupied and, holding a lighted candle in his hand, had drawn the bed curtains and stood there looking down at her. She had feared that he had come to set the curtains alight as he cried: 'Yes, you are still here. I see you are still here. I thought the Queen would be here. I know she would not desert me.' And then seeing the frightened face of Miss Goldsworthy who had come hurrying in from the adjoining chamber: 'Ah, my honest Gooley, you will take care of the Queen.' And he had taken Gooley's arm and paced up and down the room talking, talking, talking, until she had thought he would drive her mad too. It had seemed so frighteningly long before they took him away.

Now his illness was accepted and the Prince was trying to take over his father's authority.

She could not understand her emotions. She *hated* the Prince. It was incredible. This was her son, the boy whom she had loved more than all the rest of the children put together. What had come over her?

It is because I longed for his love, she told herself, *and all he has done is to despise me.*

But she would not allow herself to think such a thing. She was against him because he wished to usurp his father's power.

Miss Burney came in and, standing before her, burst into tears. The Queen stared at this unusual maid of honour, and suddenly they were crying together.

'Your pardon, Madam.'

'There is no need to ask it, Miss Burney. I thank you. You have made me weep . . . and I think it is what I needed.'

So they sat side by side and wiped their eyes and the Queen felt comforted.

'Mamma,' said the Princess Royal, 'Dr. Warren is here.'

'Dr. Warren. I have not sent for him.'

'So I thought, Mamma. But he has come and he is being most arrogant and Sir George Baker is not very pleased for he says that he is in charge of His Majesty.'

'Pray send someone to this Dr. Warren and tell him that I wish to see him without delay.'

The Princess Royal did as she was bid and came back to the Queen to present Her Majesty with her snuff box. Absentmindedly the Queen took a pinch; but there was no comfort in anything these days.

One of the pages scratched at the door and the Princess Royal bade him enter.

'Your Majesty,' said the boy, bowing low, 'Dr. Warren sends his compliments but regrets he is too busily engaged with his duties at this moment to wait on Your Majesty. He will do so at his earliest convenience.'

The page bowed low and obviously after having delivered such a message was glad to escape. The Queen's mouth tightened and she said: 'I can scarcely believe that I have heard aright.'

'Oh, Mamma,' cried the Princess, 'they are saying that Dr.

Warren is the choice of the Prince of Wales and that he is here to serve the Prince . . . that he has the Prince's authority for all he does . . .'

'Insulting the Queen, I daresay,' said the Queen grimly.

The Princess Royal sat on the footstool at her mother's feet and looked up at her anxiously. She too was remembering that dreadful scene at the dinner table when her father had attempted to murder her brother.

'What will become of us all?' she asked.

'God alone knows,' answered the Queen.

Dr. Warren and the Prince had decided that the King should go to Kew.

'There,' said the Prince, 'he will be restful. He was always fond of Kew. As for my mother,' he went on, 'I believe she should go to Buckingham House or perhaps stay at Windsor. The King is so clouded in his mind that he will be much better alone with the doctors.'

His brother Frederick agreed with him, and when his uncles Gloucester and Cumberland called they made it clear that they already regarded the Prince of Wales as the ruler.

He was gratified. No more would that mad old man dictate to him. *No one* should dictate to him; that was why he was going to teach the Queen a lesson for he was sure she still saw him as a little boy to be guided by his parents.

It was the Princess Royal once more who brought the news to her mother.

'I have heard them discussing it, Mamma,' she said. 'They are going to take the King away from us.'

'Indeed they are not.'

'Oh yes, Mamma, they are. George has given orders that they are to prepare for the journey to Kew.'

'I will see the Prince of Wales,' said the Queen.

She went to his apartments where he received her coldly.

'What is this I hear about His Majesty's going to Kew?' she demanded.

'I and his doctors think it best.'

'And I am not to be consulted?'

'No, Madam.'

'I think you forget that I am the Queen.'

'It is perhaps Your Majesty who is forgetful of *my* position.'

He was looking at her with the cold eyes of contempt. If only he had smiled at her even then, had asked for her help, her sympathy, she would have weakened. But of course he did nothing of the sort. He just stood regarding her arrogantly, implying that she was of no account and that he was the master now.

'It is monstrous that you should propose to take the King to Kew without consulting me.'

'Madam, as you will not be going with him it did not occur to us to consult you. You are to live . . . at peace either at Buckingham House or Windsor. You may take your choice.'

'How kind, how understanding of you to give me a *choice*.'

'Well, Madam, I wish to please if possible.'

'Enough of this. Where the King is there shall I be. You forget I am his wife.'

'Madam, my plans . . .'

She snapped her fingers. '*My* plan is to stay with the King and my place is at his side. I believe that His Majesty's ministers will agree with me, and would not take kindly to any plan to separate a sick husband from his wife.'

The Prince was silent.

She went on: 'It was suggested that, should there be a Regency, I should share in it, but I have said my place is to care for the King. Should I be ousted from that place, there might be another waiting for me. And if I was kept from my duty to the King I might take it.'

As she walked from the room he knew she was right and that he had been foolish to talk of separating them. He would have to give way.

The first round of the battle was a victory for the Queen.

The Prince left for Kew, having given orders that his mother and sisters with their attendants were to follow. The King was to come on later.

At Kew the Prince decided which rooms should be allotted to whom and actually wrote the names of the people who should occupy them over the doors.

The Queen's apartments were immediately above the King's and he decided that she could not occupy these for fear of disturbing His Majesty; therefore he selected a bedroom and drawing room for her which were not very commodious, but, as he said to his equerry, she would come so therefore she must make do with what accommodation there was. As for some of her maids of honour, they would have to be content with the servants' rooms.

From one of the windows he saw his mother arrive, surrounded by her weeping daughters.

At Windsor the King paced up and down his bedroom and shouted: 'Where do you wish to take me, eh, what? To Kew? I will not go to Kew. What should I go to Kew for if I do not wish it, eh, what? Tell me that! Kew . . . I do not wish to go to Kew . . .' And so on in such a strain, his voice rising higher and higher until there was little of it left and he could only croak.

Colonel Digby reminded him that he had always been particularly fond of Kew.

'No longer,' cried the King. 'I will not go to Kew. I know what you people are after. You want to shut me up there. Do you, eh, what?'

They only wanted him to be comfortable, they told him.

'You want to separate me from the Queen, eh, what? You are trying to take her from me. Queen Elizabeth . . . She's my Queen . . .'

The equerries looked mystified until Digby nodded, remembering the King's glances at Lady Elizabeth Pembroke. The poor old man was very far gone if he believed he was married to Elizabeth Pembroke.

'The Queen,' cried the King. 'I want the Queen. You have separated us. Oh yes you have. You have taken the Queen from me. You have decided that she shall not be with me, eh, what?'

Colonel Digby said: 'Your Majesty, the Queen has gone ahead to Kew. She is waiting there to welcome you.'

'Eh, what? The Queen at Kew?'

Digby assured His Majesty that this was indeed the truth; and thus was enabled to persuade him to enter his carriage. And so the poor deranged King came to Kew.

The Queen watched the King's arrival. Oh, God, she thought, is that poor shambling creature the King? And she thought of him as he had been when she first saw him: young, handsome in his way with his fresh complexion and his blue eyes, and kindly too, not letting her guess that he had married her with the utmost reluctance.

And now . . . he had come to this. There was General Harcourt and Colonel Goldsworthy with him, helping him in; she could hear his voice, hoarse and yet somehow audible; and she wondered if he had been shouting during the journey.

'Oh, Mamma, Mamma,' It was her daughter Augusta who was beside her, taking her hand and pressing it.

'My daughter,' said the Queen, 'your father has come to Kew. It is fitting that we should be together at such a time.'

Augusta began to cry. 'Everything is so different, Mamma. Everything is changed.'

'Yes,' agreed the Queen, 'I fear nothing will be the same again.'

She felt her lips tremble uncontrollably and Augusta seeing her emotion said: 'Mamma, may I sleep in your bedchamber tonight? I will have a small tent bed put up and I promise not to disturb you . . . only to be a comfort.'

The Queen pressed her daughter's hand. 'It is strange,' she said, 'that Queens should pray for sons. It is daughters who are a comfort to them.'

Immediately on his arrival in England Fox arranged to meet the Prince at Carlton House. The Prince received his old friend with tears in his eyes.

'By God, Charles, it is a relief to see you here.'

'And a relief to be here, Your Highness.'

'I had feared we should never find you.'

'As soon as I knew my services were required I came at full speed.'

'And Lizzie?''

'She is following. I doubt her return will be long delayed.'

'Now to business, Charles.'

'Indeed so, Your Highness. I hear there is a little improvement in His Majesty's general health.'

'That's true.' The Prince spoke almost ruefully and added quickly: 'In his state his death would be the best possible solution for himself more than any of us. I cannot tell you how *mad* he is, Charles. A raving lunatic.'

'Sad, very sad. And likely to remain so?'

'Dr. Warren thinks so. The other doctors hold out hope of his return to sanity. But they are doubtless primed by the Queen.'

'Her Majesty shows unusual spirit.'

'She has changed . . . completely. Now she has given up bearing children I believe she fancies herself as a powerful influence on the country's affairs.'

'She could have some influence, Your Highness. We should not lose sight of that.'

'She seems to have formed an alliance with Pitt.'

'Then we must indeed be watchful of her. Your Highness, we need Portland's assistance. It would be helpful if you could forget your quarrel with him.'

The Prince scowled. 'He showed himself to be no friend of mine over that matter of my debts.'

'Nevertheless, Your Highness, we need him.'

The Prince was silent for a moment. 'Very well,' he said. 'Shake him by the hand and tell him that I hope everything that is past may be forgotten between us.'

'Excellent,' murmured Fox.

'I will ask Maria to receive him at Pall Mall.'

Fox was silent. Would Maria receive Charles James Fox?

Oh, curse the woman! The pity of it was that the Prince had ever become influenced by her. *She* was the reason for his exile; she could now be his biggest enemy.

'Maria will see that Portland forgets his grievances,' said the Prince with a fond smile.

That may be, thought Fox, but how will she behave towards me?

At least the quarrel between the Prince and Portland would be mended and that was the first step forward.

Now, he explained, they must see that the Regency passed to the Prince with all the powers of kingship, for they could be sure Pitt would do everything in his power to curtail the Prince's.

Maria had arrived from Brighton with the Sheridans whose own house was now occupied by the bailiffs.

'Guests,' declared Sheridan, 'whom we can scarcely call welcome.'

Maria, who had herself, since her association with the Prince, suffered from the visits of such 'guests', was sympathetic.

'You and Elizabeth must stay with me until something can be done to dislodge your guests,' she told Sheridan, who was delighted at the prospect.

In his bedroom in the magnificent Pall Mall house he discussed the future with Elizabeth.

'A temporary embarrassment, my love. When the Prince is Regent, when we are in power, there'll be a very important place for me in the Government. Make no mistake about that.'

'Will it pay our debts, Richard?'

'My dearest, who is going to worry about the debts of the . . . er . . . what shall it be? What post would you choose for me?'

'I would choose that of the solvent man.'

That made him laugh. 'Elizabeth, you have no spirit of adventure?'

He took her by the shoulders and looked into her face. Now she could see clearly what dissipation had done to those once handsome looks.

Oh, Richard, she thought, where are you going?

She released herself and made a desperate effort to restrain her fit of coughing.

Maria was concerned by Elizabeth's pallor and Miss Pigot made one of her special cough mixtures for her. Maria was very fond of Elizabeth. Sheridan was witty and amusing and she believed a good friend of the Prince, but it was Elizabeth whom she loved.

The Prince had asked her to receive the Duke of Portland and she had sent an invitation to him which he had been delighted to accept, and he had shown his appreciation of her intelligence by discussing the situation with her. After that he had called several times and he, Sheridan and sometimes the Prince had had discussions together.

It would have been useful, Portland had implied, if Fox could have joined them.

It is one thing I will not do, Maria had decided. I will never have that man in my house.

The Sheridans came into her drawing room. Delightful guests, she thought. Sheridan so entertaining; Elizabeth so charming.

'We have half an hour before my guests are due,' she told him. 'Pray be seated, Elizabeth, my dear. Did you take Pig's potion? You will be in her black books if you did not.'

Elizabeth assured her that she had taken the evil-tasting concoction. 'And I have not coughed since.'

Dear Elizabeth! She needed the quiet of the country; she needed a respite from anxiety. They were of a kind. Why should they fall in love and marry—yes *marry*—men who were so different from themselves?

'Portland will be coming tonight, I suppose,' asked Sheridan.

'My dear Sherry, he almost asked himself. He seems to regard my house as the headquarters of his party, which is comical, considering my politics.'

Sheridan laughed. 'Delightfully incongruous.'

'And Portland is a little jealous of you, Sherry.'

'I know. You are too kind to us. He would like you to be as

kind to him. Perhaps if I could persuade him to pass over his fortune to me he would be in a position to entertain the bailiffs, then you might take pity on him as you are now doing on the poor impecunious Sheridans.'

'I am not sure that I should, for impecunious or not I like to think of the Sheridans as my friends.'

Sheridan rose and bowed as gracefully as though he were on a stage.

'One man I will not have in my house,' said Maria vehemently, 'is Charles James Fox. I know the Prince wishes me to, but I cannot bring myself to receive him here. When I think of the public insult he gave me, I am determined that I could never accept him as a friend of mine.'

Elizabeth's heart began to beat uncomfortably. She wanted Richard to defend his friend. All the political good fortune which had come to him had been due to Fox's influence. She wanted Richard to stand up for Fox, to explain to Maria that Fox had been forced to act as he had; but to do so was of course to cast a criticism on the conduct of the Prince of Wales and that was something he dared not do.

'Fox, I think, believed he was acting for the best . . .' he began mildly.

'For the best!' cried Maria. 'To destroy my reputation. To speak of me as though I were a . . . a street woman!'

Sheridan said soothingly: 'Oh, he's a wily old Fox. I well understand why you won't have him here.'

'No,' said Maria, 'not even for the Prince. And I do not think he is quite so fond of Fox as he once was.'

'How could he be,' said Sheridan, 'when you dislike him so?'

Later that night in their bedroom in Pall Mall Sheridan talked to Elizabeth while she brushed her long dark hair.

'Portland is jealous of me. Think of that, Elizabeth. Portland! The great Duke himself. Maria is our friend and don't make any mistake about this: Maria is going to have a big say in affairs. When the Prince is Regent, when he gives his support to the Party, then we'll be truly in power. Poor Mr. Pitt. He will depart and in his place . . .'

'Mr. Fox?' said Elizabeth quietly.

'Mr. Fox?' repeated Sheridan almost questioningly. 'Maria hates him. I have rarely seen her so vehement as she was when she spoke of him. She will have great influence. Oh, yes . . .

great influence, and she is not very pleased with Mr. Fox . . . Portland is jealous of me. Think of that Elizabeth. You see . . .'

'Yes, I see,' said Elizabeth.

'The future looks very promising. So why are you worrying about those confounded bailiffs?'

Fox out of favour, he was thinking. Portland jealous of Sheridan. Could it be? Was it possible? Was Richard Brinsley Sheridan the future Prime Minister?

Elizabeth, watching him through the mirror, knowing him so well, read his thoughts clearly.

Who knows? she asked herself. He has succeeded so well in one direction, failed so sadly in another.

And whatever the outcome, shall I be here to see it?

When Parliament reassembled in December Pitt rose to propose a committee to examine the setting up of a Regency. The King's doctors had declared his mind to be deranged, but with the exception of Dr. Warren they believed there was a very good possibility of his recovering.

'We should examine precedents,' said Pitt.

Fox was immediately on his feet. 'What is the need of a committee?' he demanded. 'The heir apparent is of age and has the capacity to govern. If the King were dead he would ascend the throne. The Prince of Wales has the *right* to govern if his father the King is unable to do so.'

What had happened to Fox? The wily politician with his expert knowledge of parliamentary procedure had made a false step, and it was one which a sharp-witted statesman such as Mr. Pitt would see at once. The use of the word *right* was the biggest blunder Fox could have made.

Pitt could scarcely contain himself for his excitement. He whispered to the man seated next to him, 'I can't believe Fox could be such a fool. This gives me the opportunity I want. I'll unwhig the gentleman for the rest of his life.'

Mr. Pitt was on his feet. He could not allow the statement of the honourable gentleman to pass. He had used the word 'right'. Mr. Pitt feared that Mr. Fox had put forth a treasonable doctrine. 'The Prince of Wales,' Mr. Pitt admitted, 'has a *claim*, but no more *right* than any other member of this community.'

Fox immediately saw his mistake. Oh, God, what a fool. Why did I use that word? All this time away from the House had blunted his wits; the journey across Europe had sapped his strength. Lizzie was right. He should have taken it more leisurely. What would a few more days have mattered . . . another week. Anything would have been better than that he should make this blunder. And of course Pitt was gleeful. Pitt had leaped into the advantage.

Fox's friend Edmund Burke, that brilliant orator, rose to defend him.

It would seem, he said, that Mr. Pitt considered himself as a candidate for the Regency. Were they now in the presence of King William IV. They should be warned lest they be guilty of *lèse majesté*.

At which Mr. Pitt did what he rarely had done before: he lost his temper. The debate had developed into a farce, he said. But since the question of *rights* had been introduced it was necessary to set up a committee to enquire into precedents.

When the debate was resumed Pitt's equanimity was restored.

All would admit, he declared, that the Prince of Wales was the most suitable person to take on the role of Regent. The situation was extraordinary; complete power could not for obvious reasons be handed to the Prince for at any moment the King might regain his health. Therefore he suggested that rules should be drawn up and that should the Prince agree to the conditions decided on by the Government the Regency should be his.

Fox, eager to put right his mistake which he realized had given Pitt time to delay a decision, declared that Pitt intended to impose such restrictions on the Regency that it would be impossible for His Highness to accept with dignity.

'The Honourable Member will realize,' retorted Pitt maliciously, 'that since the question of *right* has been raised there must be this investigation.'

Meanwhile the care of the King was to be in the hands of the Queen.

At Kew the Prince chafed against the delay.

'Nothing settled,' he grumbled to Frederick. 'If Fox had not raised that question of *rights* . . .'

Frederick sympathized with him.

'I am beginning to think he is of no use to me,' he said. 'First he upsets Maria by denying our marriage. Maria won't have him in her house. Then he makes this absurd statement about rights.'

'But you do have a right,' Frederick pointed out.

'But Fox shouldn't have *said* it. It gave Pitt his opportunity.

And Pitt is hand in glove with our mother. The Queen is now coming out in her true colours. She is not so meek as we once believed her to be. I am not sure what she is plotting with Pitt.'

'Can you understand this friendship between them?'

'Only that she is the Queen and that Pitt intends to use her against me. She will scarcely allow me to see the King.'

'Absurd.'

'But they have put her in charge of him.'

'You are the Prince of Wales . . . soon to become Regent . . . if you wish to see the King you have every right.'

'His papers and jewels are all locked away. And I am made to feel an outsider.'

'It's ridiculous, George. Come to the King's apartments now. He is safely locked away. If you want to examine the jewels and the papers you have every right to do so.'

The two brothers went to the King's recently vacated rooms and were examining the contents of drawers when the Queen appeared.

Her usually impassive face flushed with anger when she saw what they were doing.

'And what,' she cried indignantly, 'are you doing here?'

'I will tell you one thing we are not doing, Madam,' said the Prince of Wales haughtily, 'and that is explaining our actions to you.'

'These are the King's apartments; and I am in charge of the King.'

'You forget, Madam, that I am the Regent.'

'Not yet . . . not yet.'

'When my father is incapable of government it is my right to do so.'

'Your *right*!' She laughed. That unfortunate word. If Fox had not used it everything would be settled now. He would undoubtedly be Regent. A curse on Fox!

'Madam, I command you to go to your apartment.'

'My apartment! The servants' rooms which you have allotted to me here? Writing our names over the doors! I never heard such arrogance! You are not king yet, Prince of Wales. I should remember that.'

'Madam,' said the Duke of York, 'I believe you to be as deranged as the King. Come, George.'

The brothers left her and she stood staring after them. When they had gone she put her hands over her eyes. She wanted to shut out this room, shut out the scene which had just taken place.

What is happening to the family? she thought. It seems that we are all going mad.

Fox called at Carlton House in answer to a summons from the Prince who said he would ride from Kew to meet him there.

As soon as he saw the Prince, Fox was aware of the change of his manner. It lacked the cordiality to which he was accustomed.

'A weary business, Charles,' he said. 'What is Pitt up to?'

'I think, Your Highness, that he means to offer you a Regency with such restricted powers that it will be beneath your dignity to accept it.'

'And then?' asked the Prince.

'It may well be that the Queen will take it.'

'That's something I shall not allow. But this man Pitt . . .'

'He is determined to make you nothing but a figurehead.'

The Prince's eyes narrowed. He looked at Fox—very different from the Fox of a few years ago. Where was the sparkle of Mr. Fox, that irrepressible genius with words, that quick incisive mind which would have dealt peremptorily with Pitt. Gone! Left behind in Italy . . . lost in disillusion and frustration. Fox was a disappointed politician.

The Prince said: 'What if the question of Maria should be brought up?'

'We must do all in our power to prevent that.'

'And if it should be raised?'

Fox was silent. Then he said: 'It could have grave consequences. Your Highness, may I be frank?'

The Prince wanted to shout: No, you may not if you are going to tell me truths about Maria. Yet he said: 'But of course.'

'Your association with Mrs. Fitzherbert can bring nothing but harm to Your Highness. I fear that during the debate on the Regency that man Rolle . . . or someone like him . . . might bring up the point once more.'

The Prince's expression had hardened, but this was no time for prevarication and Fox went on: 'If the lady received the rank of Duchess; if she were given an income of £20,000 a year . . .'

'To desert me?' said the Prince.

Fox sighed unhappily. 'It is her religion Your Highness. If she were not a Catholic . . .'

'I am sure Maria would decline the offer you suggest, Charles.'

'Then . . .' But Fox did not finish, nor did the Prince ask him to.

The Prince walked to the window and looked out and with his back to his old friend he said: 'Charles, there was a letter I wrote to you before . . . Some years back. The one in which I said I had no intention of marrying. Do you remember it?'

Did he remember it? It was the letter on which he had based his denial.

'Charles, I should like you to bring that letter to me. I should like to have it back.'

Fox thought quickly. While he had the letter in his possession he had every excuse for his conduct in denying the Prince's marriage. He had only to produce it and there would be evidence of how the Prince had deceived him; the letter would provide vindication for the denial.

He lied: 'Your Highness, I no longer have the letter.'

'You . . . have lost it?'

'It is no longer among my papers. It may have been burned with others. I saw no significance in it . . . at the time.'

The Prince was silent for a few seconds but his manner had grown more frigid.

When Fox took his leave he knew that their friendship had suffered a severe blow.

Back to Chertsey, to consult with Lizzie.

'You see, Liz, I need not have come back post haste. Perhaps it would be better if I had stayed in Italy.'

Lizzie was inclined to agree.

'Can you imagine my making such a blunder? A *right* to the Regency. Of course he has, but it's unethical to say so.'

'It's said that you should not put your faith in princes.'

'I'm a fool to put my faith in anyone but you, Liz.'

'Well, where do we go from here? Back to Italy?'

'What a pleasant prospect! I have no desire to go to the House and be questioned by that man Rolle. You can depend upon it he'll attempt to bring up the Prince's marriage again.'

'Well, your health has suffered in the last few weeks, so what about staying at home and being sick for a while. I am an excellent nurse.'

'Excellent in all things, Liz. I have blundered and have no desire to take part in this debate. Yes, Liz, I think I'll be ill for a while.'

'A wise decision,' said Lizzie. 'I will immediately begin to nurse you.'

During the early part of the year there was little talk of anything at Court but the Regency Bill.

Society divided itself into two camps—those for the Prince and those for the King. The Duchess of Devonshire was wholeheartedly on the side of the Whigs and the Prince of Wales; everyone who came to her parties wore Regency caps. The Duchess of Gordon, a staunch Tory, gave parties at which the ladies wore ribbons inscribed with the words 'God Save the King'. Maria entertained more lavishly than ever before—the chief of the Prince's supporters.

When the Regency Bill was brought up for discussion in the House it was inevitable that the Prince's marriage should be referred to.

One of the clauses in the Bill stated that if the Prince resided outside Great Britain or should at any time marry a Papist the powers invested in him should cease.

Mr. Rolle moved an amendment to change the wording of this clause.

He wanted to add: 'Or should at any time be proved to be married in fact or in law to a Papist.'

Mr. Pitt, however, declared that the amendment was unacceptable as the clause was the same as that he had found in other Regency Bills and he believed it offered sufficient security.

Sheridan and Grey both rose to attack Mr. Rolle. The absence of Mr. Fox was commented on by their opponents and, as Fox had feared, the question of the Prince's marriage was again brought forward.

Grey stated that had Mr. Fox not been fully satisfied that his statement on a previous occasion had been true he would have risked his life—however ill he might be—to come to the house on this day.

It was an uneasy situation.

The Prince heard accounts of the debates and wondered what was going to happen next.

Maria was his great anxiety now, as she had been on that previous occasion. But for Maria he would have nothing to fear. It was entirely due to Maria that he must feel this uneasiness now. What big sacrifices he made for Maria!

He entertained guests at Carlton House or in Pall Mall every night. He went to see Fox, and finding him indeed looking in poor health his conscience smote him. Charles had been a good friend to him and when he was with him he remembered this. The ever ready tears came into his eyes as he talked to Fox of the old days. And there was Lizzie, as lovely as ever, to add a discreet word now and then to the conversation.

'When this miserable business is settled, Charles,' he said, 'you shall be my Prime Minister.'

Prime Minister, thought Charles, after the Prince had gone. It had been the dream of a lifetime.

Then he fell to wondering whether the Prince would keep his word. And he remembered the letter which he had not given up and which should be a warning if ever anything was.

For a man of his genius he had not had very much success. He had been very little in office. But Prime Minister! That would make it all worth while.

Yet he felt tired and disillusioned; he kept thinking of the olive groves of Italy and Lizzie beside him reading to him or talking of the pictures they had seen that day in one of the galleries.

The Prince was surrounded by friends.

Each day they waited for news from Kew. The Duke of Cumberland had his spies there to report on his brother's progress further along the road to madness. The Prince had promised his uncle the Garter when he came to power. And then of course there would be no more of this absurd banishment from Court, he told the Duchess.

Sheridan should be Treasurer for the Navy. A good post, thought Sheridan, but not Prime Minister of course. Fox was still hoping for that. But it was very likely that in due course . . .

He would not relinquish his dream.

So in the House the debates continued. The parties went on; the Prince made lavish promises; and while the Queen's friends prayed for a return of His Majesty to health those of the Prince talked of the Regency and looked forward to the day when it should come into force.

Then came news which was disturbing to the Prince of Wales and so pleasing to the King's supporters. His majesty's health had shown some signs of improvement; he was now enjoying periods of lucidity.

His doctors believed that there was a very good prospect of his being restored to health.

* * *

The King's periods of lucidity had been gradually increasing during January and the early part of February, and because of his passion for fresh air his doctors agreed that he might take little walks in the gardens as long as he was accompanied by one of them and certain attendants.

The King was aware of his illness and very sad because of it; he still talked rapidly until his voice grew hoarse, and although his mind was clear, on certain occasions no one could be sure when he would act with the utmost strangeness.

When his favourite daughter, Amelia, was brought to him he embraced the little girl so fiercely that she protested and made as though to escape, but he would not allow her to do this and clung to her straining her to him until she began to scream to be released. She was forcibly removed by some of the King's attendants and ran crying from the room, leaving the King bewildered and unhappy, wondering why his beloved daughter ran away from him.

But there was no doubt that his health was improving all the time the Regency Bill was being debated.

Fanny Burney who had been suffering herself from the rigours of court life—draughty corridors, long hours of attendance on the never-satisfied Schwellenburg, and the general air of melancholy which pervaded the royal apartments these days—had been advised by her doctor to take exercise in the gardens at Kew and regularly she followed this excellent advice.

She confessed to Colonel Digby that she was terrified of meeting the King on these occasions, so if he should be walking at the same time as she was she always took the precaution of enquiring which way he had gone.

'For, Colonel Digby,' she declared, 'I do not know what I should do if I came face to face with His Majesty. What should I say?'

'You would not have to speak at all, Miss Burney. The King would do all the talking that was necessary.'

'But His Majesty would expect some answers. Moreover, I dare not think in what state His Majesty might be.'

'He is much better than he was. At times quite himself.'

'So I hear . . . but . . .'

'If my duties do not prevent me perhaps I could have the pleasure of protecting you, Miss Burney, in the gardens of Kew.'

Fanny fluttered her eyelashes. Indeed, the Colonel was a gallant gentleman. Only a little while ago he had brought a carpet for her room, for there was nothing but the bare boards and the wind blowing through the ill-fitting windows was enough to chill one to the bone.

It would be pleasant to walk with Colonel Digby; but of course he had his duties. Schwellenburg had already mentioned to the Queen that Colonel Digby was constantly waiting on Miss Burney though he never waited on her; and the Queen had asked Fanny—half to her delight, half to her chagrin—why the Colonel was so frequently in her rooms. Fanny had wanted to complain then bitterly about Schwellenburg's treatment of her, but how could one complain to a poor woman who was beside herself with anxieties? If the Queen could put up with a mad husband, surely Fanny could suffer a disagreeable old woman. So she replied that Colonel Digby was a friend and they had much in common—literature for one thing. The Queen was always ready to accept an explanation of Fanny's that concerned literature. After all, was not Fanny a famous novelist?

And now Colonel Digby was unable to accompany her. She was not sure whether it was due to his duty or for some other reason. Colonel Digby had a way of avoiding duty if he wished to; and Schwellenburg had told Fanny quite frankly that Colonel Digby was as often in the company of Miss Gunning as he was in that of Miss Burney.

Fanny asked the guards at the door which way the King had gone walking, if he were in fact walking at all, and she was told that His Majesty, with his doctors and some attendants, had not long ago gone off in the direction of Richmond.

Very well, thought Fanny, then I will walk in the opposite direction. Walking, she mused on the strange behaviour of the King, the courage of the Queen, the motives of Colonel Digby—and she was thinking that it was only this last which gave her days some interest, for life at Court was not very exciting. Suddenly she was aware of some figures under a tree, and peered in their direction for she was very shortsighted. Gardeners, she thought. There were always plenty of them working in the gardens. But as she came nearer, to her great consternation, she saw that the men she had mistakenly thought were gardeners were the King with two of his doctors and some attendants.

Fanny stopped short and looked at the men. She could never think quickly in an emergency. Oh dear, she thought, what have I got myself into? Why did I take this path?

And for a few seconds she and the King looked at each other; she saw the sunken cheeks, the protruberant eyes, and she thought of all the stories she had heard about the strangeness of the King. She believed there was only one thing to do: Escape. She turned and fled.

But the King had seen her. 'Miss Burney! Miss Burney,' he called. But she ran on. She could not face him. What if he seized her as he had seized Amelia? What if he said strange things to her? She must escape.

'Miss Burney. Wait for me, Miss Burney. Miss Burney.'

But Fanny ran on. To her horror, glancing over her shoulder, she saw that the King was pursuing her, his doctors and attendants running along behind him. She heard her name called again; she heard the hoarse torrent of words; and she ran on.

'Miss Burney,' called one of the attendants. 'Stop. Dr. Willis asks you to.'

'I cannot. I cannot,' she cried.

'Miss Burney, you must. The King will be ill if he runs like this. Stop. Stop, I beg of you.'

Fanny stopped, and turning, faced the King.

'Why did you run away, Miss Burney?' he asked.

What could she say? I feared your madness? So she did not answer and he came close to her and putting his hands on her shoulders kissed her cheek.

'Now, Miss Burney. I wish to talk to you.' His hot hands were on her arm; he drew her a little to one side; she was thankful to have the doctors and attendants close at hand.

'Ah, Miss Burney, you think I have been ill, eh, what? Yes, I have been ill . . . but not as ill as people think. Do you think I have been ill, Miss Burney, eh? what?'

Fanny answered as best she could but there was no need to be anxious on that account for the King, as Colonel Digby had said, was prepared to do all the talking.

He began discussing the American Colonies and he went on at great speed with ehs? and whats? coming thick and fast. And Schwellenburg. He did not think Miss Burney was very happy with that woman. But she was not to be anxious on that account. He would speak to the Queen. And Colonel Digby? He feared that gentleman was a sad flirt . . . oh yes, he feared that. Fanny must not take that gentleman too seriously. Oh he could be a very serious gentleman . . . but he was a widower looking for a wife, and a flirt, Miss Burney, a sad flirt, and had she heard the arrangement of *The Messiah*? Handel was the finest musician in the world. Her father would know that. He could tell her some stories of Handel and she could tell her father. Dr. Burney would be very interested in the stories he could tell her of Handel. A fine musician.

He began to sing, beating time to the music, and his voice which had grown hoarse with all the talking he was doing, seemed to crack suddenly and Dr. Willis said: 'I beg Your Majesty not to strain your voice. Come along, sir. Do you not think we should go in and allow Miss Burney to continue with her walk.'

'No, no, not yet. I have to speak to Miss Burney. I have much to say to her. I have lived so long out of the world, Miss Burney, that I know nothing. You understand, eh? what?'

Fanny murmured that she understood very well and the King gripped her arm and put his face close to hers so that she trembled at the wildness in his eyes.

'Miss Burney, I pray you tell me how your father fares. Tell your father that I will take care of him. He is a good and honest man. I will take care of him, Miss Burney. Yes, I will do it myself.'

'Your Majesty is most gracious,' stammered Fanny.

'Your Majesty will get a chill,' said Dr. Willis. 'Your Majesty is progressing so favourably that it would be folly to start your illness all over again.'

'Yes,' said the King. 'Folly, folly, folly . . .'

'Then Your Majesty . . .'

'I will say *au revoir* to Miss Burney.' And with that he put his hands on her shoulders, drew her to him and kissed her cheek as he had done when at the beginning of the encounter.

Fanny was overcome with confusion, but the King's attendants were already drawing him away.

The King called over his shoulder, 'Do not fear that dreadful woman, Miss Burney. Take no heed of Schwellenburg. You may depend on me. I am your friend. As long as I live I will be your friend. You understand, eh? what? I pledge myself to be your friend.'

Fanny stood watching the King as he was drawn away, smiling and nodding to him as he turned to shout over his shoulder to her.

She made her way hastily to her apartments and when she was with the Queen repeated the conversation to her, although she said nothing of the reference to Madam von Schwellenburg.

'His Majesty still acts a little strangely, Miss Burney,' said the Queen, 'but I do believe he is going to get well.'

* * *

The Queen was right.

In the Lords the Lord Chancellor rose to declare that in view of the improved state of the King's health it would be indecent to discuss the Regency Bill further.

The King's health improved rapidly; at the beginning of April the Prince of Wales with his brother Frederick received a summons to wait on the King at Kew in order that they might congratulate him on his recovery.

The Prince of Wales behaved with absolute decorum and was more cordial to his father than he had ever been before.

The improvement went on apace. The King looked old; his speech was quick and incoherent, but his mind was lucid again.

All the royal family attended the service which was held at St. Paul's as a thanksgiving for the King's recovery. It was April and the clement weather brought the crowds into the streets. As the King's carriage rode by the people cheered wildly.

'God save the King,' they cried, throwing hats into the air and waving flags. 'Long life to Your Majesty.'

The King was touched by this devotion. The tears came to his eyes and this show of emotion only made the people cheer the more.

But for the Prince of Wales—silence.

He could not understand it. *He* was the popular member of the household. He was Prince Charming. Yet the people were greeting him with a sullen silence. It was the first time his presence had failed to rouse cheers.

He was angry. Why? What had he done but ask for that which was his right? Why should they suddenly turn against him?

It was because the people believed—in spite of the denial in Parliamant—that he was married to a Papist. Maria . . . and her religion . . . were responsible for this.

My dear love, he thought, what I have given up for you!

The Queen was elated by the Prince's reception. She had made sure that whenever possible people should be made aware of his callous behaviour during his father's illness. She had arranged that stories should be circulated of his treatment of herself and her daughters; how he had tried to separate a wife from a sick husband, how he had sought for power at all costs, how it was the anxiety over his eldest son that had driven the King mad. Mr. Pitt and the Queen were friends; and the Prince was supporting the unpopular Whigs with Fox at their head. But most heinous of all his sins was that he lived in sin with a Papist or was married to her; and neither situation was one to commend him to the people.

Ah, Prince of Wales, thought the Queen malevolently, you would not accept my love so now you have my hate.

Strange that a mother could hate the son on whom she had once doted. But Queen Charlotte had been kept so long under restraint—treated as a woman of no importance, simply a breeder of royal children—and when such prisoners were free their actions often surprised even themselves.

The cartoonists were busy. The one which attracted the most attention was *The Funeral of Miss Regency*. This portrayed a coffin on which instead of wreaths was a coronet—the Prince's—dice, and an empty purse. The chief mourner was Mrs. Fitzherbert.

When the Prince saw the cartoon he thought: Yes, Maria *is* the chief mourner. She believed that when I became Regent I would have recognized her. And if I had what would have happened? He remembered those sullen crowds at the thanksgiving service and was alarmed.

Maria could ruin me, he thought.

Somewhere from the past came the echo of an old song:

> 'I'd crowns resign
> To call thee mine.'

Coming so near to the Regency had made him realize what the Crown would mean to him. He knew in his heart that he would never resign it. And if it came to the point of choosing between it and Maria . . .

A few years ago he would have said unthinkingly: Maria.

And now?

I have already given up a great deal for her, he thought resentfully.

The Duke's Duel

The Queen was savouring her newly found power. The King's illness had shattered his confidence and he lived in constant terror of his malady returning. He had become an old man—a frightened old man—and the Queen, after years of submission, was now the ruler of the Court.

Her great enemy was the Prince of Wales and she was ready to do battle against him. She had her spies everywhere. How exciting life had become! How different this was from suffering the discomforts of pregnancy, being continuously concerned with nursery affairs, dealing with the accounts and managing her own household. Mr. Pitt was her great friend. *He* did not despise her influence; and everyone would agree that Mr. Pitt was the greatest politician of the age. Moreover, he was Prime Minister and head of the Tory Party, and the Court was Tory. When she gave a ball to celebrate the King's recovery all the ladies were in blue—the Tory colour—and the tables were decorated with devices complimentary to the Tory party; and there were even mottoes inscribed on the sweetmeats.

'The entertainment is for ministers and those persons who have voted for the King and *me*,' she announced, 'and those who have proved themselves my friends.'

A new tone, everyone noticed. Queen Charlotte could never have made such an announcement before the King's illness.

The Prince of Wales and his brothers had attended, although the Queen had shown quite clearly that she had no wish for them to come. The King, however, appeared to be pleased to see his sons and was anxious that all should be peaceful within the family.

But it was obvious from that evening—if it were not before—that there was open warfare between the Queen and the Prince of Wales and, since the Duke of York supported his brother in all things, that meant that the enmity extended to him as well.

The Queen was determined that no one but herself should have charge of the King. She knew as well as his doctors the precarious state of his health. He had at the moment recovered to some extent, but she was aware that at any moment his reason could again desert him. He was a poor, sick old man.

If he should again become insane she must be ready. In the meantime she was determined not to relinquish the smallest part of that power which she had just begun to relish.

When she was alone with the King she dwelt on the wickedness of the Prince of Wales, how he had cared only to grasp power; how he had revelled in his father's incapacity, how he had been unable to hide his dismay at his father's recovery.

'We have a rogue for a son,' she said. 'A profligate who longs to snatch the Crown from your head. I regret the day I ever bore him.'

The King wept. 'He has caused us such anxiety, but we must try to come to terms with him, eh, what?'

'Terms with him? We never shall. His terms are . . . the Regency. That's what he wants. And Frederick is almost as bad.'

The King shook his head. Not Frederick, his favourite son, the hope of the House. 'No, no . . . not Frederick . . .'

The King was looking at her appealingly and she feared he would have a relapse.

'Well, perhaps not Frederick,' she conceded, 'but he is under the influence of George and I think we should be watchful.'

'Trouble, trouble,' wailed the King, 'Eh, what, trouble!'

The tears began to fall down his cheeks and the Queen warned herself that she must be careful.

The battle between the Queen and the Prince went on and her allies saw that stories were circulated about the Prince's behaviour. Because of the King's recently pathetic condition he had the sympathy of the people.

Each day the Prince grew more and more disturbed—not by the animosity of his family but by that of the people.

Once on the way to the opera his carriage was surrounded by the mob who threatened to drag him from it. The Prince disliked violence and was alarmed and astonished that it should be directed against himself, but his greatest emotion was anger that the partisans of the Queen should have spread such stories about him that the people who had once admired him should have turned against him.

He looked through the window of his carriage at those jeering faces.

'Pitt for ever!' came the shout.

'Damn Pitt!' retorted the Prince. 'Fox for ever.'

The crowd was startled by his reply and the driver seized the opportunity to drive on. As they passed through the shouting crowd the Prince began to think of what might have happened. It was very unpleasant.

But one thing was clear to him. He was no longer the popular idol.

One early May morning the Prince, who was at Carlton House, was awakened by his brother's coming into his bedroom and flinging himself on to a chair by his bed.

The Prince started up, crying: 'Why, Fred, what on earth has happened to you? You look as if you've seen a ghost.'

'It might well have been you who was seeing a ghost at this moment, George. My ghost! Less than half an hour ago I faced death.'

'What are you talking about?'

'My dear George, I have just come from Wimbledon Common where I faced Colonel Lennox in a duel.'

'Frederick, you fool,'

'You say that, George, but something had to be done about these rumours and slanders . . . all directed at you.'

'Good God, Fred, what if . . .'

Frederick laughed at his brother's dismay.

'Well, you see me here safe and sound.'

'Thank God for that. And Lennox?'

'Equally unharmed. But at least we have had satisfaction though no blood was drawn.'

'Fred . . . this is going too far.'

'I tell you something had to be done. You know how friendly the Lennoxes are at Court. Lennox's mother is hand in glove with the Queen and the Colonel is a great favourite of our old toad of a mother, too. He has been abusing us right and left for months. Of course we know who is behind all this. I let it be known what I thought of Lennox and he challenged me . . . so what could I do? We met on Wimbledon Common. I refused to fire. But Lennox's ball grazed my ear. Oh, nothing to be startled about. It singed one of my curls. No other damage, I do assure you, brother.'

'Fred, do you think our mother asked Lennox to challenge you?'

'It could be so.'

'The woman's nothing less than a monster. I shall see the King about this.'

'There's no need. The matter is over, except that the Queen will know that at least her sons are not afraid to face her friends in duels.'

'The wicked creature! Leave this to me.'

Frederick sat back in his chair, laughing at his brother's concern for his safety. The affection between them was as strong as it had been all through their lives.

The Prince called at Kew and demanded to see his father, but although he was respectfully conducted into the King's apartments it was the Queen he found there.

'Madam,' said the Prince, 'I wish to speak to the King.'

'His Majesty is not well enough to receive visitors.'

'Then his son should be with him.'

'Not if his wife decides the meeting might upset His Majesty.'

'Madam, have done with this overbearing attitude. I have come to tell you that you are responsible for what has happened at Wimbledon this morning.'

'What . . . has happened?'

'Your son, the Duke of York, fought a duel with your *favourite* Colonel Lennox. Madam, are you a mother or a monster? What pleasure do you find in sending your sons . . . to death.'

The Queen turned pale, and the Prince went on: 'I demand to see His Majesty.'

'Frederick is . . .' The woman was shaken, thought the Prince. She is really frightened now. Let her be.

'What I have to say I will say to His Majesty.'

'I did not ask Colonel Lennox to fight a duel. I . . .'

'Madam, the blame for what has happened lies at your door. You have slandered your sons and the Duke of York has fought a duel with one of Your Majesty's servants who has been most active in spreading lies about us. I hope you are satisfied and I intend to give a full account of the matter to the King . . . and to make sure that he is aware of the part you have played in it.'

The Queen was truly frightened. She thought of Frederick, the rash young adventurer, who was capable of any foolish act. He was her son, and her only complaint about him was that he had placed himself on the side of his brother. If he were dead . . . Oh God, she thought, I will in a way be responsible for his death. But he is not dead. George would not be so calm if he were. He is enjoying this. He could not be if Frederick were dead. Selfish and careless as he is, at least he loves his brother.

The Prince saw his advantage and pushing the Queen aside went through to the King's bedchamber.

The King was resting, but he started up when he saw the Prince and cried: 'What's this, eh, what?'

'Your Majesty, I have come to tell you that the Duke of York, unable to endure any longer the ridiculous and wicked slanders which have been circulated about myself and himself has today faced, with pistols, Colonel Lennox—a *creature* of the Queen's—to demand satisfaction.'

The King gasped. 'What? What's this? Frederick . . . in a duel. He can't. royal dukes can't . . . But he has, eh? what? Frederick? Oh, my son . . .'

The Queen had hurried to the King's side and was trying to soothe him and the Prince said quickly: 'It is all right, Father. He is unharmed. Lennox's bullet grazed his ear and that's an end of the matter. The Duke did not fire. He just wished Lennox to know that he would accept his challenge and that was that. He had no wish to take life . . . only to defend his honour.'

But the King was staring wildly before him.

'Frederick,' he said. 'My son Frederick . . . the Hope of the House. Frederick . . . my son. He's dead. Oh, yes, he's dead . . . I know it. You're deceiving me. You've come to break the news gradually, eh, what?'

The Prince said: 'He is alive and well, sir. He is outside in my carriage. I guessed you would wish to see him to make sure that he had suffered no harm. I had no wish to upset Your Majesty, only to bring home the point to some people that these wicked slanders are dangerous and must *stop*.'

'So he *is* dead,' said the King, 'eh, what? So you have come to tell me my son Frederick is dead.'

The Prince immediately sent an attendant down to the carriage to tell the Duke of York to come at once to the King's apartment.

When Frederick came the King embraced him with tears in his eyes.

'I'm here, Father,' cried Frederick. 'Alive and well. But I had to accept Lennox's challenge. You wouldn't have a coward for a son, would you?'

'Never thought you were that, son. The Hope of the House I always said. The best of the bunch . . . Wish you'd been the eldest, eh? what?'

'I'd never have cut such a fine figure as George,' said the Duke, grinning at his brother. 'Now Your Majesty is satisfied, eh? But there shouldn't be this trouble in the family. I'm sure Your Majesty agrees.'

The King continued to embrace his son and the Prince watched his mother through narrowed eyes.

She was discomfited. This was a bad business. But the Prince of Wales and the Duke of York need not think that she was going to be ousted from her position because they happened to have scored this time.

The occasion of the King's birthday ball was coming nearer. The news of the duel was common knowledge and everyone had been particularly interested in the Queen's attitude towards Colonel Lennox who might so easily have killed her son. It was astonishing, but she had received him warmly, even affectionately, and he had not been reproached for challenging a royal duke to a duel.

The Prince of Wales who must, of course, appear at such a function did not believe that the Queen would allow the Colonel to attend the ball; and on receiving the information that the man would most certainly be there, he arrived at the ball at seven o'clock, although it was not due to start until eight, and demanded to see the Queen.

She was dressing, he was told, and was unable to receive him.

By God, he thought, am I the Prince of Wales or am I not? He pushed aside her attendants and strode into her dressing room.

She sat at her mirror and her cold gaze met his through the looking glass.

'So . . . it is the Prince of Wales.'

'Madam,' he said, 'when I wish to speak to you I will do so. The King is still an invalid.'

'Thanks to the anxiety caused by his sons.'

'Perhaps his wife is not entirely blameless.'

'What do you mean?' the Queen demanded shrilly; and the Prince thought that this was another change in her character. In the old days she used to be calm; now she lost her temper easily. Madam is no longer in control of her feelings, he thought.

'That is a question, Madam, that you best can answer. I have not come here to discuss it, but to tell you that Colonel Lennox should not be allowed to come to the King's birthday ball.'

The Queen shrugged her shoulders. 'It is too late now to cancel invitations.'

'So you mean that you have asked this man to the King's ball?'

'Colonel Lennox is a member of the household.'

'Colonel Lennox is the would-be murderer of your son.'

'Prince of Wales, you are too dramatic.'

'I should have thought a mother might have shown some concern at the prospect of her son's murder.'

'I know full well that Frederick provoked the Colonel. I have investigated the matter and have learned that it was the Duke's own fault. He showed more eagerness to fight Colonel Lennox than the Colonel did to fight him.'

'Madam, I have not come to argue with you but to tell you that Colonel Lennox must not come to the ball.'

'I could not cancel the Colonel's invitation until I have consulted the King.'

'I know full well who decides such matters nowadays.'

The Queen was exultant. Yes, it was she who decided now; she, who in the old days had never been allowed to give an opinion. How that had changed!

'You are aware of the state of your father's health. I could not disturb him with such a request. I will wait until Mr. Pitt arrives. The decision can rest with him.'

The Prince said coldly: 'I shall not expect to see at the ball tonight the man who wished to murder my brother.'

And with that he left his mother.

The King's birthday ball! Who, a few months ago, would have thought it could have taken place; but here was the King receiving his guests, happy to be among them, looking a little strained and fatigued it was true, and perhaps there was a wild light in his eyes and all felt wary of him—but still he was able to attend.

He received his sons with affection; and he was delighted to have his daughters with him.

He could scarcely bear his youngest daughter Amelia out of his sight and he kept her at his side. Amelia had forgotten how frightened she had been when he had embraced her so tightly and seemed as though he would hug her to death. She now talked lightheartedly to him in a manner which delighted him.

The Queen was triumphant. She had told Mr. Pitt of the Prince's demand that Colonel Lennox should not be allowed to attend the ball and she wished Mr. Pitt to confirm her opinion that there was no reason at all why the Colonel should not attend. This Mr. Pitt had been happy to do, and consequently the Colonel was present.

She made a point of receiving him with very special favour and during the evening was seen to kiss her fan to him. This was deliberate and calculated to annoy the Prince of Wales, which it undoubtedly did. The inevitable crisis came when the Prince was partnering his sister, the Princess Royal, in a country dance. The Prince and his sister must trip between two rows of dancers and the Prince must dance with each lady in turn and the Princess with each gentleman.

When the Prince reached Colonel Lennox and his partner he bowed low to the lady and said: 'Madam, I crave your pardon, but this dance is over. This is not meant as an insult to you. I think you will understand.' And with that he took the hand of his astonished sister and led her back to the Queen.

The Queen said: 'But what has happened? Your Highness is tired?'

'By no means,' replied the Prince.

'Then you find it too hot?'

'Madam, in such company it is impossible not to find it too hot.'

'I suppose you wish me to break up the ball.'

'I do wish it, Madam.'

The Prince bowed and left the ballroom and the Queen had no alternative but to bring the ball to a close.

In a way, a victory for the Prince.

He went back to Carlton House, angry and dissatisfied.

He knew what he would do. He would leave all this—and go to Maria in Brighton.

There was no lack of warmth in the welcome he received at Brighton. Everywhere he went he was cheered, and the people were glad to see him back. There he could forget his troubles, for his friends rallied round him and sought to make him forget his disappointment at not having acquired the Regency and the humiliations he had suffered at the hands of his parents.

There was Maria, comforting and motherly—his Dear Love waiting to give him her devotion. There was his Marine Pavilion, always a joy, and he delighted in planning new alterations to it; there were his friends. The Sheridans were there and the Barry family ready to amuse him with the wildest pranks. The Lades came to greet him and talk of horses; he was surrounded by his old friends; the only one who was absent was Charles James Fox. He was indisposed, he wrote the Prince, and was living quietly for a while at Chertsey.

The King had gone to Weymouth, there to recuperate and enjoy a little sea bathing, taking with him the Queen and the three elder Princesses.

Weymouth! thought the Prince with a sneer. How different from fashionable Brighton.

Brighton was wonderful. The sun seemed to shine endlessly; every morning there was old Smoker waiting to superintend the Prince's bathing, always with a wry remark to amuse him; and then there were balls and banquets, the strolling along by the sea and the races. Always the races. He enjoyed driving out of Brighton with Maria in his carriage drawn by four grey ponies and when they reached Lewes there he would be received by the High Sheriff of the County; he gambled recklessly; he was constantly in the company of the Lades; he was seen more and more often with the reckless Barrys; he seemed determined to enjoy every minute of that summer.

'Hellgate,' the eldest of the Barry brothers, was constantly thinking up the wildest diversions to amuse the Prince. He often behaved like a madman and liked to drive through the streets cracking his whip and lashing out at the houses as he passed; a favourite 'joke' of his was to ride from London to Brighton with his brothers and shout as they went 'Murder!' 'Rape!' in such high pitched voices that they would give the impression that a female was being abducted. If anyone stopped them in order to rescue the woman they imagined was being abducted, the brothers amused themselves by thrashing the would-be rescuer. Their idea of fun almost always included physical violence in which the Prince had no wish to partake; but the wildness of the brothers amused him, and although he did not share their cruel adventures, he liked to hear of them.

Not so Maria. She wished to be gay and enjoy those summer months, but as she told the Prince, she could find no pleasure in Hellgate's kind of fun.

Instead she had arranged that the Old Theatre in Duke Street should be used by amateur actors who believed they could do well on the stage if given a chance. Let them act their plays, she said, and London managers could come down and watch them and perhaps discover their talent. The people of Brighton would provide them with the audiences they needed. And since it was her idea that this should be done, they must, she told the Prince, support the theatre.

Often she and the Prince could be seen together in their box and the antics of the actors so delighted them, unpractised as they were, that they often laughed until the tears rolled down their cheeks.

A much better way of enjoying life, commented Maria, than the sort of dangerous horseplay indulged in by Hellgate Barrymore.

That summer the refugees were arriving from France, for that country was now groaning under the onslaught of fearsome revolution.

The Prince and Mrs. Fitzherbert received them warmly and the influence of French aristocracy was obvious in Brighton.

Those were happy days for Maria and she felt a determination to enjoy them to the full. She sensed change. She was thirty-four—no longer young, and she was growing fat. So was the Prince; but the six years between them seemed more marked now than they had before. Perhaps it was because he so enjoyed the company of people like the Barrys and the Lades, and those who wished to please the Prince must enjoy his pleasures. It was no use urging him to spend less recklessly; she herself had her money difficulties, for she had added her resources to his and received an income from him. This he often forgot to pay and her expenses were prodigious. This worried her, for she was the sort of woman who left to herself would have lived within her means, for the thought of owing money was abhorrent to her; and yet since she must maintain her royal style how could she do anything but fall into debt?

But for one glorious summer at Brighton she must forget such things. She must try to keep up with the pace set by her spectacular husband. She must dance, ride, laugh and be merry; and she must be there to comfort him when he needed her. Because that was what he expected of her.

She became more and more aware of the clouds . . . distant so far, but nevertheless showing themselves on the horizon. He was not faithful. Maria heard whispers of his amours. But he always came back to her, and although he never mentioned his infidelities she sensed his contrition. She was his Dear Love, as he constantly addressed her. She was there to receive him back into the home after his adventures. Maria must know that however many women there were in his life she would always be the first and the most important of them all—his Dear Love—the woman whom he had defied the law to marry, the woman for whom he had once been ready to resign his crown.

It was her dream that she would lure him away from the friends who were of no use to him—the profligate Barry brothers, the eccentric Major Hanger, the coarse Letty Lade and her husband. Fox would have been a better friend. As for Sheridan, he had become as wild as the Barrys and the Lades, following the Prince into many a foolish adventure, drinking, gambling . . . and she supposed amusing themselves with women.

Sometimes he would be unconscious when they brought him home. How she hated his drinking! It was humiliating to have to share in his horseplay and she avoided it whenever possible. When she heard him coming in with his friends in a merry mood after an evening's drinking she would hide herself perhaps under a sofa or in the heavy curtains at the windows hoping that, finding the room empty, they would go away. It was no use. The Prince would cry: 'Where is my Maria? Where is my Dear Love? Come out, Maria, if you are in hiding.' And then they would search the room, pushing their swords and canes behind curtains, under sofas until they found her and drew her out—when with shouts of triumph they would expect her to indulge in whatever sort of maudlin fun they fancied.

There was undoubtedly change.

She was anxious, too, about his position with his family. He had always been in conflict with his father, but it was particularly disconcerting that now his mother should be his enemy. She had heard that the Queen hated her son so much that she was ready to do anything to bring about his downfall. There was a rumour that she, Maria Fitzherbert, was to be accused of praemunire for violating the Royal Marriage Act by going through a form of marriage with the Prince of Wales.

She reminded herself that she had known that if she became involved with the Prince of Wales she was going to be very vulnerable to attacks from all directions.

'Why did I?' she asked herself.

The answer was that she loved him.

Yes, she did. She must face the fact. Perhaps it would have

been easier if she had not. Perhaps she would have been wiser in her conduct towards him. Perhaps when she heard of those infidelities she would have left him.

But how could she? She considered herself married to him; she had sworn to love, honour and obey him; and she was a woman who kept her vows.

And fundamentally—she loved him. Even sensible women did not stop loving a man who they knew was not worthy of that love.

He could charm her with his gaiety, with his gallantries, with his gracious manners, with his protestations of devotion. They were insincere, but she made herself believe them because she wanted to. She had heard a remark Sheridan had made of him which had wounded her deeply, the more so because she knew it to be true.

'The Prince is too much every lady's man to be the man of any lady.'

How true! she thought. How sadly true!

There was a not very characteristic recklessness about the manner in which she determined to enjoy that summer.

Debts. They were her constant thoughts.

One morning she was awakened by her maid in her house at Pall Mall to be told that two gentlemen were below and insisting on admittance.

'Two gentlemen?' she asked. Was it a joke of the Prince's?

Miss Pigot came running into the room, her face long and indignant.

'It's the bailiffs,' she cried. 'They're demanding immediate payment of this.'

'This' was a bill for one thousand eight hundred and thirty-five pounds.

'Oh, Pig, how did I accumulate such a debt?'

'I don't know, but we've got to find it unless we want these men with us for weeks.'

It was even worse than she had anticipated as she soon discovered. The debt had been long outstanding and her creditors would wait no longer. Unless she could find the required sum before the day was out she would be conveyed to the debtors' prison.

'Oh, for God's sake, call the Prince. Go to Carlton House at once and tell him what plight I am in.'

* * *

He came at once. That was one of his most lovable qualities. He would always be gallant and a lady in distress would receive his immediate compassion. A lady in distress! She was his wife. And the debts incurred had been through entertaining him.

He was with her in as short a time as it took to come from Carlton House.

'My dear, dear love, what has happened? These wretched people are bothering you.'

Prison! For his dear love! It was ridiculous.

But they would have to find the money, Maria told him.

'Leave it to me,' he replied, embracing her; he was always lighthearted about money. He never took it seriously. Debts? Oh, they were one of the little pinpricks in the life of royalty. One incurred them and they were settled.

Perhaps for princes, Maria reminded him. But what of people like herself?

'No one is going to bother my dear love,' he told her. 'I will go with all speed to the moneylenders.'

He was back not long afterwards with the money.

Beaming with satisfaction he paid the debt and the house was free of its unwelcome visitors.

He then explained that the Jews had refused to advance him the money until some of his own outstanding commitments had been met.

'So, my dear, what do you think I did. I've pledged some of the jewels and plate from Carlton House.'

'Your jewels and plate!'

This was a situation that appealed to him. With tears in his eyes he declared that he would pledge his life for his dear love.

He stayed with her; they laughed; they were lovers as they had been in the first days after the marriage ceremony.

She was as happy as she had rarely been.

But those were uneasy times.

The Quarrel

Early the following year the matter of the Prince's debts had become so acute that he had no alternative but to appeal once more to his father.

The King received him with sorrow. Since his illness he wanted to be reconciled to his son and as he himself had become more mellow, the reconciliation might have taken place had not the Queen been determined to present her son to his father in the worst possible light.

But the quarrel between the Court and Carlton House was having disastrous results on the Monarchy and both the King and the Prince realized that it was unwise to show their dislike of each other so blatantly. This was brought home to them afresh with news of the terrible things which were happening across the Channel.

The Princess Royal, now twenty-five years of age, was aware of the harm the family quarrel was doing and tried to reason with her mother, but the Queen, having so recently acquired her influence, was not going to allow her daughter to interfere with it. Her dislike of the Prince of Wales was like a disease. It possessed her and it seemed there was no cure. She was delighted at the scurrilous reports of his liaison with Mrs. Fitzherbert which filled the newspapers, and when the Princess Royal pointed out that that lady had always behaved with the greatest decorum the Queen poohpoohed the suggestion and said that of course the woman was a scheming adventuress who hoped to take advantage of the Prince of Wales's folly. When Maria brought an action against one pamphleteer the Queen read the accounts with glee; but when the writer was fined and imprisoned and the affair appeared to be a warning to others not to incur further penalties, the Queen was disappointed.

How like the Prince to commit the ultimate folly, thought the Queen. To marry a commoner . . . and a Catholic. If he had had any sense of his duty he would be married now to a suitable German Princess and have one or two lusty sons to ensure the succession as his father had done.

The best way of disturbing the Prince was to force public enquires into his so-called marriage with Mrs. Fitzherbert. Let him be disturbed. It was only right that he should be called on to do his duty.

When she was walking with the King in the gardens she mentioned the delicate subject which she knew would upset him, but she was determined to speak of it.

'The Prince of Wales is approaching thirty. Is it not time that he thought about giving us the heir to the throne?'

The King's brows were drawn together into a worried frown.

'There is this affair . . . this woman. She seems a good woman. If he is married to her . . .'

'Married to her! How can he be married to her? He cannot marry without your consent and he has never asked it. Therefore he cannot have had it. He is *not* married to this woman and therefore he should be married to a German Princess.'

'Yes,' agreed the King. 'It is true . . . He should marry.'

The Queen nodded. She was thinking that her niece Louise, Princess of Mecklenburg-Strelitz, would be a very good match. How comforting if her own niece were Princess of Wales! How grateful she would be to Aunt Charlotte who had arranged this marriage for her! She would defer to her aunt in everything. Yes, it must be Louise.

'There is another matter,' said the Queen. 'He sets himself up to be the patron of the Whigs. He should be made to receive Tories at Carlton House as well as Whigs. His debts are constantly settled by the Treasury and yet he turns his back on Tories. It is a ridiculous situation,'

'A ridiculous situation, eh?' agreed the King.

The Queen happened to know—for now that she was a woman of influence she had her spies everywhere—that the Prince's creditors were getting so impatient that he would soon again be begging the King's help in the settlement of his debts. At such times he was more humble—by necessity of course. Well, when he came he would have a shock waiting for him.

* * *

The King received the Prince. Mr. Pitt had suggested that there must be a formal reconciliation because the constant bickerings in the family were dangerous to the country's reputation abroad.

Tears filled the King's eyes; he wept more easily than ever nowadays, and his memory failed him so that at times he was living in the past. This was George—the precious infant, the first-born, who had brought such joy to his parents—handsome, charming, healthy, sound in mind and body, the child for whom he had planned and schemed. What has gone wrong? the King asked himself.

The Prince too was moved. This poor old man who rambled frequently, who wept without reason, who was obsessed by the fear of falling once more into madness, was a shadow of the martinet he had once been; and the Prince, whose emotions were superficial, and who wept as easily as the King, found himself wishing for a reconciliation.

In a humble tone he told of his debts.

The King nodded without reproaches and said that there would have to be conditions if the debts were settled.

The Prince enquired what conditions.

'It is time you produced the heir to the throne.'

'But I have many brothers.'

'The country expects the Prince of Wales to provide the heirs unless he is unable to do so. I do not believe, my son, that you suffer from such a disability.'

'Good God, no.'

'Then . . . there should be a marriage. A German Princess would be most suitable.'

'A German!' cried the Prince in disgust.

'She must be Protestant. You realize that.'

The Prince turned pale. 'I would resist such a suggestion with all my might.'

The King nodded. He understood. The Prince had gone through a ceremony of marriage with that woman, who was a good woman. She was a Catholic and had insisted on the ceremony. He understood; and he had no wish to embarrass the Prince.

'Well,' he said, 'since you are so set against it let us hope that we may shelve that matter for a while. But there is another.'

The Prince was so relived that he said impulsively: 'I will endeavour to meet Your Majesty's wishes on all other matters except this one.'

'You must receive Tories at Carlton House,' said the King.

'By making it a Whig stronghold—and yourself nominal head of the Whigs—you offend the Government.'

The Prince was thoughtful. Anything . . . just anything to stop this talk about marriage. And what of the Whigs? What had they done for him? Fox . . . Fox had denied his marriage in Parliament, he had ruined his case for the Regency by talking of rights. What did he owe the Whigs?

'Yes, Father,' he said, 'I will receive Tories at Carlton House.'

The King nodded; and the two smiled at each other, on better terms than they had been for many years. But the Prince knew who had suggested those terms to his father and he hated the Queen more than ever.

Shortly after the debts of the Prince of Wales had been settled Frederick, Duke of York, presented himself to the King with a similar request.

'Money, money, money,' cried the King. 'Can you never have enough of it?'

The Duke of York placed his hand on his heart and bowed. 'Never, sir,' he said vehemently.

The King eyed his favourite son with affection.

'Now,' he said to him: 'There is one condition I must make before your debts are settled, my son.'

'Name it,' cried the Duke. 'I accept it.'

'Without hearing what it is, eh, what?'

'The pressing demand of my creditors are the most urgent consideration in my life, sir.'

'It's marriage,' said the King. 'You must marry without delay.'

The Duke grimaced. 'Well, I'm ready to consider it, sir.'

'More sensible than your brother.' The King's eyes were clouded suddenly. 'You are all a great worry to me. There's William setting up house with a play-actress . . . a Mrs. Jordan . . . and aping a respectable married man.'

'Better than aping a disreputable one, sir.'

These sons of his disconcerted him. They could not be serious when situations demanded seriousness. 'There's your brother, the Prince of Wales . . . Oh, I don't know . . . I do not know. I can't sleep of nights thinking of you all and wondering what will become of you. You understand that, eh, what?'

The Duke said gently: 'Don't fret over me, Father. I will marry when you wish and whom you choose for me.'

The King embraced his son. 'Frederick . . . I always said you were the Hope of the House. I always knew you would not fret me as your brother does.'

'George does not mean to, Father. It's easier to be the Duke of York than the Prince of Wales. Besides, George is more flamboyant than I am . . . Larger than life, that's George. He's a fine fellow at heart. You can't blame him.'

'You always stood together, you two.'

'We never forget we're brothers.'

The King was weeping silently. Then he said: 'There won't be much delay. The Princess Royal of Prussia is the lady suggested for you, Frederica Charlotte Ulrica. You must make your preparations without delay for I think your brother's reluctance to consider providing us with an heir to the Crown makes this a necessity.'

He would do it, said the Duke, not only for the settlement of his debts but for the sake of his dear brother George.

Frederick left almost immediately for Berlin where he was married to his bride. He was not very pleased with her for she was small, exceedingly plain and badly pockmarked; and she was no more pleased with him than he was with her. If he thought that he was doing her an honour by marrying her, she implied, she wished quickly to disillusion him. He might be the son of the King of England but she was the daughter of the King of Prussia—and in her eyes Prussia was of no less importance in the world than England.

The Duke shrugged his shoulders, went through the ceremony and consoled himself with the thought that marriage was not going to interfere with his life very much. He would do his duty—if possible provide an heir—and then go back to the pleasures of his bachelor existence. When he looked at his ugly little wife who constantly smelt of the animals which she kept in her apartments he consoled himself with the reminder that he had done it for George.

The wedding ceremony over they set out for England but unfortunately were obliged to travel through France—where the Revolution was raging. On more than one occasion their retinue was held up by a bloodthirsty mob and only the proof that they were not French royalists attempting to escape but an English prince and a German princess who had no concern with French internal affairs saved their lives, though the royal trappings were torn from their carriages and only then were they reluctantly allowed to escape.

It was November by the time they reached England and there another ceremony must take place; in this the Prince of Wales was selected to give the bride away.

The night before the ceremony the Duke of York was at Carlton House where he gave an account of his adventures to his brother.

'By God, George,' he said, 'revolution is a fearful thing. One doesn't realize it until one is in the midst of it. If it came here . . .'

The Prince was horrified at the thought.

'The royal family of France . . . treated as they are. If you could have seen those people . . . I never saw such fanatical hatred. It brings home to you how quickly the mob can rise up. The mob is always there . . . that element of the people that wants to take what others have, the envious, the bloodthirsty. By God, George, when those people surrounded our coach it was an experience I shall never forget. One has to be watchful of the people. One has to please the people one rules. No doubt of it.'

The Prince thought of the crowds which had surrounded his carriage after the King's recovery. Murderous lot! They wanted their rulers to behave according to a certain code. The Gordon Riots which had happened some years ago . . . that was the nearest England had come to the sort of thing that was happening now in France. The cry of 'No Popery' had filled the streets. The people of England wanted a Protestant monarchy; they had turned out the Stuarts because they were Catholics. And he, the Prince of Wales, had gone through a ceremony of marriage with a Papist. Maria . . . everything came back to Maria. He was unpopular with the people because of Maria.

He changed the subject hastily. He hated to talk of unpleasant things.

'Well, here you are safe and sound—and a bridegroom. Do you love your wife?'

The Duke grimaced. 'To tell the truth I do not know whether I shall even be able to tolerate her. She is an arrogant little creature, very much aware of her dignity. And she is threatening to surround herself with animals . . . dogs . . . not one or two . . . but twenty of them. And monkeys, if you please. She prefers them to the human animal, I do declare.'

'My poor Frederick!'

'You may well condone. Lucky George with your Maria.'

'Maria is a woman in a million. I shall expect your Frederica to receive her and treat her with the dignity due to . . . '

'To the Princess of Wales? You can be sure I shall do my best to insist on this. But she is a self-willed woman.'

'Maria will expect to be treated as her sister-in-law.'

'I will do my best,' promised Frederick.

The next day at the marriage ceremony the bride was given away by the Prince of Wales. The streets were lined with people to see the bride and groom, for it was believed that since the Prince of Wales had contracted a marriage with Maria Fitzherbert which could never be acknowledged, this plain little German Princess might well one day be the Queen of England.

Frederick was soon wishing he had never married. He had believed that at least he could tolerate his wife, but that was not possible when she filled their house with animals of all descriptions. He lost count of the number of dogs, whose habits were none too clean; she had cages of parrots in every room; monkeys roamed through corridors and hung on bedposts and banisters.

Moreover, although she had received Mrs. Fitzherbert she showed quite clearly that she considered her merely the mistress of the Prince of Wales and that she had no intention of becoming on intimate terms with a woman in such a position.

Maria was incensed. It was not often that she lost her temper but she did over the Duchess of York. How dared the plain malodorous creature treat her with such haughty contempt! The Prince must insist that she stop that.

That Prince spoke to the Duke of York who declared that he had done everything in his power to make his wife treat Maria with due respect; she simply refused.

'But, Fred, you could insist.'

'I do assure you, George, that I cannot make her do what she has decided not to. She is the most stubborn, arrogant creature you ever set eyes on.'

'Try,' said the Prince, 'because it upsets Maria.'

The Queen was delighted with the Duchess's attitude towards Maria and encouraged her in it because she knew it upset the Prince. As for the Duchess, who in any case was determined to have her own way, she maliciously made it more clear than ever that she regarded Maria Fitzherbert as her brother-in-law's mistress. She herself stood a very good chance of becoming Queen and she did not forget it. No one was going to dictate to her.

She quarrelled with her husband over it. But then she quarrelled with him over many things. He hated her beloved animals and was always pointing out their unclean habits. If he did not like it he could go, she told him. They were more important to her than he was.

The Prince of Wales believed that Frederick could have insisted on his wife's accepting Maria, in spite of Frederick's vehement assurance that he could do nothing; and for the first time in their lives a coolness sprang up between the two brothers.

Frederick retaliated by leaving his wife alone as much as possible and seeking new friends with whom he could continue the life of wild extravagance he had led before his marriage, and the Prince of Wales brooded on the deterioration in his friendship with this beloved brother.

It all came back to Maria, he told himself. Memories of the mob which had surrounded his carriage; echoes of accounts told by his brother of the journey through France; he should have been a model prince married to a princess; they should have children. Children! That was what he missed. His friendship with Fred was impaired. Who would have thought that possible?

And all because of Maria.

Sometimes a thought came into his head which he tried not to examine too closely.

It was: Is she worth it?

The Prince consoled himself by going down to Brighton. He would arrive in early spring and stay until late autumn. He came to London only when it was absolutely necessary and a large portion of Carlton House was closed for the greater part of the year. Maria was constantly with him, living in the house close to the Pavilion. He made extensive alterations to the place and it was beginning to look like an oriental palace and very different from old Kemp's Farm which Weltje had discovered some years ago. The people of Brighton, in contrast to those of London, continued to treat him as though he were their king—and Mrs. Fitzherbert their queen.

Racing provided one of his most enjoyable pastimes until a scandal at Newmarket interrupted his pleasure in the sport. Two days before a big race his horse, Escape, was beaten by two outsiders, with the result that on the day of the race the odds were against it. There was great consternation in racing circles when Escape effortlessly came in first, and unpleasant comment followed when it was learned that the Prince and his jockey,

Sam Chifney, had each made a fortune on the race. The murmurings were, in fact, against Chifney rather than the Prince,
but when an investigation was made, nothing could be proved
against the jockey. The rumours, however, persisted and the
Prince, so humiliated and disgusted, sold his stud and gave up
racing, although he kept a stable of hunters which he used regularly.

The scandal was repeated throughout the country to the delight
of the Queen, who could never hear a word against her eldest
son without showing her pleasure. As for Maria she was not
sorry that he had lost interest in racing which was responsible
for a large part of his financial embarrassment.

They were both disturbed by the news from the Continent
which was growing worse; and when it was known that the King
of France had been executed a feeling of horror swept through
the whole country. Refugees began arriving at Brighton in their
hundreds and the Prince and Maria agreed that every hospitality
must be afforded them.

When news reached the Prince that a party of nuns had arrived at Shoreham in a pitiable condition, having been several
days crossing the Channel in fishing boats, he and Maria between them arranged that they should be brought to Brighton
and housed at the Ship Inn until he could make some arrangements for them.

Together he and Maria collected money for them; and when
they arrived at the Ship Inn and their sad condition had been
alleviated he went to see them.

They did not know how to express their gratitude and the
tears fell copiously on both sides, but the Prince was genuinely
sorry and it was he who arranged for the nuns to find a home in
a Somerset convent.

All during that summer the refugees continued to arrive and
no one was more zealous in offering them assistance than the
Prince of Wales—with Maria at his side. This task of helping
the refugees brought them closer together.

When the beautiful twenty-one-year-old Duchesse de Noailles
was found on the beach, exhausted and shocked from the crossing, Maria took her into her home and looked after her. This
the Prince applauded, but when Maria found that his interest in
the beautiful Duchesse was becoming too intent, she tactfully
arranged other accommodation for the lady in London.

The Prince often brooded on the fate of these refugees and
discussed the conditions which had brought about the Revolu-

tion with men like the Dean of Rouen and the Archbishop d'Avranches to whom he was able to offer hospitality in their dire need.

Could it happen here? he asked himself; and the smiles and cheers of the people of Brighton were more welcome than they had ever been. But rulers must constantly please the people whom they rule for it was the people who decided how long they should continue to be rulers. It was a lesson one must never forget. And what had he done? He had displeased the people because he had gone through a ceremony of marriage with a Catholic. If it were known . . .

Oh Maria, Maria, what have I done for you?

He was becoming irritable with her, and as she was aware of his increasing infidelities she was tense and nervous and sometimes unable to control her temper.

A young lady named Miss Paget was the cause of a really violent quarrel between them. She was a young woman of good family whom Maria had wished to launch into society. There was nothing extraordinary in this. Maria had launched many daughters of her friends. She enjoyed pleasing them; and she was fond of young women.

Maria had discovered the letter on the floor of her dressing room. She had read it before she realized that it was addressed to the Prince and certainly not meant for her to see.

'Miss Paget regrets it is not in her power to comply with the wishes of His Royal Highness to their fullest extent, but in a matter of so much delicacy there is not anything Miss Paget would not do to accomplish this purpose which he has in view and thereby contribute to his personal happiness. As secrecy in a matter of this kind is of the greatest moment, if His Royal Highness will confer on Miss Paget the honour of meeting her at the faro table of the Duchess of Cumberland on Tuesday, the business may be arranged to the entire satisfaction of His Royal Highness.'

Maria read the letter and a rare anger took possession of her. There could be no mistaking the meaning of the note. He had been unfaithful before, but he was carrying on this affair under her own roof and with a girl who was her protégée.

She would hide her suspicions, however, and the following day accompanied the deceitful Miss Paget—who was playing the innocent girl with such perfection that Maria thought she must have imagined the whole affair—to Cumberland House, where they were received with pleasure by the Duke and Duchess. In due course the Prince arrived. Maria watched him closely; he did not speak to Miss Paget but she fancied their glances met and that the arrangement was made.

The Prince roamed through the company bestowing his smiles liberally, chatting with Maria, as affectionately as ever until the Duchess asked the company if they would care to pass to the card tables, as play was about to begin. And suddenly there was the Prince beside Miss Paget and as they passed into the card room, the pair disappeared. It was impossible for such an illustrious guest to disappear without notice and speculative glances were exchanged.

So Maria Fitzherbert's young guest was the new young lady, was she? Poor Maria! What she had to put up with from their naughty Prince!

Maria nursed her resentment during the game and as early as possible said goodbye to her hostess and, not waiting for Miss Paget, she went back to her house in Pall Mall.

After a sleepless night Maria arose determined on action. She took a dish of chocolate in her room, being unable to eat anything, and then going down to her drawing room sent one of the servants to Miss Paget's room to tell her that she wished to see her as soon as possible.

The young lady appeared looking innocent and undisturbed although she must have been surprised that Maria had gone home without her on the previous night. Who had brought her back? wondered Maria. She could guess it was the Prince.

'Good morning,' said Maria coolly.

'Good morning,' cooed Miss Paget.

'I have sent for you,' went on Maria, ' to tell you that you are no longer my guest and it will be agreeable to me if you select another place of residence.'

'But . . .'

Maria turned away. 'I will tell one of the servants to pack your bags without delay.'

'But where . . . ? What . . . ?

'I do not think you need further explanation,' said Maria. 'And I have no wish to discuss the matter.'

Miss Paget burst into tears; but long association with the Prince had led Maria to distrust this form of emotion.

She walked out of the room and in half an hour Miss Paget's

bags were packed and Mrs. Fitzherbert's carriage was waiting to take her back to her family.

Miss Paget went instead to Carlton House where amid floods of tears she told the Prince what had happened.

He was alarmed. Miss Paget was a pretty creature but not worth a quarrel with Maria. She must go back to her family and he would see that she had a handsome husband who should make up to her for all she had endured.

Somewhat mollified Miss Paget left and the Prince went at once to Maria.

He went straight into the attack. 'How could you be so ungracious to a guest . . . and a guest who is almost as much my guest as yours. To turn the girl away . . .'

'Don't waste your sympathy on her. As you will have discovered she is not so innocent as she appears.'

'She was a guest.'

'A very special guest of Your Highness's.'

'No, Maria, this is foolish jealousy on your part.'

She told him of the letter she had seen. She had read it and she remembered every word. There was no doubt in her mind what it meant . . . and then his conduct with the brazen creature . . .

'My dear Maria, it was unpardonable of you to read a guest's letters.'

'I found it, so naturally I read it.'

'Most unnaturally! It was most dishonourable and the height of bad manners.'

'And what of your manners in seducing a young girl in my care?'

'Seducing the girl? What nonsense!'

His lies were as facile as his tears.

She told him so. 'Do you think I cannot see through you? Do you think I'm a fool?'

'My dear love . . .'

She threw him off. 'Perhaps these women believe your protestations. I have learned to distrust them.'

Maria was magnificent in her fury . . . like a queen of tragedy. A damned attractive woman, Maria; and no other light affair could ever compare with his marriage to her. In his heart he regarded it as a marriage and always would, he told himself. But he must placate her. Now what was this letter. He could explain everything.

And he did in most glib manner.

'It's those debts, Maria, those damned debts. The bane of my life. They are bothering me again. Why cannot these people exercise a little patience? They'll get their money in time. I did something rather foolish, Maria. This Miss Paget of yours . . .'

'Of mine.'

'Your guest, my dear love, and she is nothing to me . . . absolutely nothing.'

'You will have to convince me of that.'

'I can . . . with ease . . . the utmost ease. I was telling you of these debts. Her family is very rich, as you know, and I am getting desperate. I can't go to my father again . . .'

'Oh, these debts,' cried Maria in exasperation. 'Why cannot we live within our means?'

'I should like that, Maria . . . the two of us in a country house somewhere like the Pavilion.'

The Pavilion! She laughed. That costly country house on which he was spending a fortune!

'Just the two of us, Maria. Well, I was foolish enough to ask Miss Paget for a loan of £10,000. Now you wondered why we disappeared together at Cumberland's. She had brought me some of the money . . . as she said in the letter. But not all. She brought seven thousand pounds, which is very useful as you can realize, Maria.'

'Very,' she said, 'if she ever gave it to you.'

'I am telling you what happened.'

'And I am telling you that I don't believe a word of it.'

'Now, Maria, are you telling me that I am a liar?'

She pushed him from her and walked to the door. 'Yes,' she said, 'I am. I have long known that you were skilled in that art.'

'This is no way to talk to your husband.'

'My husband,' she said. 'Will you go to your family and call yourself that? I must endure sly looks. I must be insulted by your brother's wife. And you allow it to happen. Please go now before I lose my temper.'

'Before you have lost it? That is a joke.'

In a sudden irresistible irritation she took off her shoe and threw it at him. It caught the diamond star on his jacket.

He stood staring at it as it lay on the floor.

Then he strode out of the room and went back to Carlton House.

Lady Jersey

Shortly after the Paget affair the Prince made the acquaintance of an extremely fascinating woman. This was the wife of the Earl of Jersey who had become his Lord of the Bedchamber and Master of Horse.

Frances, Countess of Jersey, had attracted him largely because she was as different from Maria as a woman could be. She was small and dainty; a woman of the world; a leader of fashion, a beauty possessed of a pungent wit, an undoubted aristocrat. She was considerably older than the Prince—nine years in fact—and was the mother of two sons and seven daughters, some of whom were already married and had made her a grandmother.

But no sooner had the Prince set eyes on her than he was enchanted, and Lady Jersey was scarcely the sort of woman to indulge in a light love affair.

She was the daughter of an Irish Bishop and from her earliest youth had been expected to make a good match not only on account of her outstanding beauty but because of her intellect. She had been known as the beautiful Miss Frances Twysden and no one had been surprised when she had become the Countess of Jersey.

She was soon moving in the highest circles and through her friend Lady Harcourt—an intimate of the Queen—she had very soon gained the confidence of Charlotte herself.

Lady Jersey was ambitious. She was looking for adventure and more than that—power; and she knew that her husband would be complaisant. Her children were all growing up and she needed the diversions she visualized through an association with the Prince of Wales. But she was not the woman to take second place, which was what every one of the Prince's mistresses had been obliged to do. He had always gone back to Maria Fitzherbert, the erring husband asking forgiveness.

But it was not going to be so with Lady Jersey.

The Prince sensed this and in spite of his quarrels with Maria, in spite of those moments when he told himself that all his troubles came through his association with her, he regarded her as the wife to whom he had made his vows and believed in his heart that however much they quarrelled she would always be there in the background waiting to comfort him when he, penitently, returned to her.

He was a little afraid of this quick-witted woman with the alluring body, with the beautiful intelligent eyes—this clever Lady Jersey. He believed that if she finally took possession of him she would never wish to let him go—and how was he going to explain that to Maria?

Lady Jersey had her own ideas. He would not *have* to explain, because this was going to be the end of Maria Fitzherbert—the end of that ridiculous marriage which was no marriage. Fat, complacent Maria could say goodbye to her Prince and go back to being the virtuous widow she had been before she met him.

The Prince avoided Lady Jersey, but she would not allow that. She contrived to be wherever he was; and she began to fascinate him so that he looked for her at every house he visited. In time hostesses knew that unless she was present he was bored and listless.

The whole of London was watching the effect the mercurial Frances was having upon the Prince of Wales.

There followed the inevitable result which the Prince had sought. Now, he had thought, it would be like every other affair. He would enjoy it for a while, grow tired of it, and with satiety would come repentance. He would go back to Maria; there would be reproaches and recriminations, then they would be reconciled and he would be the good and faithful husband until the next charmer came along.

But it was not quite like that. The more he made love with Frances, the more he wished to. It was a strange emotion which he felt for her. By no means the romantic love he had felt for Maria . . . nor even that which he had known with Perdita Robinson. This was different; this was an irresistible fascination which astonished him because he was not in love; and he was a romantic who had always looked for love.

This was different. It repelled and attracted, yet he could not resist it. When he was with Frances he was enslaved.

Maria knew of the relationship between the Prince and Lady Jersey.

Another of them! she thought. When it is over he will come back to me full of repentance. And I shall forgive him. Why does he behave in this way?

But what was the use? What could she do? Only wait for the attraction to pass as it had passed so many times before.

Lady Harcourt talked to the Queen.

The Queen felt at peace with Lady Harcourt who was one of her oldest friends. She had confided in her during the old days—the time before she had become an important figure at the Court. Lady Harcourt knew of the slights she had suffered when the King had kept her shut away from Court, and she had lived quietly at Kew, bearing children. So now if anyone could speak to the Queen of the intimate affairs of her family, that woman was Lady Harcourt.

'Well,' said Charlotte, 'what is the news of my son's latest amour?'

'It progresses, Your Majesty.'

'Mrs. Fitzherbert cannot be very pleased,' said the Queen with a smirk.

'Pleased, Your Majesty? She must be well nigh frantic.'

'So Frances Jersey has really replaced the woman?'

'He has not abandoned her . . . yet.'

'Frances should work harder,' said the Queen with a wry laugh.

Lady Harcourt was surprised. The Queen had changed so much recently that her friends scarcely recognized her. A short while ago she would have been deeply shocked by Frances Jersey's behaviour; now it seemed to amuse her.

'Frances *must* work harder,' she amended. 'It is long since I saw her.'

'She is a little disturbed as to what effect these rumours may have had on Your Majesty.'

'She thinks I am shocked by her conduct with my son?'

'She does think that, Your Majesty.'

'It might be exceedingly patriotic conduct. I do believe that Lady Jersey could be of great use to the country.'

Lady Harcourt was silent and the Queen went on: 'It is imperative that the Prince take a wife. I wonder the King does not insist. But he is a sick man . . . a very sick man. Sometimes I fear . . . But we were talking of the Prince. He *must* marry and I have the very bride for him. Until that ridiculous liaison with Maria Fitzherbert is broken he never will. It must be broken. You see that?'

'Yes, Your Majesty.'

'Once he has repudiated the woman . . . left her . . . well then everyone could be prepared for his marriage to a suitable wife.'

Lady Harcourt was silent and the Queen went on: 'You must speak to Lady Jersey,' she said. 'Tell her of my regard. Tell her that I wish her to turn the Prince's thoughts *completely* from that woman. Frances should be able to do it. She is a most fascinating creature. And when it is done . . . and he is married to the wife of my choice . . . Frances shall still hold her place. She will not lose by it.'

Lady Harcourt was astonished. That the Queen should be capable of such cynical deductions was amazing; and yet, she reasoned, for the good of the country, for the Prince's own good, he should marry. And what did the means matter as long as the end was achieved?

'I will see what can be done, Your Majesty,' she said.

The Test Case

The fates were against Maria.

While the Prince was at Carlton House brooding on his relationship with the fascinating Frances and at the same time longing for the comfort Maria alone could give, his brother Augustus, the Duke of Sussex, came to see him in a state of great agitation.

The Prince was alarmed at the sight of his brother. Augustus had always been one of the weaker members of the family and as a child had suffered acutely from asthma, which the King had tried to cure through constant canings. Augustus had always aroused George's pity; and the *camaraderie* between the brothers had persisted through their lives, so that it was natural that when they were in trouble they should consult each other.

'Augustus,' cried the Prince of Wales, 'what on earth is the matter with you?'

'I'm in trouble, George. Great trouble. I'm married.'

'Oh, God!' cried the Prince of Wales.

'Yes. I can't imagine what the King will say.'

'It's the Queen you have to placate now. You'd better tell me about it from the beginning.'

Augustus nodded. The Prince knew that he had been to Rome to escape the English winter. Staying there were the Countess of Dunmore and her family and Augusta was the eldest daughter.

'And Augusta is the lady you have married?'

Augustus nodded. 'Lady Augusta Murray. She is beautiful and witty, George.'

'Of course,' said George sympathetically.

'I asked her to marry me and at first she refused, but at last she gave in. We were married by a clergyman of the English church there . . . a man named Gunn.'

'Whatever his name was is not going to help you, brother,' said the Prince sadly.

'We were married without witnesses and when we told Augusta's mother she talked about the Marriage Act and said we should keep it secret and we did . . . and as Augusta was going to have a child when we came to England we were married again at St. George's in Hanover Square. George, what am I going to do?'

The Prince said: 'If I were King you would be in no difficulty whatsoever. But I'm not, Augustus; and I think there is only one thing you can do and that is go to the King and beg his leniency. After all, you're the fifth son. It's not like being myself or Fred or even William.'

'Is there nothing else I can do?'

'I cannot see what, Augustus. If I could help, I would, but you know how I am received there. I should go and see the King. Explain to him and for God's sake try to keep out of our mother's way. She's become a virago. If you try to persuade the King that he must accept this marriage, who knows, you might succeed.'

'I might explain,' said Augustus, 'that Augusta is of royal blood; she's connected with Henry VII and William of Orange. Surely that should count.'

'Of course it will, Augustus. Go and talk to our father. I am sure you will put your case to him in a way he will understand. And the best of luck. I wish I could do more. When I am King I will do something for my family . . . find husbands for the girls and repeal that obnoxious Act. You will see.'

'George, if only . . .'

The brothers clasped hands, and with George's good wishes ringing in his ears, Augustus set out to face his father.

It was impossible to see the King alone and when he and the Queen heard Augustus' story they made no secret of their anger.

The King wailed to Heaven, asking what he had done to deserve such sons. George, living with Mrs. Fitzherbert, married or not he did not know—and either was equally disgraceful; William was living with a play-actress. And now Augustus had dared do this wicked thing. Even Frederick was creating scandals by not living with his wife and letting it be known that she preferred dogs and monkeys to him. But this was shocking, quite shocking. Had Augustus never heard of the Marriage Act?

Augustus had.

And did he not know that by going through a ceremony of marriage without the King's consent he was breaking the law?

Augustus did know it.

And yet he had done it! He had defied the law and his father!

Well, he would see what would happen. This marriage would be annulled.

The Queen said: 'I suppose this is the influence of the Prince of Wales.'

'George has been kind to me,' stammered Augustus. 'No one could be kinder than George.'

It was the worst thing he could have said. So the Prince of Wales was behind this, was he? He was supporting Augustus in his disobedience. It was to be expected.

'It is his example,' said the Queen. 'You are making the King ill.'

Augustus began to breathe with difficulty and the King was alarmed for his son, so the Queen peremptorily dismissed him; and when he had gone she led the King back to his apartments and said he should not be worried by such affairs and should leave them to her and his ministers.

The whole Court and the whole of the country was talking of the marriage of the Duke of Sussex and Lady Augusta Murray; but while the fate of the two was considered, that of the Prince and Maria was in everyone's mind.

The King had announced his intention of having the marriage annulled as it could not be legal since it was a breach of the law. The Court of Privileges was instructed to give a verdict and it became a test case; the Court agreed that the ceremonies which had taken place in Rome and in England were null and void. Augustus was deeply distressed; he implored the King to allow him to give up any right to the succession, but this the King refused.

Augustus was not married and his child was illegitimate.

His brothers consoled him, particularly the Prince of Wales.

'Ignore the ruling,' said the Prince. 'Set up house together. I will see that you are received wherever you wish to go and once I have ascended the throne . . .'

Augustus thanked him, but he was bitterly unhappy.

* * *

Throughout the Court they discussed the case.

Then, it was said, if the Prince and Maria actually did go through a form of marriage they are not, by the law of the land, man and wife.

What could be clearer than that?

Lady Augusta belonged to one of the highest families in the land; she could trace her descent to royalty; and yet she was not acceptable because the King had not given his consent.

How much less acceptable would be Maria Fitzherbert, for her so-called husband was the Prince of Wales.

This was indeed a test case. Maria Fitzherbert would never be regarded in law as the Prince's wife.

No one was more aware of the implications than Maria herself, who saw clearly that she would never be acknowledged.

She was worried. Her position was becoming unendurable. The Prince was growing closer to Lady Jersey. She saw him rarely now, and when they did meet there was friction between them. He, because he wished to placate his conscience, seemed eager to make a shrew of her; and she, anxious and fretful, could not control her temper.

The happy days were over. Crisis loomed ahead.

The Fateful Decision

The Prince drove his phaeton through the park. People standing about in groups looked at him in silence. There were no cheers. How different it had become. He remembered how they used to jostle each other for a glimpse of him.

'God bless the Prince of Wales!' He had heard it so constantly that he had grown tired of it. How he would like to hear it now!

He heard a shout of 'Papist woman . . .' and he urged the horses to a greater speed.

It had all changed. The people no longer loved him.

He called on Lady Jersey. When he had embraced her she regarded him with some amusement and asked him what had happened.

'Happened?' he cried. 'What do you mean?'

'I can see you are disturbed. Pray tell me.'

She knelt at his feet and raised her beautiful eyes to his face in gesture of mock supplication. How different from Maria who would have been truly concerned. But when he tried to imagine Maria in such a position he thought how ridiculous she would look. Frances was so willowy, so graceful.

'It's nothing,' he said. 'Merely that riding through the park just now I thought the people looked hostile.'

Frances was on her feet and perching on the arm of his chair.

Maria would have soothed him. Frances said: 'Of course they are hostile! They're learning to hate Your Highness.'

She was indeed a disturbing woman—like a wasp . . . no, a beautiful dragonfly whose wings are of the most exquisite colours, who flies and hovers with a fascinating grace and has a sting in the tail.

318

'Why in God's name?'

'Very, very simple. Because you have displeased them.'

'I . . . what have I done to them? I have always smiled on them, talked to them whenever possible. I suppose it is my mother's spies who have been circulating stories about me.'

Frances smiled. She was, in a manner of speaking, one of those spies, for Lady Harcourt had conveyed to her the Queen's wishes. How clever of her to be the friend of the Queen and the inamorata of the Prince of Wales . . . all at the same time.

'You have provided the material for those spies to work on, my dear one.'

'I, Frances? By God, you go too far.'

'That is why you love me,' she told him. 'I go that little farther . . . in all things. Is it not so?'

'Frances, you are a devil.'

'So much more interesting than the angels, do you not agree?'

'Oh, stop this. What can I do? Do you know at one time they only had to see my face to set them cheering.'

'I know, I know. But then you had not accumulated a mountain of debts . . . or they didn't know of it.'

'I had. I have always accumulated debts. It's due to the miserable allowance I'm given.'

'The first time they're lenient. Prince Charming . . . dear extravagant Prince Charming! But even Princes can bore with repetition.'

But she was not eager to talk of his debts because she was an avaricious woman and she believed that the Prince should pay handsomely for the services she gave him.

So she said: 'You are growing old.'

'I am nine years younger than you are.'

'Which is why you lack my experience. But my age is of no importance. I am not the Prince of Wales. When you were young . . .' She smirked. 'When you were younger, your exploits amused the people. Now they are no longer amused by those frivolities which are so charming in the very young. You could win back your popularity tomorrow if you wished.'

'How?'

'By marrying and presenting them with a little prince who in his turn would be their adored Prince of Wales.'

'Marrying, but . . .'

She laughed at him slyly. 'I know. You're thinking of that absurd affair with the fat lady.'

'Frances, please do not . . .'

'But you asked that I should. Shall I go on or cannot you bear to hear the truth?'

'There is no point in going on. I could not marry the fat German *frau* they would choose for me.'

'Why object because she is German?'

He was not going to discuss Maria in these terms even with Frances. Maria had grown . . . plump, but she was still beautiful. There would never be anyone like Maria . . . and he wanted to tell Frances this.

While he sought for words Frances went on: 'Face the truth. You're unpopular and you wish to be popular. Kings cannot be *un*popular too long. You have an example of what can happen to kings across the Channel. There is one reason why the people of this country are beginning to hate you. I'm going to risk displeasing Your Highness by telling you in two words: Maria Fitzherbert.'

The Prince was silent. He wanted to protest, but he was saying to himself: It's true. But Maria had been faithful to him. Maria regarded herself as his wife.

Frances went on reading his thoughts in that diabolically clever way of hers: 'Why do you think she clings to you? Why do you think she meekly suffers your infidelities, eh? Why does she receive you back with open arms after all your little adventures? Shall I tell you? But of course you know that it is in the hope of the rank which will one day be hers. Princess of Wales? Queen of England! Well, at least a Duchess. She could expect that, couldn't she?'

'I think you are wrong about Maria.'

She looked at him pityingly. 'Fall in with the King's wishes. Marry. Give the country an heir. What harm will that do to the friendship of your *disinterested* friends.'

He was silent and she took his hand and looked at him mockingly.

'I would be there,' she said, 'to comfort you.'

On his way back to Carlton House the crowds seemed more sullen than ever.

They really hate me, he thought. They had given their devotion to the King now—the poor old King who had won their sympathy by going mad for a while and then regaining his sanity. Not that he was likely to cling to that for long. The people were fickle. He was well aware of that and they had grown tired of him and his debts and the wild tricks of his friends for which they often unfairly blamed him; but they were most weary of all of his marriage with Maria.

If he announced his betrothal to a German Princess these people would shout for him as they now shouted for the King.

And if he did not they would grow to hate him. He went to his drawing room in Carlton House and gazed unseeingly at the Chinese yellow silk on the walls. He thought of money. Debts, mounting debts. Why could he never keep within his allowance? The position was growing desperate. Something would have to be done.

So Maria tolerated him for the sake of the rank she would one day have? How many times had he told her what he would do for her when he was King . . . or Regent? All this time he had thought she cared for him. But of course she cared for him. Maria was not a seeker after that sort of advantage. She had been happiest when they had been poor . . . well, when he had sold his horses and shut Carlton House and they had attempted to economize! And yet . . . her temper was almost unendurable these days. She suppressed her feelings for weeks and then gave vent to a violent outburst. She did not mince her words then.

Oh, Maria! He wanted to go to her now. He wanted to explain to her: You see, my Dear Love, I have to marry. It is my duty. The people expect it. They are sullen now because I don't marry. Frederick will never have children. He doesn't live with that woman of his—and I don't blame him. William is chortling with glee because he is the third son and can enjoy married bliss with Mrs. Jordan without the benefit of clergy. Even young Augustus has his matrimonial difficulties. It is my duty. I am the eldest. I must marry, Maria. I must give the country the heir it needs. Then my debts will be settled and if they are not, they will be putting me into a debtors' prison.

The Prince of Wales in a debtors' prison. The idea was absurd. His father and the Parliament would never allow that.

Yet if he did not fall into line, if he did not do his duty . . .

A prince . . . a future king . . . is in the hands of his people . . .

He thought of that king across the water who had fallen into the hands of *his* people and the stories he had heard of that Terror haunted him.

You see, Maria. You see, it has to be.

If he went along and explained to Maria. But it was one subject which could never be explained to Maria. She saw it only through her own eyes; she could see no other point of view. Her religion insisted.

Maria, it is selfish of you. You must see my point of view too. You may have your religion, but I have my duty to the State.

It was no use talking to Maria. She would lose her temper. He would not discuss his affairs with her. He would act first and she would accept what he did as a *fait accompli*.

He was meeting her that evening at the house of the Duke of Clarence at Bushey.

He had almost made up his mind how he must act.

Maria was waiting for her carriage to take her to Bushey. Miss Pigot sat with her, watching her anxiously.

Dear Maria, thought Miss Pigot, how sad she was because of the Prince's behaviour! This Lady Jersey was a wicked woman and no one was going to convince Miss Pigot that she was not.

'All will be well, Maria,' she said wistfully.

Maria laughed without pleasure. 'My dear Pig, it's the old pattern which I have learned to know so well. He becomes enamoured of some woman; he make a public scandal with her; and then when it is over he comes back full of repentance. It will never happen again . . . until the next time.'

'He always comes back,' said Miss Pigot.

'To find me patiently waiting.'

'He trusts you, Maria. He relies on you.'

'He relies on me to respect my vows although he breaks his constantly.'

'He is young. He is a prince. Perhaps in time he will settle down. Give him time, Maria. It will all come well in the end.'

'You're a romantic optimist, Piggy. And here's the carriage.'

'Perhaps he will come back with you tonight.'

'I doubt it, Pig. The moment has not yet come.'

'And you will be gentle with him.'

Maria's face flamed in sudden anger. 'You ask too much. I shall be cool, I hope. I shall try to show him that he has no power to hurt me.'

Ah, sighed Miss Pigot to herself. If only that were true.

William, Duke of Clarence, received her with the deference he would show to the Princess of Wales. All the Prince's brothers were her friends; and even though there was a coldness between Frederick and the Prince of Wales—because of Frederick's wife's treatment of her—that had not prevented Frederick's remaining her very good friend.

The company was awaiting the arrival of the Prince of Wales, none more eagerly than Maria. She was always excited at the moment when he entered a room—so graceful, and in spite of the fact that he was putting on weight alarmingly, so elegant. A prince—every inch of him, she thought with pride.

Oh, this affair will be over like the others and then the reconciliation.

But they must stop. They impair his dignity no less than mine. I shall be firm. I shall tell him that they must stop and that this is the last time I will tolerate his infidelities. If he does not remain my faithful husband I shall leave him. I shall go abroad again. Where? To France? Oh, not that pitiable country! To Switzerland, perhaps.

Where was the Prince? William was puzzled. He had promised to come most definitely.

Something must have happened to detain him. And here was a messenger with letters. One for William and one for Maria.

So he has remembered to send a message to his wife, thought Maria with satisfaction.

She opened hers. The words in that familiar handwriting would not make sense. Such words were impossible. They could not be true, for they told her that he would never enter her house again.

She smiled faintly. They must not guess . . . not yet, though of course they would soon know.

So . . . she was dismissed. She was treated as a mistress of whom he had tired. His vows were to be discarded.

It wasn't true. It was a phase inspired by that wicked Jersey woman.

William was looking at her in some consternation. She smiled.

'So the Prince is unable to attend,' she said.

'Shall we go in to dinner?' replied the Duke.

Sensing calamity, Miss Pigot was waiting for her when she returned.

'Maria . . . Maria . . . my dearest Maria what has happened?'

'It is the end. He is never coming here again.'

'It can't be true.'

'He has given me my . . . dismissal.'

'No, no. I can't believe it.'

'Read this, then.'

Miss Pigot read it; then she threw herself on to a couch and covered her face with her hands.

'Be calm, Pig,' said Maria. 'We should have seen this coming.'

'That woman . . .'

'Is no ordinary woman.'

'He'll come back. There have been quarrels before.'

'Too many quarrels.'

'Oh, Maria, Maria . . . What shall you do?'

'I have to think. I have to think very clearly.'

Quickly, thought the Prince. Before I change my mind. I dare not pause to think. I dare not look back now.

He went to see the King and naturally the Queen was present.

'I have made up my mind to marry,' he said.

The King smiled. 'That is good . . . sound good sense, eh, what? The people will be pleased. We shouldn't delay.'

'Fortunately,' said the Queen, 'there is a charming Princess available—talented, beautiful and a Protestant. I refer to my niece, Louise of Mecklenburg-Strelitz.'

Her niece! thought the Prince. Never. One woman from Mecklenburg-Strelitz is enough!

'You are very fortunate indeed,' said the King. 'You have a choice. My niece or the Queen's. Louise of Mecklenburg-Strelitz, daughter of the Queen's brother, or Caroline of Brunswick, daughter of my sister. And once your promise has been given officially to accept one of these ladies there will be no hesitation in the settlement of those debts.'

A choice, thought the Prince. And one German frau was as good as another.

The Queen was looking eager. Oh, how much she wanted him to take her niece! No, Madam, you should have behaved differently if you had wanted concessions from me. Certainly I'll not take *your* niece. It will have to be this other. Caroline of Brunswick. He was beginning to hate her already!

The King was patting him on the shoulder. Everything was going to be all right now. The Prince had come to his senses.

All sow wild oats when we're young, thought the King. No longer a boy. People will be pleased. Debts paid, settle down, produce an heir. Rather late but better late than never. All that talk of marriage with that woman . . . good woman, but of course no marriage . . . all that over and done with.

'Good, good, eh, what?' said the King. 'Mustn't lose any time. Go ahead now . . . Summon Pitt . . . Country will be pleased.'

The Prince sought comfort with Frances. He had been wise, she told him. So had she. The Queen was delighted with her. She would be very well received at Court; and her position as Prince's mistress would be unimpaired by the marriage. Madame Caroline would have to accept Lady Jersey.

He would see the change in the attitude of the people when his betrothal was announced, she assured him. And soon he would be married, for they would lose no time in bringing Caroline over.

The Queen was furious because he had not chosen her niece so that gave him some satisfaction. But all the time he was thinking of Maria. He rehearsed what he would say to her.

'It had to be. The people expected it. A Prince of Wales must constantly consider the people. You understand, Maria. You must understand.' That note about not entering her house again. Of course he hadn't meant it. She should have known he hadn't meant it. She was his true wife. He would never forget it. This was just a State affair. She must understand. He could never be completely happy unless she did.

Maria heard the news. The Prince of Wales was to marry Caroline of Brunswick.

She did not rage against him; she was very calm, but this frightened Miss Pigot more than her rage would have done. She was broken-hearted, poor Maria, because whatever she said of him, however much she quarrelled with him, she loved him.

And he had told her publicly as clearly as he could that he did not consider her his wife.

'I should have known, Piggy,' she said. 'It was clear, wasn't it, when Fox denied the marriage in the House of Commons? He accepted that then. He never meant to acknowledge me. Oh, Piggy, I have been so foolish . . . so fond and foolish.'

'It will be all right, Maria. He'll come back. He will come back. I know it.'

'I shan't be here. We're going away. We're going at once.'

'But where?'

'What does it matter? It only matters that we are gone . . .

should he come back. But he won't, Pig. He will never enter this house again. He has said it.'

'He will,' said Miss Pigot firmly. 'He will.'

The Prince came to the house in Pall Mall. The furniture was covered with dust sheets; the blinds drawn.

'Mrs. Fitzherbert has left, Your Highness.'

'Where has she gone? Where? Where?'

'She left no information, sir.'

So she had gone, deserted him, and he was left alone to face this situation.

How could she have treated him so. Tears filled his eyes. Maria . . . his *wife*.

He went back to Carlton House. They were showing him portraits of a pretty girl, the German Princess who was to be his wife.

I have never been so wretched in my life, he said. No one could comfort him. Lady Jersey? He was only fascinated by her. Maria should have known that. It was the comfort Maria alone could give him that he wanted. Why couldn't she understand?

But he was a prince, and a Prince of Wales, and he had given his word to marry.

Soon his bride would be here and he must do his duty.

In Switzerland Maria heard that the Princess Caroline of Brunswick was coming to England to be married to the Prince of Wales.

'This is the end, Piggy,' she said. 'This is the final repudiation.'

But Miss Pigot shook her head. 'That is not true,' she said. 'It is not the end. Something tells me it is not. I know in my heart that whatever happens he will always come back to you.'

Maria shook her head and, smiling, tried to hide her unhappiness, trying foolishly—for how could she hide her feelings from the faithful Pig?—to pretend she did not care.

But in her heart she believed it, too. She was his wife. The bond between them would never be severed while they lived.

It was not the end. He would come back to her.

About the Author

Jean Plaidy is Victoria Holt. Under the Plaidy pseudonym she has written over forty-five historical novels for Fawcett Books, including the Georgian Saga, the Plantagenet Saga and the Queens of England series. Ms. Plaidy resides in England.